I0672190

The Shaman's Song

Evans Bissonette

The Shaman's Song

Copyright © 2013 by Evans Bissonette

McCoy and Sextant, Publisher

Printed Book ISBN 978-0-9890714-2-0

EBook ISBN 978-0-9890714-3-7

All rights reserved. No part of this book may be used or reproduced by any means, graphic, electronic, or mechanical including photocopying, recording, taping, or by any information storage retrieval system, without the written permission of the publisher. An exception is made for brief quotations embodied in critical articles or reviews. Your support and respect for the property of this author is appreciated.

This book is licensed for your personal enjoyment only. It may not be re-sold or given away to other people. If you would like to share this book with another person, please purchase an additional copy for each recipient. If you're reading this book and did not purchase it, or it was not purchased for your use only, then please return to an authorized seller and purchase your own copy. Thank you for respecting the hard work of this author.

The characters are productions of the author's imagination and are used fictitiously. Any resemblance to persons, living or dead, or places, event or locales is purely coincidental.

All trademarks or registered trademarks are the property of their respective owners

Dedication

To Bright Moon... for sharing her story

Thanks to my wife, certainly my biggest cheerleader, for all her support and for reading and re-reading multiple versions of my manuscript. A big thank you to all my family and friends for the encouragement they provided as it made the goal obtainable.

Special thanks to another willing cheerleader, my friend Dave Jones. I want to acknowledge my friends in my local (Troy-Birmingham Writers and the Writers' Connection) and online (Critique Café – Adventure Writers) support groups for their helpful suggestions and guidance.

Finally, thanks also to the staff at McDonalds (Long Lake and Dequindre) for their willingness to pour me a cup of fresh decaf and take a few minutes to chat when time allowed.

.

Table of Contents

Shaman: *A "medicine elder" (not always a male) who uses naturally occurring products, such as herbs, to treat the ailments/illness of their tribe. In order to attend to the tribes' physical, spiritual, and mental needs, they had to be adept at reading body language and using primitive psychology. They were often required by situations to think and act quickly.*

Chapter 1: Caravan

North America, Early Spring, 13,500 BCE:

Chilled to the bone, Silver Waters pulled her animal-hide robe closer in hopes of avoiding another fit of coughing. Two days travel from the Great Ice[1] and Wawakin's[2] cold breath still reached out to clutch at her. An unrelenting predator, the wind, slowly drained the old woman's strength, but not her will to go on. Her dreams had told her this was how her life would end. Insistent, the wind would continue its pursuit until her last drop of life was gone. Just as obstinate, the old woman would fight it to her final breath.

With her free hand, Silver Waters held aloft a flaming branch from their campfire. The stars had not left the sky. Their radiance, together with the flickering glow of this flaming stick, provided scant light for her daughter, Bright Moon. She watched the young girl scurry from person to person, look over their work, and give instructions or words of approval.

"I see you're new to this task," Bright Moon told a scrawny youth. "Use a travois[3]. You'll need to make a

---

1 The glacial ice-sheet, in their view, an area that the people saw as seemingly going on forever.

2 Their name for cold wind which blows off of the Great Ice.

3 This is structure small enough for one person to handle. Generally made of wood in a triangle shape, it was used to drag loads over land, ice, or snow. A travois made it possible for a person to transport more weight than could be

1

frame with two poles, both longer than walking sticks. Tie the top ends together, these will go over your head and rest on your shoulders. Tie a rawhide from here to here and make a strap to slip your arms through," Bright Moon whispered. "But first, wrap fur around each strap to keep them from cutting into your shoulders. To support the mountain of hides you have, tie more sticks, crosswise, near the middle and the bottom to support the hides. It will be easier to drag your load than to than to carry it."

Moving to the next person, a young woman just a couple of summers older than herself, Bright Moon hefted her bundle. "The fever's still with you. This load's too heavy for you to carry." Quickly, Bright Moon undid the bindings, slipped out a handful of furs, and retied the remainder in a neat package. "I'll add these furs to mine," she explained and then stifled the woman's mounting protest by adding, "Things will get better. You can return the favor when your fever's gone." The fact that Bright Moon's influence as a chief's daughter still carried some weight, at least with their own people, was currently the only positive feature of Silver Water's drab life.

A figure, hardly more than an outline in the dim light, stumbled out of the darkness, found Bright Moon and bent to whisper to her. "Two more of our people sleep *the-sleep-from-which-no-one-wakes*[4]," he said. In the darkness, a death wail started. It was soon followed by another.

Bright Moon nodded. "We'll have to split their load between us." Having gone through similar occurrences almost daily since the night they were attacked, she spoke without emotion. "Put a portion over there. I will wrap them with mine when I finish here. Divide the rest between the others. Hurry or Long Tusk will cut our food rations if we're not ready when the caravan starts or if we

carried on the back.

4 Death was associated with sleep, and is referred to as "the-sleep-from-which-no-one-wakes" as well as "the-long-sleep".

can't carry our share of the load."

Bright Moon stole a glance at the horizon. False dawn[5] was beginning. She had to hurry. Soon, at the place where the dark meets the earth, the sun would peer over the rim of the world. Though it would barely provide enough light for them to pick their way across the rough terrain, Long Tusk would bellow the order for his caravan to begin. The sun would join them in their travels as it raced across the sky and then sink below the opposite horizon before the caravan stopped for the night. There would be few rest breaks along the way.

Silver Moon watched as her people hurried to follow her daughter's directions. Seeing them grovel, hearing their conversations, a great sadness overcame her. These remnants of Great Elk's once proud people had survived a night attack only to be reduced to pack animals for Long Tusk's caravan. Her people did not complain, but willingly followed her daughter's directions and hurried to repackage the groups of furs. Bright Moon, pleased with their efforts, knelt and began looping rawhide bindings around her own stack of pelts.

It was not what Silver Waters wished, but it was as it had to be. After the girl's father, her mate[6] Great Elk, went into *the-sleep-from-which-no-one-wakes*, she became sick with the fever. It grew worse every day. Her daughter, less than three hands old[7,] had become the parent and the

---

5 False dawn, also called the Zodiacal Light, is a faint, roughly triangular diffused white glow seen in the night sky that appears to extend up from the vicinity of the Sun along an imaginary line called the ecliptic or zodiac. It is best seen just after sunset and before sunrise in spring and autumn when the zodiac is at a steep angle to the horizon. It is caused by sunlight scattered by space dust in the zodiacal cloud.
6 To be joined together as in marriage.
7 In this culture, counting is done in sets of five. One hand is a count of five; two hands are a count of ten, three hands would mean a count of 15.

leader of the remainder of their tribe, while she, the mother, had become the child.

I must give my daughter some glimmer of hope in this moment of darkness, she thought. "Daughter, I had the dream again last night." Silver Waters leaned on her walking stick and smiled as she recalled it.

Bright Moon knew her mother had many dreams. Her hands seemed to fly through the task of grouping and tying the hides. Her mother had told the story so many times since the night the marauders attacked the girl knew it by heart. Glancing up from her work to return a smile, the girl teased her mother. "The dream where I get lost in a storm of white-rain[8] while crossing the Great Ice, fall through and have to swim in icy waters. Is that the dream you're speaking about?"

"Yes daughter, I see great things in store for you. Crossing the edge of the Great Ice, it swallows you, but you find a treasure floating in a blue...."

"We just crossed the edge, honored Mother, like we had so many times in the past. It always seems to go on forever, but no one fell through. There was no storm, only this bitter cold wind which still chases us and brings sickness. Our people, what's left of them, suffer greatly; but Long Tusk and his people will do nothing for them." The bitterness in her voice did little to hide the disdain she had for the caravan master.

"This caravan, Long Tusk's caravan, just crossed the Great Ice, but, in my dream, you were alone and...."

Long Tusk's bellowing interrupted further comment. "Bright Moon! Bright Moon! Where are you? Why do you disappear when there's work to be done?"

At the sound of the old man's voice, Bright Moon grimaced. Gritting her teeth, she thought, *yes, there's work to be done... and just what do you think I'm doing?* "I'm coming," she called dutifully, showing only a slight sign of

---

8 To distinguish it from regular rain, snow was called 'white-rain' as they knew that when it melted, it was water.

4

irritation in her voice.

"Careful, my daughter," Silver Waters warned through wheezing breaths. "The distance between hate and love is but one short step."

Bright Moon rolled her eyes. "Love? Him? Never! Not if he was the last man on Earth," she said and then made a sign as if to vomit.

Unamused, her mother waved a hand to include the remnants of their tribe scattered around them, "Only a few of us survived the attack and we lose more of our people every day. We were too few and too weak to survive on our own and had to become part of Long Tusk's caravan." Her mother dropped her raspy voice, "With your father, Great Elk, sleeping the-sleep-from-which-no-one-wakes, we are lucky Long Tusk agreed to take us in and look after us. Like it or not, he's the one we must depend on for food and protection." She bent to grab the packages meant for her to carry and broke into a fit of coughing.

Bright Moon stopped her work and gave her mother a sympathetic look. *My beloved mother is too sick to make today's trek let alone do any work.*

The young girl finished combining the parcels in front of her and then hoisted it and her mother's burden to her shoulders. "I must go now, Honored Mother," Bright Moon said and bent to pat her mother on the shoulder. "I will take your parcels today so you can rest. Take care of yourself and remember I love you."

Smiling, Silver Waters looked up into her daughter's face and caressed the hand on her shoulder. Her daughter staggered slightly under the load before she regained her balance and nimbly picked her way across the rough terrain toward her place in the caravan.

Rounding the end of the string of porters[9], Bright Moon could make out the bulky shape of the old caravan master. Even in the dim light, she could tell he waited

---

9 A person, or people, whose job is to carry burdens or baggage

impatiently for her.

"There you are; where have you been?" Long Tusk, hands on his ponderous hips, fixed her with an icy cold stare.

"Two more of our people have begun the sleep-from-which-no-one-wakes. I've gathered up the hides they carried and split them between myself and another, sir."

"Likely story," he snapped. "You and your people are weak and lazy good-for-nothings. You should have divided their bales long ago." A quick flick of his wrist brought his quirt[10] soundly across her bare legs raising yet another welt.[11] "Your indolence will cause us a delay." He drew back, ready to lay another blow alongside the first when Bright Moon shifted her burden, sliding the packets off her shoulders and between them, a defiant signal she would not take further abuse.

Enraged, Long Tusk glowered at her; but, towering over him by a head, Bright Moon held her ground and returned his venomous look with one of her own. "My people have struggled to do all you asked," she said, "yet you cut their rations and treat them miserably."

The deadlock was broken by a tussle among the porters up the line. "I'll tend to you later," Long Tusk said. His eyes burned with rage and hatred as he turned and waddled off in his distinctive shuffle to quell the disturbance.

Her anger under control, Bright Moon shifted her burden in order to slip her arms through the bindings and carry it on her back. With the bundle in place, she walked toward her group in the porter line. The sound of the caravan master's steps hung in her mind, haunting her. Bright Moon didn't know why.

---

10 A weighted, short-handled, whip usually made of braided rawhide or leather.
11 A raised mark on the skin (as produced by the blow of a whip), also called a wale.

Seeing her approach, Mochni[12], the out-walker[13] who oversaw these sections of porters, scowled at her and sneered, "You're late again. What's the problem this time?"

As an out-walker, it was Mochni's job to watch over a portion of the porters and keep discipline while on the trek. Out-walkers who handled the job well were rewarded; those who didn't were demoted... or worse. Mochni took her responsibilities seriously. She liked rewards and feared demotion. Her dark eyes set deeply in her pasty face, darted back and forth as she tried to keep an eye on everyone and everything.

"My mother is still weak from the fever and she needed my help." Bright Moon offered, knowing whatever she said would be unacceptable to the out-walker.

Mochni made a face as she examined a pointed end of her walking stick, "If your mother is too weak, she will be left behind. She might be set upon by bandits or become food for the wolves who trail after us," she sneered. "Long Tusk will not put up with her slowing the caravan down." The out-walker leaned in closer. Her scorn was evident in the hatred flashing in her eyes as she spoke. "He only tolerates her now because she is a Shaman[14] and has magical powers... and he wants to make you his woman."

"Make me his woman?" Bright Moon shuddered at Mochni's words. "He already has several women." She could not believe her ears.

"Not as a mate, you fool; as trade goods!" In disdain,

---

12 Hopi name meaning "talking bird."
13 A guide or escort, especially one employed to keep porters from acting up, running away or getting out of control. On occasion, they may be sent to catch runaways.
14 A "medicine elder" (not always a male) uses naturally occurring products, such as herbs, to treat ailments/illness. To become a Shaman, a person would apprentice themselves to a teacher for 20-30 years.

Mochni leaned over and spit. "Given the chance, he'll trade you for animals—goats maybe—certainly something more useful than you!" The out-walker broke into a fit of cackling before suddenly, deciding her attentions were needed elsewhere. She left Bright Moon alone to mull over her words.

In shock, Bright Moon watched the out-walker's chubby frame move up the line of porters, speaking to some and ignoring others as she went. *Trade goods?* She was stunned. *Long Tusk is planning to trade me for goats? I am a chief's daughter. How dare he consider such a thing!* Was Mochni serious or was this some twisted joke? Bright Moon was not sure.

From up the line, Long Tusk roared, "All right, let's move out!" Satisfied his presence had resolved whatever caused the disturbance, he eagerly bawled the order to begin the day's trek. The caravan—porters carrying trade goods, women carrying camp supplies, young children, slaves, herds of sheep and goats—started forward. At the same time, his scouts fanned out in several directions to look for game, water, and other tribes: those who were friendly and willing to trade, as well those not-so-friendly and should be avoided.

Alongside this procession walked Long Tusk's out-walkers armed with heavy sticks, sharpened on both ends, their points hardened in campfires. These were used to prod caravan members, especially porters, along. Long Tusk would not tolerate delays. The out-walkers did not tolerate stragglers.

Long Tusk excused their actions claiming the out-walkers were a second line of defense. By keeping the caravan together, it would be easier to defend against attack. Beyond the line of out-walkers, along each side as well as at the front and rear of the line, marched clusters of Long Tusk's warriors. "For protection," he said. "The first line of defense," he said.

Ever present, these moving walls surrounded the caravan. It took time, but Bright Moon now realized the out-walkers were not for protection. Her people had become prisoners. These two walls were there to keep her people from bolting.

The sun was high in the sky by the time they stopped for a short rest break. Hurriedly, women and children brought water pouches and dried food to their friends and family members among the porters. Silver Waters, a pouch in each hand, found Bright Moon resting on a fallen log. "Here daughter, take this to keep your strength up."

She shoved a water pouch and a bag of pemmican[15] at her. Bright Moon accepted the water, took a long drink, and then splashed some on her face and arms. She refused the food, saying, "No, Honored Mother, you keep it. You need it to grow strong."

"I've already eaten," her mother said and took the water back, hoping her daughter didn't see through her deception. Setting the container aside, Silver Waters resumed her efforts to get her daughter to take the pemmican. "You carry a heavy load, both our packs and more. You will need this to stay strong," she pleaded with her daughter. "Right now, food is scarce, but Long Tusk told me it will get better. In the meantime, you know whatever I have is yours."

"I know our people are hungry while Long Tusk's

---

15 A concentrated mixture of fat and protein (usually meat) used as a nutritious food as a mainstay while on the trail or as a supplement when other food was available. Traditionally pemmican was prepared from the lean meat of large game such as buffalo, elk, or deer. The meat was cut in thin slices and dried over a slow fire or in the hot sun until it was hard and brittle. Then it was pounded into very small pieces, almost powder-like in consistency, using stones. This was mixed with an equal amount of fat. When available, nuts and dried fruits were pounded into powder and then added to the meat/fat mixture. The resulting mixture could be packed into rawhide pouches for storage until needed.

people are well-fed. That's what I know!" Bright Moon snapped back. Regretting her tone, she reached up and patted Silver Waters' hand gently. "I'm sorry, Honored Mother, but it's the truth. I spoke to others of our tribe. You must eat and gain your strength so we can leave... or you could share it with our people. They could use it as much as I."

"We are so few and so weak I don't think we could survive if we struck out on our own." Silver Waters confided and dropped her head in dismay.

Mochni's harsh voice broke into their conversation. "All right, everybody on your feet, it's time to move on," she yelled. "You," the out-walker singled out Silver Waters, "get back to your group, you're holding us up."

Silver Waters stood up as if to leave and nodded toward the bundles Bright Moon would carry. "Are your packs still tied tight?"

Still seated, the girl twisted to look at the bindings. Silver Waters smiled and dropped the bag of pemmican into her daughter's lap, then turned to scurry off and join the women and children.

Bright Moon snapped around when she felt the pouch land. Tricked by her mother again! She could only shake her head and smile as she watched the woman disappear into the crowd.

Mochni glared at Silver Waters' retreating figure making sure she was out of sight before turning to face Bright Moon. The young woman, like the others in her group, was just getting to her feet. The out-walker leaned on her walking stick and watched Bright Moon shift her pack to a better position and then fasten a pouch to her belt.

"Here you, what do you have there?" Mochni challenged.

"Some extra food my mother brought me."

"In this caravan, there's no such thing as extra food." Mochni's eyes remained fixed greedily on the pouch. Always hungry, she knew extra food would help quiet her growling stomach. "You have what you're given so it must be stolen. That's why you're trying to hide it. Give it here."

"No, it's not stolen and I'm not hiding it. It's mine! My mother gave it to me." Chin up, Bright Moon glared back at her, thinking, *If this food goes to anyone, I want it to go to my people and not this oaf.*

Still leaning on her walking stick, Mochni bent forward to grab at the pouch. "I said, give it here, you thief!"

Bright Moon turned away, causing her assailant to lean in further. She caught her nemesis by the wrist and took another step back, pulling the out-walker off balance. Surprised, Mochni landed in a heap accompanied by a heavy thump.

Still holding on to her walking stick and now shouting obscenities, Mochni staggered to her feet. Hatred poured from her eyes. Bright Moon slipped out of her pack. The out-walker brought her stick up ready to strike; but Bright Moon grabbed it in both hands, twisted her attacker around, and pushed forward. Mochni went down again. Porters gathered around yelling, cheering, and laughing as they watched the scuffle.

"What's going on here?" Long Tusk shouted as he and two guards pushed through the crowd. The porters grew silent and backed away, hoping to escape any punishment that might be dealt out.

Bright Moon, her opponent's walking stick in hand, stood over the prostrate out-walker.

"She stole food!" Mochni shouted as she clamored to her feet. "Then she attacked me when I discovered her theft."

"Not true," Bright Moon said. "My mother gave me part of her meal." Nodding to Mochni, she added, "She tried to take it for herself."

Long Tusk looked from one to the other and back. Making a decision, he looked Bright Moon in the eyes and said, "Strokes[16], two hands' worth; one hand for attacking my out-walker and one hand for holding up my caravan."

He turned to the guards and said, "Tie her to that tree and get her ready."

---

16 Typically imposed on an unwilling subject, this is a form of corporal punishment which involves methodically beating a person or animal. It has also been called flogging, whipping, birching, and caning. Some specialized implements for it include rods, switches, and the cat o' nine tails.

Chapter 2: Punishment, Courage, Discovery

Long Tusk's words still ringing in her ears, Bright Moon felt the guards' fingers close around her wrists. A guard on each side, they pulled her to the base of a nearby oak. The men stripped her to the waist before pushing her face-first against the tree trunk. The bark dug into her bare skin. To keep her from backing away, one man shoved a hand in the middle of her back. The other guard tied a rope around her right wrist, ran it around the back of the tree, tied it around her left wrist, and pulled it tight. Pressed so firmly to the trunk, she was barely able to breathe and could not turn her head.

Even with her limited view, she knew Mochni was close by. The pudgy out-walker filled the air with her insane cackling, gleefully anticipating her next task while she waited for the signal to proceed. A low murmur of voices signaled the other caravan members had been gathered and would be forced to watch. Public discipline was Long Tusk's preferred method of keeping order.

Heavy footsteps, dimly familiar, shuffled across gravel and stopped out of her range of vision. Panic flowed over her, stifling all thoughts. She was sure she had heard the sound of those steps, the rhythm of that gait, before today.

Long Tusk leaned in close. Even before he spoke, she could tell it was him by his foul breath. "If you continue to rebel, I will break you," he whispered hoarsely. The caravan master stepped away. "Begin!" he ordered.

His words, echoing in her head, did not cover the sound of his footsteps as he retreated. She didn't deserve a beating, and certainly not one as brutal as what she was about to get. She grew weak in the knees picturing what would happen next. Her stomach churned and she had to fight the urge to retch. Mochni, pretending she was unfamiliar with the instrument, cackled as she snapped and cracked the leather whip in the air. Bright Moon was sure it was not the out-walker's first performance. Stillness fell over the crowd in anticipation of the first blow. The demonstration the women put on was to instill fear in the onlookers and break the victim's will. Bright Moon would not let this happen to her. Determined not to show fear or pain, she bit her lip and held her breath while she waited for Mochni to begin. She did not have to wait long.

Behind her, a hefty grunt shattered the air. Bright Moon could picture the out-walker swing her whip-arm back over her shoulder and strain to put all her being into bringing it forward. A hissing sound filled the stillness as thorn-laced leather cut through the air to burn a path across her shoulders. Pain, burning pain, she wanted to scream, to cry out, but clenched her teeth instead. Bright Moon buried her face in the bark, took another breath, and held it. *Don't think about the whip,* she told herself. *Think about something else, anything else.*

"Da!"[17] Nearby, one of Long Tusk's guards began to count loudly as each blow fell. The other guard, a hand held high in the air raised a finger and circled the crowd for all to see the official count.

Another whirr, another burning pain, tears came to her eyes, but she did not cry out.

"Jar!" The guard called. She could picture the second guard, holding up two fingers, as he strutted in front of the gathering.

Bright Moon focused on what had happened the

---

17 In this culture, counting is done in sets of five. One hand is a count of five; two hands are a count of ten. Individual numbers are: Da (1); Jar (2); Cha (3); Tug (4); and Mux (5). Numbers six through ten uses Pra plus the count, as Pra-Da (6), Pra-Jar (7), etc.

night her father's caravan was attacked. *Camped near a small creek, on the border between forest and grassy steppes, the caravan felt they had an ideal place to stop for the night. For the last several nights, her mother's dreams had been filled with dark visions of pending doom and she had not been sleeping well. Always cautious, Great Elk posted guards.*

The whip bit into her skin again. "Cha" The guard's voice broke into her thoughts.

Another voice, it was Long Tusk this time. "Come on," he urged, "put your back into it!"

Mochni wheezed heavily. Bright Moon pictured her, beads of sweat covering her fat jowls as she strained to make a good show for Long Tusk. The rawhide cut through the air. Searing pain slashed across her back and into her consciousness, but she refused to cry out, refused even to whimper.

Great Elk was always so careful, how did this happen to them? It had been a long, hard day's march, she recalled. After evening meal, Father ordered the fires banked and the caravan settled in for the night. Quiet fell quickly over the encampment.

The whip sliced through the air, raising another welt and laying her skin open.

"Tug," the guard called.

Bright Moon's hammock was slung between branches in a pine grove. Her mother and father slept nearby. It was dark when she woke not knowing what disturbed her. Half asleep, she fought against dozing off as she lay still and listened. The night fires were out. Why were they out? Those on guard always kept the fires going. She heard new noises, unusual at this time of night. Heavy, shuffling footsteps, crunching gravel near the creek, and twigs crackling. Sleep had become a thing of the past. The sounds were coming closer to where she lay curled up in her hammock. The sounds she remembered were the same as those she heard when Long Tusk approached her moments before. She was sure of it.

Another whir and the rawhide exploded across her back. Bright Moon bit her lip.

"Mux," the guard called. She pictured the second guard holding up one hand, fingers spread wide to signal the completion of one hand's count. One more hand's count to go. Her head swam, her legs grew weaker, and then darkness engulfed her.

The smack of cold water brought her sharply awake. Bright Moon's breath came in gasps.

"Is she awake?" Long Tusk questioned. Someone splashed her with more water. Remembering where she was, Bright Moon struggled to her feet and hugged the tree tightly.

"She's awake," Mochni replied. "Do you want me to continue?"

"Continue... If you have the strength," Bright Moon spat out, taunting her tormentors and interrupting anything Long Tusk would have said.

Robbed of the decision, afraid of losing face if he backed off, Long Tusk strode forward and grabbed the whip from Mochni's hands. Bright Moon listened to his footfalls as he closed the distance to the tree and leaned in close to ensure his venomous whisper filled her ears. "Your father, Great Elk, wouldn't listen. I had to break him, teach him a lesson. He fought me to the end, but I won." His putrid breath filled the air around them. "You want more?" He waved the coiled whip in her face. "I'll give you more," he hissed.

He turned away and she heard his distinctive shuffle fade as he moved back, cracking the whip menacingly as he went. Egged on by her words, he would be harder on her than Mochni had been, but by baiting him, she gained another chance to listen to his footsteps. It confirmed her suspicions.

The rawhide split the air, burning a fresh streak across her back, opening another wound.

"Pra-Da," the guard called half-heartily.

Marauders exploded from the darkness falling on Great Elk's caravan. The air was filled with screams and shouts. Caught off-

guard and in the dark, many of his people became victims of swinging clubs, jabbing spears.

The whip carved a new path across her back before the sound of its travel through the air arrived. She gritted her teeth, against the need to cry out.

"Pra-Jar," called the guard.

Under the onslaught, a few members of her father's caravan fled to the safety of the forest. It was daybreak before any of them crept back to what had been their campsite. In the darkness, the raiders had grabbed whatever they could before they disappeared, swallowed up by the night.

Another stroke burned across her back.

"Pra-Cha," called the guard.

Many were wounded. Some of the wounded suffered before dying. Others had been killed outright; Great Elk, her father, was one of them.

Long Tusk wheezed under the effort. The strokes were coming slower, but they were still coming. With great effort, he laid another mark across her back.

"Pra-Tug," called the guard.

Bright Moon acted as Shaman and tended the wounded. One was her mother, Silver Waters. Wounded, more in spirit than in body, she had been sick with fever ever since the attack.

Again, the rawhide cut across her back.

"Pra-Mux," called the guard. Bright Moon could picture the second guard holding up both hands. The beating over, she embraced the tree and waited to be cut down.

Two, maybe three days after the raid, Long Tusk's caravan arrived. His people seemed concerned for their welfare. They helped gather up and care for the remaining survivors. In the beginning, food and protection were offered and little was asked in exchange.

Because they were in no condition to look out for themselves when Long Tusk was ready to move on, he agreed to take them in and make them a part of his caravan, but only if they would agree to certain changes. In the beginning, he requested able-bodied men, women, and children act as porters and perform other tasks. As the days wore on, further changes were made, their significance wasn't obvious then, but, by the time three moons' had passed, Great Elk's people had become slaves within the caravan. Occasionally, some of their members disappeared. Bright Moon's people were told these individuals had grown tired of caravan life and decided to remain behind in the last village. Bright Moon now realized they had been bartered away—forced to trade one type of slavery for another.

Through sweat-blurred vision, Bright Moon saw one of the guards swing a stone ax. The ropes holding her went slack. The beating over, she relaxed and felt her legs go weak. Pretending to offer support, her guards each took an arm, turned her away from the tree and let go. Bright Moon heard a familiar cry and managed to stumble three steps toward her mother before going to her knees. Darkness closed in on her. The last thing she saw was the ground rushing up. She put out her hands to break her fall.

Chapter 3: Confirmation

Tears streamed down Silver Waters face as she knelt over her daughter's inert form. "You had no right to beat her like this." She stopped searching through her medicine pouch to look up at Long Tusk' sweat stained face. "Do you hear me, you had no right."

"No right!" Long Tusk sputtered. "No right!" He raised clenched fists and shouted, "I am Caravan Master. I have every right."

"Being Caravan Master does not give you the right to deprive my people of food and warm clothing, nor does it give you the right to beat someone into unconsciousness."

Frustrated by his inability to break the girl and now faced with her mother's demands, his rage rose even higher. "Your people are lazy... greedy... and... and ungrateful. If I knew then what I know now, I would not have come to your rescue."

Silver Waters, unwilling to back down, clamored to her feet to face this wretched man. "If you had known...? If we had known, we would have taken our chances without your help. Maybe more of my people would have survived. You work us to our deaths."

Nosily, Long Tusk sucked in a deep breath through clenched teeth. "Your people die because they are not used to honest work. I've taken food from my own people to share with yours and only asked your clans carry a share of our burden. But your people are a bunch of complaining weaklings who do nothing but complain and hold up my caravan."

On the ground where the guards dropped her after cutting her down, Bright Moon moaned and stirred. Silver

Waters quickly fell to her knees and began quieting the girl.

"Hush, my daughter," she told Bright Moon. "Lie still and let me finish my work." Stone-faced, Silver Waters gave Long Tusk a cold, dark stare before finally speaking. "You concern yourself with your caravan, but because of what you've done, this girl will be of no use to you. I looked into your future and see you die, falling from the sky covered in flames. Delay should not be your biggest worry, Caravan Master." She held her gaze on him for a moment longer and then bent to tend to her daughter, dismissing Long Tusk as if he weren't there. Shaken by her prediction, he turned and left, hoping to put as much distance as he could between Silver Waters and himself.

Silver Waters put aside her Shaman's role and became a mother once again. Gently, she cleaned Bright Moon's wounds with water and a flood of tears. As a Shaman, she had balm for the wounds and would finish by covering her back with soft hides. The wounds would close over and, in a few days, the lash marks would be invisible. Bright Moon gritted her teeth and lay still while her mother tended her.

Waiting for the signal to start, clan members huddled in small groups and spoke in low voices. They heard Silver Waters' prediction and believed every word. Her words were on everyone's lips.

At the head of the caravan, an agitated Long Tusk, still sweat covered and wheezing, stared at the ground and paced about impatiently. His complaints filled the air. Even in his rage, he was unable to break the girl, and now her mother, the Shaman, predicted his death. *A fiery one*, she said, *he would fall from the sky*. It was an absurd story, but one that had enhanced the idea the woman was more than a shaman. *In the eyes of his people, she was a witch with magical powers*. He knew he had lost face with everyone in the caravan, even his own people. Now he must plan some way of recovering his power even if it meant he had to rid himself of the girl.

Rid himself of the girl! This was the answer to his problems. All he had to do to resolve the problem was to arrange for this trade to happen. I will give her as a gift and receive a gift in exchange. He smiled broadly. His future looked brighter than it had for some time.

Long Tusk wheeled about and started back the way he had come. On the way to the head of the caravan, he had walked past a scout, the one called Kaliska[18], lounging idly in the shade of a tree. He entertained some youngsters by balancing his war-club on top of his head while hopping from one foot to another.

The young man, an exceptional scout, had joined the caravan just two moons back. He was given to Long Tusk by an old chief in payment of a debt. As an outsider, the scout was not yet trusted to participate in any night raids. Those were handled in secret by Long Tusk's people. He didn't know Kaliska well, but certainly the man could be trusted with this task.

Arduously, Long Tusk waddled over to confront the scout. The sentinel, a lean, muscular, young man, immediately came to attention. "I need you to pay a visit to my friend Askook[19], Chief of the Mattocks." Long Tusk paused to roll the idea over in his mind. He delighted in its promise. It was so simple; he should have thought of it earlier.

"Yes...?" Unconsciously, the young man shifted from one foot to another waiting for Long Tusk to recover from his fantasy and continue.

The caravan chief dropped his voice and started again. "I need you to pay a visit to my friend Askook, Chief of The Mattocks. Tell him I wish to present this girl as a gift." A quick nod of his head confirmed he meant Bright Moon. "She is strong and young, less than three hands old," he continued, "and will have many years of childbearing ahead of her." Delighted with the idea, he

---

18 Miwok name meaning "coyote chasing deer."
19 Native American Algonquin name meaning "snake."

almost danced at the sound of his words. "Tell Askook we will be at the place where the river meets the Great Ice. It's where we've met before." Long Tusk held up both hands, fingers spread and added, "We'll be there in two hand's time and will have goods to trade... and the girl as a present."

As a scout, Kaliska wasn't in camp very often; a situation he preferred since it gave him more... time; time to gather information; and time to plan his revenge for what Long Tusk had done to his family. Kaliska was repayment of a debt, but he had a debt of his own to settle.-

He knew of the girl, having seen her around the caravan; he also heard the gossip and had seen how badly she and her people were treated. With the rest of the caravan, he was forced to watch the beating and flinched as each stroke fell. The girl defied her tormenters and he cheered inwardly. *But give her as a present!* Calm on the outside, Kaliska did his best not to show the rage he felt on the inside. *This evil man, unable to break the girl, now wants to give her away as a present! Perhaps she would be better off with this new man.* He shuddered. *If Askook was truly a friend of Long Tusk's then she might be no better off. Maybe, if I built her up as a shaman, one with magic powers, Askook's treatment of her might be better than she currently receives. Who knows?*

"Do you understand what you're to do?" The Caravan Master questioned.

Jarred out of his own reverie, Kaliska quickly summarized the task he'd been given. "I am to visit Askook, Chief of The Mattocks, with this message: in two hand's time, you will meet him where the river meets the Great Ice." The scout's answer barely hid his true feelings, but the fact went unnoticed by Long Tusk.

"Yes, our usual meeting place. We can trade goods and I will give him the girl as a present."

The scout left to carry out his task and Long Tusk called Mochni over. "The girl is barely able to walk, let alone carry anything. I will not have my caravan held up. As trade goods, she still has value. You started this so now you get to carry her burden." He held two hands in front of her face, fingers spread wide, "You are to look after her this long," he said.

Surprised, Mochni's mouth dropped. Ten days! She wanted to protest; but, fearing the same fate as Bright Moon, she kept silent.

Putting the girl in Mochni's care assured Long Tusk he would have somebody he could trust to watch her. This would work until he heard if Askook would become the answer to his problem. If not, he would come up with a different plan... a better plan. He turned and squinted into the sun, now above the horizon, and then nodded to his bodyguards saying, "Get the procession ready to go. We've lost enough time."

Mochni strolled over to her charge. "Get on your feet," she spat. "We're ready to move and Long Tusk in his mercy has asked me to carry your burden." Making no effort to hide her disgust, she grabbed the girl's packs, hoisted them up onto her shoulders, and wobbled off under this unaccustomed load.

As Bright Moon watched her persecutor stagger away, a slight smile played at the corners of her mouth. Even though she had suffered, she had won this battle against both foes. Her mother, having smoothed out the balm, covered the wounds with strips of soft rabbit skin. It would do for now.

They left the grassy plains and entered rolling hills. These were followed by forest-clad foothills beyond which they could see the edge of the Great Ice creeping out of mountain valleys.

The trail twisted back and forth as it wound upward toward the summit and their trek became more rigorous with each step. Reaching the top, they would follow the crest for two days, before descending. At times, a cold, biting wind swept off the glacier and covered their path with white-rain. It would turn to mush and disappear under the sun's gaze, but not before they were soaked to the skin.

The route they traveled, new to Bright Moon, skirted the edge of a gorge. Large birds, someone called them 'Condors', would launch themselves from the ledge where they roosted and glide effortlessly through the air. The birds were huge. Each of their wings looked longer than a man was tall.

Leaning on her walking stick, Bright Moon watched the plodding movements of the procession stretching out in front of her. The sun was setting. They would be making camp soon.

"Are you going to stand there all day?" Mochni growled. "I don't want to be the last one in camp again tonight."

"Do these birds make you nervous?" Bright Moon taunted her.

"No they don't," Mochni snapped. "The best food will be gone by the time we get there. I'm tired of missing out."

Bright Moon heard the words the out-walker spoke, but noticed she kept a close eye on the birds.

"The trail is easy to follow. I can find the encampment myself. If you want to go ahead, I'll follow along."

"Be sure you do," came Mochni's sour reply. "Unless you want another beating." Bending low under the weight of Bright Moon's packs, the out-walker wobbled on, complaining as she went, but wary of the birds.

After a few moments, Bright Moon fell in step

behind, where the out-walker couldn't see her smile. She enjoyed watching Mochni struggle under the load while she healed and she would enjoy this change in roles as long as she could.

"Finally!" Mochni staggered into the meadow where the caravan would spend the night. Still a few paces behind, Bright Moon watched the out-walker single out a porter, drop her packs at his feet and demand he stow them with the others. No longer concerned with this burden, she staggered off, grunting and groaning about her aches as she went.

It had been three days since Bright Moon's flogging. Silver Waters had grown weaker with every step, but still found the energy to wash and dress her daughter's injuries each night. Because of her care, the girl's wounds were healing nicely.

During these sessions, Silver Waters showed Bright Moon the medicines in her pouch, described each, where it could be found, and its uses. The way her breath rattled in her chest, Silver Waters knew her time to pass on knowledge to her daughter was limited.

Bright Moon found her mother in the care of another woman. "Her fever has grown worse and she is weak," the woman explained.

"My daughter," Silver Waters said. "It is good... you're here... there are... so few of us left... you have much to learn... I will soon join...."

A startled yell and screams interrupted her.

"Trouble," Silver Waters said, her trained ear recognizing the sound. "Take my pouch...," she wheezed, "and see what you can do." She pushed her shoulder satchel[20] to Bright Moon.

---

20 This is a bag with a cover, similar to a saddlebag, but often with a strap. The strap is often worn so it diagonally crosses the body, with

The girl looked at her dumbfounded. "Why... what...." Lost for words, she stumbled trying to make sense of her words.

Her mother looked down, gathered herself and then, raising her head to look her daughter in the eyes, she said, "I am not able to help... I will probably... be joining your father soon. You are Shaman now... I see greatness for you.... It is your duty... your calling. You must go and help... I must rest now."

Silver Waters, slumped back on the mat and closed her eyes, dismissing her daughter. Weighted down by her new responsibilities, Bright Moon picked up the pouch and hurried off. She would do her best as fast as she could and return when she finished.

Across the camp, a crowd had gathered. Elbowing her way toward the center, Bright Moon reached an inner circle where she saw a young woman on the ground, her head cradled in a sobbing man's lap. "I am the Shaman," she shouted. "Let me through!"

Surprised, the crowd parted and allowed her access. Bright Moon dropped to the ground next to the couple. "What happened?" She asked.

"She was making a place for us here. She did not see the snake and... and...." He broke down in tears, unable to continue.

"Snake! We must act quickly, where did it strike?"

Weakly, the young woman stretched out a leg and pointed.

"Light, I need a light here." Bright Moon searched the pouch and found what she needed. Someone arrived with a torch. She motioned them to bring it closer and leaned in to inspect the exposed limb. Just above the

---

the bag hanging on the opposite hip, rather than hanging directly down from the shoulder. Satchels are most commonly made of leather or cloth.

ankle, she found a swollen area with two small fang marks.

Moving quickly, she wrapped a rawhide cord above the marks and twisted the ends tightly to make a tourniquet. "Hold the light here," Bright Moon commanded and, flint bladed knife in hand, she enlarged the wounds the snake had made. Blood flowed as she worked the flesh around the wounds with her fingers and then bent to suck the poisoned juice, spitting each mouthful aside. She performed this action until she could no longer taste the snake's bitter fluid. Grabbing her bag, she applied ointments and herbs to the wounds and wrapped them in a soft leather skin from her pouch. She removed the tourniquet, and watched color flow back into the young woman's lower leg.

"The balm I applied acts as a poultice[21] and helps draw the poison out. She will be weak, may be feverish, but should be alright in a day or...."

"What's going on here?" Long Tusk pushed his way through the crowd, shoving anyone out of the way who did not move fast enough on their own. He was trailed by his two guards. Mochni followed in their wake.

"The woman was bitten by a snake," said a voice from the crowd. "The Shaman saved her." Others nodded and voiced their agreement.

Long Tusk looked around, but only saw Bright Moon kneeling near the woman. "Shaman? What Shaman? What are you talking about?" Long Tusk was beside himself with what he considered trickery. Mochni, straining to get a better look, bounced around behind the guards.

Rising to her feet, Bright Moon lifted her chin defiantly and said, "It is I who saved her. I am the

---

21 A Medicine that might be converted to a paste and applied as a salve or, used dry, worn in a small bag. Its purpose is to heal bruises, break up congestion, reduce inflammation, withdraw pus, toxins and embedded particles in the skin, and to soothe irritation.

Shaman now. She must rest here for two days."

Caught off-guard, Long Tusk's jaw dropped. Mochni, still behind the guards, yelled, "She's not the Shaman. She's nothing. A porter... and a thief! She can't be the Shaman."

Prodded by Mochni's retort, Long Tusk's anger boiled over. "You! Shaman? Never!"

He took a threatening step toward Bright Moon, but she held her ground. A protest rose from the crowd, most of whom were not part of Long Tusk's original tribe. Their behavior let him know she had their favor and he did not. To regain control, he would have to take action in secret and do so quickly.

Chapter 4: Vengeance

Long Tusk focused his caustic gaze on Bright Moon. She didn't flinch. With the crowd behind her, there was little he could do right now. "All right," he agreed, "we'll make camp here for two days." Waving his quirt under her nose, he warned, "By that time, everyone will see if a Shaman or a fake stands in front of them."

The woman, embarrassed to be the center of everyone's attention and the cause for the delay, tried to raise herself on one elbow. Bright Moon placed a hand on her shoulder, cautioning, "Lie back, you need rest and quiet."

The crowd rallied around the couple as individuals presented words of encouragement and offers of assistance. Long Tusk quietly motioned Mochni to follow him and he pushed his way out of the throng. Bright Moon looked up in time to see the pair, trailed by the guards, melt into the chaos. She knew they were plotting but didn't know what and would have to always be on the alert. Right now, it was time to check on her mother. Turning to the couple, she gave the man final instructions on caring for his mate, gathered her bag of medicines, and made her way through the crowd.

Long Tusk waited until he and Mochni were out of earshot before he spoke. Even then, he kept his voice low, barely above a hoarse whisper. "The girl is nothing but trouble. I had been hoping she would come around, hoping she would understand her place. I believed I could barter her for trade goods when I reached my friend in the land of the Mattocks. I even sent word ahead. I think I could strike a good bargain, but she has grown into too much of a problem." He shook his head in despair over the lost opportunity and looked over at Mochni. Was she listening?

The out-walker gave him a side-glance. It confirmed he expected some kind of response. Not sure what to say, Mochni finally choked out an answer, "What... what are you planning to do now?"

"My plans are to do nothing," he said sharply. "Your plan, however, is to make her disappear."

Make her disappear! Shock and then excitement filled Mochni as her mind raced on. She tried to listen to the Caravan Master as he continued his rant, but his words were lost. *Long Tusk is willing to entrust me with this great task. It could mean much to my future. His rewards will be generous.* Mochni smiled, *Generous, yes!*

"Mochni! Are you listening?"

Mochni snapped her head around and looked at Long Tusk. "Sorry, sir."

"You've been with her. She's grown accustomed to you being around. We're walking along a gorge. Before we next make camp, drop back from the caravan and, when you have the opportunity, a gentle nudge should take care of your problem." Long Tusk looked at his out-walker. Had he sized her up correctly? Locked in his cold stare, he watched her face as she struggled with the turmoil boiling within her.

Mochni gulped. She wasn't a stranger to the raids and the fights that went with them, but she swallowed hard at the prospect of just pushing somebody off a cliff. Taking a deep breath, she said, "Yes. Yes, I can do it."

Bright Moon, wooden cup in hand, sat with her mother. They watched the rising moon as she recounted the details of that afternoon. "...so, after I located the fang marks, I tied off her leg, made small cuts over the wounds and sucked out as much of the poisoned blood as I could." She smiled warmly at Silver Waters and leaned forward to offer her mother more warm broth.

Weakly, her mother held up a hand rejecting the nourishment. She returned the girl's warm smile and whispered, "You have done well, daughter.... I knew you would... be able to handle... the situation... whatever it was... you would at least give it your best... our people... those who are left... will be proud." She lay back, exhausted from her little speech.

"You're weak, you need to eat and get stronger." Bright Moon coaxed as she pushed the cup toward her mother.

Silver Waters closed her eyes and turned her head away. "Yes... I am weak," she finally agreed. "But, you must... prepare yourself.... It is my time.... I probably... will not last... through the night."

Shocked, Bright Moon was at a loss for words, but finally stammered, "But... you must eat and get well...."

Her mother shook her head. "No,' she said, "it is my time. I will join your father... in the-sleep-from-which-no-one-wakes.... Prepare yourself now."

"I will stay by your side and keep watch. If you drink this soup, you'll get better." Bright Moon offered her the cup, again.

"No soup. I need you... to come closer now." She raised her head weakly, and whispered, "I have things... to tell you." Obediently, Bright Moon bent close and strained to hear her mother's words.

"I have heard rumors," Silver Waters said. "Long Tusk leads his men on raids... attacking villages. I believe it was... they who attacked Great Elk. They may be preparing... for such a thing tonight. Keep your eyes open. If it is true... avenge your father... and our friends."

"Honored Mother, I believe you are right. I have spoken with our people and have come to the same conclusion."

Silver Waters nodded. "You are wise beyond your years, but... you must be wary... lest your wisdom... gives you a false confidence.... It will be your downfall." With great effort, she drew a breath. Bright Moon caressed her mother's hand, bringing it to her own tear-streaked face. Silver Water's fingers stroked her daughter's cheek. "My daughter.... I love you.... I go now... but my spirit... will watch over you... always."

She slumped back, her breath escaping in one long sigh and she entered into the-sleep-from which-no-one-wakes. Bright Moon fell across her mother's body, wishing her tears could pull her mother's spirit back, but to no avail.

It was long past dusk by the time Bright Moon finished tearfully lacing her mother's body into the sleeping-robes that had become her burial shroud. Fires, a small one near her mother's head and another at the foot of her wrapped body, did little to push back the darkness.

Exhausted from the day's trek, camp activity died out and the stillness of night fell over the area. Here and there, night fires burned. In the morning, she would get help to create a burial site.

From somewhere in the darkness, muffled footsteps and low voices caught her attention. She stopped her work and peered into the darkness, straining to locate their source. Staying low, she got to her feet and started forward. No one else was awake. Quieter than a great cat, she kept to the shadows as she moved along. There were no guards around the night fires. It soon became obvious to her none of Long Tusk's people were in camp. Ahead lay a gully, outlined by the soft glow of a campfire. Getting on her belly, she crawled silently until she reached the rim.

Long Tusk, his guards, warriors and out-walkers-- Mochni among them—were gathered around one side of a fire. Facing them across the flames, a scout gave his report. Bright Moon was only able to hear a few words, but from those she understood a scouting party had found another caravan. It was in a village not far off their route. This scout returned with the news while the others in the scouting party stayed behind to keep watch. Excited by the report, Long Tusk smiled broadly and rubbed his hands together as he danced a little dance. Others joined him in the celebration. *Yes*, if they *attacked the village and the train together and they could gather riches, trade goods, and slaves from both.*

In preparation for the raid, Long Tusk's people donned tunics of animal hides turned inside out. The hides' smooth inside, naturally ashy in color, reflected what little light there was, enabling them to identify themselves in the dark from their victims.

So, it was true and not something she imagined! Long Tusk and his people had attacked her father's caravan only to return a few days later, play innocent and act as if they were concerned for the welfare of the remaining survivors. He took them in, but made them slaves. What she witnessed tonight confirmed they had been duped. It was apparent this was not a new undertaking for Long Tusk, but one he had played many times.

The caravan master had heard enough. His plan was in place. His people knew their roles, and everyone was ready. Weapons in hand, men, and women followed their leader, his guards, and the scout out of the gully. Bright Moon waited, listening as the sounds of their movements was swallowed by the night, and then slid over the lip of the gully to fall in, unnoticed, behind them. *Tonight, she would have her revenge!*

Chapter 5: Raiders

Thanks to the light color of their tunics, Bright Moon could see the ghostly outlines of Long Tusk's people as they padded along the path. It was good they stayed on a well-worn trail. She needed to follow close enough not to lose them, but not so close as to be discovered. She failed.

The terrain was rough and Bright Moon tripped. A woman, the last person in Long Tusk's group, heard the commotion and turned to see Bright Moon getting to her feet.

The woman beckoned, "Hurry, or you'll be lost in the dark," she whispered. "Where's your tunic?" Not waiting for a reply, the woman, believing Bright Moon infirm and incapable of keeping up, reached out, grabbed her hand and pulled her along.

Having executed their plan before, Long Tusk's people had grown so confident of their success the woman never gave Bright Moon a second glance. Caught in her grip, Bright Moon had little choice but to go along.

The raiding party did not slow their pace until they reached the flat meadow. There, the remaining scouts, the ones who had stayed behind, poured out of a copse[22] of trees to join them. Long Tusk's raiders split into groups, spread out in a line and crept forward toward their intended victims. Unable to separate herself from the others, Bright Moon stayed low to the ground and sought the protection of shadows to keep from being recognized.

The campsites of the unsuspecting villagers and the visiting caravan members were disbursed among clumps

---

22 A thicket of small trees or shrubs; a coppice.

of trees prominent in this area. Ahead, the lights from their night fires were the only signs of life.

The raiding party came to a halt at a place just outside the main encampment. Long Tusk's scouts, carrying skins of water, crept further into the sleeping settlement. They intended to douse the fires and leave their intended victims in the dark and confused. A crescent moon hung low in the sky and neither it nor the stars provided enough light to give them away. Bright Moon knew those in front would attack without warning as soon as the scouts extinguished the fires unless she could do something. Her heart in her throat, she cupped her hands around her mouth and, in her deepest voice shouted, "Attack! Attack! Attack!"

Up to this point, Long Tusk's raiders had expected this assault, like the ones they had made before, would be successful. Shocked by this outburst, they froze in place. Their scouts had not had time to quench all of the fires. In the encampment, voices—one, two, then more—rose up in alarm. Recovering from the surprise, Long Tusk's people launched their attack, leaping forward, yelling, and waving weapons. Their intended victims rallied quickly and the bedlam of hand-to-hand fighting in the dark began. In the village, a fire broke out, its flames silhouetting the combatants locked in their struggle.

The woman who had taken her hand earlier charged Bright Moon, but she danced out of the way and looked for an escape. Unsatisfied, her opponent clutched at the air and became entangled in the Shaman necklace. Desperate to get away, Bright Moon ducked under the woman's arm and swung her fist, catching her assailant in the gut. Her adversary gasped and stumbled backwards, still clutching the necklace. The girl had to act quickly before others joined in. Unable to free her necklace, Bright Moon hunched over and slid out of the ornament.

Free of her attacker's grip, Bright Moon looked for an escape but was completely lost in the dark. In the village, another fire flared up, its flickering fingers vainly attempting to push back the night. A figure jumped in front of her, blocking the path. There was no way around this new menace. Before Bright Moon could change directions, another form stepped out of the shadows, swung a club, and cleared her path. With his free hand, the club-swinging man—Bright Moon could not make out his features—grabbed her hand and pulled her behind him. Then he turned and tripped the nearest person, pushing their falling body into another opponent. Before the individual hit the ground, a body-block added another to the pile.

Still shielding her behind him, her protector motioned toward the mass of bodies thrashing around and yelled, "Quickly, there's the one who called out. Don't let him get away." Changing direction, he quickly guided Bright Moon along the edge of the mêlée while, behind them, irate, club-swinging, people descended on the wad of fallen bodies. Still holding her hand, he led her through the fracas before coming to a halt, somewhere in the vacant darkened meadow. Leaning in close, he whispered, "This is where we go our separate ways."

Bright Moon peered at her protector. Mud camouflaged his face, leaving only his dark eyes and broad smile visible in the dim light. She could not make out any other features, but was sure he was not someone she would recognize even in daylight. The conflict still raged behind them, but it was not Long Tusk's plan to fight an even battle. His forces would melt into the night soon and beat a quick retreat.

As if her guardian had read her mind, he said, "The battle won't last long. You'll have to hurry to get back to camp before they do. When he gets there, Long Tusk will want to know who gave the alarm. You'll have to convince him you never left. Do you have another necklace like the one you lost?"

Bright Moon took a deep breath before nodding. *Yes,* she thought, *I know where there is another necklace just like the one I lost... and I know what I will have to do to get it.*

Her guardian smiled. "This is the path the raiders used to cross the meadow. The camp is just a little ways from here. I've done all I can do." He gave her a gentle push and she started up the path toward the camp. A glance over her shoulder allowed her to see him turn and melt into the darkness.

Stunned by his sudden appearance, she had listened to him but hadn't spoken a word, not even to ask his name. *Who is he? Would she see him again? Was he one of Long Tusk's tribe or was he one of the intended victims? What was he doing here? Since he knew she lost her necklace in the fray, how long had he been there watching her? And why did he choose to help her?* She had no answers and it was too late to ask, but she did remember his eyes and his smile. For now, that would have to be enough because she had to plan her escape from even greater problems. The answers to these questions would have to wait.

Bright Moon didn't know what happened to the woman who accosted her, but the loss of her necklace would be a problem. If Long Tusk suspected her, Bright Moon would not live to see the sunrise. She would have to have an unquestionable alibi. This meant she would have to do something repulsive—something she was reluctant to do.

Along the way, she picked up some firewood and a pine tree limb. It was almost as long as her leg. She clutched the limb in one hand. Her fingers and thumb barely touched wherever she grabbed it. The wood was green and slow to start burning, but burned well once afire. This limb would make a fine torch. It was a particularly important part of her plan. She smiled at her good fortune.

###

Cautiously, she slipped back into camp and the place where her mother lay. All appeared to be quiet. If anyone saw her she hoped it would appear to them she had been out gathering firewood. The two fires left to keep her mother company were reduced to glowing coals. She stirred them and added wood to each before kneeling beside her mother's shroud.

"I am sorry Honored Mother. I do not wish to do this. In my heart I truly beg your forgiveness." She untied the knot holding the shroud closed and drew back the robe. "I mean no disrespect, but I must do this," she repeated. Taking a deep breath, she grasped her mother's Shaman necklace—one identical to her own—and yanked it free. Necklace in hand, she checked to make sure her action left a mark around her mother's neck. Satisfied, she laced the shroud closed and retied the cord. Finally, she tied the broken ends of the necklace strands together, donned the ornament and tucked it inside her own tunic.

With her mother's necklace in place, she used a piece of firewood to dig a hole, stopping when she reached clay. She slipped one end of the tree limb in the hole and pushed the excess dirt, except for a small amount of clay, around its base to hold the shaft upright while she worked. Bright Moon wrapped bundled twigs and tinder[23] around the exposed end and bound them in place with strips of fat-drenched hide.

On the side facing her, she inserted more tinder, pushing it deep inside the fat-drenched cap. To add more moisture to the clay, she spit on it before kneading it in her hands then smoothed it out thin and flat. Using a set of twigs like pincers, she worked an ember free from the fire and dropped it in the middle of the flattened clay. Loosely wrapping the glowing coal in the clay, she tucked her creation in the tinder. At the right moment, she hoped it would come to her rescue.

Voices, angry voices, accompanied by the sound of many feet announced Long Tusk and his raiders had returned. She wiped her hands clean, threw her digging stick in the fire, and straightened up her camp in

---

23 Fine, dry grasses and other materials for starting a fire.

expectation of her guests' arrival.

When they found her, Bright Moon was sitting cross-legged near her mother's shroud. With heavy heart, she swayed rhythmically while slowly passing a lit branch over a bedroll. It was part of the ancient ceremonial dirge her people performed over those who now slept the-sleep-from-which-no-one-wakes. Tears began to flow as the girl said her final good-bye to the woman who had looked after her all these years.

Even accompanied by the others, Bright Moon could pick out the sound of Long Tusk's ponderous shuffle long before his entrance. She did not look up when they arrived, torches in hand. He came to a halt in front of her, but she continued waving the branch and singing softly.

The two small fires cast more shadows than light, but it would not have made a difference. In his rage, Long Tusk did not recognize the ceremony. In the flickering light, he did not see the tears glistening in her eyes nor the ones forming rivulets down her cheeks.

Her routine was disrupted when Long Tusk tossed the necklace in her lap. "Explain this?" He barked. "Is it yours?"

Bright Moon looked at the necklace in her lap. "No," she said softly. After a slight pause, she added, "It is my mother's. Where did you get it?"

A murmur went up from the crowd and Long Tusk grunted his dissatisfaction. "Your mother's...?" He looked at her dumbfounded. Recovering, he challenged, "Then where is yours?"

"Right here," Bright Moon said. With her free hand, she dipped into her tunic and pulled out the necklace she wore. "Where I always have it."

"The Shaman is needed. Where is she?" he demanded. *I cannot believe the old woman, sick with fever, could travel that far, fight as hard as my people claim, and then hide*

39

herself so well. I found the necklace she left behind. I will find her and she will get the punishment she deserves... they both will.

Bright Moon did not look up, but continued to wave the flaming wand. "Right in front of you," she replied softly. "I am the Shaman now."

Disdainfully, Long Tusk spat. "Not you, girl. Your mother! Where is she?" His fists clenched in rage.

Tear-streaked face, she looked up at him, the epitome of sadness and mourning, she replied, "My mother is here also.... In front of you... she sleeps the-sleep-from-which-no-one-wakes...." Their eyes locked and she added, "I am the Shaman, now. What is your need?"

Long Tusk looked at the tear-stained face of the girl sitting behind the bedroll and finally realized she had been conducting Silver Waters' funeral when they arrived. Disregarding her grief, he turned to his guards and pointed at the bedroll. "Open it!" He commanded.

Shock came across the two men's faces. Desecrate the place of one who sleeps the-sleep-from-which-no-one-wakes. They had heard of others who had done this and became sick, finally falling into this unending sleep themselves. The guards cringed at the idea of this happening to them.

"I said, open it!" Long Tusk growled. Neither man moved. The caravan master could feel his stature fading. He could not let that happen. Anger getting the best of him, he took his knife and lurched toward the bedroll.

"No!" Bright Moon screamed. She tossed her burning wand away and threw herself over the body. "You cannot desecrate the body; those who do, risk being cursed forever."

Anger twisted Long Tusk's pudgy face making him even uglier. Straightening up, he glared at her and said, "I want it open. I want to see the body."

"I... I will do it," Bright Moon sniffled.

She made a show of shaking while untying the knot. With tears running down her face she unlaced and pulled back the sleeping robe. Murmurs rippled through the crowd of onlookers.

Taking a torch, Long Tusk bent and examined Silver Moon's corpse. She wore no necklace and her neck carried a mark... as if one had been torn from it. He reached out and touched the body. Cold to the touch, the remains were lifeless and had been so for some time. *His people claimed a frail, old woman had joined them. There was no way Silver Waters could have been on the raid tonight. Yet his people swore she gave the alarm.* Those close by could see what he saw and the crowd passed a hiss of whispers between them.

Long Tusk straightened up. "Close it," he said disdainfully. He looked about to see if he could recapture some of his lost prestige.

Bright Moon was not about to let that happen. "Wait!" She said in a loud voice, "I wish to return my mother's necklace to her. Where did you say you found it?" Long Tusk did not answer. She smiled inwardly knowing she had planted another seed of doubt undermining Long Tusk even further. Bright Moon fastened the necklace in place and smoothed out the folds of Silver Waters' tunic before she closed the bedroll.

Even in the undulating light of the campfires, it was not difficult for Long Tusk to read the faces of those around them. He had lost another battle with this girl. He could feel his power melting away. "The necklace belonged to someone else. It was nothing." He spat. "Your mother was nothing."

"Not true. My mother was a great Shaman. Her spirit is with us even now. I can feel it, and she is angry at the things you say and do." Another murmur rippled through the crowd.

Long Tusk's heart leaped at the sound of her words. Now he had a chance to turn the tables, trap the girl with her own words, and show everyone she was nothing but a fake. Driven by the rage for this insolent girl, he spat his venomous challenge, "You claim to be a Shaman and tell us your mother, the great Shaman, is with us now. So

Shaman, show us your power and call her if you can. Have her show herself."

Bright Moon, still seated cross-legged looked up at Long Tusk. The caravan master stood in front of her, arms crossed defiantly across his huge stomach and waited. The throng that accompanied him also waited. Her mother's warning—*You are wise beyond your years, but you must be wary lest your wisdom gives you a false confidence. It will be your downfall*—rang in her ears. In her mind, she voiced a silent prayer; *Mother, please don't let this be a trap I built for myself.* In front of her stood the unlit torch, the ember's bright red glow seen only by her. Bright Moon stretched her arms out to her sides, closed her eyes to mere slits, and began to sway and chant.

The chants were nonsense words, made-up words, words condemning Long Tusk and noises she thought sounded exotic. More importantly, they contained numerous breathy words. In the crisp night air, she could see the vapor mix with the campfire's smoke. This mix floated gently toward the clay-encrusted ember embedded in the torch less than a hand's thickness away.

Everyone, even Long Tusk, watched. Captivated by her motions and the idea that Silver Waters' spirit would make itself known, they remained unaware of the unseen coal glowing redder with each puff.

A sudden gust of wind, when there had been no wind, gave the needed assistance and the tinder caught. The torch exploded into flame and filled the air with sparks. The crowd, frozen until now, let out a loud shriek; some fainted, while others ran away in a panic. As suddenly as the wind came, it died, leaving all still, not a leaf moved.

New words rang in Bright Moon's mind, *My daughter, I love you. I go now, but my spirit will always watch over you.* Bright Moon said a prayer of thanksgiving and then got to her feet. "Thank you, Honored Mother, Great Shaman of the people," Looking beyond Long Tusk, she asked those that remained, "Is that proof enough?"

Long Tusk's stomach tighten in knots and he tasted the bitterness that comes with defeat. He had tried to trick her; tried to corner her but she had bested him again. Rage contorted Long Tusk's face. He flexed the fingers of both hands in his desire to strangle this impertinent girl, but he could not carry out his wish in front of the crowd. He would have to rely on Mochni.

"Get your medicines and follow me," he finally said through tight lips. "We've had a bad hunting accident." The lie he told didn't bother him, but his humiliation at having to tell this story, and ask this girl for help, left a bitter taste in his mouth. Mochni had to act. That's all there was to it.

He wheeled about and the crowd quickly parted to allow him passage. The two guards, his constant shadows, trailed closely after him. Bright Moon quickly gathered her mother's—now her—medicine bags and fell in behind the guards before the crowd closed in around them. Was her protector among them... watching her? She looked the gathering over. Most faces were just a blur, but here and there, she saw one she recognized and could eliminate right away.

One individual stood out immediately, but she quickly dismissed him. This stranger was an older, lanky man, bald except for a single long braid and was dressed in odd-looking garb, nothing like the furs her people wore, and certainly not the dress or build of her unknow protector. Not far from him, near the place where firelight gave way to darkness, stood a younger man, a scout she thought. Suspiciously, he seemed to watch her with measured disinterest. She shook off the idea as paranoid and scurried after the caravan leader. If her protector was there, he did nothing to signal his presence.

Chapter 6: Aftermath

Bright Moon, Long Tusk at her side, did a quick inspection of the wounded. It looked like all those who had accompanied him on the raid sported cuts, lumps, and gashes. Some were injured so badly, they had to be carried back. Their raid had failed, thanks to her undercover participation, and, aided by an unknown protector, she had gotten away. Now, she had the opportunity to see the impact of her efforts. A quick spasm of guilt rose within her and just as quickly was pushed aside. She would not accept blame for her actions nor allow herself to relish the results. More importantly, she had to play ignorant of what really happened lest they find out she was the one who had caused their downfall.

Bright Moon turned to face Long Tusk. "What were you hunting, mastodons?" Her voice dripped with sarcasm. She did not wait for his answer, but ordered, "Have everyone line up so I can take a better look at their wounds. I'll treat the most serious injuries, first."

Long Tusk, bristling under the yoke of submitting to her orders, glared at her before bellowing instructions to the wounded.

Without asking, she turned to the guards and ordered, "Get torches. I'll need light, lots of light."

Should they follow the girl's order or not? Perplexed, the pair looked at Long Tusk. His back toward them, the caravan master was busily ordering the wounded to line up and offered no help. Shrugging, the men gave up and went separate ways, returning shortly with several torches.

Once he got his people organized, Long Tusk made himself scarce, hoping his absence would not be noticed. It would give him time and privacy to vent his rage and plot his next move.

Long Tusk's disappearance did not bother Bright Moon. With him out of the way, she was able to work without interference. Night became morning; morning became afternoon. Focused on the work in front of her, the passage of time, her hunger, her weariness went without notice. The sun was beyond mid-sky before she reached the last one in line.

From the corner of her eye, she saw Long Tusk, flanked by his two guards, return. A noisy crowd of those wishing favors surrounded the trio. Ignoring his approach, she turned slightly, so her back was squarely toward his party, and dallied over her last patient.

When Long Tusk was an arm's length away, he stopped and held up a hand. Those following him fell silent.

"You! Girl!" The caravan leader would not call her by name and certainly not by title, least the recognition grant her even more prestige among the caravan people. "How long before we can move on?"

Bright Moon held up one hand, fingers spread. "One hand," she said without stopping her work... and without looking at him. When it comes to failing to show respect, two people could play this game.

The wounded man, feeling the blame for the delay fall on his shoulders, fidgeted nervously under the scathing stare of the caravan leader.

"No," Long Tusk was emphatic. "We need to move on sooner or we could be attacked."

She turned, gave him a cold stare, and raised an eyebrow in question. "The mastodons would attack you?"

His lie discovered, the caravan leader squirmed slightly then caught himself. "We tracked a herd, made our kill, and then encountered another tribe who wanted the animals we had slain. They attacked us. With this many wounded, I want to move on before they come back."

She knew he lied, but he lied so much and so

45

skillfully, even he believed it. "We should be able to move in three days if you arrange litters and travel slowly. It will give me time before we leave this place to replenish my medicines. I will need them to care for the injured while we're travelling."

Long Tusk folded his arms across his chest and scowled at her. He could not have this insolent girl tell him how and when he should travel. "We'll move on in two days," he declared, pleased he had grabbed the initiative. He smiled broadly and searched the faces of those who surrounded him for the admiration he deserved. "I'll send Mochni along with you. That should speed up your collection."

"She knows nothing...."

"She knows how to follow orders and you seem to be good at giving them." His curt reply cut off further complaint. "Gather your collection bags. I'll talk to Mochni." Turning, he shuffled off. His actions caught her by surprise. Mouth hanging open, she stared after him.

Long Tusk finally found Mochni. Sprawled on a robe in the shade of a tree, the out-walker was sound asleep and didn't hear him approach. He woke her with a sharp kick to her bare arm.

Startled, the out-walker sat up quickly, and scowled at the interruption.

"Wake up!" Long Tusk ordered. "I have a job for you. Come, walk with me." He signaled the guards to stay there and he turned and strolled away. Mochni scrambled to her feet, and trotted to catch up still clutching the place where his long, dirty toenails had broken through her skin. *It is long past the time you should have replaced those foot coverings*, she thought. *What have your wives been doing to neglect you so?*

"The longer we stay here, the greater our risk of attack," he explained. "We have many wounded." He looked over at Mochni. Always eager to please him, she matched his step pace-for-pace. "The upstart girl, the one who tries to pass herself off as a shaman, has been up all night tending to them." Making a face, he added, "She wants to stay longer so they can rest and she can gather medicines." He came to an abrupt halt and turned to face the startled out-walker. "It's risky, but I've decided to let the caravan rest here for two days before we move on. At the start of the third day, the wounded will have to keep up or fall behind. While we rest, she can go out and find what she needs. I told her you will go with her to help."

"Me...? Help her? Why?" Mochni, not the quickest of his followers, needed time to grasp Long Tusk's strategy.

The caravan leader ignored his out-walker's questions. "We are close to the gorges. They are deep. While you're out helping her, you can help yourself by keeping your promise." Long Tusk looked at her expectantly, hoping she'd decipher his meaning. She didn't.

"Promise? I... I... I don't understand."

"When we reached the gorges, you promised to eliminate her as a problem, even if you had to push her over the edge. I had hoped you'd live up to your word, but if you want out...." Stroking his chin, he paused playing on her emotions. "I guess I could find someone else more dependable."

Struggle and turmoil clouded the out-walker's face. *She knew the girl was a problem for Long Tusk, but he was asking her to deliberately push Bright Moon into a gorge. Did she promise that?* Frowning, she wrestled with the idea. *It was true, she had participated in many raids and taken on other tasks for him, but this was different. This could be a chance to become something more than just another out-walker.* Her frown faded. "No, I can do this," she said.

"Will we eat soon?" Mochni asked. Shooing away

flying bugs, she licked her lips in anticipation of a meal.

Bright Moon, forked stick in hand, eyed the tufts of grass along the edge of the swamp, "We've got too much work to do now," she answered curtly. "Probably won't eat before we get back to camp tonight."

"You killed rabbits and birds and we're not going to stop and eat them?" Mochni couldn't believe her ears.

"I didn't kill them to eat. I need them for medicine." With her free hand, Bright Moon held out a piece of pemmican, "Chew on this if you're hungry."

Mochni grabbed the food Bright Moon offered and bit off a piece. The satchel at her side, its contents slowly turning to water, had grown wet and uncomfortable. "Why did we collect white-rain[24] along the ridge and carry it with us down to this marsh?" She was puzzled by this seemingly useless effort and suspected it was only meant to aggravate her.

"I need to keep some of the things I collect cold," Bright Moon answered. A movement in the grass caught her eye and she jumped forward, jabbing the forked end of the stick downward at the spot. "Quickly, open the bag with the white-rain and bring it here."

While she waited for her pudgy companion to follow directions, Bright Moon let her prey thrash around in the grass until it grew tired. Mochni finally presented an open bag.

"Use your fist to make a pocket in the white-rain and then hold the bag out," she told Mochni.

The out-walker made an indentation in the parcel's cold, white contents and looked at Bright Moon. Reaching into the grass, Bright Moon quickly pulled her hand back. In it, she held a snake, her fingers pinching it just behind its head. It wriggled and whipped back and forth. Fanged mouth agape, it had a dark calico[25] body

---

24 To distinguish it from regular rain, snow was called 'white-rain', as they knew when it melted, it was water.

25 Any small repeated print design. This was probably a Water Moccasin, also called a Cottonmouth, and is poisonous.

with a white, ribbed-belly. Wide-eyed, Mochni drew back. "Hold the bag open," Bright Moon commanded, "but get ready to close it when I put the snake inside."

Quaking, Mochni held the bag with outstretched arms while Bright Moon gave her catch a new home and then quickly ordered the bag closed. Pleased with her find, Bright Moon made sure the satchel's cover was tied down before holding it out to Mochni.

Still wide-eyed, the out-walker shrank away, shaking her head, refusing to get near the package.

"Go ahead and take it," Bright Moon cajoled. "The snake can't get out and the cold will probably put it to sleep soon."

Mochni took another step backward.

Near exhaustion, Bright Moon glared at her reluctant assistant. "Long Tusk sent you to help me," she yelled. "I've already got a bunch of bags and need my hands free to collect more medicines." Mochni made no move toward the bag. Bright Moon could see she was not going to get anywhere at this rate. Using her forked stick and a piece of rawhide, she secured the bag to the end of the stick and held it out to the wide-eyed out-walker. "Now, take this or I'll tell Long Tusk you refused to help," Bright Moon threatened. Intimidated, Mochni finally complied, but held the bag away from her body.

"Okay, let's get a move on. There are more things I need and we've got a lot of work to do." Turning, she started off. Mochni, satchel separated by the full length of the stick, fell in step behind her.

As the day continued, the pair traipsed up and down hills, through glens, back and forth across meadows, and along the marshes. Mushrooms, birds' nests, wildflowers, mosses, lichens, and small game all became candidates for the pouches both girls carried.

When they first started, Bright Moon had named each item and talked about how it could be put to use. After a short time, she realized Mochni wasn't interested and would never be interested. Bright Moon resigned herself to replying to Mochni's questions and then with only the simplest of explanations.

Even this was lost on Mochni, who understood little of what she was told and had no interest in learning. She just wanted to get through the day and do so quickly. Her focus was on accomplishing the task Long Tusk had given her. It was something she understood.

"Chief Long Tusk, your friend, Askook, Chief of The Mattocks, received your message and is eager to view his present," his scout, Kaliska, reported. "He asked me to escort this warrior here to claim her for him. We arrived while you were on the night hunt."

The stranger gave the scout a short side glance at the report, but otherwise remained expressionless.

Long Tusk eyed his scout and stranger who accompanied him. Did either of them know what actually happened last night? He couldn't read anything in their expressions. The outsider who accompanied his scout was, in many ways, a stranger. Not because he was an older man with a wiry frame, but because of his shaved head except for a long braid. Added to this was the fact he didn't wear the usual animal skins, not even treated hides such as a chief like Long Tusk wore. Instead, it appeared he wore something like finely woven mats. This strange man would bear some watching.

"What have you to say?" Long Tusk challenged him.

"It is as your scout told you," the foreigner said. "Askook wants to view the present you offer and is preparing for the journey to the meeting place. I, Wikvaya[26], will bring her to him there as he requested."

"Not so fast," Long Tusk replied. Did he hear the man correctly? *Bring her to him there...?* Askook was not only interested, he was eager. This was a new wrinkle. To

---

26 Native American Hopi name meaning "one who brings."

take advantage of the opportunity, he needed to be there when Askook met the girl. Long Tusk had to think fast. If he pushed the caravan, really pushed them, they might get there in time to present the girl before Askook lost interest.

"The girl is a Shaman, the caravan's Shaman. She is our only Shaman." He let his words sink in before he continued. "What is Askook offering in trade?" *The girl still might have some value,* he reflected. *If I work this right I could get rid of her and get a reward in return.*

"Trade...?" Wikvaya acted puzzled. "Askook was told she was a present. He will not like this news."

Long Tusk had sent Mochni to carry out his intentions. *If she is successful, he will be out a treasure, and Askook could become upset at the loss. If I would be rid of the meddling girl,* he thought, *it would be worth Askook's disappointment.* Long Tusk, not one to be out-maneuvered, rethought his approach. *Neither Askook nor his representative is familiar with this troublesome girl so he could always substitute another girl or two in her place,* he concluded. *It might still get me a reward.*

"We had a hunting accident. The injured required all her medicines." He tried to sound consoling. "She's out looking for replacements."

"If she is suitable, I'm sure Askook will be generous with his rewards, especially since she is a Shaman," Wikvaya said.

Generous with his rewards, Long Tusk smiled at the idea as he thought about what it might entail. From somewhere in the distance, a long, drawn-out scream interrupted his reverie. *Sounds like I'm going to have to change my plans and select another girl,* he thought. The crowd, frozen for a moment, now broke into action. Grabbing weapons and torches they started for the place where they thought the sound originated.

###

Driven by Long Tusk's time restriction, Bright Moon had moved briskly all day and took few breaks. It had been a long time since Mochni worked this hard. She did her best to keep up, but still lagged behind.

"Wait... please, wait," Mochni begged. "I cannot go another step without a rest." Bright Moon looked over her shoulder at the struggling figure behind her.

The sun was low in the sky, but they were close to camp and would easily be able to get there before dark. A productive day, one that had sapped most of her energy, Bright Moon felt she could relax now before returning to camp life and tasks there. The plump out-walker carried few satchels, but still labored as if heavily burdened. Bright Moon shook her head at the sight, but relented.

They had traversed a slope that ended in a chasm. Ahead, an outcropping provided an inviting place for Mochni to sit and rest. While she relaxed, Bright Moon could scrape moss from nearby boulders, a task she wanted to complete before the light faded completely. Had Mochni asked, Bright Moon would have explained that *moss was useful when you had to stop the flow of blood from wounds*. Mochni didn't ask.

"You can rest here," Bright Moon told her and put her own bags down near the outcropping. "I want to get some of this moss before we return. It won't take long. We're not far from camp and should be home before moonrise."

Covered in sweat and dirt, Mochni was quick to struggle out of the satchels' harnesses. She wheezed out a long sigh and plopped down on the rock shelf, sore legs stretched out in front of her. Looking around, she sized up their situation. Goats agilely roamed the peaks around them. The depths of the valley were obscured by clouds. A big bird, a condor, circled overhead while another, perched near the rim of the gorge, busily devoured some carrion[27]. She smiled. Long Tusk had suggested such a

---

27 (From the Latin caro, meaning meat) refers to the carcass of a

place as this as a good location for her to act... and act she would.

While Mochni rested, Bright Moon wearily crouched near a boulder and scraped moss. She stuffed the scrapings into a satchel her reluctant assistant had cast off and then moved to the next patch, nearer the lip of the ravine. Devotion to the wounded throughout the night and now collecting all day had taken their toll. Her will, seemingly the last of her strength, was draining away. She lacked focus. It took longer for her to compose her thoughts and carry out her work. Less than alert, her reactions slowed by fatigue, she did not realize Mochni had crept next to her...until it was too late.

Bright Moon was unable to get to her feet before Mochni shoved her. She toppled sideways landing hard. Mochni continued forward, striking at her victim with her walking stick. Caught off-guard, Bright Moon rolled away from the blows. Her path took her to the edge. Her body left the comfort of solid ground. Her feet flailed the air as she slipped over the brink. Desperate for something to hold her, her frantic fingers closed around the lip of the rim, but she could not hold on.

A scrawny thorn bush, its roots having found a home amid a crack in the rock wall, poked her sides and she grabbed for it. Its prickly thorns dug into her flesh. With its perch nearly as precarious as her own, she could feel it slowly ripping loose. "Mochni, help me!" She begged.

"No!" came her assailant's curt reply. Mochni stood near the lip looking down, watching Bright Moon fight for a better hold. The out-walker calmly put her walking stick between the bush's trunk and the ledge and began to pry it loose.

Wide-eyed, Bright Moon screamed, "What are you doing?"

"Working this loose," Mochni said unconcerned.

---

dead animal. Carrion is an important food source for large carnivores and omnivores in most ecosystems.

"When this is gone, you're gone. I'll be sure to throw your precious medicine bags after you, so you'll have them while you're sleeping the-sleep-from-which-no-one-wakes."

"Why are you doing this?" Bright Moon questioned. Terror drove her frantic efforts for a better grip, one that would carry her weight when the tree could no longer do so. "What have I done to you?" Her feet examined the rough surface of the gorge. Rubble from its pockmarked face clattered down the stone walls and was swallowed by the clouds below. Her efforts were rewarded when her feet found a small ledge. Even better, a scrawny tree, young and supple, jutted out from the stony-faced wall giving her a foothold. Not much reassurance, but they would hold her.

"Long Tusk asked me to get rid of you," Mochni replied. "He even told me what to do." She paused in her work long enough to add, "Unlike you, I do as he asks." She threw her head back and laughed.

As much as Bright Moon hated hearing her boasting, distracting her antagonist would give her a chance to come up with a plan. "Does that include attacking villages and caravans in the middle of the night?"

"Yes, that and more," Mochni cackled. "We get most of our trade goods and slaves that way." She paused in her efforts to catch her breath and then went on with her explanation, "Long Tusk asked your father to join him, but he wouldn't, so we made sure to slay him and many of his people when we attacked his train. Both your father and your mother now sleep the-sleep-from-which-no-one-wakes and soon you will join them."

Bright Moon's search of the gorge's face yielded additional handholds. They might be enough to let her hang on; maybe even give her a chance to climb out, if it weren't for her assailant standing over her. Distraction would not be enough. She had to lure her into a trap.

Bright Moon looked away, as if she pondered a great loss. "When I go, no one... no living thing will know the secret."

"Secret? What secret?" Mochni scoffed at the idea, but, she had seen the girl perform magic and it might be worthwhile. Eager to hear the details, she stopped working.

Bright Moon looked up, locking eyes with the out-walker and put on her most sincere face. "Why... how to become invisible of course."

"How.... How to become invisible? I don't believe it. There is no such thing." Mochni attacked the tree again.

"Yes, yes, it's true." Bright Moon stirred a little excitement into her words. "How do you think my mother was able to follow you without being seen? She told me she was there when Long Tusk was ready to attack a caravan at a village. Just as the scouts moved in to douse the night fires, she jumped up and sounded the alarm."

Mochni stopped working on the tree, eyes widened as she heard these words. "Yes, and then what...?" She wanted more proof.

"Yes, she told me she shouted 'attack', 'attack' and Long Tusk and his people were discovered. Everyone turned to silence her, but she made herself invisible again so no one could find her."

Mochni had been part of the raid. She heard these words shouted and then the one who gave the alarm disappeared. Convinced now, Mochni forgot about the tree as she leaned forward, eager to hear the details. "Tell me, how is it done?"

"It's a secret passed down through the ages from shaman to shaman."

"Is this a trick for you to get free?"

"No, my mother told me before she slipped into the great sleep. I am the last to know it." Bright Moon dropped her head and quietly added, "So, when I'm gone, the secret is gone."

"No, no! Tell me."

Bright Moon looked at her sharply as if she were

about to scold Mochni, but then soften. "Well.... Well I guess it would be better than losing the secret altogether. But first...."

"Yes, what is it? Ask anything." Thinking of all the possibilities, Mochni danced with excitement.

Bright Moon tested the spring of the branch under her feet. It was flexible and seemed to be strong enough to hold all her weight. "You have to promise not to tell anyone or anything." Face serious, she raised her eyebrows, expectantly waiting for an answer.

"Yes, I promise I will never tell anyone else."

Bright Moon scowled. "Not only anyone, but anything else. You don't want the game you hunt to become invisible do you?"

Mochni was shocked. "No I won't tell anyone or anything. I promise."

Bright Moon looked left and right quickly as if checking to make sure they were alone. "Come close," she said. "I will whisper it so the secret will be safe. You will be the only one, the only living creature to know this secret. Guard it well. It will give you great power."

Mochni hesitated, but Bright Moon kicked some rubble loose then appeared to slip down a little. "Quickly," she ordered, panic written on her face. "I'm slipping. I can't hold on much longer. You must come closer."

Getting to her knees, Mochni leaned over the rim in order to get even nearer. "Yes, tell me the secret. I am ready."

"You start by saying...." Bright Moon said, and then yelped as she sent more rocks clattering down the ravine. Planting one foot firmly on the ledge, the other on the branch, she went into a slight squat, her face taking on a terrified look. "I'm slipping. I can't hold on much longer. Get closer so I can whisper to you and no one else will hear."

Believing the secret was on the verge of being lost, Mochni quickly leaned over the rim, unknowingly putting herself exactly in the stance Bright Moon had hoped for.

"You start by saying...," Bright Moon began as she pushed off from the ledge. The bough bent down under the force and then, recoiling, it shot her upwards. One hand gripping the edge of the brim in front of her, she reached up with the other and grabbed Mochni's tunic.

Having been propelled to the maximum by the spring of the tree, she now started downward, still gripping Mochni. Caught by surprise, the out-walker tried to back away but could not straighten up. She had leaned over too far and was off balance.

Plunging downward, Bright Moon's weight pulled her assailant forward. Foot now planted securely back on the ledge, the crafty girl gave a final, hearty yank. "...Good-bye!" She completed her statement as she let go of her attacker's tunic.

Surprised, shocked, Mochni, arms flaying, somersaulted past Bright Moon. Before she realized what had happened she was falling and only recovered enough to scream as she disappeared into the clouds.

The sound echoed up and down the valley startling the condor. Carrion gripped tightly in its talons, the giant bird tipped into the open air of the canyon, flapped its wings a few times, caught the updrafts, and made off toward some distant quiet spot to enjoy its meal.

Shaking, Bright Moon pulled herself up over the lip of the gorge, fell on the ground and sobbed.

Chapter 7: Explain

Noise from the approaching crowd brought Bright Moon to her senses. Quickly, she dried her tears and began gathering the satchels Mochni had cast aside.

Out of breath, Long Tusk shuffled up, followed by his guards. A mixed group of caravan members—some of Long Tusk's tribe and some not—and a stranger, trailed after them. A few carried torches against the fall of night.

The caravan master plopped down on the rock shelf—the same one Mochni had sat only moments before—to rest. "We heard a scream. What happened?" He asked between asthmatic breaths.

Seeing Bright Moon still here left him with mixed emotions. He would not have to disappoint Askook, but she could still present him with problems. If only Mochni were more reliable, Bright Moon could be kept in line. However, Mochni continued to fail him. He would have to think up a suitable method to discipline her for failing her duties. Then, he'd have to tell her about the change in plans he had to make because of her failure.

Catching his breath, he finally looked around for Mochni, but could not find her. Icy-fingers seemed to close around his spine. Was she the one who screamed? True, his out-walker was not the brightest, but she did possess a certain amount of cunning. Could this upstart girl have worked her trickery against Mochni? He sat dumbfounded considering the idea while Bright Moon silently finished gathering her satchels. Taking a torch from one of the spectators, the girl picked up Mochni's walking stick and turned to start back to the encampment.

Mochni was nowhere to be found and Bright Moon was leaving. The fact hit Long Tusk like a club. "Wait!"

He shouted after her, "Where is Mochni?"

Already well up the path, Bright Moon paused for a moment and nonchalantly waved the torch toward the now distant condor. The bird flapped away into the twilight, a dark silhouette in the distance, its kill dangling from its talons. "There she is," Bright Moon said. Stone-faced, her voice cold, she turned to look at him. In the flickering light of the torch she added, "She had an evil heart and attacked me. She said you told her to do so. She also told me you and your tribe attacked my father's caravan in the middle of the night and you have attacked others in the same manner."

Her words brought about a murmur of discontent from among the onlookers. Guilt clearly painted on their faces, Long Tusk's people hung their heads and drew back.

"To defend myself, I had to use my powers as Shaman and called up the great bird," Bright Moon added. "At my command, it carried her off."

She did not give Long Tusk time to reject her statement, but quickly turned and hurried toward camp. They would arrive at their conclusion without her, and then she would deal with it. Right now, she needed to get away.

Long Tusk looked at the bird as did everyone else. They were sure there was something clutched in its claws, but it was too far away, the light too poor to make out more. Clouds obscured the bottom of the gorge. Whatever might be there was hidden from their view.

Murmurs rippled through the crowd as everyone voiced their opinions. They asked themselves, '*Is the girl telling the truth?*' *If so, then was what she said about Long Tusk also true?* They looked around for some sign of Mochni, but found none. The condor and its prey were now a tiny spec in the fading light.

Wikvaya, stranger among these people, did not know what happened but believed it was safe to say Mochni would not be seen again. He recognized Bright Moon as quick-witted and would use a situation to her advantage. He smiled inwardly as he watched the tribe and Long Tusk's reaction to her words. Yes, she was tricky. He would keep an eye on her until he could get her to Askook. When his task done, he would be free of his obligation and could return to his own people. The girl would be Askook's problem. Suppressing his smile, he signaled Kaliska he was ready to be escorted back to camp.

Bright Moon held the torch close to the ground as she picked her way along the animal trail in the vanishing light. Long ago, herds carved these paths. Migrating tribes, hunters, and caravans now followed the routes animals had laid down and were still using.

Tired, she almost missed the paw print in the fading light. A wolf's print, alone in the soft dirt... so fresh the animal must have just made it and slunk away. But, a wolf seldom travels alone. Looking around, she found signs that a pack followed the caravan and were close by, ready to pick up any scraps.

A spark of an idea caused her to pick up her pace. If she could get to camp before the others, she could keep her trickery going and continue to mystify everyone. That would undermine Long Tusk even more.

Medicines gathered that day could be put to use in ways not originally intended. While she trotted along the path, Bright Moon dropped bodies of the small game taken earlier in order to bait her trap. She saved the last one for her own use. It was dark, the time night prowlers began to roam. She knew the scent of these small creatures would attract them. She counted on the wolves being drawn to the trail she was leaving.

It seemed like a lifetime ago when Long Tusk's group followed the path along the ridge and arrived at the meadow, but much had happened since then. When the caravan halted for the night, they made camp on a small plateau along the crest of the ridge. One side sloped off to the valley while the other backed up to a ragged rock wall. Bright Moon and her mother had built their shelter adjacent to its base. Their choice of locations, near a small gully which led to the ravine where Long Tusk and his people gathered before their raid, was purely accidental.

Reaching her shelter, she gently put the satchels down and planted the torch's shaft in the dirt. A piece of bark became a suitable digging tool. Bright Moon used it to create a shallow hole in the sand along the edge of the gully. Laying a bed of grass and leaves at the bottom, she carefully opened the bag of white-rain.

Disturbed, the snake stirred, but remained dormant. Until it warmed up, it could do little more. Satisfied it was still asleep, Bright Moon picked it up and gingerly laid it in on the grass bed in a circular fashion. She covered it with a layer of grass, topped it with sand, and then flung the remainder of white-rain into the undergrowth behind her.

Bright Moon turned to the game she had kept. Cleaning it and removing the hide, she prepared to cook her supper by mounting it on a spit. Placing sticks and tinder together, just behind the snake's lair, she used the torch to get a small fire started.

As a final touch, she picked up a dead branch as long as her arm. One end tapered off to finger thickness, but grew to finger-to-thumb thickness over the rest of its length. She held it up and smiled. Not only was it just the right size, it was also gnarled. The bark, all but gone, gave it a stained and weathered surface. This, she lay next to her sleeping-robes.

Angry voices from across the encampment confirmed she had completed her tasks just in time. Even in the dark, she could tell from the ruckus Long Tusk and his followers were entering the camp. With them here, Bright Moon added more wood to the fire and set the skewer[28] in place. As the fire blazed, she positioned herself, back to the wall, where she could turn the spit and look beyond the fire toward the torches marking Long Tusk's approach.

The caravan leader, and those that followed him, found the girl in her campsite. She sat on a mat at the edge of a gully, back against the wall, roasting her dinner. The girl continued to stare into the fire, seemingly oblivious to their arrival.

"Where's Mochni," the caravan master bellowed.

Wikvaya and Kaliska, having accompanied Long Tusk, his cronies, and the rest of the crowd, could see the caravan chief did not react well under pressure. On the other hand, the girl was calm and had control of the situation. They picked their way through the group and found a spot to watch.

"It is as I told you. I am Shaman and I used my powers to have the great bird carry her off." Bright Moon spoke quietly, unperturbed by their presence or Long Tusk's state of mind.

"I don't believe you. You're no Shaman." Long Tusk edged forward, arms crossed defiantly over his ponderous belly, and stood across the fire from her.

Bright Moon got to her feet. Her deceased nemesis' walking stick in hand, she stood her ground. "You looked around, did you not?" She glared at him. "Did you find Mochni anywhere?" Her voice, now a hiss, she asked, "Did you find any sign of her other than what I pointed out?"

The fire cast a small oval of light, barely illuminating their features before being swallowed by the night. The burning wood crackled and popped, filling the air between them with glowing embers.

"You are not a Shaman," he repeated. You can't call animals.... They are not at your command."

"Oh, they aren't?" The timing couldn't have been

---

28 A wooden shaft used to secure or suspend meat and/or vegetables during cooking.

better. The moon, full and bright, just crested the next rise. She tilted her head back, cupped her hands to her mouth, and sounded a loud, "Ay.... Ay.... Ayeeeeeee."

The wolf-like sound rolled and echoed across the canyon walls. She was taking a big chance, but it was necessary. The crowd pushed closer to Long Tusk. Everyone waited in silence. Heart in her throat, Bright Moon remained outwardly calm, concealing any signs of doubt on her part.

A heartbeat... maybe two... and then, close by, another voice, a wild, throaty voice broke the silence as a wolf answered her call. "Ay.... Ay.... Ayeeeeeee." Far away, another wolf voice joined the first. Then, farther out, a chorus of still other voices joined the serenade. Bright Moon concealed her smile.

Startled, Long Tusk jumped back at the sound and looked around nervously. A murmur whispered through the crowd.

The caravan master finally composed himself. "That's nothing," he bellowed. "It's a trick known to most hunters. Anyone can imitate the wolf's call. Anyone can do what you have done," Long Tusk looked at the crowd and then back at Bright Moon. "If this is how you command animals, you do nothing special." He edged near the fire, cupped his hands to his mouth, and attempted to copy her. The air was filled with a screeching noise that broke midway. Muffled snickering rolled through the crowd but no answering wolf call was heard.

While he demonstrated, Bright Moon glanced down. The fire had warmed the sand around it. Along the edge nearest Long Tusk, it was beginning to stir, to show some sign of movement. She raised her eyes to lock on his.

"If anyone can do what I have done, can they also do this?" She raised the walking stick in the air, cried out unknown words in a shrill voice followed by, "Arise, show yourself and strike at this evil one!" Bringing the walking stick down, she planted the end in the ground next to the fire and the rim of the nest she created. Warmed out of its dormant state by the fire and jarred from its slumber, the snake erupted from its hiding place.

Long Tusk turned and tried to draw back, but the crowd had pressed in too close. He stood frozen in fear, his mouth agape, eyes bulging and watched as the form lunged forward. It sank its fangs into his calf. He screamed, more in shock than pain, and tried to brush it away. The snake released its grip, dropped to the ground and began to slither off. Long Tusk cradled his leg as he slumped to the ground in front of the fire.

The throng, which had encompassed Long Tusk, quickly parted. Normally, a serpent in their midst would have been slain immediately. However, they believed this one magical and drew back.

Leaving the walking stick in place, Bright Moon grabbed her sleeping-robe. In one quick motion, she concealed the branch in its folds, stepped over the fire and brushed by Long Tusk. Under the crowd's watchful eyes, the girl bent down and fanned out her robe covering the snake. Before it could escape its new confinement, she scooped up the robe and the snake, singing as she twirled around in a little dance. Cloaked by the robe, the snake squirmed under her fingertips while she chanted gibberish words, her voice rising and falling rhythmically. Bright Moon let the robe spread out filling the air in front of her as she edged away from her onlookers and closer to the brush near the ravine.

Her cookfire flickered, increasing the mystery but did little to chase away the darkness. With a flick of her wrist, she sent the stick flying toward the crowd. It hit the ground in front of them and bounced twice before rolling to a stop near the fear-struck group. Expecting to see a threat rise up, they gasped and stepped backwards, all eyes fixed on it. While they were engaged, Bright Moon casually laid her robe aside secretly releasing the snake. Under the cover of night, it slithered off into the brush at the lip of the ravine.

"You are safe," Bright Moon shouted to the crowd. Her words jarred them out of their frozen state. A braver member of the crowd crept forward to peer at the bough.

"It's a stick," he yelled excitedly. "She turned it into a stick." In unison, the mob gasped and then exploded in a cacophony of noise as each member tried to tell the others what they witnessed.

"Stop!" Long Tusk yelled. "I am dying."

"Tie your leg off above the bite," Bright Moon told him. "Cut the bite marks. Get the poison out. Then remove the tie." She tossed him a pouch containing a balm. "Put this on and wrap the wound."

"Aren't you going to help me?"

"I just gave you all the help you'll get from me."

Wikvaya smiled. Bright Moon was quick-witted, crafty, and determined. He would definitely have to keep an eye on her.

Chapter 8: Kidnapped

Long Tusk's wives were not there when the snake bit his leg. They had no knowledge of the events that led to it. However, within the camp, gossip flowed freely. Because each bearer added their own unique details, the stories told were often less than accurate and never timely. Still, the news eventually reached his wives. In time, they would learn what had occurred before his guards carried the bellowing old man into their midst.

The guards had Long Tusk recline on a mound of furs. His wives brought food and drink to quiet him, and then began working on his wound. For the time, his women only knew that their ill-tempered master had been bitten, was in pain, and received little aid from the young shaman; a fact that made him grumpy, disrupted their lives, and set them against the girl.

Calmed by the attention, Long Tusk began issuing orders. "I need some men to act as an escort. Select those that are good but have fallen out of favor. They'll be willing to do anything to regain their position." A sinister smile curled his lips as he continued to roll out his plan. "Send for the scout, the one who brought the stranger from Askook's tribe," the caravan master growled. "I need to talk to him about the trip back. After I speak with him call the stranger and I'll lay out my plan... at least the part he needs to know."

###

"It was bad enough when the girl was just an irritation," Long Tusk told Wikvaya. "Now she's gotten out of hand. The problems she's created have become

66

unbearable."

On either side of Wikvaya, the caravan master's guards fidgeted uncomfortably. They were present when their leader suffered the snakebite; they had watched as it erupted from the ground and sank its fangs into him *at her command*. It was not hearsay. It was not some wild story told around campfires. They were there! They saw it with their own eyes. If Wikvaya was not standing next to them, Long Tusk would have given them the job of handling the girl and her magic. If that happened, they could end up being carried off like Mochni. Luck was on their side. Wikvaya stood between them, and that changed things because he would be the one to handle the witch. She would be his problem. They were safe.

Wikvaya threw his hands up, hoping to show his rejection. "She's only a girl. Just one girl," he chided. "Yet, it seems that everyone fears her. Why is that?"

Ignoring his questions, Long Tusk replied, "She undermines my authority. I cannot allow her to stay here any longer." He paused while he thought out the process and then spoke, "I'll pick some men... some good men... one hand's worth should do it." He paused again, while he thought. "Yes, one hand's worth of good men should do it." As an afterthought, he added, "I'll send a scout along as a guide."

Perplexed, Wikvaya tried to refuse the offer. "I'll accept your offer of a guide; however, I think I can manage one girl, even a reluctant one."

"Don't be a fool. She's cunning," Long Tusk said, "not to mention dangerous." How dare this stranger defy me. He glared at Wikvaya and added, "If you lose the girl, Askook won't be happy... and neither will I."

Wikvaya was not one to back down under threats. "Consider how foolish it would look if I marched into Askook's settlement with that many men guarding one girl." He gave the caravan leader time to picture the scene his words painted. "I'll accept two men and tell Askook that you sent them as an honor guard. He'll be pleased and will show his generosity."

Show his generosity. Oh how Long Tusk loved the sound of those words. It spurred him on; his mind racing ahead as he pictured the events that should take place... must take place. "I will send five men with you. If you have things under control, just before you reach Askook, dismiss three." This was a good compromise. One that would insure the girl would arrive without trouble.

Wikvaya did not see a need for the number of men Long Tusk suggested, but he realized the caravan leader was determined. *Did he think Askook's generosity would be greater if he sent more men? Or, was it because Long Tusk was afraid of the girl?*

"You don't seem to understand what I'm offering you," Long Tusk roared. "I will arrange for my best guards to get the girl quietly out of camp. My scout, Kaliska—the one that brought you here from the land of the Mattocks—will lead you to a place where you can meet the guards and continue on from there."

Disgusted, Wikvaya wanted to reject the idea, but he would answer to Askook if he failed to deliver. Still, Long Tusk's plan seemed so unnecessary. "Couldn't we just tell her to come along?"

"Oh no," Long Tusk shook his head. "She is so full of tricks she might raise an alarm, stir up the rest of the caravan, and then bolt[29] in the confusion."

Before Wikvaya could reply, the caravan leader motioned and Wikvaya turned to see the young scout and a pair of torchbearers approach. When the old tyrant had summoned him Wikvaya thought that Long Tusk was laying out this scheme as he thought it up. With the arrival of the scout and torchbearers, Wikvaya realized that the old master had already made the arrangements and this meeting was only for show. There was no point in continuing the conversation. Long Tusk would not be swayed without losing face, and that was not going to

---

29 To run off quickly; to depart in haste

happen. Glumly, he turned back to face the girl's adversary.

Long Tusk, a wicked smile painted across his face, said, "Go with Kaliska now, and I will take care of getting the girl out of camp."

Wikvaya sighed as he gave up and joined the scout. They followed the torchbearers into the darkness.

Long Tusk stood quietly and watched the glow of the retreating torches become small circles of light bouncing rhythmically in the dark. A noise behind him interrupted his thoughts and he turned to see his chief guard emerge from the darkness beyond the campfire's light.

The man slapped his chest in salute. "I thought it best that I wait until the torchbearers led the stranger away before I present the men selected to escort." Behind him, one-hand's worth of men stood at nervous attention.

Long Tusk nodded to his guard, signaled a wife, and limped over to inspect the line of men. She picked up a brand from the fire and followed behind.

Various cuts and bruises guaranteed these burly men were tough and probably quicker to fight than to think. They met with his approval.

"The girl," Long Tusk said, "the one who claims to be a shaman, is to be presented as a gift to my good friend Askook in the Land of the Mattocks. You've been handpicked to insure she gets there safely and in one piece. I'm told that she sleeps now, so there'll be no trouble taking her." Long Tusk rubbed his hands together, smiling at the prospect of surprising the witch. "Don't let her cry out; it could rouse the rest of the caravan and they would object. Bind her tightly and make sure you're off long before the sun returns to the sky."

The caravan leader peered into the darkness. In the distance, light from the torches combined to make one small point in the gloom and then decided to add a little incentive to their task. "That man, Wikvaya, irritates me." He spat the words out like food with a bad taste. "He does not have to complete the trip. Askook should reward you greatly for doing what his man was not able to do." Mentally, Long Tusk ran through the list, making sure he had covered everything. "When you present her to my friend, Askook," he concluded with a laugh, "tell him that I'm giving her as a present... one that he will find very interesting."

Exhausted from the day's events, Bright Moon was happy when Long Tusk's guards carted him away and the crowd dispersed. She forced herself to eat and then settled in for the night, soon falling into a deep and dreamless sleep.

Still excited by the night's events, the crowd fanned out from Bright Moon's camp fire, stopping by their friend's fires to trade stories and refreshments before finding their own camps. Finally, they settled down and quiet fell over the caravan.

Just before false dawn, while everyone else in the camp slept, the guards descended on her.

"Ahuug." Startled awake, Bright Moon's scream was muffled by a hand clamped over her mouth. She bit at it and was rewarded with a cry of pain. The hand was pulled from her mouth, but quickly replaced by a rawhide gag. Other hands grabbed her and she realized there was more than one attacker. Arms and legs flying, she struck out in the dark hoping to find a target, fight free from their clutches and escape.

Someone pinned one of her arms to the ground. She rewarded the holder with a fist, raining a series of blows until someone caught her wrist and bent it down to the ground. Bucking, she kicked at unseen targets but her assailants grabbed her ankles and restrained her.

Arms and legs pinned to the ground, her attackers

held her down while they tied her hands in front of her and hobbled[30] her feet. She squirmed without success as a blindfold was tied over her eyes. They rolled her over, face down, and a bony knee in the middle of her back held her in place. The guard leaned on her, his weight forcing the air out of her lungs. Her breath whooshed out of her. She was barely able to suck air in.

Though Bright Moon had fought them like a wildcat, the guards had her gagged, tied, and blindfolded before she could cry out. Her head spun, her stomach churned, and she fought to keep from being sick. She could guess who was behind this, but had no idea of her attackers' plans.

Grunts, accompanied by low, muffled voices—Bright Moon was unable to make out what was said—then the men, still panting from their efforts, yanked her to her feet, lifted her off the ground and slung her over an attacker's shoulder. The group started off at a quick walk, giving Bright Moon a bouncy ride. By placing her hands between herself and the man's back, she was able to cushion the blows from his jarring gait. *How many men were there? If it were two working together, perhaps they would tire quickly and she could escape.* Bright Moon tried to count, but the soft ground muffled their footsteps.

Her captors took turns carrying her. When they left camp, their steps were smooth, and there were long periods between changes, but now the changes had come more frequently and the ride had grown rougher.

From the start, she counted four-hand's worth of changes; four-hand's worth of being manhandled from shoulder to shoulder; four-hand's worth of being held close to their sweat-soaked, stinking bodies—before they came to a halt.

A few whispered commands and she was allowed to

---

30 This is a device, such as a rope or strap (around the legs of a horse, for example) used to impede action and restrict, but not prevent, movement.

slide off the guard's shoulder. Her landing on the hardpack[31] knocked the wind out of her. She let out a surprised grunt when she hit. Unable to stop, she rolled across the rough ground while rocks and sticks dug into her flesh. She suspected this was not a well-traveled path. *Wherever they're taking me, they want to avoid running into others.*

Not allowed a rest, her assailants pulled her to her feet before she could catch her breath and tied a leash around her waist. *Ahhh, move quickly and quietly, stay off regular trails,* she thought, *until far enough away from camp to feel safe ... then ... then ... what? What could be next?* She had no answer for that.

A yank on the leash jerked her into action, and she stumbled forward. Restrained by the hobble, she was barely able to walk and unable to see through the blindfold. She did her best to move in the direction she was being pulled. *Don't fight them now,* she kept telling herself. *Save your energy. There'll be a better time to resist. When they think you're beaten into submission, when they least suspect anything from you, then you can make a move. Yes, there'll be a better time....*

Bright Moon stumbled over the rough ground, frequently falling; her falls accompanied by taunts and muffled laughter from the men. Sharp tugs on the leash and the continued nip of a rawhide cord followed until she regained her feet.

She could not tell how far they traveled or how many falls she'd taken since their departure. Hands tied in front of her, she was able to use her hands and arms to break her falls, but rocks and sticks at each landing left their marks on her.

Exhausted, it was no surprise that she fell again. She heard the sound the rawhide made when it cut through

---

31 Soil that has been packed down either by feet or nature, into a firm layer of dirt that is structurally developed enough to prevent much penetration or deformation. It is the most common soil condition if the weather has been dry, and the trail is in good condition without much loose dirt on top.

the air as her handler raised the cord and she braced herself for its biting sting, but this time it was different.

Ahead of them, new voices, one with a thick accent. "Stop!" came the sharp command. The blow she expected never came.

Chapter 9: By Force

Pressured by Long Tusk, Wikvaya's group made a hasty departure from camp. In the lead, Kaliska, Long Tusk's scout, directed the torchbearers downhill along a well-worn path. They reached the meeting place before false dawn.

After Kaliska gathered wood, the torches provided the spark of life for the campfire. Their task completed, the torchbearers turned and left. Wrapped in robes, scant protection against the chill of night, the men huddled over their small fire and quietly waited the arrival of Bright Moon and the escort guarding her. Wikvaya, still upset over Long Tusk's methods, brooded over the distasteful task ahead.

Kaliska was the first to break the silence. "When the others arrive, I will scout the trail ahead."

"Do you expect problems?" Wikvaya, concerned for their safety, knew they would not be in a position to fight if set upon by raiders. Even if they fought bravely, the girl might be captured or killed. Or, she could take advantage of the opportunity and escape. His stomach tightened in knots. Unless he delivered the girl, his family would suffer at the hands of Askook. His task grew harder at every turn.

"The path from here isn't hard to follow." Lost in his own thoughts, Kaliska played with a stick from the fire. In the flickering light, the scout did not appear to notice Wikvaya's turmoil and went on describing the trail ahead. "It slopes down until you reach a shallow canyon—a gorge, really—that cuts through a heavily forested ridge. There, it splits: one branch climbs up the ridge through the forest and down the other side; the other leads into the ravine."

"Which path should we take?"

"When I first met with Askook, I told him the girl was a great shaman with magical powers," the scout confessed sheepishly and tossed the stick into the fire. "I believe he wants her powers for himself and is anxious for the meeting to take place. Long Tusk is eager because he sees big rewards."

Wikvaya made a face. "So you're saying that they both want the meeting to happen, and quickly. Which trail would be the quickest?"

The scout shrugged. "The gorge is the quickest, but it could be a problem if you encounter bandits or animals. The safer way is to climb the ridge and follow the rim, but it's the longest path and a steep trip uphill. The path down the other side isn't any better. You'll have to drive your group hard or you'll never get to the meeting place on time. If you're late, that won't sit well with either Long Tusk or Askook and they won't care how many problems you faced."

Concern lined Wikvaya's already furrowed brow. "So, which path would you take?"

Kaliska brushed off his companion's concern. It really wasn't his problem. "I'll scout ahead. From the top of the ridge, I can check both the trail and the canyon for signs of trouble. If you arrive and I'm not there, look for a cairn[32] to mark the direction I'm taking."

Wikvaya stared into the fire. *The scout*, he thought, *isn't much help. But, what can I expect? The man is loyal to Long Tusk and doesn't care what happens to the girl or if I am able to deliver her to Askook.*

"What do you think of the girl?" Kaliska asked softly,

---

32 A pile of stones used to mark a path for walkers and climbers.

interrupting Wikvaya's musings.

"She is brave... and quick-witted." Knees drawn up, Wikvaya, cushioned his chin on folded arms and went back to staring at the flames. "Too bad she has to go to Askook."

Wikvaya's words caused Kaliska to jump as if struck by a burning ember. "I had hoped she would be better off with Askook. Is this not the case?" He tried to suppress the concern in his voice.

"Askook is a worthless villain. Before he descended on us, my people lived in peace with neighboring tribes. The scoundrel demands tribute and holds whole families hostage."

As he listened to Wikvaya, the scout's shoulders hunched over and he appeared to withdraw. His youthful, energetic, boastfulness disappeared. Finally, Kaliska spoke, his words quiet and almost apologetic. "I thought the girl's future would be brighter with Askook, but it sounds like she will be no better off; perhaps even worse." He shook his head in dismay.

"Aren't you a member of Long Tusk's tribe?" Surprised, Wikvaya's eyebrows arched upwards. "I thought your loyalties lay with him."

"No!" Kaliska spat out the word like a foul taste. "Long Tusk claimed my uncle owed him a debt. Villain that he is, he held my uncle's family hostage. Many died while captives. Long Tusk still demanded payment." Kaliska looked closely at Wikvaya. *Could he trust his man? How much?* "I am here to pay the debt for my uncle... and his family."

Wikvaya nodded. He understood Kaliska's message—both the spoken and unspoken words. "At the ravine, after Long Tusk's out-walker disappeared, the girl claimed she was attacked and that Long Tusk was the instigator." It was his turn to look closely at his companion. "She went on to say that Long Tusk's people attacked her father's caravan. Do you believe her?"

"Yes," Kaliska nodded. "I heard rumors long before she confronted him. I am not a member of his tribe. If they did as she said, they kept it secret from me."

Spotting movement in the early morning darkness, the scout rose to a crouch, his war-club in his hand; Wikvaya grabbed a spear. The pair turned to face the oncoming shadows. Long Tusk's guards emerged from the darkness and the duo relaxed.

"They're late, but they're finally here," Kaliska said. "At this rate you'll never make the meeting in time no matter which path you take."

Wikvaya nodded. The specter of failure seemed to lurk around every turn.

Just as the lead guard called a halt, the girl tripped and landed flat on the ground. Her plight confirmed the cause of the party's delay. The guard acting as her handler raised a rawhide cord.

"Stop," Wikvaya commanded. Surprised, the man brought the whip up short.

On her own, Bright Moon rose slowly to one knee and was able to stay in that position for the time being. She sensed a change, but was unsure of the situation. *If I listen closely, what can I find out? It sounds like another man, maybe two, has joined the group.*

With controlled anger, Wikvaya planted the butt-end of his spear upright in the ground. "All of you will have some explaining to do if the girl isn't in good condition," Wikvaya told the guards. Scornfully, he picked up a fiery brand and walked over to examine their charge.

The new men approached; Bright Moon had heard their footsteps; she felt the heat of a torch held close as someone circled around her before moving away. Another meeting, more muffled voices—one with an angry tone heard above the rest. Bright Moon knew the new people were not happy.

His exam complete, Wikvaya motioned to the guards'

leader to join him at the campfire. "You're late," Wikvaya said.

"We had trouble getting the witch here in the dark," the guard mumbled. "She slowed us down." By passing the blame, the guard hoped to sidestep any trouble.

"One hand's worth of armed men to escort a girl who is hobbled, gagged, and blindfolded and you can't get her here without using a whip", Wikvaya hissed through clenched teeth. "The girl, the one you call the witch, is our reason—our only reason—for being here, but only if we make the meeting on time and she is undamaged."

The guard, his muscular arms crossed defiantly over his chest, sneered at his scrawny challenger, "Our instructions were to take her out of camp quietly and bring her to you. Then, we are to escort you and the girl to Askook." Hands hidden from view, he clenched and unclenched his fingers, suppressing his immediate desire to strangle this stranger. "We carried her out of camp and part way here," the guard's voice grew louder as he spoke and he began waving his hands around. "The men grew tired. It will be a long trip and they must save their strength so she had to walk. The whip was to keep her from slowing us down."

Wikvaya made a show of spitting to show his disdain. "Neither Askook nor Long Tusk will tolerate delays, but you have a bigger problem. They will see how you treated her. You can explain how she got the bruises and whip welts when you explain the delay. Long Tusk is expecting a big reward for her delivery. If she's delivered late or damaged, Askook won't be happy. If he's not happy, my guess is that Long Tusk won't be happy."

"I'll scout the path ahead," Kaliska said. For the benefit of the guard, he added, "You need to keep this bunch moving. Any more delays and you won't have time to climb the ridge. If you have to take the gorge, you'll need to get there early in order to get out the other end before dark. You won't want to be in there after the sun goes down."

Wikvaya nodded. Kaliska took to the trail, fading into the lingering darkness.

The guard remained silent and impassive, but the scout's words had raised his hackles and he shot poisonous looks at the retreating figure.

"You heard the man," Wikvaya chided. "We've got a long way to go and because you were so late getting here, we're short on time. You need to decide on a way to move her quickly without hurting her."

Angrily, the guard rejoined his men. He assigned one at each side of the girl to help her along. The other two were to follow behind. Bright Moon heard whispered grumblings followed by a tug on her leash. She got to her feet and was surprised to find a guard on each arm to guide her and smiled to herself; things were starting to go her way.

Wikvaya lectured the guard but didn't bother looking his way. "If your men are ready, let's get moving." He put the fire out and started along the trail Kaliska had taken.

The chief guard shot a smoldering glance after Wikvaya's disappearing form. *Maybe*, he thought, *just maybe, neither the stranger nor the scout will complete the trip.* Stone-faced, he took the lead, but inwardly began planning ways to get rid of this upstart stranger… and then the scout. The guard and those escorting the girl, followed. Sunlight, a thin golden line, exposed the rim of the horizon.

###

It was late morning by the time they found the place where the trail split. Wikvaya called a halt and the men collapsed in the cool shade under a clump of trees. "Kneel," Bright Moon's handler ordered and then smirked as he watched her struggle.

Ignoring them for the time, Wikvaya studied the trail in front of him. Just as Kaliska said it would, the path split. One branch dipped down into the winding close-quarters of the gorge. The other branch climbed up, fought its way through the tangle of brush to the forest. From there trees covered the ground to the summit embracing the rim along the way. To reach the far side of the ridge, they would have to push their way up hill through the brush to the forest and then thread their way along the narrow lip of the gorge to reach the crest. Once there, they would have to make their descent to the river valley through terrain similar to that they had just traveled.

The scout told him the trip along the rim would take time. Wikvaya could see why. While there would be cool breezes along the rim and shade in the forest, there were less appealing features to consider. If they were attacked, with their back to the gorge there would be no escape. They would also have to keep a close eye on the girl to keep her from stepping over the edge and ending her plight. The trip along the rim would not be easy with the girl bound and he could not risk untying her. He would have to watch the guards, least they push him over. Yes, that route would be full of problems and take time. It was time he did not have.

Bright Moon knelt on the ground and listened for clues, but it was useless. The men didn't speak, or spoke only in whispers. She raised her bound hands toward the blindfold. It would be good to see again, if only to keep from tripping once they resumed their journey.

"Leave it!" her handler growled and reinforced his command with a quick flick of the rawhide tether across her bare arm.

"Yhaaag!" Her surprised yelp, muffled by the gag across her mouth, amused her keeper and he gave her another sharp smack.

"Yhaaag!" Wilting away from her tormentor, Bright Moon's protests were greeted by more laughter.

"Enough!" She heard another voice command. An unknown, his words were thick as if spoken by a stranger to this land. *Who was this person?* She asked herself. *Was he the one she had seen with Long Tusk?*

"The witch was trying to free herself," her tormentor replied.

"Long Tusk didn't send you along to beat her. Watch her carefully, but no more beatings," the stranger commanded. "Askook will not accept damaged goods."

The sharp sting of the rawhide faded, but the blindfold remained. Still, she had gained valuable knowledge from this exchange: *The group included a stranger, probably the one from the last place they stopped—maybe the one she had seen with Long Tusk—and he was in charge. It also confirmed what she had suspected—Long Tusk was behind this plot and, as trade goods, the amount of abuse she would suffer would be limited.*

On the other hand, she could only guess at her surroundings, but made a mental list of what she did know. The high-meadows were gone, replaced by rough, rocky ground and the air lacked the cool mountain breezes. The calls of night-creatures had given way to those of day-hunters. The calls of crickets and grasshoppers had all but disappeared.

The night's chill had been replaced by the sun's warmth. Fidgeting, she slowly shifted her position around and tilted her head to the side, letting her long hair drape across her chest. The sun's warmth now bathed her back while her front cooled. She had not made a mistake. The rising sun was behind her.

"Be still," her tormentor growled. Unhappy that he could not apply the lash, he satisfied himself by jerking on her leash.

Bright Moon sat still, but smiled inwardly. She now knew the general direction of the rising sun and, from that, she might figure out which way they were traveling. When she escaped, it would be knowledge she would need.

Wikvaya checked the position of the sun. Already well along its daily journey, it would soon reach its high point before its decline to the far horizon would begin. It was hot, yet the hottest part of the day was still in front of them... and so was the whole length of the gorge.

Kaliska said the fastest route was through the gorge and to Wikvaya this trail appeared to be the most inviting. He also said that Wikvaya's group would have to move quickly to be at the other end before dark.

Though the gorge's twists and turns varied in width, the trail was unimpeded, even by the stream it contained. Hardly more than a trickle, this pathetic creek meandered through the rocky cut, sometimes spreading out, sometimes forming pools, but so small it could be easily stepped over or trod through. It would not hamper their travel.

As hot as it was here, the trip through the gorge would be even hotter. Breezes would not exist there. The rocks would be as hot as if they were in a fire. Sweat trickled down Wikvaya's back. He knew that his robes, woven from plant fibers, were cooler than the guards' animal-hide tunics. But, the trip through the gorge was necessary if they were going to make the meeting ... and then he would be done with all of this and his family would be freed.

The guards, though restrained, chafed at their task and did not like taking orders from him. Both paths provided an ideal place for them to launch an attack. Regardless of the path, it was clear to Wikvaya that he would not be able to turn his back on Long Tusk's men....

Unaware of the stranger's thoughts, the chief guard continued to entertain himself with thoughts of his own: *If the stranger chooses the ridge route, a slight shove at the right moment and over the rim he goes....*

The cairn Kaliska left pointed toward the rim. Wikvaya didn't like the canyon's close confines, and was even less comfortable with its twists and turns that offered many places for ambush. Still, it offered swift passage and a chance for him to be done with this task. He put his feelings aside, had the men fill their water pouches and rebuild the marker to show the scout the direction he chose. If they hurried, they would be out before dark. He was confident of that.

Bright Moon's thoughts were interrupted. Whoever led the group must have decided they should continue, as there were noises of several people moving, and then a tug at the leash. "Get on your feet," her handler growled.

Dutifully, Bright Moon got to her feet and, a guard on either side, they started off.

The wind died. It grew warmer and then stifling hot. Though she could not see anything around her, by the sound of their footfalls, she guessed they were in a closed area. The air seemed thick with blowflies and gnats. The sound of crunching gravel echoed back replacing the previous soft pat, pat, pat of treading on grass covered rocky dirt. Their downhill descent became even steeper.

Where were they going? How far would they have to travel to get there? How could she escape? She thought about these questions but did not know the answers.

The day wore on and the heat grew more severe. Thirst and the overpowering heat drove Bright Moon into an impassive daze. She was barely able to shuffle along.

Thoughts of her captors, the direction they traveled, even of escaping, faded. Loose rubble replaced gravel making walking difficult. Even with the men by her sides, her falls came so often that there was little laughter. Ridicule replaced taunts.

The group continued its pace, herding her along without rest, sapping her strength until she could go on no more. These conditions finally overwhelmed her. Bright Moon felt her legs weaken and give way. Tripping, she slipped out of her escorts hands and fell, tumbling out of control until she crashed into a boulder. She felt a tug on the leash but did not move. The tug turned into a jerk, but she continued to lay there. Yanking ceased. In a heat-driven stupor, she was aware that her assailants called a conference Muffled voices—some low and controlled others loud and sharp—buzzed around her.

Finally, rough hands seized her, pulled her up, sat her on a log and then leaned her back against a boulder as if her handlers were now concerned for her comfort. Her blindfold was removed.

Dirt-caked and covered with dried sweat, she blinked and slowly brought her bound hands up to shield her eyes from the bright sunlight. Motionless, she sat there in this near lifeless state in case those surrounding her were watching. Slowly, Bright Moon shifted her gaze to take in her surroundings. She was able to count five men—all were Long Tusk's people—lounging about.

They were in a rock-strewn gully with steep, ragged walls. In its descent from the crest, its width varied between wide and narrow as it twisted and turned. Their confinement offered little shade and no breeze. Heat, rising from rocky surfaces, made the air shimmer and dance. The only relief offered was a small creek, barely a trickle, near her feet. If she had the strength, if it were a little larger, she would have sat in it, lay in it, splashed its cool waters over herself, but she was too exhausted to do anything but sit there.

"Leave her tied, but remove the gag." Startled, she jumped at the sound of a slightly accented voice behind her.

A lanky stranger leaned against the canyon wall. Thinking back, she recalled seeing him lingering at the edge of the crowd when Long Tusk was bitten by the snake. It had not meant anything to her then; but now, this man, realizing he had surprised her, flashed her a smile—more like a smirk—and took on an air of confident smugness.

An older man, he was tall, slim, and handsome in a rugged sort of way. His head was shaved except for a long braid, gray in color. He wore the trappings of an unfamiliar tribe. In place of the skins or hides most men wore, his tunic appeared to be made similar to mats, but finer. It appeared that he had been watching her closely.

The one with rough hands, one of Long Tusk's guards, removed her gag, but left her hands tied and her feet hobbled. The stranger casually strolled over and held out a water pouch. "Here," he said, still beaming, "drink this."

Unsure of his motives, Bright Moon hesitated. *Could this be a step toward her escape?* Holding up her bound hands, she showed her helplessness. Would he recognize an inability to hold the pouch? Her eyes pleaded with him for leniency.

"No," he said, "you're too tricky to untie. Drink this. Refresh yourself. Do the best you can."

Clumsily, she accepted his offering. Her plans for immediate escape fading, she put the pouch to her cracked sun-dried lips and took a long swig. Dumping more over her head, she moaned as she let the cool water run down her body. She would have liked to wash the dirt off and clean her cuts and bruises, but could not with her hands still bound. Maybe she could pry some information out of the stranger. "Where are you taking me?"

"Long Tusk has made you a present to Askook, Chief of The Mattocks. We go there." The one who gave her water took the empty pouch and offered pemmican in exchange. "Eat this," he said and he handed the pouch to another guard. "Take this," he told the man, "make sure all the pouches are replenished. We'll be leaving soon."

Behind them, there was a sudden noise, the clatter of a rock tumbling across the rubble-strewn canyon floor. Everyone came alert; clutching their weapons, they turned to face a possible attack.

Kaliska stepped from behind a turn in the canyon. He was the one who had thrown the rock. She remembered seeing him at Long Tusk's camp.

The scout's tone showed his disdain. "If I were a gang of bandits or a pack of animals, most of you would be dead." He let them consider his words before going on. "You're less than half way through the canyon," he scolded. "To be out by sundown, you'll have to travel faster."

"Move on in this heat?" The men scoffed at his remarks and showed no interest in continuing just yet. The sun bore down on them. Its heat intensified by the rock walls. Everyone felt like they were being cooked.

"In these close quarters, you're vulnerable to attack from hostile tribes... from animals... from the weather." The scout's words met with contempt from Long Tusk's men.

Coming to the scout's aid, Wikvaya said, "While you are reluctant to move on in this heat, I am sure that none of you want to face the Long Tusk's wrath or be in the company of the witch any longer than necessary and certainly not after dark." They grumbled but it stirred them into action.

Wikvaya weighed blindfolding the girl again, against making better time through the gorge with her able to see.

Trussed up like she was before, the girl would be unable to play tricks, but would fall more and that would slow them down. Released, she could return to her old ways. He had misgivings, but they were behind schedule. He wanted to get to the end of this canyon before nightfall. Striking an air of confidence in front of the others, he made his decision and nodded to the chief guard.

"Everybody on your feet," the guard said, "it's time to move."

Her guard, the one who had held her leash, picked up the blindfold and gag as he started toward Bright Moon. Wide-eyed, apprehensive about being confined again, she stiffened but remained docile hoping for compassion.

"Don't bother with that," Wikvaya instructed. "There's no one around to hear her yell and we'll make better time if she's not tripping over everything."

"But she's a witch and will cast a spell on us," the guard protested.

The stranger turned to Bright Moon and smiled. "Don't cast any spells, don't play any tricks and you won't have to wear your headdress." His demeanor hid his strength. He pulled her to her feet and effortlessly lifted her into the air before planting her gently on the ground. "Now tell Wikvaya you understand?"

Surprised by his actions, she found her heart in her throat. Regaining her composure, she signaled him with a nod. *Yes*, she thought, *I understand. I don't agree to your terms and will try to get away as soon as the opportunity presents itself, but I understand your conditions.*

Ignoring her, oblivious to her condition, Wikvaya turned to her guard and handed over the leash with a smile. "Watch her carefully. She may play tricks, but I don't believe she can cast spells."

###

Mid-afternoon found them still in the twisting, turning confines of the gully, but without the blindfold, Bright Moon—still bound and hobbled and with a guard at each elbow—was able to avoid obstacles. They made better time. Wikvaya was pleased with his decision.

Bright Moon took inventory of her environment, noting that she had sat on a log at their previous stop. As they moved downhill, she noted that brush and logs tucked in nooks and bends were common. Her companions seemed unaware, at least unconcerned, that the path they followed had been used by floodwaters. A heavy rain, and their ignorance, could work to her benefit.

The sun beat down. In the close quarters of the ravine, there was little air movement. They walked in the shade where possible, but it did little good. It went from stifling to oppressively hot. Water pouches were soon drained dry. Their eyes burned from sweat streaming off their brows.

Plump, dark clouds slithered in and covered the sun. Fire-from-the-sky[33] finally announced the storm. Rain followed it. Large, fat, drops fell. Only a few at first and then the air was filled with rain intermixed with hail. They were soon soaked to the skin. The wind, absent until now, picked up. Never constant, it seemed to come from every direction, sending rain in sheets, blinding them. One hand against the canyon wall, they felt their way along until the guards found a niche large enough for the men to crowd in and be out of the weather. There was no room for Bright Moon.

"Tie this end of her leash securely," Wikvaya ordered, "and let the rest out so she can search for shelter."

Long Tusk's men watched Bright Moon make her way through the downpour. She finally found a place near

---

33 This is how lightning is described because they recognized that it sometimes started fires.

the wall, between it and a boulder. She settled down there, back to the weather and the men, and seemed to shiver in the cold.

Seeing her condition improved her guards' morale. They laughed at her plight, joking about "How the witch must like being wet or else she would have cast a spell for better weather." Believing she was secure, they turned their backs to her.

From his place, Wikvaya peered through the waves of rain until he located the girl. She had not moved from what little shelter the boulder provided. Wet and apparently cold, she shivered quietly near the end of her leash. It was unfortunate, but the exposure might take some of the fight out of her.

Satisfied that she was secure, Wikvaya turned his back to her and the weather and settled in with the others to wait. It had been his experience that storms, as fierce as this, never lasted long. But, he was anxious, anxious to get started, anxious to get out of the gorge, anxious to reach his goal and be done with this burden. This was a delay and even though he tried not to let it show, he was unhappy with the delay. Now, they would have to travel even faster to reach the river valley before nightfall. Stymied, confined in this tiny crevasse, he chafed at the delay.

Lightning and hail continued. Rain formed rivulets that flowed downhill. Bright Moon sat on the ground, huddled next to a boulder, her back to both the driving rain and her captors. She sat as far away as the leash would allow, but it was not their taunts that drove her here.

At her feet, an upturned stone--half buried in the dirt--presented a sharp edge. She eased the rawhide that hobbled her over its lip. Quietly, using very little body movement, she started pulling the cord over its blade-like rim. It didn't take long to free her feet. She glanced over her shoulder but was unable to see through the pounding rain. Satisfied that she had not been discovered, she set to work on the cords that bound her hands and they soon parted.

The downpour was thinning. If the men looked her way before she finished freeing herself, her efforts would be worthless. More than that, the men, unfamiliar with this terrain, didn't realize how much water would be coming down the gorge. She knew and she knew she had to work fast.

She cut the cord at her waist. It was then that Bright Moon's attention was suddenly drawn to a small, dark figure darting nimbly over the nearby rocks. A scorpion, driven out of its nest by the rain, searched for a drier spot. A parade of others followed the first.

A dry spot, she thought, *I'll help you find a dry spot!* With her thumb and forefinger, she grabbed the closest by its upraised telson and flung it into the niche where the men sat. Grabbing another, she did the same. Several more soon joined the first two. They would give her captors something to think about while she made her getaway.

A dead tree-trunk, swept down by previous floodwaters, stood upended against the wall, the remains of branches stuck out like ribs picked clean. Above it, bushes sprouted out of the rock surfaces. From these she could gain a ledge and a series of handholds that would take her to the top. Having mapped this route, she was on her feet and at the timber in an instant.

From the ground, the handholds above had appeared plentiful, but she had not figured they would be this slippery. Not one to quibble, she dug her fingers and toes in, clawing and pulling herself along the slick surface until she reached the rim. Sliding over the lip, she slipped under the bushes and lay in the grass while she caught her breath.

Free! She was free from her tormentors. Her heart beat so strong, it felt like it would burst. She had not dared to let herself believe it until now. She was lightheaded and as giddy as if she drank too much chicha.

Bright Moon heard a distant, dull roar, something like rolling thunder. It grew louder and she could feel a slight tremor in the ground beneath her. Hidden behind the brush, she could creep safely away. What held her there was the knowledge that one man, the stranger, stopped the abuse she received and shown her a small amount of kindness... something that she should repay. She could not leave him to the fate they were about to suffer even though the others deserved it. She would give him a fighting chance, even if only a little one, and even if it meant warning Long Tusk's guards.

The rain abated as Wikvaya knew it would. He turned to check the weather and his charge. The girl was nowhere to be seen. Startled, he sat upright and peered through the drizzle. Could he be mistaken? Did she find a better shelter behind the boulder? No, that was not it. The cord that had acted as a leash floated leisurely in the rain-pocked stream, its frayed end pointed at the clouds, mocking him. His jaw dropped. Earlier, when he thought she was shivering from the cold, she was cutting the cords that bound her.

From behind a bush, Bright Moon peered down into the gorge. The downpour had become a drizzle. Water covered the floor of the gorge where she had been sitting only moments before. A flash of Fire-from-the-sky struck near the opposite rim. The thunderous boom split the air. Bright Moon cupped her hands around her mouth and called as a wolf calls, "Ay...Ay...Ayeeeeeee."

The sound echoed off the stonewalls. She watched the men's surprised faces poke out of their niche. The stranger, the one called Wikvaya, bolted out of his dry spot into ankle deep water and looked around, trying to locate her.

From her hiding place, she yelled, "Don't bother to look for me. I am gone... invisible... but I left my friends, the scorpions, to keep you company until the waters I called up get here." Another bolt of Fire-from-the-sky sounded, adding emphasis to her words.

The men, wide-eyed and pale-faced, crouched in their relatively dry space and looked around in disbelief. One spotted a black menace crawling on him and screamed. "There it is! It's on me! It's on me! Get it off!"

Almost as one, the group erupted from the crevasse, landing with a splash in the deepening water. She heard Wikvaya yell to them and then watched as he turned to splash toward the timber she had used.

Intent on making sure they were scorpion free, Long Tusk's men ignored Wikvaya's warning as they danced and splashed around in the deepening water. A yell from the chief guard changed their focus.

"Get him," their leader commanded, "he set the witch free; he brought this on us." He threw his spear at Wikvaya. The others joined in. Absorbed on skewering the stranger, they didn't see the wall of water that thundered around the bend.

Bright Moon didn't need to stay longer. Having shouted her warning, she felt her obligation to the stranger discharged. It was up to him to survive. She didn't wait to see what happened next.

Chapter 10: Survival

Pushing and shoving their way out of their refuge, the guards threw off their robes to make sure they were scorpion free. The fact that they landed in knee-deep water went unnoticed.

Wikvaya heard a low rumble, something like distant, rolling thunder. The sound grew. It sent a chill down his back. Few had experienced this danger and fewer lived to talk about it. He had to change tactics and do so quickly.

A log—the remains of a tree washed down and abandoned by previous floods—leaned against the canyon wall. It could provide a path to the rim and may have been the route the girl had taken. With the water now waist-deep, the girl wasn't Wikvaya's biggest concern at the moment. Instead, he wallowed along, hands outstretched, toward the tree. It was as if he ran in mud and would never reach his goal, but he knew he must. Reaching it would be his only salvation. He splashed through the deepening waters yelling, "Quickly, to the tree... hang on."

"Get him," the chief guard commanded, "he set the witch free. He brought this on us."

A spear flew over Wikvaya's shoulder and dug into the water in front of him. He dodged to the side and another spear hit the water where he would have been. Close to the timber, but not close enough, Wikvaya gave up running and dove under water, hoping it would hide him. Intent on skewering the stranger, the guards didn't see the wall of water that thundered around the bend.

Wikvaya surfaced in time to see the timber shift and tumble into the torrent. His spirits sank with the log as it disappeared under water but rose again when it bobbed to the surface. Caught by the current, the log began to move away, its branches churning the water as it picked up speed. Frantically, he struggled to reach its safety before it was carried forever out of his reach. Lunging forward, his fingers closed around one of the limbs and locked on while he clawed for another grip with his free hand.

Caught in the current, the timber began its brisk downstream journey. Wikvaya clung to a single branch and scrambled desperately for a better hold. His task, made more difficult by the slippery, moss-covered surface, was finally resolved when he found a tree hollow.[34]

Undeterred by his efforts, the log tumbled along the gorge carrying its passenger through the turbulent waters into another curve in the ravine. A last glance over his shoulder showed the stream was no longer a pathetic trickle, but a raging wall of water thundering around the bend behind him. If the men had failed to heed his warning, those too slow to react would be caught, slammed into a wall or swept under the foamy mass, never to be seen again.

The deluge caught Wikvaya and the timber, taking them on a wild ride down the ravine. Buried in froth, the pair charged forward even faster, hitting walls, outcroppings, and boulders along the way. Each strike jarring Wikvaya, often submerging the timber he clung to, and putting him in danger of losing his grip.

During all of this, one thought ran though his mind. *Had the girl caused this? He didn't want to believe that, but....*

From her hiding place, Bright Moon shouted a

---

34 A tree hollow or tree hole is a semi-enclosed cavity which has naturally formed in the trunk or branch of a tree. These are predominantly found in old trees, whether living or not. Hollows form in many species of trees, and are a prominent feature of natural forests and woodlands, and act as a resource or habitat for small animals.

warning to her captors and now slithered on her belly, backwards, away from the rim. Getting to her hands and knees, she scrambled even farther back until she reached a point where she could safely stand without being seen from the floor of the gorge.

Did anyone survive the flood? She didn't know, but she knew she was free. To stay that way, she needed to remain out of sight—no one would know if she survived or not—and then decide on her next course of action.

The path in front of her ran parallel to the canyon. One way would take her toward Askook; the other would take her to where the caravan last made camp. She did not want to end up in either place, but needed to throw potential pursuers off her trail before striking out in another direction. The rain continued to fall, but had settled into a slow steady pattern. If she were careful, it might help cover her trail. The ground, from the lip of the gorge to here, was covered with marks that shouted her presence; marks where she had slithered backwards on her belly like a snake; marks where she moved backwards on hands-and-knees to the point where she now stood.

It would take too long to cover these tracks, to brush them out and make them disappear. The next best ploy would be to walk around in circles, first one way and then the other, to confuse any followers in the direction she went and her intentions.

At the apex of the circle, she hopped up on a fallen log and cautiously traversed its length taking care not to break any branches along the way. A boulder, partially submerged in a bed of gravel, provided a convenient place to step off. Tiptoeing across the gravel, she reached the grassy trail that was her goal. A glance over her shoulder allowed her to inspect her steps. The marks left when she climbed out were now buried under a myriad of tracks leading every direction. "Good," she whispered with smug satisfaction.

If no one survived the flood, she had nothing to worry about. If anyone did survive and came looking for her, she'd give them tracks to follow, something that will take them in another direction.

Satisfied, she turned and walked up the trail toward Long Tusk's last campsite. Now and then, she would leave a sign to mark her path. If she were being tracked, this would give the impression she was hiding her trail while searching for the caravan. She wanted to appear a little careless without it being obvious that she was misleading her pursuers. In the excitement of finding her tracks, they would believe that she was headed for the caravan and miss the place where she doubled back. Eventually, they would realize she had tricked them; but, by then, she would be long gone.

Wikvaya lost track of time. How long had he hung on, he couldn't say; but it had finally ended. Exhausted, he raised his head to look around. The floodwaters had carried him out of the gorge and abandoned him in a pond, the far end of which emptied into a river.

Compared to those in the canyon, these waters were placid, giving Wikvaya the opportunity to weakly paddle toward shore. The log reached shallow waters, bumped aground on a sandbar, broke loose, and then grounded again. He lay on it and eyed the distance to the shore. Beyond the sand bar where he lay, more water separated him from the sand-and-gravel beach that hugged a rocky knoll. It looked appealing, but to get there he had to leave this safe place and cross the remaining water. Did he have the strength?

Wikvaya struggled to his feet and started forward, focusing on the shore. He stepped off the sandbar into knee-deep water. Three, maybe four steps more and he found himself up to his armpits. The current swept him off his feet, carrying him downstream. He thrashed around until he snagged a low-hanging branch, pulled himself into shallow water, and then stumbled ashore.

Exhausted, he collapsed on the sand-and-gravel beach and passed out.

He did not know how long he lay there when his rest was disturbed by a rock hitting the sand nearby. He sat up with a start. Was it an animal or an enemy?

"I was afraid you were dead," Kaliska said. Hands on his hips, the scout stood on an outcropping overlooking the beach.

"I never had a ride like that before. I wasn't sure I was going to survive." Wikvaya watched as the scout made his way down.

"I reached the mouth of the gorge and heard the storm coming. By the time I climbed out and turned back to warn you, the wind and rain were on me," the scout explained. "I had to find shelter until it passed." Squatting across from Wikvaya, he held out a piece of jerky[35].

Wikvaya eagerly took the offering. "What brings you here?" He asked, between bites. Kaliska offered him a water pouch.

Wikvaya shook his head, rejecting the scout's offer. "I've had enough water for a while," he said, "but, I'll take more jerky."

Kaliska laughed good-naturedly. "My friend, whatever I have is yours."

Wikvaya bit off a piece of the dried meat and then asked, "How did you know where to find me?"

The scout sat upright and thumped himself on the chest. "I am Kaliska, a great scout... and the best one Long Tusk will ever have," he added immodestly. Kaliska shot a smug look at the waterlogged man and continued

---

35 Meat that has been cut into strips, trimmed of fat, marinated in a spicy, salty, or sweet rub or liquid, and dried or smoked with low heat (usually under 70°C/160°F). Occasionally just salted and sun-dried. The result is a salty, savory, or semisweet snack that can be stored for a long time without refrigeration. The word "jerky" comes from the Quechua term Charqui which means to burn (meat). Jerked meat was one of the first human-made products and was a crucially important food preservation technique for survival.

with, "I knew what would follow the storm when I had to find shelter. I waited for the floodwaters to recede then I searched toward the mouth of the gorge for survivors. You're the first person I found. Did any of the other men escape? What happened to the girl?"

The scout's jabbering seemed endless. His questions came faster than they could be answered. Wikvaya made a face. *Maybe*, he thought, *it was because the scout was alone so much he felt starved for conversation.* He held up a hand and Kaliska grew silent.

"To make better time," Wikvaya explained, "I told the guard to leave her blindfold off. They were against it because they felt she was a witch and would cast a spell. I insisted they leave it off."

The scout raised his eyebrows in question.

"Blindfolded," Wikvaya rationalized, "they thought she couldn't see to cast her spells and they'd be safe." Wikvaya shrugged. "Before you last found us, even with a guard on each arm, she was stumbling over everything. The men propped her up, but didn't tell her where to step so she still tripped. Having them at her sides was little better than when they weren't there. Their irritation and the delays grew each time she fell."

Kaliska leaned forward in rapt attention. "So, then what happened?"

"I didn't think she could cast spells and knew that we'd make better time if she could see." Wikvaya paused and took another bite of jerky. "It worked out. Once she could see where she was walking, we made good time. Then the rains came. The men found a place big enough to hold everyone... but her."

Kaliska nodded. "What happened next?"

"I had her guard tie the leash to a rock so she couldn't go too far but was free to seek her own shelter." Wikvaya paused for a moment, seemingly lost in thought. "The men saw her huddled against a boulder and shivering in the rain. Believing she could not be a witch, they grew more confident. I thought that being wet might make her less tricky and easier to handle."

"Did it?" Kaliska leaned in, wanting to hear every detail.

Wikvaya scoffed. "I thought she was shivering in the cold, but not everything is as it seems."

"What was happening?"

"Her back turned to us, she was cutting her binding."

Kaliska broke into laughter, full-throated, head back, roaring laughter. Wikvaya stopped his narration to wait for scout to pull himself together. It finally played itself out and the scout composed himself enough to say, "Yes, yes, go on. What happened after that?"

Wikvaya tried to suppress a smile as he fought to remain serious. "She climbed out of the gorge, shouted a warning, and slipped away just before the water hit." He pointed to the timber. "I made it to the log, but lost sight of the others so I don't know if anybody else survived."

"Long Tusk wanted to meet Askook at the place where the river meets the Great Ice. With her gone, neither one will be happy." The scout ended his flood of questions with, "What do we do now?"

"We still have a few days before the meeting. I'll need your help to go back and check for survivors and see if we can pick up her trail," Wikvaya replied. "If we can catch her, we can make the meeting with the girl." If *we can't catch her*, Wikvaya thought, *I will be forced to watch as Askook makes my children slaves and gives my wives and daughters to his friends as gifts; then, when he's had his revenge, I will be put to death.*

"Maybe we'll find that she ran into a bear." Kaliska suggested. To Wikvaya, it seemed like the scout was secretly happy to hear the girl was alive and free.

Wikvaya scoffed "If she did, I'd feel sorry for the bear."

Some distance up the trail, Bright Moon stopped for

a rest. It would be nightfall soon and she needed to make preparations. She sat on a fallen tree and surveyed her surroundings.

The recent storm brought the tree down and turned its long, straight branches—the ones that had once fanned out over the earth—stretching for the sky while others lay crumpled and shattered, a victim of the tree's descent. Getting to her feet, she searched through the rubble until she found two long shafts sheared off by the fall. Each was almost as long as she was tall and of sufficient girth to make good spears. A short piece, stubbed at one end and with a wye[36] at the other, would become the handle for her ax.

A sandstone ledge, weathered and cracked, provided a makeshift blade. She forced the blade between the arms of the wye and tied it in place with the remnants of the rawhide that once bound her. The ax, heavy and not as sharp as she would have liked, worked to remove the bark, clean branch nubs, and give the shafts pointed ends. As a final act, she tied rawhide cords around fist-sized rocks to make a bola[37]. These tools are what she would depend on to provide protection... and food. Her stomach growled loudly, supporting this last idea.

After leaving the impression that she continued in the same direction, she turned and started along the path back the way she came. Earlier, she had passed a fork in the trail. The new branch led uphill, toward the forest and the mountains beyond. It led away from Long Tusk's caravan, away from Askook, and away from the certain bondage they both represented. Careful to leave nothing to indicate her change in direction, she headed for her new objective.

---

36 The name of the letter Y; A wye-shaped object: a wye-level, wye-connected.

37 Weighted cord for entangling an animal's legs: a strong cord with weights attached to the ends, used for catching animals, large or small, by throwing it to entangle the animal's legs.

###

At first glance, the forest in front of Bright Moon looked thick, dark, uninviting. Sunlight filtered through the tall trees allowing patches of light to perforate the darkness under the canopy of leaves. A breeze whispered through the branches causing leaves to flutter. Bird marked their territories with song. Squirrels chattered. Somewhere, a woodpecker announced his search for food with its rhythmic tapping, and the path leading into the forest was well worn.

Yes, she thought, *the forest is dark, but not as dark as the life I just left behind.* Fortified by that thought, Bright Moon took a deep breath, threw her shoulders back and marched forward, fingers wrapped securely around the shafts of her spears.

Afternoon turned into dusk. Bright Moon needed a place to stay for the night. In a clearing, she found a tree suitable for climbing. Actually, it had been a clump of trees that had grown together, becoming one. The collection stood in the center of a clearing near a small creek and towered over the trees around them. When darkness came, she would be safer high in the tree, tied to a limb, than on the forest floor with the night-stalkers. For protection against biting insects, she covered her exposed flesh with heavy coats of mud from the creek before starting her climb. Hunger gnawed at her. Tomorrow, when she had more time, she would check the creek for fish and try to spear a couple.

With darkness closing in, she selected a comfortable set of branches for her overnight home. Tucked away in her lofty nest, hidden by the draping foliage and moss, her location gave a good view of the surrounding area. Insects buzzed around, but the mud coating her body provided protection. She was pleased with her foresight, even though it made her skin itch as the mud dried and cracked.

Treetops spread out around her like a green carpet

leading up to the whiteness that was the Great Ice. Satisfied that she could see, but would go unseen, she used the rope that belted her tunic to fasten herself securely to the tree and settled in for the night. Her nest swayed gently in the breeze as she drifted off to sleep.

Noises! Bright Moon woke with a start and listened to the sounds. There were people on the forest floor. Was it her captors? The sound flowed up the hollow between the trees. She peered through the branches and watched their movements. Family groups, one hand's worth, probably a clan, their leader used strong, harsh words as he directed the band setting up shelters for the night. Their tents, huddled together near its base, encircled the tree. Their presence would keep predators away. They were unaware of her existence. It would not be advisable to go down and join them.

A group of hunters, carrying a deer slung on a pole, emerged from the forest and shouted their greetings. People gathered around them. Excitement grew as the carcass was divided up among the families. Eventually, the air filled with cooking smells and her stomach grumbled so loudly she feared it would give her away. Her last meal had been before she was snatched away from the caravan. How long ago was that? During the night, she might be able to drop down and grab something to eat, perhaps grab a rope, a warm robe, or anything that would help her.

Morning came to her treetop earlier than to those on the ground. Guards had kept watch through the night so she had not been able to move without being caught. Cooking smells filled the air once again. Her stomach growled even louder.

"What's that?" On the ground, a man's voice questioned the strange sound that broke the early morning stillness.

The men grabbed weapons and formed a block. Women and children stopped their work, frozen in place. Bright Moon, on the verge of being discovered, pressed herself closer to the tree hoping to blend in. The rich, warm, smells of cooking meat filled the air stirring her hunger. Her stomach growls sounded even louder this time. Those on the ground looked around... and then looked up.

"The sound comes from the tree," their clan-leader, said. His voice, a hoarse whisper, she heard him clearly as if he were right there, lips to her ear. Bright Moon realized the sound came up the hollow between the trees.

Turning her face to the hollow, she moaned long and low and then whispered, "Who dares come to my forest?"

The cluster of men drew back, forming a block, weapons at the ready. Inside the block, women and children formed an even tighter group. Wide-eyed children clung to their mothers.

"I am Hantaywee[38], leader of this clan. Who are you? Come out and show yourself."

Bright Moon moaned again, and then added, "I am Howahkan [39], the Spirit of the Forest. I live in the trees in this clearing. Why are you here?"

Hantaywee turned and addressed the tree. "We are travelers and have come a long way," he said.

"You've come across the Great Ice. I've watched your travels through my forest," Bright Moon intoned. "Where did you come from?"

"You watched us?" The man couldn't believe his ears. "We came from a valley in the mountains. We crossed the Great Ice on our way to our summer camp."

"I watched you cross the ice and the bog[40] that

---

38 Sioux name meaning "faithful"
39 Sioux name meaning "of the mysterious voice".
40 Wet spongy ground; especially a poorly drained usually acid area rich in accumulated plant material. Also known as a mire or "muskeg", bogs consist of a thick ground cover layer of sphagnum

borders it. I saw you enter the forest. Your men slew my deer."

"We meant no harm and will be going now."

"Wait! You have used my forest. You have sacrificed one of my animals. Before you go, you must leave a tribute."

"A tribute? What would you like us to leave?"

"Leave medicine, rope, a robe, a parfleche[41] of jerky and pemmican, a pouch of water, an ax and two spears. Then strike your tents and be on your way."

It was a strange list. Hantaywee turned away, giving orders and assigning tasks as he did. The tribute demanded was piled near the tree's base. With their equipment hastily packed, the group departed.

Bright Moon waited, giving them time to leave. She would have liked to have waited longer to be sure that no one lingered, no one hid nearby, no one returned to see if they were duped, but hunger won over caution.

Judging her safety by the fading sounds of their travel, she darted down, grabbed the food and water, and returned to her loft. Safe once again, she bit off a chunk of pemmican and settled back to wait longer. Night fell. Morning came. Belly full, satisfied she had not been discovered, Bright Moon descended again to look over the rest of the tribute the departing clan had left her before she headed to the creek to wash her muddy coat away.

---

moss or similar growth. Acidic in nature and very low in nutrients they may support thin amounts of black spruce, Pin Oak, or Tamarack Larch forest. Open water is rare, but the water table is very close to the surface and the ground soft with many hidden sinkholes that act similar to quicksand.

41 A Native American rawhide bag. It is similar in construction to an envelope but can be as large as a suitcase. They were often painted and decorated and used to carry personal and ceremonial objects. In everyday use, they were typically used for holding objects such as dried meats, jerky and pemmican

Chapter 11: Tracking

Crushed grass, a broken branch, an imprint in the soft dirt; on one knee, Kaliska, read these signs and then turned to face Wikvaya. "From the place where she climbed out of the gorge, she came this way and stopped here."

"You're sure it was her?" Wikvaya questioned.

"We found the place where she climbed out," the scout repeated tiredly. "She left many tracks—on her belly, on her hands-and-knees, finally standing—it was hard to miss. Rather than cover them up, she tried going around in circles to confuse anyone following her before stepping on the fallen tree, then stones, before starting this way."

"What makes you think she came this way?" Wikvaya was not convinced.

The scout got to his feet and looked around with disdain. "She is very good, but I am better. An over-turned stone told me that she traveled this way, toward the caravan," Kaliska beamed. Hopefully, his companion, new to the art of tracking, would understand.

"Why do you scout for Long Tusk?"

"It is as I said. My uncle's clan traded with Long Tusk. One day, Long Tusk claimed my uncle owed him a debt. He seized my uncle's family, which was most of the clan, and held them captive. Many died while under his control. Still, Long Tusk demanded payment. He knew I was a good scout and he agreed to release the others if I scouted for him. Scouting lets me roam free. I can stay out away from the caravan and all that goes with it." His demeanor changed and he paused to spit, as if discharging a foul taste. "I will scout for him until I am able to repay the debt. But, now we need to find the girl."

Wikvaya mulled these words over in his mind. *She was not going toward Askook. That was no surprise, but it seemed strange she would want to return to the caravan and Long Tusk—a place she liked even less.* Leaving that mystery, he signaled the scout to continue.

"She stopped over there to rest," the scout said. Pointing at the rubble around the fallen tree, he added, "It looks like she made something here...." The scout scanned the surrounding area. "Pulled stones loose from that ledge... there's old bark and broken branches...." His voice trailed off.

"Okay, you found where she climbed out," Wikvaya said. "You could see where she tried to hide her tracks. She stopped here to make something... probably weapons... and you're sure these tracks are hers."

Kaliska looked down at the tracks and shrugged. "She's not standing in them right now, but I'm sure they're hers."

Wikvaya signaled his acceptance. "Where did she go from here?"

Kaliska pointed up the trail toward the last place the caravan had camped. "She is still being cautious and hiding her tracks," he said. "But, if we go that way, we should catch up with her."

"The Land of the Mattocks, if she could find it, offers her a fate at least as bad as the one she left. I can understand her not going there." Wikvaya looked at the tracks and then in the direction Kaliska pointed. "Long Tusk has already lost his patience and will certainly slay her. Why would she return to the caravan?"

###

The Great Ice had pushed its way through a gap between the mountains. From her vantage point, a clearing on the hillside, Bright Moon looked over the terrain. Beyond the ice, the mountains and valleys that were her goal, beckoned. There, she knew that leaves rustled softly in the warm spring breeze; there, she knew that she would be safe from Long Tusk and Askook.

Shading her eyes against the glare, she scanned the ice in front of her. White, wide, unbroken, it bridged the gap between the mountains as it stretched to the horizon.

A single sparse line of pine trees, cut and set in the ice at intervals, provided the only change in color. Like the ice, the row of trees stretched out to disappear over the horizon. The elders said that long ago, a local tribe began the tradition of marking the safest path with trees. This line would help her find her way, but she would need more than a row of trees to survive the journey across the Great Ice.

I'll need a place to stay while I'm here, she mumbled to herself, somewhere I can *set up camp for a night... or two... maybe even more depending on how my luck flows.*

Yes, echoed the little voice inside her head, you *could use a change.*

My efforts haven't been going well, lately, she admitted, but silenced that little voice by adding, *like the moon changes her face, my luck will also change.* She knew it would, she could feel it. Down deep in her bones, she could feel it. Maybe because of the dream that had haunted her mother now plagued her own sleep....

Still searching, she stepped forward and tripped on a root hidden in the grass. It sent her sprawling, somersaulting down the slope until she came to a stop on the till plain.[42] Looking up, she found what she sought. It was a place to stay. Her luck was turning. This was good.

This location, tucked under the crest of the hill, lay hidden from view. The ebb and flow of the glacier had left a mix of sand, gravel, boulders, and rock-slabs to create a pocket, an alcove, where she would set up camp. High ground, it would be dry and the outcropping would

---

42 A gently irregular plain of till--mixed grain-sized sediments-- deposited by an actively retreating glacier.

give her protection from weather, predators, and prying eyes. Happily, Bright Moon cleared rocks and debris from a spot in the cleft[43].

Sinking one spear in the ground, she tied the pouch of pemmican to the upright end. After collecting her remaining belongings—the tribute left by the migrating tribe—she dropped them in her new home and stood back to look at her work.

Yes, she told herself, *this was a good place to make camp for the night… or for however many nights she needed to stay.*

The sun sat low in the sky. She would have to act quickly, daylight was fading fast and she had work to do. To cross the Great Ice, she needed to locate a special type of tree. The tree did not have to be a big one, just the right one. She would also have to gather firewood. Yes, there was work to do and it was getting late.

Glacial melt waters had turned the shallow valley into a mosquito-filled bog, pockmarked by brush, stunted trees, bottomless mud pits, and dark, hidden, pools. It lay between her and the forest. To get here, she crossed this treacherous ground by using the butt of her spear to search out these traps. To gather the needed items, she would have to go back the way she came… maybe several times before dark.

Her ax and a spear in hand, she started for the swamp and, if necessary, the forest beyond. It was not long before she returned, dragging a tree behind her. Leaving it there, she retraced her steps to gather firewood.

Wikvaya and Kaliska sat across the fire from Chief Honovi, their host. "Chief Long Tusk was sending his friend, Askook, Chief of The Mattocks, a present,"

---

43 Geologically, a crack or a long narrow opening in a rock face; an opening, fissure, or V-shaped indentation. A hollow between ridges or protuberances.

Wikvaya explained. "During our travels, our group was swept away by a flood. We have been searching for survivors but I fear everyone was lost. Have any of your people come across strangers or have they encountered anything out of the ordinary?"

Chief Honovi nodded to his advisor, Tolinka[44], who then left. Before speaking again, Honovi relit his pipe. "This high meadow is our summer hunting grounds," he explained. "When the white-rain fades away, my people come back here until the cold wind warns us it will soon return."

In Tolinka's absence, two women entered. One passed around wooden bowls of stew; the other delivered drinking gourds of chicha[45].

Honovi, silent while his guests enjoyed their meal, watched the fire and puffed on his pipe. Finished, his guests set their bowls aside and the chief continued, "When we are on the move, the tribe travels in small groups, each taking their own path. A small band can live off the land easier than a large group," he explained. "Larger groups scare the game away. To answer your questions, Tolinka is talking with each of these groups to see what they know. "

"Honovi is a kind and gracious host to go through this trouble for us," Wikvaya acknowledged.

"Was yours a large party?"

Wikvaya shook his head. "One hand's worth of warriors. That is all...." He stared into the fire, recalling the floodwaters rushing at them.... "I fear they are all lost."

"One hand's worth... what were you taking to

---

44 Miwok name meaning "flapping ear of a coyote."
45 A term used for several varieties of fermented beverages, most commonly made from maize, grapes or apples, but which also describes similar non-alcoholic beverages. Chicha may also be made from Manioc root (also called Yucca or Cassava), or fruits, and other ingredients. The drink is often consumed during festivals or provided to visiting guests.

Askook that would require that many warriors." Chief Honovi was curious.

Wikvaya, unruffled by the question, replied, "A girl."

Kaliska shot a glance his way.

Honovi blinked. Could this be true? "A girl? That's all? Five men taking one girl." He was astounded.

"Not an ordinary girl," Wikvaya admitted. "Long Tusk wanted to...."

"No, this one is a witch," the scout interrupted.

Honovi grunted. "Scratch the surface and you'll find that most women have that capability. I believe it's in their blood," he acknowledged philosophically.

"This one is full of tricks," Wikvaya countered. "The men thought she was a witch. Myself, I don't think so. All the same, I would rather have escorted a pair of saber-tooth's than deal with her."

Tolinka's return interrupted further comment. He was followed by another man.

"Great Chief, no one reported any strangers," Tolinka gestured toward the other man, "but this one did have an unusual meeting along the way."

Aware that everyone's attention was now on him, the man stepped forward. Wikvaya could see this barrel-chested man, slightly graying, wore the trappings of a leader. "I, Hantaywee, led my clan across the Great Ice. We followed the path along the morning side laid out by our ancestors and did this without incident."

Honovi concurred. It was a familiar route they all had traveled at one time or another. There would be more to the story, he knew, and did not rush the speaker.

Hantaywee appreciated his chief's acknowledgement. "We crossed the bogs along the edge of the Great Ice, the swampy place where the trees are sparse and stunted, and finally reached the forest where game is plentiful and the ground solid." He looked at his audience. They understood his description and were attentive. "Our fresh meat was almost gone. We sent out a hunting party while the rest of us pushed on. By nightfall, we had crossed half of the forest and camped in a clearing near a stream. Our hunters found us there. It was a good spot... or so I thought."

Eyebrows rose and they waited for Hantaywee to continue. "The hunters were successful and brought a young deer to divide. We were happy to have fresh meat to cook. Some heard strange sounds that evening."

"Strange sounds?" Wikvaya was curious. "What kind of strange sounds?"

"Low, rumbling noises like a great animal's breathing. I posted extra guards. It was quiet throughout the rest of the night."

Honovi and Tolinka nodded their approval of the man's diligence. Hantaywee quietly accepted their recognition and continued, "Morning came... and the noises returned, even louder this time. There was one clump of odd-looking trees in this clearing and we had pitched our tents around it."

"Odd looking? What made them odd looking?" Wikvaya questioned.

"They stood all by themselves in the center of the clearing and were tall, taller than any around, and different," Hantaywee explained.

"Different? In what way?" Wikvaya couldn't picture how a tree could be 'different'.

"They appeared to be several trees—maybe one hands' worth—that merged together as they grew. The tree's foliage was thick, the branches vine-covered. Heavy moss draped down, touching the ground in many places." Hantaywee grew a little wide-eyed. "Then, the tree called out to me."

"Called out to you?" Wikvaya looked at Kaliska. It sounded like an all too familiar story. The scout was silent, but a small smile confirmed he knew what was coming. "Who called out to you?" Wikvaya asked.

"It was the spirit of the forest. It lived in the tree. We slew one of its deer so we must offer tribute and then leave." Hantaywee explained.

"Tribute? What kind of tribute?" Kaliska asked.

"Food, water, a robe, two spears...."

"What did you do?" Wikvaya interrupted.

"I had the objects placed at the foot of the tree. Then we packed up and left. I sent my best hunter back to see what happened," Hantaywee said. "He hid himself nearby and lay in wait for some time before he saw an ugly creature with long wild hair and molting skin. It dropped from the tree like a giant spider, grabbed the food, and disappeared into the branches again, all in one quick movement."

"It's the girl," Kaliska shouted. "She's a witch!"

Wikvaya looked at Honovi. "I told you she is wily."

Honovi nodded and turned to the clan-leader, "Our guests will rest here for the night. Tolinka will arrange supplies for them. At dawn, you and your hunter will lead them to the place where you camped. Then you can return and our guests can pursue this spirit if they wish."

Chapter 12: Crossing

Bright Moon sat cross-legged in front of her small fire and chewed a piece of pemmican while she stripped a tree limb, first of its branches, then its bark. Finished, she stood up, stretched, and then hefted the shaft.

Taller than she was by half, the shaft was well-balanced and felt good in her hands. Crossing the snow, she would use it to test for hidden crevasses from a safe distance. It would make a fine companion on her journey. With a quick jab, Bright Moon planted the walking stick upright in the sand next to her spears.

Muffled sounds in the dark. Bright Moon froze in place and listened. Before dusk had faded to night, she had scanned the horizon for signs of pursuers and found nothing. Even now, the darkness failed to show a telltale twinkle of a campfire or an approaching torch. No surprise—a person would be foolish to cross the bog in the dark.

More sounds, a startled squeal, scurrying feet, a scuffle. These she recognized as the sounds predators and prey make as each fights for survival. Realizing she had been holding her breath, she relaxed and returned to her fire.

Spread out on the buffalo robe were the remains of the tribute she had tricked a clan into leaving. Bright Moon knew that tribes never wasted anything. Animals were the source of hides, furs, and meat. Small bones or porcupine quills could become awls and needles, and even the tough tendons and intestines were dried and cut into thin strips. These were twisted and woven together with rawhide to form a strong, but light, rope. Bright Moon cut a piece of the rope from the length left by the clan and separated the rawhide from gut-string[46].

After separating the green, willowy branches from those that were thicker and less limber, Bright Moon plopped down next to the fire and began bending the supple green branches into an oval. When she was very small, her father taught her how to tie the ends together and measure her work against her leather-clad foot. Her egg-shaped creation proved to be slightly larger than her boot. It was the beginning of a nice pair of snowshoes. He would have been pleased.

Bright Moon made the frame stronger by binding additional branches to the first and wrapped this framework in a rawhide flap. The sides were held apart by crosspieces made from thicker branches. *I'll add a set of rawhide laces to bind the shoe to my foot and the first one will be all done.*

Tired, she wanted to sleep but there was work to finish. She began bargaining with herself, *I'll finish the pair of snowshoes before bedding down for the night. In the morning, I'll make a rawhide face mask. It would cut down the sun's glare on the snowfield and protect me from cold winds. After that, depending on the weather, I will start across the Great Ice.* The idea got her excited and this gave her a new spurt of energy. *A good beginning, this is a good new beginning and I am free*, she thought and she began to sing to herself while she worked.

###

Hantaywee's hunter signaled a halt near the edge of a clearing. The group crouched low, peered through the foliage, and surveyed the meadow in front of them. "This

---

46 This is a tough thin cord made from the treated and stretched intestines of certain animals, especially sheep, and today is used for stringing musical instruments, tennis rackets and for surgical ligatures

is the place where I lay in wait, the place where I saw that... that wild thing," the hunter told them.

Wikvaya studied the distant tree and its surroundings. The tree, rather several trees that grew together, stood alone near a small creek and towered above the trees in the neighboring forest. Moss covered branches drooped down. Prior to the incident, the tree's posture was thought to provide a convenient shelter from the elements. Now, however, its canopy appeared like so many tentacles waiting for the opportunity to snatch an unsuspecting victim.

"We came from the mountains and crossed the Great Ice to get here." Hantaywee explained. "The trail we followed lies on the other side of the clearing. It is easy to find and well-traveled."

"You're sure this is the place?" Wikvaya questioned.

"Yes." Hantaywee replied. To have this stranger question his abilities was insulting. If his chief had not given him this task, he would have handled the matter differently. Instead, stern-faced, the clan-leader suppressed the urge and responded, "I'd wager a stack of prime hides on it. This is the place where we camped. I had our people spread their tents all around that tree."

Anger overcame his reluctance propelled the clan-leader forward. "Come, I will show you signs of our being there." Wikvaya and Kaliska quickly followed while Hantaywee's hunter cautiously brought up the rear.

They reached the tree and circled the base. The hunter, spear poised and ready, kept a wary eye on the tree itself while the others checked the ground for clues.

"There are too many footprints here to tell the story," Kaliska said. He jabbed the butt of his spear in the ground. Satisfied that it would stand upright on its own, he jumped up, grabbed a low branch, and pulled himself up into the tree.

"Stop!" The clan-leader yelled. "Stop this foolishness

before the tree spirit grows angry." But Kaliska continued his climb, leaving the others to watch him clamor up the trunk and disappear into the overgrow foliage.

Hantaywee leaned back to see how high Wikvaya's scout had climbed, and then whispered, "He has climbed very high without finding anything."

Overhead and barely visible through the leaf covered branches, Kaliska waved to them before climbing higher. Seeing that nothing had happened, Hantaywee's hunter, spear still handy, appeared to relax.

"Found something," the scout finally called.

Hantaywee was puzzled. Other than the tree spirit, what else could he find?

A noise, low and menacing, came from the tree. The clan-leader jumped back. The hunter, sure that a giant spider-creature was about to show itself, raised his weapon and braced for the attack.

"The tree spirit! I found where the tree spirit rested," Kaliska's voice, now a whisper, seemed to come from near the base of the tree.

Wikvaya held a hand up for silence and bent to examine the base. *Kaliska was high up in the tree, but he sounded so near. Where was his voice coming from?* "Are you okay? Can you hear me? He asked. "Talk some more." *Your chatter goes on and on so it should be no problem for you,* he thought.

"I'm okay," Kaliska chuckled. "I'm sure the girl was here and up to her tricks again. I can see a long way, but I don't see any sign of our charge. Did my growl and whisper sound like what you had heard before?" His one-sided conversation continued to fill the air.

While his scout spoke, Wikvaya stepped closer and began circling the tree, stopping back where he started. He took Kaliska's spear and parted a bundle of creepers[47]

---

47 A clinging plant especially one that grows by means of tendrils,

and scrub[48] growing near the base to reveal a tree hollow partially hidden in the foliage. "Do you see anything else?"

"No," the scout said. "I'm coming down now." Branches rustled as he descended, dropping to the ground near the trio. Seeing the scout safe and unharmed, the hunter finally relaxed and lowered his weapon.

"What did you find up there?" Wikvaya asked. Hantaywee and his hunter stepped closer to hear.

"Someone, probably the girl, wanted to spend the night in the tree and tied themselves to the branches," he reported. "Their rope wore some bark away. They must have covered themselves with mud to avoid bug bites. Small branches were broken where they nested and other branches had traces of mud. Even as high as I climbed, I could hear you. You heard my words?"

"Yes. Your words sounded like they came from that hole there," Wikvaya said, pointing at the tree hollow.

Kaliska nodded. "Near the nest, there is a hole like that one, but smaller. It's where I heard your words and so it's where I spoke."

Wikvaya turned to Hantaywee, "Go back and tell Chief Honovi that the girl we were to deliver fooled everyone into believing she was a tree spirit." *The girl is quick-witted and full of tricks. Even Long Tusk recognized that in her,* Wikvaya thought.

"What are you going to do?" Hantaywee asked.

"We will continue our pursuit and try to catch up with her," Wikvaya said.

"You could go after her but you probably won't catch her," the clan-leader replied. "She's had too much of a head start."

"Two men can travel faster than a migrating clan. If

suckers, or roots that anchor it to a surface
48 A stunted tree, shrub, or bush.

she thinks she threw us off, she may relax, slow down, and take it easy," Kaliska said.

"True, you'll make it through the forest quick enough, but just before the Great Ice, the forest dips down into a shallow, flat valley... a swamp, really. From the forest to the Great Ice, the trail twists and turns, often disappearing as it crosses the fen[49]. You have to go slow and test the spongy ground or end up in a bog with no way out. Then, if you make it across, there's the weather...."

"What about the weather?" Wikvaya asked.

Hantaywee pointed to a mountain peak, its tip just showing over the trees. "See that plume?" he said. "The mountain's cold breath is blowing. When it reaches down to the ice, white-rain will blow around so heavily you can't see an arm's length away. If you don't freeze, you'll probably fall into a chasm." The clan-leader, experienced with this trail, shook his head. "If the girl made it through the forest, she had little chance of making it across the bog and no chance of crossing the ice. You should go back and report to your chiefs that she's gone; anything else would mean certain death."

A soft blue-white glow punctuated the darkness. Ahead, silhouetted against ghostly walls, a dark form danced softly, just out of her reach. It was not anything she recognized, but she knew that somehow it would be the key to triumph in her trip. Somehow, it would mean wealth and success for her. She moved toward whatever it was slowly, but with high expectations. When she was close enough, she reached out. Gingerly, her fingertips explored its rough surface. It felt wet, cold and....

---

49 An area of low, flat marshy land where decomposing plants accumulate, forming peat

"Ay... Ay... Ayeeeeeee." A wolf's howl split the night startling Bright Moon awake. Throwing off her sleeping robe, she sat bolt upright, a hand clamped around her spear. "Ay... Ay... Ayeeeeeee." From somewhere nearby, the animal's cry tore through the air again.

Her panic flared up—the fire was almost out—no wonder the wolves were close. Taking a branch, she hastily stirred the embers, bringing their warm, red, coals to the surface, and placed a few dry twigs there. Bending low, face near the coals, she gave a few meager puffs and was rewarded by the flicker of flame as the twigs began burning. Bright Moon slowly added more sticks, larger sticks and, as they caught, a log and then another.

Light and warmth returned to her little alcove. As it grew, its light spread out pushing the night back. In the dim fringes, near the border of dark and light, a glowing pair of eyes appeared. It was joined by another, then another. Warily, soundlessly, the wolves moved with a smooth flowing motion. Bright Moon jumped up. Bellowing, she cut the air in front of her with her spear. The wolves scattered and then disappeared into the darkness.

Wrapping herself in her robe, she sat down, leaned back against the rock wall, and stared into the fire. It was that dream again, just like her mother's. She didn't understand what it meant—only that it was her destiny and it lay somewhere in the darkness ahead of her. Eventually, eyes heavy, she drifted off to sleep.

Wikvaya and Kaliska stared aimlessly into Chief Honovi's campfire. At a sign from the Chief, women brought bowls of stew and gourds of chicha for everyone. Hantaywee and his hunter eagerly accepted the food.

"What are your plans now?" Honovi asked, putting

aside his pipe.

"We'll return to Askook's settlement and then locate Long Tusk's caravan," Wikvaya said. "They'll need to know what happened." He shrugged. "Maybe, Long Tusk has another girl to offer."

Honovi turned to Tolinka. "They will need supplies. Make a dugout[50] ready for them." Turning back to Wikvaya he said, "Travel by river will quickly get you closest to the land of the Mattocks."

"You are very kind and generous," Wikvaya said.

Honovi waved his hand dismissively. "You saved me a lot of trouble by identifying the tree spirit as your lost girl," he said. "Rumors were already getting started and my people were leery of traveling that way. Now it is being passed off as a joke, even one that Hantaywee's clan laughs at, although not as much as the others."

Bright Moon adjusted her facemask. The eye-slits, small as they were, allowed her to see; the pair of slits below them let her breath escape before moisture could collect inside the mask and freeze to her face. Reaching down, she tugged at the laces that bound the new snowshoes to her. Mentally, she ran through her preparations. Everything was ready.

Bright Moon glanced over her shoulder. Her robe covered the remainder of her possessions—pemmican, ax, and spears—piled on her makeshift skid[51]. She slipped

---

50 A dugout or dugout canoe, is a boat which is basically a tree trunk that has been hollowed out. A variety of tools, such as axes and an adze, may be used. Controlled fires might also be used to soft and burn out the area to assist in creating the hollow.

51 A plank, log, etc., often one of a pair or set, used as a support or as a track upon which to slide or roll a heavy object. A low pallet on which goods are loaded for handling or transport.

on the harness, fashioned from the last of the rope, which she would use to pull the skid. It would leave her hands free to handle the walking stick. She needed it to probe the snow for hidden crevasses.

The alcove where she camped was empty. Hardly a sign of it being occupied existed. Her last fire had used the remainder of the branches and bark, and she stirred the ashes, burying their spent remains. Beyond the alcove lay the bog that separated her from the forest, potential pursuers, and captivity. There was no going back. Bright Moon turned to face the Great Ice and the line of trees that marked the trail toward the mountains and valleys across this white expanse. Once again, she threw her shoulders back, took a deep breath, and started her journey.

Two days travel put most of the ice field behind her, but it was two days with nights spent without the comfort and warmth of a campfire; two almost-sleepless, dark nights spent wrapped in her robe, ax in her lap, clutching a spear and perched atop her skid. It was this sacrifice that brought the mountains ahead closer, much closer.

When she started, she did not think crossing the Great Ice would be this difficult. The weather was clear then. Now, a plume of white reached out toward her from the mountain peak she used to mark her bearings. It was not a good sign. The mountain's cold breath was blowing her way. She would need to complete the crossing before the plume reached down to the ice.

Indeed, she had hoped to cross by now, but had not planned on the delays caused by the need to detour around the many fissures. Because it was a time when the ice sometimes shifted and stirred in its endless sleep, each step was not without its hazards. Places, even those close to the tree-marked path that might have been solid before, could suddenly become traps. The white plume was also closer and much heavier. She put that out of her mind and carefully probed the snow ahead with her walking stick.

When the storm hit, the mountain on the far side, the horizon, the line of trees marking the trail, were all lost, swallowed in swirling snow kicked up by howling, gale force winds. The cold cut through her like a knife and drained the warmth from her body.

Numbed to the bone, Bright Moon peered into the storm-driven bedlam from behind an upheld arm hoping to find relief. In any direction, for as far as she could see, everything was white... nothing but white. To continue in this weather would be a mistake. She could not see the mountains that rose up so close in front of her, nor was she able to make out the line of trees that marked the safest path.

The only choice I have is to hold my robe close and hunker down until the storm blows itself out. She planted her walking stick and snowshoes upright in the snow next to her skid. *I will make a ball of myself,* she thought, *bundle up, and let the snow bury me. I will be warm and it will protect me from the cold wind until the storm passes. Then I can continue.* She crouched down and began trying to pull the robe around her.

However, the forces that set the gale against her continued their assault. Ripping the robe from her numb fingers, the wind sent it tumbling across the field of white. She gave chase knowing that without it she would surely freeze. It flaunted the robe just out of reach leading her a few steps farther before swallowing it in the all-pervasive blinding white. Too late, she realized her mistake.

Crack! She clearly heard the sound even above the

howling wind. Another snap, louder than the first, punctuated the air, adding to her anxiety. Before Bright Moon could back away, she felt the ice-covered snow beneath her feet give way. The sickening feeling of treading open air followed. Then snow, ice, and the woman dropped as one through a once-hidden fracture.

Chapter 13: In the Dark

Streams of water poured out of the face of the glacier and splashed into the pond below. From there it would flow around a peninsula and empty into the river. This neck of land was a convenient meeting place for Askook and Long Tusk. The terrain where they sat was a wide, flat meadow joining a low hogback[52]. It rose up to a tree-lined ridge. The opposite side of this finger of land, the riverside, had a steep slope down to a narrow, sandy beach.

"I've heard that the girl you are providing is a witch," Askook said. He watched Long Tusk's expression. If caught off-guard what would the old caravan leader reveal?

"The woman... a witch?" Long Tusk paused a moment, as if mulling over the idea. "Aren't they one and the same?" He forced a laugh at his own joke hoping to make light of the subject. "Where did you hear such nonsense?" *Askook must have spies everywhere.*

"Word gets around. Your people told my people and they told me." Askook watched Long Tusk lick his lips nervously.

How much did Askook know? Long Tusk wondered. *How would this affect his reward?* "Mere stories... exaggerations," he said. "My people must be spinning stories again. They shouldn't have wasted your time." *My well-deserved reward will disappear if Askook is unhappy.*

"They said that she commanded a great bird to carry away one of your out-walkers." Askook persisted.

---

52 A ridge formed by tilted strata; hence, any ridge with a sharp summit, and steeply sloping sides.

"No one saw this happen. There was no proof. We only have the girl's word," Long Tusk fired back. "The out-walker came up missing, but she was very clumsy. It was nearly dark. I think she tripped and fell into the gorge, but we'll never know."

Askook persistent questions did not waver. "She called up a pack of wolves."

"Many hunters have done the same." *If I go without a suitable reward, I will have my guards find the ones responsible for telling these tales, and they will be punished.*

"Any hunter? I heard that you tried and failed."

"I have not done this for a long time, and I am without practice...."

"There's also the matter of the snake." It was Askook's crowning piece of information.

"Snake? What snake? I don't recall a snake." A bead of sweat broke out on Long Tusk's brow.

"You don't recall the snake that she commanded to rise up and bite you in the leg... the leg you've been favoring since you arrived here. You don't recall that snake?"

"Well... uhm ... I can explain." Long Tusk knew he would have to talk fast in order to reclaim some level of reward from this disaster. "She will make a good wife. She is young, with many childbearing years ahead of her... and a Shaman, too. I'm sure you'll be very...." He was cut off by a wave of Askook's hand.

"I have wives... many wives. They are a bother. I don't need one more," Askook said.

"She's also a Shaman," Long Tusk added, desperately trying to rescue his reward.

"So you said. No matter, I already have a Shaman and I don't need another."

Long Tusk's face drooped. His hopes of being rid of the girl and gaining a reward in the process were dashed—trampled as if a herd of mastodons had trod over them.

It was time for Askook to turn the tables. "If the girl

were more than a Shaman... if she truly were a witch, one that could work this magic, then I would be interested. "

Long Tusk couldn't believe his ears. *Askook was only interested in Bright Moon if she was a witch and could work magic. The reward that had slipped out of my fingers, now returned.* "Why, yes," he said, "I can see where a witch who could work this magic would be of interest. March her out and let her perform for us." *If she performs a trick or two, and Askook is impressed, I will be rewarded... and she will no longer give me problems. If she fails, I never said she was anything but a girl. Askook will punish her. My reward will be her punishment.*

"I will, as soon as they get here, but they haven't arrived yet."

"Your emissary[53] hasn't arrived with the girl? How could this be?" Long Tusk questioned Askook. Suspicious by nature, the caravan leader feared that Askook may have received the girl and decided not to offer anything in return.

It was Askook's turn to challenge his counterpart. "If they left the caravan as you said, they didn't arrive at my village, and they aren't here." He thumped a forefinger solidly against Long Tusk's chest. "Your man guided them, so you tell me where they are."

"We left after they did and took a different route." It had been some time since Long Tusk had seen Askook this angry.

"You took a different route? Why did you do that?" It was Askook's turn to be puzzled.

"A caravan as large as mine moves slowly. If we let our guard down, we risk being attacked. I have to be careful which paths we take. As it were, I had to push them to get here by now."

"If the man and the girl traveled alone, wouldn't they run the same risks?"

"I sent warriors, one hand's worth, with your man

---

53 Someone sent on a mission to represent the interests of another person

and the girl. My scout went with them to mark the way. A small group like theirs can travel faster than my caravan and follow the quickest routes." Long Tusk explained.

"Travel faster and follow the quickest routes...." Seeming to mull the thought over, Askook repeated the words. "Which way would they have gone?"

"They could have climbed over the ridge, but to reach you quickly, they would have taken the gorge." Pleased with his explanation, Long Tusk sat back, a look of smug satisfaction on his face.

"The gorge? In this weather?" Askook didn't believe what he had heard.

"Yes, well," Long Tusk waved a hand, "the weather was good when they left and you seemed so anxious to meet the girl...." His voice trailed off. He had hoped to stall long enough that the group would show up. He would breathe easier once that happened. Since it had not, he had to think of an excuse, something that would let him shift the blame elsewhere, anywhere, to anyone but him. "My scout is very good, but new," Long Tusk offered. "Perhaps they just got lost. I will send people out to look for them."

A search party, Askook nodded, *yes that would appease me... to have Long Tusk go through this effort because of me would raise my stature in the tribe and among other tribes. Everyone fears me now, but they would fear me more if bodies were found. I will act irate and Long Tusk would have to offer more—and take less—to satisfy my anger. My stature among others would certainly increase. I could demand more tribute from them and, in their fear, they would give it.*

"What about your man?" Long Tusk said. "How well do you know him? Can he be trusted?" *Askook has grown soft and suspicious in his old age, and maybe I can work this to my advantage*, the wily caravan leader thought. "Who's to say that your man's not the culprit?"

Askook made a face and lapsed into silence while he pondered the idea. *I have dealt with Long Tusk enough to know when the old rat was scrambling for a way out, but I realize*

Wikvaya is a stranger who could ruin my standing among the other tribes.

"I hold Wikvaya's family hostage," *Askook said,* "to force him to carry out the task." *If Wikvaya does not turn up, the tribes might believe that he ran off with the girl. If they believed this one man had the nerve to steal a prize meant for me and he goes unpunished, they might also feel that they could stand up to me. I would lose their respect and their tribute. In my younger days, I rose to this position by success in battles, bluffs, and bargains. If I lose prestige now when I'm older and soft from easy living, I'll lose my empire... and I am too old to rebuild it.*

"They are delayed, perhaps lost. Let's send out search parties." Long Tusk, made nervous by Askook's silence, hoped to offer an acceptable solution least he becomes a victim of Askook's wrath. "We should set a feast in anticipation of their arrival."

The forced enthusiasm in Long Tusk's voice told Askook that he still wielded fear, at least in this man. *Time,* he thought, *Long Tusk needs time for the searchers to find the girl and the others... or find their bodies. If they're not found, then I will have to demand more of Long Tusk and hope that the caravan leader will not recognize I am bluffing.* "We should celebrate our gathering," Askook agreed. "Our peoples should begin trading. When that is done, if the girl has not arrived, then send out search parties." *Time, this would give Long Tusk time to find his people... and time for him to worry if he didn't find them; and, because of my generous extension, no one will complain about the wrath I lay on him.*

The crevice opened beneath Bright Moon's feet. It sent her plummeting downward. Arms flailing, her hands clawed the air, unable to grab anything solid. Bright Moon hit bottom and became part of the mound of rubble being swallowed by the Great Ice. Engulfed in debris turned-slush, she rolled to the side and scampered away from the deluge. Loud bangs and a final roar followed by silence signaled the end. The place she had occupied when she first came down now lay buried.

Scant light, diffused by airborne snow, shone down from above. Whimpering, her heart in her throat, Bright Moon forced herself tighter against the safety of the tunnel walls. She waited longer in the quiet dusk before getting up, lest she start another cave in. It was then she realized how fast her heart beat.

Pull yourself together, her little internal voice told her. *Check yourself out. No twists, no sprains, no broken bones, no cuts. You're buried, but in good shape and out of the freezing cold wind. Calm down. Look around. Find a way out!*

Slipping and sliding over the wet, debris-covered ice, she crept through the semi-darkness to a place near where she had landed. Blocks of ice filled the area, and snow filled the spaces between them. A few shafts of light did their best to fight off the darkness.

Here I am, she thought, *at the bottom of… the bottom of… of what?*

No matter, her inside voice answered. *There's light overhead, that's good. When I climb up there, I'll be back on top and on my way again.*

Stepping up onto a chunk of ice raised her confidence. Her second step found her floundering in knee-deep snow.

Too soft and treacherous, her inner voice said. *It won't hold your weight.*

Back on the floor, Bright Moon buried her numb fingers in her armpits seeking warmth while she thought. Her inner voice began a constant barrage of complaints:

What a mess you're in now. You could have gone to Askook.

Never! Bright Moon mentally shouted back at that nagging voice.

You could have gone back to the caravan.

Never! Bright Moon's anger rose until she realized she was standing there all alone having an argument with herself.

Her internal voice switched from unpleasant

suggestions and said, *Well then, stop standing around and get out.*

How?

If the snow is too soft, pile the big ice chunks up and climb out.

Bright Moon tugged tentatively at the nearest block. It showed no sign of budging. Trying another tack, she braced her back against the wall, feet against the block and tried again. It broke loose and slid out of reach. Her efforts were rewarded with rubble from above tumbling down, nearly burying her. When the torrent stopped, she tried once more, but another round of falling wreckage forced her to abandon the idea.

"Now what?" She said aloud as she freed herself. Her voice echoed back through the darkness, but did not provide an answer.

Face the facts, her little friend told her. *You're not getting out the way you came.*

She took stock of her situation. Snow and chunks of ice, the remains of the collapsed roof and walls, lay piled in the center of the chamber where she first landed. Indeed, she would have to find another way out. *There was no getting back the way I came.* Adding to her problems, water began seeping around the edges of the heap, slowly at first, then heavier[54]. *Wherever the water is coming from, it hasn't stopped flowing just because the walls fell in the way.* In the dim light, Bright Moon watched a thin trickle squeeze out

---

54 Glaciers form because snow collects faster than it melts. Time, cold, pressure from the weight of the snow, and additional water, turn some of the snow into ice. The surface may appear as one continuous expanse, but seasonal changes cause the ice to push forward or draw back, creating fissures. These may be partially or fully buried under a shroud of snow. The glacier's immense weight, combined with the friction of its movement, produces heat which creates small amounts of water. Fast flowing rivers may have been swallowed but not frozen. Beneath the surface, protected from the intense cold, the water collects, drips down, trickles, and forms rivulets. The rivulets combine to form creeks, streams, and rivers. They burrow ravine-like tunnels and eat away at the snow and ice overhead.

from under the debris and flow down the passageway connecting to puddles along the way before disappearing into the darkness. A water droplet hit her head, confirming her suspicions. *Water falls from above; before I arrived, this was a river and a deep one. It's blocked now but not for long.*

###

Kaliska complained, "We've been on the river since dawn, let's put ashore on that beach? I think we're getting close to Long Tusk's meeting spot. We can stretch our legs and get our bearings."

The sandy shore, a spit of land,[55] jutted into the river near the glacier's base, provided an inviting place. Wikvaya had to admit he too needed to get out and stretch. The heavy dugout nosed into the soft sand, and both men jumped out and began tugging it farther ashore.

"Invaders! Hold up there," a voice from behind commanded. "Stop what you're doing!"

They stopped tugging on the boat and looked up. Five men emerged from the bushes near the beach. Four had spears pointing their way.

"What's wrong?" Wikvaya asked. "There's no need for spears."

"I am Kolenya[56], Warrior of the Mattocks, and you are now my prisoners."

"Captives? We've done nothing wrong." Playing their current situation by ear, Wikvaya found himself buying time as he tried to think of something, anything which would work to free them. If he could figure a way to lull their captors off guard, they might be able to turn the tables on Kolenya and his spear-toting thugs.

"You invaded our lands. You are here to spy on us."

---

55 A peninsula, possible an island, that appears to protrude from the main land mass.
56 Miwok name meaning "coughing fish."

"No, that's not true. We journey to the land of the Mattocks, to the village of Askook, to bring a gift from Long Tusk, the Caravan Master."

"Askook...?" Kolenya was confused and needed time to think.

Wikvaya realized that the guard was picked for his brawn not his brain. "Askook and his friend Long Tusk had agreed to meet, and we're on our way to join them. We started our trip too early and did not offer sacrifices to the river or the great glacier before we started." Wikvaya directed his attentions, not to Kolenya, but to those holding the spears. "Our failures angered the spirits and their anger brought us trouble." To emphasize this, he jabbed a finger at each of the spear wielders and concluded, "If we are gone, the evil that has plagued us from the beginning will be on each and every one of you until it is satisfied."

"Save your breath," Kolenya said. "Askook and Long Tusk are here. They agreed to meet at this place so our people can barter goods. They will be happy to know that you've arrived."

What I need is some dry wood so I can start a fire, get warm, make a torch, and see what I have in front of me. Bright Moon stood, numb hands tucked in her armpits once again, peering into the darkness in front of her, ignoring that little voice inside that said, *No, don't waste time looking because there's no dry wood. What you really need is to concentrate on getting out of here.*

Before Bright Moon crashed through from above, melt-water, lots of it, had carved the tunnel. Now, snow, ice, and the remains of the walls lay in the passageway, cutting off further flow.

Aloud, almost in answer to that nagging voice Bright Moon continued, "Can't tell for sure how far the tunnel goes, but it looks like it slants down slightly. That makes sense."

Behind the debris, the pent-up water carved new, larger channels through the rubble. The trickle turned into a flow heavier. It didn't matter where the tunnel went; she knew she would not be able to stay here.

Well, that much water had to go somewhere. Her only means to find a way out—her only hope for survival—would be to follow the water. With that, she took the first tentative steps into the darkness.

A scraping noise behind her, followed by a low rumble, caught her attention. She looked over her shoulder. The light was dim, but enough for her to see the icy mound begin to move her way. As it moved, jets of water erupted from around it. Blocks of ice tore loose and were caught in the stream cascading toward her.

A gusher of water swept her off her feet at the mouth of the tunnel. She went down with a thud and a splash and started a trip down the incline into the black abyss.

The melt-water was freezing and the pathway slippery. It was a wet sled run with Bright Moon twisting and turning from back-to-belly, belly-to-back. Her screams filled the dark tunnel until she was ejected into a deep, cold, pool of water. Behind her, the tunnel resounded with a loud boom as blocks of ice, too large to follow her through the portal, crashed into the opening, blocking the way.

Chapter 14: Meeting Place

Long Tusk, eager to appease Askook, ordered his wives to supervise the preparations for a celebration feast. Such tasks required the work of many hands.

The women had a shallow depression dug and lined with wet, green reeds. These became the bedding for the meal's ingredients. It was too early in the season for fresh vegetables. Dried onions, carrots, and potatoes were added by the basketful before topping the furrow off with more wet canes and covered with sand. Firewood piled on top was set on fire. The coals left behind baked the contents of the trench.

Meat and fish, skewered between poles, hung over campfires. Children were given the job of turning the poles to provide even cooking. Containers—made of wicker baskets covered with baked mud—hung over glowing coals. They held a variety of stews made of a mix of meats and vegetables in a porridge-like[57] base.

An endless supply of fresh water poured from holes and crevasses in this white wall. It fed the pond separating the promontory from the glacier.

While they waited for the feast to begin, Long Tusk's people mingled with Askook's people in the meadow next to the pond. They traded stories while eyeing up available goods—hides, weapons, or slaves—and later, after feasting heavily, they would begin bargaining in earnest.

The crowd parted as Kolenya and his thugs arrived with their prisoners. Thoughts of trade were put aside as the crowd, expecting entertainment to soon follow, fell in

---

57 Depending on availability, they boiled cereal meal (oats, rice, semolina, etc.) in water, milk, or both.

behind them and escorted Kolenya, his guards, and their prisoners to where the two chiefs and their advisors sat in the shade. Long Tusk's wives darted around among this group of dignitaries or hovered about in the background.

Kolenya had his men herd their prisoners forward to a spot near the end of the long cooking trench and in front of Tusk and Askook. The chiefs' relaxed demeanor changed when Wikvaya and Kaliska were shoved forward.

"Where is the girl?" the two leaders chorused.

Wikvaya answered, "There was a flash flood. Everyone was swept away."

"You survived," Long Tusk accused. "How come she didn't?"

"I was against your plan from the beginning," Wikvaya said, "but, because you told me she was a mere girl, not a witch, I had her tied up in the manner you directed." By pointing a finger at Long Tusk, he hoped to be spared any wrath. "If she freed herself and survived, she would have had to be a witch... more than a witch, she would have had to work magic," Wikvaya continued. "The spirits were against your plan from the beginning. It was ill luck that carried her away. The spirits need to be appeased, and soon, before more trouble befalls us... before more..."

"He speaks nonsense." Kolenya cut him off. "He told that story when we found the two of them."

Without waiting, Wikvaya extended his arms upward, turned to face the glacier, and began to chant, swaying side-to-side and slowly turning around in a circle as he did. "Oh Great River Spirit, oh Great Glacier Spirit, send your servants a sign," he chanted.

From somewhere up on the glacial plateau, a dull boom rose and rolled through the air. The sound echoed along rocky walls until it reached Wikvaya's ears like an answering voice. He knew everyone else heard it, too.

Kolenya jumped and turned toward the glacier. The mob fidgeted and eyed each other nervously. Wikvaya started in on the chant again. Kaliska, knowing that this was a show to appease their leaders, joined in on the chanting and lay flat on the ground as he did. As if in response, the water flowing from openings in the glacier slowed and then all but died. A shriek, more a long drawn out wail, came from that direction and filled the air. One by one, the mob, mimicking those they held captive, fell on their faces while Wikvaya chanted. Through all this, Kolenya stood staring, open-mouthed. Beads of sweat broke out on Long Tusk's brow and Askook looked around nervously.

Still swaying, circling, and chanting, Wikvaya scanned the group. Could he convince them that the girl used her magic to escape? It might work out, maybe even better than he expected; but, to keep things going his way, he needed a surprise, one big enough to give him the upper hand.

Deposited in an icy cold pool and driven by panic, Bright Moon thrashed the water for a few moments before she realized it was only chest deep.

Her body racked with shivers, she turned around to look over her new surroundings. Icicles coated the walls and hung from the ceiling. Her elk-skin clothes, thoroughly soaked, made her feel as if she carried the animal that once wore them. The cold drained her energy. She knew she could not stay here long. *What kind of place is this?* She asked herself.

When it came, the glacier crawled across the land like a giant turtle, swallowing everything in its path that didn't or couldn't move. A stony canyon, one that nature had laced with crags and overhangs was one of its victims. Collected melt water had wormed its way through the fissures and crevasses and found, next to the canyon wall, the spaces under the overhangs.

The combination of water and overhangs created a high-ceilinged room. The meltwater spilled into the room and excavated a pool before moving on. A faint blue-white[58] glow—sunlight shining through thin ice overhead—contrasted with the blackness that had been the tunnel. In the dim light, she could see that her movements created ripples in the water, casting shadows across the soft light dancing off the walls.

I... I don't understand. This place looks vaguely familiar. Maybe the cold is taking its toll; playing tricks with my mind, but this seemed to be the place my mother described. Here is the place that haunted both of our dreams. Ahead, in the shadows, a dark form bobbed softly, aimlessly, up and down. She could not make it out clearly, but, with high expectations and heart drumming in her chest, she decided to move toward the core of her dream, whatever it was.

Finally, close enough, she reached a hand out and touched it's wet, cold, rough surface. *This time it was not a dream. It was real. It was real!* She smiled. *Honored Mother, here is the dream we share.*

"Enough!" Askook shouted. It was time for him to step in before this renegade made a fool of him.

Interrupted by this outburst, Wikvaya stopped chanting and the others slowly rose to their feet.

"Did you see the girl get swept away?" Askook questioned Kaliska.

"No, I was scouting ahead of the group," the scout replied.

"Did you see the girl's body?" Askook persisted.

"No. After a long search, I came across Wikvaya. He would have drowned had it not been for a fallen log,"

---

58 Why is Glacier Ice Blue? In simplest of terms, think of the ice or snow layer as a filter. From the surface, snow and ice present a uniformly white face because almost of the visible light striking its surface is reflected back. Light that is not reflected is scattered by the icy grains filtering out most of the light spectrum. If the ice is thick enough, mostly blue light makes it through.

Kaliska said. "We went back and searched, but found no others…." He spoke the truth, but hesitated. During their travels, he and Wikvaya had become friends and he knew that their situation was serious. Should he tell more or leave that to Wikvaya?

"You did not find the girl." From long experience, Askook had learned to ask direct questions. He knew questions like these would whittle away at the unknown leaving only the truth when finished.

"No."

"Did you find her body?"

"No."

"What did you find?"

There was no way out for Kaliska now. "We found signs that somebody, probably the girl, climbed out of the gorge," he said.

Askook nodded. He knew there had to be more to the story. "Did you see her?"

"No, I never saw her. I never saw anyone until we arrived at a friendly village,"

"Why do you think it was the girl?"

"After climbing out, she tried to cover her tracks and mislead us." Thinking about it, Kaliska added," She made it appear she was headed for the caravan, but doubled back. We never did catch up to her."

Askook thought it over for a moment and then motioned to Kolenya. "Bind Wikvaya, hang him by his hands from a tree. Bring firewood." Turning to Wikvaya, Askook said, "You told us the girl was swept away, but I find out that you knew she climbed out and hid her trail. I think you helped her escape and know where she went. Tell us what you've done with her while you still can."

The dim light limited her view. The water was deeper here, but no warmer. Shivering from the cold, Bright Moon felt the rough texture under her fingertips. The object bobbing in the water next to her seemed to be little more than a tree trunk. Her heart sunk... a tree trunk? Her dream had been about something great, not about a tree trunk. She was sure that the dream was special, certainly more than a tree carried away by floodwaters. Tears burned her eyes. Her disappointment formed a lump and lodged in her throat. She leaned her head against the rough surface. *A tree trunk! Nothing but a tree trunk, how could that be?*

Anger and bitterness replaced the disappointment. At least she would not drown. She could climb up and get out of the cold water. Pushing off from the bottom, she reached up, searching for some kind of handhold, and made a new discovery.

This wasn't just any tree swept away by a raging river. No, not just any tree at all! This one had the feel of being worked, shaped, carved, and decorated. Her spirits rose. Running her fingers up the side, beyond the curve of the trunk, she found a lip, an edge that marked an opening.

"Is this a dugout?" Her teeth chattered. Her lips, blue with cold, but Bright Moon managed to say it aloud and her voice, echoing off the walls, reassured her. She felt beyond the lip and along its edge to confirm that it was not just a hole made by birds or insects, but something actually carved out of the trunk by human hands. It was a dugout!

"I can use this," her excited voice continued to echo off the walls. She grabbed the lip of the hull with both hands and pulled herself upwards until she was high enough to be able to lean forward and tumble in. Exhausted, Bright Moon lay in the bottom while she worked to catch her breath. Rocked by waves and current, the craft rhythmically bumped against the wall. It would be so easy to lie there and go to sleep.

Shaking from the cold, she forced herself to sit up. With numb fingers, she fumbled to untie the rawhide belt wrapped around her waist. "Have to get out of these wet clothes."

Next to come off were her ankle-high moccasins. They squished when she moved and felt like stones tied to her feet. She peeled off her tunic and leggings and wrung them out before laying them out to dry.

She had emerged from the water trembling from the cold. Getting out of her clothes had taken considerable effort, but it warmed her. With that finished, she began to examine her find. The dim light that filtered down wasn't a big help, but she was able to make out a few details and was surprised by each.

The craft was nothing like she had ever seen. A dugout straddled by two slightly smaller ones, the three were lashed together to make a barge. A platform, made of hides stretched over logs, bridged the hulls. A totem, the likeness of a bull's head, was carved into a post and occupied the front of the larger craft.

On each vessel, sheltered below the lip of the deck and tucked under the canopy, sat low baskets filled with clay and partially burnt logs. Their position there provided protection from the weather. These were fire pits, but built more for cooking than warmth. *Food and heat, I could use both, but right now I'll settle for heat.*

Shaking, her fingers numb, she felt around in the dark. Bright Moon hoped to find tinder and small branches for a fire. She was rewarded with both. Even better, flints, secured by rawhide tethers, hung conveniently close. *Ahhh, held nearby so they wouldn't get lost. Somebody was thinking.*

Arranging the tinder in a loose ball, she began awkwardly striking the flints, pointing the flashes created toward the ball until she spotted a spark's telltale red glow in the tinder's midst. Bending close, Bright Moon gently puffed a breath of air. The spot glowed bright. Another, patient, gentle puff and the spot increased and then the first flicker of real flame came to life. Bright Moon added more tinder followed by a few small twigs. The flames grew enough that she could add larger sticks. *Not too big but it will do.*

Crouched closer to the growing flame, she cupped numb hands around it, remaining there, huddled over her small fire to soak up its warmth. Her eagerness to examine her treasure trophy did not let her linger long. As soon as the chill was gone, she took a brand[59] to light her way while she inspected her treasures.

Strewn about the platform, littering the bottom of the dugouts were large and small clay jars. This cargo lay in disarray, probably caused by the ship's erratic downstream trip and the sudden grounding that brought the trip to a halt. Like the design of the vessel, these were nothing like she had seen before. She wanted to know more, to examine each item closer, but the light of the flickering brand was too poor. Downstream from where she was stranded, the gap between the ice and the rock wall widened. There, the snow-covered roof, if there had been one, must have collapsed. The sun shone through the opening, bathing that area in golden light, making the tunnel beyond seem all the darker.

"Well," her voice echoing off the walls, "If I could get this over to the light I'd be able to see what I've got."

The barge would not move. One end was hung up on a rocky outcropping. The whole vessel could swing freely in the stream but it would not move forward.

A change in the wind direction allowed a warm breeze to sift through the opening and blow across her face, taunting her. The storm had died and she was in possession of a boat loaded with goods. Things were looking better. Smiling, she said, "Looks like that patch of sunlight's where I need to be." With that, she leaned out over the edge to examine the obstruction.

Had the water been just a little deeper here, the craft would have skimmed over this shelf. As it was, the force of the current had worked the barge along for some distance. Given time, or deeper water, it would be freed without assistance.

---

59 A piece of burning wood.

Bright Moon didn't want to wait. Sitting up, she felt around for something she could use as a pry. Nothing in the first dugout, but she found a long heavy pole in the second. It was just what she needed. Returning to her starting point with the pole, she prodded the submerged reef to test its strength and the depth of the water.

Satisfied, she stepped overboard. The ledge was sturdy, the water shallow, and the current rapid. Getting one end of her pry under the hull, she squatted under the other end and strained to push up. The end of the dugout rose up a little and then slid forward, but not much. Placing the pry under the hull again, she did the same squat-lift motion, moving it less than a finger width. Shaking her head, she thought, *At this rate, I will be an old woman before the vessel is free. I'd better look for another way.*

Moving forward, she stowed the pole and went to inspect the dugout's position. It was difficult to tell in the dim light, but it looked like half the vessel's length rested on the ledge. "Were you sitting over this shelf when the water went down or did you get washed here by a wave?"

Bright Moon could ask questions all she wanted, but there would be no answers. She could go back to using the pry but the distance she had to cover was too great. She could also start tossing things over the side to lighten the load, but what kind of prize would an empty barge make?

Naked, shivering, exhausted, on the verge of tears again, she shook her head in despair. Swallowing the bitterness, she felt, she moved forward. With her next step, she disappeared under the surface. Bobbing to the top, gasping for air, she found she had been jarred back to her senses.

Floating alongside, she followed the boat's length to the far end. Half of it was hung up on the ledge while the other half, along with the other two hulls floated free. If she transferred things from this dugout to the other two, she would lighten the load on it and it might float free.

Well, she hoped it would. It certainly was one thing

that she hadn't tried yet. It held some promise. Her head filled with ideas brought a burst of excitement to her tired body. Bright Moon pulled herself back along the hull to the end and scrambled aboard. Her small fire had died down to smoldering coals. She stirred them, adding tinder, twigs and larger pieces of wood. When her vessel was free, she could sit in the sunlight and enjoy its warmth while she examined her prize. At the moment, even though chilled and trembling from her cold swim, she was too excited to take time to warm herself thoroughly before she began looking for things to move.

The first to go were clay jars. Some of these were filled with powder and others with unknown liquids. A few jars had tipped over spilling their contents. The inside of the dugout was sticky. She could not move without stepping in it. Barefoot, her feet soon became coated as she climbed between vessels while shifting the load.

She moved the first set, placing them on the platform near the fire pit. Bright Moon had never seen jars made like this. In the villages they visited, containers were simple baskets made of willows or reeds woven together, covered with mud, then hung over a fire to bake the mud skin without burning the frame. These were different. Made entirely of clay—they didn't use any kind of framework—and each was decorated with its own bright colors and ornate designs. Later, she could spend time inspecting them, but now she had work to do.

Behind her, unnoticed, there was a low, grinding, rumble. Ice and snow blocking the passageway shifted under the pressure of the pent-up torrent it held back. This massive plug began moving her way, slowly at first, but it picked up speed as it moved. Streams that had been but a trickle earlier now started to flow in earnest. Here and there, places that had been dry began producing waterspouts that grew in intensity, further eroding snow, and ejecting ice chunks. Together, they weakened the plug's ability to hold back the torrent. The splashing and gurgling created was lost in the cacophony of sounds already echoing through the cavern.

Having moved all lighter items, Bright Moon began the work of transferring heavier objects. Carefully, wrapping her arms around a container, she stood up and stepped into the middle dugout just as the floodwaters slammed into the barge. It was lifted free and pushed downstream in one huge lurch. Behind her, another rumble—louder this time—as more ice and then volumes of water gushed out of the portal.

Finally, a muffled roar announced that the pent-up river was to be contained no longer. Water and ice began their trip downstream, the wave washing the boat ahead of it, blocks of ice followed along, banging against the walls as they did.

Caught off-guard, Bright Moon went down, knocking over other containers as she landed on her back in the pit of the dugout. The container she held, having slipped from her grasp, overturned, spilling its contents on her. From head to toe, she was now covered in a thick, greasy, red, glop.

The barge bounced off the walls as it shot downstream. The jars, the ones she placed near the fire pit earlier, spilled, spreading their thick, black, oily contents over the deck and into the pit where she was thrown and was not being tossed around like a child's toy. Bright Moon's red, glop-covered body now became coated in this black, oily substance. Spreading over the deck, the oil reached the edge and dropped into the fire. It snapped, crackled, and then burst into flame, quickly spreading over the bow of the vessel. Sparks hit the coating on her and she too started burning.

Smoke and sparks filled the air. The barge was not only free it was ablaze and rushing headlong through the tunnel. Jerked around, Bright Moon was unable to gain her feet. She caught a glimpse of a patch of blue sky as it whizzed by. It was followed by alternating light and dark times as the whole assembly, twisting and banging along, raced down the tunnel on the crest of the wave.

Having her own fire to fight, Bright Moon could not concern herself about the blaze aboard the boat, it was all she could do to flail away at the flames that spread across the coatings her body wore. Surrendering to her despair, she began to wail at the top of her lungs.

Wikvaya stirred a bit. Someone doused him with water. He opened his eyes slightly. Kolenya, cudgel[60] in hand, stood nearby.

"This is your last chance," Askook spat out, "where did you hide the girl?"

"I told you…" Wikvaya, hung by his hands over a small fire, started to speak, but was cut off by a blow from Kolenya's club. The blow knocked him back, set him swaying, and opened another wound.

His rage getting the better of him, Kolenya prodded Wikvaya's chest with his club. "No more of your lies, none of your tricks. We have been patient long…"

The wail and the drumming noise began again, louder this time. The sound cut his words short. Kolenya, fear written across his face, looked toward the glacier and slowly began backing away from his victim. *Perhaps Wikvaya was right*, he thought. *Perhaps he had provoked the Glacier's spirit.*

Openings that had gone almost dry just a short while ago began spewing water once again. Everyone stopped what they were doing and turned toward the wall of ice and snow, not more than two spear-throws away. Wide-eyed, some more than others, they were in time to witness a burning barge explode through the glacier's wall.

Rumbling, a torrent of snow and ice, once the covering of this tunnel, collapsed under the force of the vessel's impact, coating it. Snow-covered, the vessel made a shallow nose-dive into the pool. Before the bow

---

60 A short heavy club: a heavy stick used as a weapon.

resurfaced, water washed over the jars, extinguishing their flames, filling the air with putrid smoke. At the glacier, torrents of water and ice spewed out of the exit the barge created. Then, all was calm, but not for long.

Bright Moon stopped screaming when the barge hit the wall, not because she wanted to, but because snow partially buried her. After surfacing, the barge skated across the pond's surface until it lurched to a halt in the shallow water near the shore ending her ride. Lying in the bottom of the craft, she brushed the snow away and opened her eyes. Above her, she saw light and sky. It took a moment to register. She was no longer a captive of the glacier. She was free!

Bright Moon jumped to her feet and spat out a mouth full of snow. Tilting her head back, she raised her arms to the sky and let out a series of long, loud whoops. The snow that had covered her body fell away like molting skin, extinguishing the remaining flames still caressing her painted form. She began dancing around joyfully.

Still in shock from the barge's explosive entrance, the mob was confronted with the sight of a wild, snow-covered girl with disheveled hair. Some fainted; the rest, not knowing if they were in the presence of a witch or a Great Spirit, dropped to the ground, and lay prone to await their fate.

Chapter 15: Retribution

Wikvaya, suspended from a limb over the fire, did a double take. It was the girl, the one he had lost. She had found him! In her excitement, she was unaware of his situation. He had to get her attention before anyone else recovered from the shock of her entry and hope she could take advantage of the situation. "Oh, thank you Great Spirit for hearing the call of Wikvaya, your faithful servant," he yelled.

Startled, Bright Moon stopped her dance and looked around. She knew that voice. Onshore, men, women, and children lay prone. They knew they waited for something, but she did not know they were waiting for.

A warrior, cudgel in hand, slowly edged away from the man hanging from a branch over a fire. The person over the fire, called out again. "Come Great Spirit and order Long Tusk and Askook to release your servant, Wikvaya."

Long Tusk? Askook? Wikvaya? Behind those on the ground, surrounded by their toadies[61], sat the men she had tried to avoid. *How far had she traveled to get away from them only to end up in their hands? What kind of evil trick was this?*

Was this person a witch or a spirit? Kolenya didn't know, but it could be his opportunity to gain favor in Askook's eyes. He dropped his club, picked up a spear and threw it

---

61 A person who flatters and ingratiates himself in a servile way; sycophant: to fawn on and flatter (someone).). A servile self-seeker who attempts to win favor by flattering influential people.

at her.

Normally, the spear would have flown swiftly to its target, but an unexpected puff of wind created a momentary dust devil[62] that stirred the sands on the beach. Caught in this draft, the spear seemed to hang in the sky. Kolenya watched, open-mouthed, as the girl plucked the shaft out of the air.

Unconcerned, Bright Moon twirled her prize over her head and then struck a pose as if she were about to send the projectile back. Seeing this, Kolenya dropped to the ground, hoping to blend in with those around him.

Suspended over the fire, Wikvaya called out again, hoping to draw her attention to his plight. "Great Spirit, finder of my lost vessel, come, release your servant, Wikvaya. Free him from his misery."

Circumstances had changed. The one who had been her captor was now the one trussed up and at the mercy of others. Spear over her shoulder, she crossed the sticky deck. Her feet made soft slurp-slurp-slurp sounds as she walked to the bow and jumped to the grassy slope. Ashore, a wry grin playing on her lips, a sparkle in her eyes, she sized up the situation.

The rope that held her former captor suspended was looped around a tree and tied off at the trunk. Not far away, in the shade of another tree, at the foot of a long cooking trench, sat Long Tusk and Askook, their advisors, and their wives. Hardly able to cast a nervous look her way, men, women, and children lay on the ground waiting for her to decide their fate.

Sand and dry grass clung to the soles of her feet. She walked toward Wikvaya between rows of prostrate bodies roasting in the sun. Their fear hung in the stifling air. Black clouds, signaling a pending storm, crept over the

---

62 A miniature whirlwind strong enough to whip dust, leaves and litter into the air

hogback. Good! Its presence would be something she could claim to have brought about should the need arise.

Reaching him, she stopped and looked up. In a whispered voice, she said, "*Your* vessel?"

"Get me down," he whispered, "we can talk later."

She nodded and then replied loud enough for those nearby to hear, "I heard your call, Wikvaya, my faithful servant."

"Hurry. It's a little warm here," Wikvaya whispered.

With one foot, she swept the burning branches aside and then walked through the remaining ashes toward the tree anchoring the rope. Ash and hot embers clung to the coating on her feet. Kolenya, the spear-thrower, lay trembling in her path. Without breaking stride, she showed her disdain for him by stepping squarely on his back.

Surprised by her actions, he winced. The slight sound he made caught Bright Moon's attention. She looked back and spotted embers still sizzling on his back where she stepped.

With a casual glance at her feet, she saw the dry grass under them smolder and char. A murmur rippled through the crowd. *They saw that where I step things burn,* she thought. *But they don't know that dirt clings to the sticky coating on my feet and protects me.*

Before she reached her destination, Bright Moon bent and picked up a stone ax. Its owner did not object. One hearty swing severed the rope. Wikvaya hit the ground noisily and began working to free himself.

Discarding the ax, Bright Moon turned and started toward the place where Long Tusk and Askook sat.

Wide-eyed, Long Tusk, Askook and their cohorts, held their breath. They had witnessed a burning vessel explode from the side of the glacier. It slammed into the pool disappearing in a shower of water mixed with snow only to appear at the shore fire extinguished.

Now the girl, the ship's only occupant, her naked body decorated in red and black, with a spear over her shoulder walked defiantly toward them. The group emitted a collective gasp as they witnessed her walk the length of the cooking trench over hot coals. She stepped off the end and stopped to glare at her nemesis.

Freed, Wikvaya slunk over to a secluded spot where he could watch events unfold and, perhaps, come to her aid in the slight chance he would be needed.

Before they could challenge her, Bright Moon demanded, "Why are you here?"

Nervous and pale, Long Tusk licked his lips, but was unable to choke out a reply. Coming to her tongue-tied husband's aid, one of Long Tusk's wives yelled, "She's a fake. It's a trick anyone can do."

"If it is a trick anyone can do, then get up and follow in my footsteps." With a sweep of her hand, Bright Moon threw out the challenge and waited for the woman to accept it or admit defeat.

Forced into action by her own words the woman rose slowly to accept the dare, wishing instead that she had had the sense to remain silent. Bright Moon stepped onto the coals and walked to the opposite end. There, she waited for the woman to make her move.

The woman, all eyes on her, stepped on the coals and winced. The glowing embers hissed as the soles of her feet touched them. A quick step forward kicked up ash and set more coals hissing their protest. Two more quick steps followed. Then, screaming in pain, she jumped off to roll around on the ground, wailing. Bright Moon walked back over the coals, stepped off the path and stopped in front of Long Tusk. She did not let on, but, by the end of the last trip, she could feel the heat and knew that she would not be able to make the walk again.

Long Tusk, unable to look at her, wishing he were somewhere else, remained silent. Askook, however, was so excited he could barely get his words out. "That girl is magic," he said. "I will take her. She will be mine. I will make her secrets mine!"

He bubbled over with joy. Dreams of power made him light-headed. *He would learn her secrets. With them, he would expand his empire. No one would be able to stand against him. Yes, he would have her secrets!*

Turning, Bright Moon whipped the spear off her shoulder and brought it to bear short of Askook's throat. "You may *take* me," she said, her voice low, her tone menacing. "But, you will never *have* me! My secrets will remain just that… MY SECRETS!"

"Hold your tongue girl!" Askook roared. "My warriors are here. At a wiggle of my finger, they will bind you. I could have you flogged."

The irate leader made a hand motion, quick and emphatic. He had made this same gesture many times before and it always got results. A few of those surrounding him started slowly to their feet, looking around, hoping that more would join them.

The afternoon heat abated under the pressure of a sudden cold breeze. The clouds Bright Moon spotted earlier rolled across the sky, blocking the sun. The shadows covered Askook and his followers. Those that had risen were now back on the ground, hiding among the others, hoping their actions went unseen.

Askook's mouth dropped as fire-from-the-sky filled the air with painted streaks of white-hot intensity. Thunder exploded through the air, its concussion setting birds to flight.

"You call your warriors…" Bright Moon began. The next bolt drowned out her words. It split a tree that had towered above the others along the crest of the ridge and sent it crashing down. The ground beneath their feet seemed to shake and the hairs on the back of everyone's necks stood on end. "… And I'll call mine."

Those around her flinched at the spectacle, but Bright Moon stood fast, as if nothing unexpected had happened.

"Wha... what would you have of me?" It was Askook's turn to cower.

"What do you want?" It was Bright Moon's turn to question.

"I want power like yours... magic like yours."

"If you are not worthy, it could mean your death. Are you sure that's what you want?"

Askook nodded, unable to speak.

"If you wish to have my magic, to be my equal then begin by making me your equal. Have your people swear their allegiance to me for as long as they live, just as they have sworn so to you," Bright Moon said.

"That's all?" Askook couldn't believe his ears. "That's all?"

Bright Moon shook her head. "That's not all, but it's a start."

"Not all... what else?"

"Two tasks," she said. "First, Long Tusk and his people must be banished immediately from these lands, forever, under the penalty of death."

"No... you can't." Long Tusk interjected, but a look from Askook told him that protesting was useless.

"Consider it done," Askook said. "What is the other task?"

"There is a ceremony, performed in the full-of-the-moon. Those willing must drink a potion. If you are worthy, if you want this bad enough, and if you're strong enough to survive, you'll have the power."

"Let it be done then." Askook, absolute in his decision, didn't bother consulting his advisors.

###

Wikvaya found a sullen-faced Kaliska squatting in the shade. An assortment of pemmican lay on a robe spread out in front of the scout. He busied himself bundling and packing this staple into a parfleche.

He had lost contact with the scout after Bright Moon's sudden arrival. "Are you planning on going somewhere?"

"Long Tusk and his people have been banished," the scout said. "I will be going with them."

"You told me you're not one of his people," Wikvaya offered. "You don't have to leave."

Kaliska nodded. "I have my uncle's debt to consider. I still need to repay Long Tusk and it is a debt I will honor." Working on the last bundle, Wikvaya watched the scout put extra effort into pulling the cords tight and guessed there was more to the payment of debt than the scout mentioned. Kaliska didn't want the caravan leader dead; he wanted him broken, powerless, and alone.

"When that is done,' Kaliska paused—possibly to give him time to think about the debt and his method of payment—before adding, "I will be free." Satisfied with the contents of the parfleche, he began rolling up the robe. "How about you?" He asked, "Now that the girl is here, is your family free?"

"No," Wikvaya said, "Not yet."

Kaliska stopped what he was doing. "Not freed? Why not? With the girl here, I thought Askook would be satisfied and let your family go."

"It is not as bad as it was before. When we couldn't catch up with her on the trail, I was troubled. I had hoped Askook would accept my efforts and free my family. Instead, he hung me over a fire. While I hung there, I knew that he would treat my family to the worst conditions and I would not be able to stop him."

"And now...." Eager to learn what new conditions Askook had laid on his friend, the scout interrupted.

"You've met his demands, why didn't he free your family?"

"He wants to be all-powerful. The girl convinced him she needs to gather medicines for the potion to be used in the ceremony. Not wanting her to get away, he wanted to send a large escort, but she told him that those that came along might learn the secret and then everyone might become powerful." Wikvaya smirked. "Understandably, he didn't want that to happen so he agreed to a compromise. He will continue to hold my family, and I will go along with the girl to make sure she doesn't run away."

Lost in thought, perhaps regretting his past decisions, Kaliska dabbled in the loose dirt in front of him then shrugged. "It is like I told you before, when I first met with Askook, I built the girl up as a shaman, possibly a witch with magical powers. I didn't know Askook, but I thought she might be better off with him and wanted to free her from Long Tusk. I should have guessed that anyone Long Tusk befriended anyone that he offered a tribute to, would be just as bad or worse than he. Perhaps, if I didn't tell Askook she was magic, he would have accepted any girl. That could have made it easier on you."

"It may not have changed anything," Wikvaya said. "Even after he had offered Bright Moon as a prize, Long Tusk had his out-walker try to shove her over a cliff. Had the out-walker been successful, he would have substituted as many girls as needed to get a reward from Askook." A smirk on his face, Wikvaya added, "What Long Tusk didn't know was that Askook was only interested in the girl because he heard she was magic. Everything comes down to the fact that Askook wants power and Long Tusk wants a reward."

Ahead of them, a horn trumpeted. Kaliska stood and the two clasped arms. "That's Long Tusk's signal to start forward. After my debt is paid, maybe we'll meet again. In the meantime, look after our girl."

"My people will do our best to look after Bright Moon. It is my hope that we meet again, and soon. Among my people, you will always be welcome."

"I don't understand what we're doing hiding here," Wikvaya whispered. Camped in a small hillside grove, they were alone, but he took no chances least his voice would carry, giving their place of concealment away.

Busy with her cooking, Bright Moon stirred in more ingredients. Lost in thought, she finally said, "Stick to being a lookout and don't worry about me. I need some time to work up the details of my plan."

"Plan? What plan? Since your arrival, we've chased around the countryside, collecting plants and... and... and all sorts of items." Wikvaya's hoarse whisper failed to hide his exasperation.

"I had three reasons to take us away," Bright Moon replied. "First, it kept us away from Askook and the others. If I were in his village, underfoot, he might ask me to perform some magic. I don't want him finding out that I can't."

"Yes, well, maybe that was a good idea, but we could have used the time..."

With a wave of her hand, Bright Moon motioned toward the stew being brewed. "Second, I needed to collect some herbs, berries, and mushrooms for the potion I'm making for Askook's celebration."

Bewildered, unable to see a solution, Wikvaya scowled. "What's the third reason?"

Looking up from her work, she smiled at him. "It was so we could spend some time together. I needed to find out if I could trust you."

"Trust me? What about you? I ask about your plans

every day but you haven't answered. You don't trust me enough to share, yet the full moon rises tonight. When that happens, Askook expects to become magic; to have great power. What then? What will you do then?" *What was she planning? He could only guess.*

Trust you? Trust the person Askook and Long Tusk entrusted to carry me into captivity? Did he realize what he was asking? "I had him send Long Tusk and his people away." Dreamily, she stirred the brew. "They are banished forever on pain of death. He is humiliated and won't be here to poison Askook's thoughts against me."

It was a simple statement, but hearing it only frustrated Wikvaya more. He grimaced. "What good did that do? He's still out there." *What are your plans, woman. What happens next affects me, affects my people.*

Eyes flashing anger, she turned to him, waving the wooden ladle under his nose. "Yes, he's still out there. I wanted to punish him for what he did to my father, to my family, to my tribe. I wanted to take my revenge, but I couldn't. I was powerless to act against the two of them." Bright Moon looked over the remaining ingredients on the nearby hide: Chopped roots, crushed grains, and a paste of ground flowers. She scooped up a handful of each and dropped them into the brew. "I couldn't leave the two of them together as allies. Askook thought I was magic and wanted me—or at least my powers—for himself." She paused to take a breath, or maybe swallow the bitterness she felt, before she continued. "I knew he would never let me go. Neither would he want to share my powers with Long Tusk and his tribe. That's why I knew he would agree to banish them from these lands. In his greed, Askook wants power and places a high value on becoming magic. He was more than ready to agree to make me his equal. At the time, it was the best I could do."

"Do you think that will keep Long Tusk away?"

"No, but when he returns he will face death."

Wikvaya mulled that over. *Right now, she's upset, but I need to test her resolve.* "We should've taken the vessel and sailed out of here. We should have gone somewhere far away."

"Your family is held hostage. Am I supposed to believe that you'd leave them to suffer whatever fate Askook doles out?" Bright Moon snapped. Angry fire flared up in her eyes and then disappeared as she calmed down again. "After what it's been through, the boat's in need of repair. Even if it was in good shape, we wouldn't be able to sail far enough, fast enough and we would go leaving Long Tusk and Askook united against us once again." Laying a hand softly on his arm, Bright Moon gently added, "To save face, they would not, could not, let us go unpunished. They would search everywhere. Eventually, we would be found. When that happened, I wouldn't be able to fool them. With them split up, they can be dealt with one at a time."

Wikvaya looked down. He wanted to appear remorseful or lost in thought. "The ship floats. It would not take much to get it ready," he said. *Would this coax her into talking about her plans?*

Bright Moon changed the subject. "What were you doing, I mean, before you fell in with Askook?"

"I was born in a small fishing village. It was on the shore of a great sea near a grassy plain. There came a time when the fishing went bad. There was no rain. The herds went away and crops failed. The village, no longer able to scrimp out a living, was making ready to leave when a strange ship, similar to one you found, arrived.

It was unlike anything we had ever seen. The only people onboard, an old man and his woman, offered to trade with us, but we had little left to trade. They persisted, offering to trade goods for a child—whichever child they selected. After testing all the children, they took me with them."

He paused in his narration as if remembering things he didn't want to remember. "The trader was not what he appeared to be. A wise man in disguise, I became his student. The three of us traveled from village to village to see what we could learn and collected samples of what they made."

"What did they collect?" Bright Moon paused in her work and gave Wikvaya an emotionless glance before going back to her work.

"All the items you found on the vessel were part of the treasure they collected, the items you found on the vessel, and the items that covered you from head-to-toe. Lucky for both of us, the vessel also contained the items I used to clean you up." He paused to watch a hawk soar lazily through the sky. *How do I end this and convince her that my fable is real?* "Before Askook's men found us, we'd lost our ship in the rapids. Until you arrived, I didn't think I would see it again."

Bright Moon looked up, gave him a stony-look, and sighed, before going back to her cooking.

"What's the matter?" He asked.

"You talk about running away from this, but, when I ask you to trust me; you spin some story like we were sitting around a campfire. I've watched you command men. You do it with great ease. You were never a child from a poor fishing village, I can tell that much. I was hoping you trusted me enough to tell me the truth, but you choose to lie."

Wikvaya stabbed at the ground with one foot. *She caught me. There was no point in denying it. I had hoped this story would sway her my way.* It was his turn to change the subject. "So, the path we mapped out is set and everything is in place. Tonight when the moon's full and the celebration starts, what happens then?" He asked softly.

She stirred the cooking pot; lifting the ladle from the

bottom and pushing it back down before she answered. "Askook... and all of his cronies... die."

Chapter 16: New Beginning

While Bright Moon spoke, Askook, in the center of the group facing the girl, fidgeted. *Get on with it, woman,* he thought. *You went through all of this in front of the council, clan leaders, and the people. When I get the power, I will have everything I need and get anything I want... and I will have you, as well.*

Bright Moon had gathered the group near the top of a craggy ridge, one of the many that bordered the foothills. Torches, varying in height and set in patterned rows, encircled the group. Flames flickered in the soft breeze blowing across the hillside. If nothing else, it increased the eerie feeling.

"When we're finished, you will either be powerful... or dead," she said.

Askook looked bored. Unlike their leader, the men behind him—two council members and two clan leaders—were solemn-faced, emotionless. With Askook's hunger for power, Bright Moon thought he would have included a much smaller group. Did he need them there or did they demand to be there? She did not know, but at this late date, it did not matter. The decision to go on would be theirs and theirs alone.

Continuing in a solemn voice, Bright Moon added, "I want to give everyone a chance to back out, to walk away."

Slight movement came from a man in the back. Was he just shifting weight from one foot to the other, or was he watching to see if anyone stepped forward before revealing his own concerns? She could only guess, but felt that if one worked up the courage to leave, others might follow. She hoped that would happen. It did not.

Agitated, Askook—wanting to pick up the pace—

spoke up. "Nobody's going to leave. We all want powers like yours."

Bright Moon took a deep breath. She knew what she had to do. "It can be a painful process. If you are worthy, if you want this enough, and if you're strong enough to survive, you'll have the power." A murmur, accompanied by light, nervous laughter, rippled through the group as they encouraged each other.

Bright Moon paused and waited for their voices to subside. "Those willing must drink this potion in the light of the full moon. Drink it before her golden hue fades to silver," she said. "Does everyone understand?"

"Where's your cup?" Askook questioned.

"When I was very young, I was given this potion to drink. If I do so again, I will lose all my powers, age before your eyes and turn to dust," Bright Moon explained. Quickly changing the subject, she exclaimed, "Behold, Sister Moon is rising. Is everyone ready?"

"Yes," Askook bellowed. "Let's get on with it." The group roared their agreement.

"The tonic is ready. Sister Moon is full and golden, but will turn to silver soon. Gather 'round now and fill your cups. The extent of your power will depend on how much of the brew you swallow. I urge you to drink deeply, drink quickly, and gain the power you desire."

Bright Moon stepped away from the stew pot as the others eagerly crowded around it. Lifting filled cups to their lips, each person willingly, wildly gulped down the contents and hurried to get more before the cauldron emptied. *Drink deeply*, she thought. You'll never quench your thirst for power, but it will dull your mind and, one way or another, it will give you the power to help you enter the-sleep-from-which-no-one-wakes.

###

In the shade of a large willow, Long Tusk sat with Chochmo[63] and his council. Nearby, a group of Long

Tusk's wives turned a skewer over a cook fire. Long Tusk did not want to be here, to deal with these people, but they were the only tribe he could turn to for support.

Chochmo's people were like his own in disposition, but more primitive. Stocky, bandy legged, people who wore little more than a loincloth[64]. Chochmo and council members set themselves apart by adding a simple tunic[65]—little more than animal hides with a hole for the person's head and belted around the waist—to their attire.

Chochmo's tunic, like those of his council, was home for untold numbers of vermin: lice, roaches, other bugs crawled in and out of its folds. Those that didn't live there, overflowed into his matted, unkempt hairy body. A heavy coat of mud covered any exposed skin. "Guards against bug bites," he explained.

They could have met in Chochmo's village in the tribal council house, but Long Tusk knew the stench accompanied them would be overpowering. Instead, he met them in the open where the wind was free to clear away the smell. "I'm telling you, the woman is a witch," he told them. "She is a danger to all of us."

He scanned their faces. Did they believe him? Did they believe anything he said? At the risk of over-playing his hand, Long Tusk added, "She was about to cast a spell on me when one of my wives came to my aid. You saw the burns on her feet."

Long Tusk motioned toward the group of his women. One lifted her feet to show Chochmo's people her blisters, the other wives howled in sympathetic misery.

"The witch enchanted my long-time friend, Askook. He banished me and my people from his lands." With a

---

63 Native American Hopi name meaning "mud mound."
64 A one-piece male garment similar to a breechcloth, sometimes kept in place by a belt, which covers the genitals and, at least partially, the buttocks.
65 A short, usually to hip line or slightly longer, sleeveless, straight, tubular garment, gathered at the waist, sometimes belted.

dramatic sigh, Long Tusk added, "I risk immediate death if I return."

Long Tusk spoke in great detail about how she wronged him, how she wronged his people. He didn't mention that on his departure from the Land of the Mattocks, he sacked three small villages, stripping them of everything of value and enslaving those not killed outright. It was their furs Long Tusk's people would offer in trade... and their captives as slaves. He mentioned none of this.

Even if he had, it would not have surprised nor would it have offended Chochmo or his council, because they also raided, robbed, and made slaves of survivors. Pillaging and plundering were their way of life, but if they knew of Long Tusk's actions, they might demand greater payment.

"What would you have of us?" Chochmo asked. He stroked the coat of his favorite hunting dog, an animal that was nearly as mangy[66] as he.

It was the opening Long Tusk hoped for. "We must work together to rid ourselves of this witch before she grows even stronger."

Pensive, Chochmo considered Long Tusk's appeal. *I must be careful. I have dealt with Long Tusk before and know that he exaggerates his successes and his challenges—even to the extent of calling on his clan leaders and wives to support whatever claim he wanted to make. In the tales he tells, the animals he faced were bigger, his enemies were more cunning—and, in every one, he rose up to beat them. He fails to talk about the friends he sacrificed to get his way.*

"We are too few to attack a witch that powerful," Chochmo finally said, "especially if she has Askook and his people under her spell." Chochmo did not get to be old or the chief by letting his guard down.

---

66 A condition caused by a class of persistent contagious skin diseases caused by parasitic mites. These mites embed themselves either in hair follicles or skin.

Long Tusk shook his head. "I thought I could count on you… on our friendship…."

"We are friends… have been for a long time," Chochmo shot Long Tusk a cold stare, "and you can count on me… to be wise." He signaled a young man near the forest's edge. "We need to talk to other tribes," he continued. "Enlist their aid. When we have enough support, we can act."

Smiling to himself, Long Tusk nodded. Chochmo would sponsor his efforts with the other tribes. With the old man's help, he would get his revenge.

At Chochmo's prompting, the young man had disappeared into the woods. Now he and another emerged leading a string of horses. Long Tusk knew many tribes kept animals for food or pack animals, but these didn't seem to fall into either category. He was puzzled by their actions.

"We go now," Chochmo announced without ceremony. Getting to his feet, he started for the horses.

"Wait!" Long Tusk shouted.

Startled by this outburst, Chochmo, at the side of the first animal, stopped and looked back.

Long Tusk was unsure of Chochmo's plans for the animals. If it was food they wanted, at his directions Long Tusk's women were roasting meat and had readied other dishes. Providing a meal would bring Chochmo one-step deeper into their bargain. "My women have prepared food. We should eat together and seal our pact."

Chochmo turned, put his hands over the horse's back, and pulled himself up in one well-practiced movement. The young man handed the reins to him and then headed for his own mount. Behind them, his men mounted their steeds in a motion too fast to follow and made ready to leave. "We'll eat together another time," he said. The pack of dogs accompanying him milled around by the horses, but were careful not to get in the way of flying hooves.

"Wait!" Long Tusk shouted again. His outburst made

the horses prance nervously at the sudden noise.

Mounted, Chochmo was able to look down on him. "What now?" He asked gruffly.

"I've seen a few others use horses as pack animals, but I've never seen anyone ride them."

Chochmo shrugged. "My people have a way with all types of animals," he said. "We start when they're young. Carrying a person is not much different than carrying a pack... if you know how to train them." Throwing his head back, he gave a hearty laugh as he turned his horse in a tight circle. His men joined in the laughter.

When they had arrived, Chochmo had dismounted in the forest, leaving the horses there, hidden from view. He wanted riding them to be a surprise. It had worked! Long Tusk wanted such an animal. Chochmo could read it in his face. The caravan leader would give anything to have one. Bringing his animal to a halt, he leaned over and looked Long Tusk in the eye. "If you're interested, we could work a trade," he offered.

Long Tusk's eyes lit up at the prospect. They were willing to trade for this animal. He was in luck, but what would he have that Chochmo's people would want? "What would you like to trade?"

Chochmo made a face. His forehead, caught between long dirty bangs and heavy dark brows, furrowed in thought. Finally, his leer exposing the decay of his broken teeth, he said, "Women. My tribe could use some new women. The ones we've been getting are weak and don't last long... some of them ended up in our cook pots."

"Women! I've got plenty of them," Long Tusk said. Indeed, among the slaves he captured in his latest raids, there were women of all ages. So far, having them meant more mouths to feed, even though he didn't feed them very often. "How many do you want?" He asked Chochmo. It would be a fine trade. "When next we meet, I will bring a group so you can choose."

Chochmo smiled warmly. It was a good offer. "I'd like that," Chochmo said. "We have many fine horses as good as this one. I will let you choose. Bring one hand's worth of women for each horse you want." Waving, he turned his horse and led the way into the forest."

The Moon's golden hue faded to silver and it slipped behind a mask of clouds. The five men, having scraped the last of the potion from the caldron, turned to face Bright Moon. "Follow me," she commanded. Grabbing a torch, she turned to lead the way through the darkness.

Two days ago, while collecting the medicines for the potion, she and Wikvaya selected this route and placed unlit torches along the course. As she passed by, she used her torch to light each one. "We must give the potion time to sink in before we can test your new powers at a place I've selected."

Askook eagerly fell in line behind her and his followers took up places after him. Flat, broad and smooth at the start, their route soon developed into an incline and became more taxing. In the beginning, Bright Moon set a slow pace. She glanced over her shoulder now and then to check the faces of those behind. Shortly, beads of sweat broke out on pasty brows. The set of their jaws didn't completely hide suppressed pain. The potion was starting to have its effects.

"You should begin to feel changes taking place," Bright Moon shouted over her shoulder. *Giving them that bit of reassurance would encourage them to keep up the pace,* she thought, *and tolerate the pains they are beginning to feel. They would keep on... until it was too late.*

Switchbacks[67], narrow and steep, wound around the hillside as the path climbed upward. The darkness hid the depth of the gorge they now paralleled. As she continued, she began going faster so that they would not have time

---

67 A path, as in a mountainous area, having a series of tight zigzag curves arranged for climbing a steep grade.

to think. Following her—gasping for breath, moaning from pain—the group of five continued their efforts to keep up, but fell farther behind with each step.

Stopping at a curve, Bright Moon looked back as she lit the torches there. She wanted the light bright enough that they would not see well in the darkness around the bend.

Behind her, the group stumbled along in painful stupor, their desire for power draining the last of their energy. They moved without thinking beyond the next step, ripe for the final blow.

"We are at the last bend," she yelled. "The first people to arrive will get the greatest powers."

Her message gave the group new life and they stepped up their pace. Bright Moon, resolved to carry out the last phase, took a deep breath, and jogged around the bend. She stopped when she reached the rope Wikvaya had strung across the void between the bends and twists of this curve.

A carrier, little more than a basket filled with rocks, hung suspended there, waiting for her to attach her torch. With it in place, she gave the device a nudge. It slid forward on a rope well lubricated with animal fats. She watched as the torch swung out over the chasm, propelled by the stones' weight.

Satisfied that it would continue, she placed one hand on the rock wall to guide her through the darkness until she reached the opposite side of the S-curve. Wikvaya, holding a second rope—this one attached to the carrier—waited for her there. In the darkness that filled the void, the torch equipped carrier crept forward.

"Should I start now?" Wikvaya asked.

"Wait till they're closer."

Across the way, the group's huffing and puffing announced their arrival.

"Okay, begin pulling it steadily, but not faster than a person could run," Bright Moon said.

Hand-over-hand, Wikvaya tugged the rope. The

torch, suspended over the chasm, moved toward them with a slight bouncing motion as if someone were running through the darkness with it.

"Quickly!" She yelled. "Your time is near. Be ready to accept your powers. Step out and fly."

Eager to gain their powers, minds dulled by their efforts and the effect of the potion, the men charged after the bouncing light ahead. At this new urging, the last of the group stepped off into the darkness before their first member realized they were falling, not flying, and began screaming. The noise echoed off the rock walls, splitting the night.

Hands over her ears, Bright Moon tried to block the sounds of their cries. From behind her, a slight scuff sounded. Before she could react, Wikvaya's strong arms cradled her. "It was quick and merciful, much better than the slow death the poison would have given them," he whispered.

Chapter 17: Changes

Exhausted and still in shock, Bright Moon let Wikvaya lead her through the darkness to a campsite. Tucked away in a clump of trees, a small lean-to filled with pine boughs awaited their arrival.

"I knew we would be tired after the night's events," he explained, "so I prepared a place for us to rest."

He spread sleep-robes over the boughs and they climbed into the shelter. *A perfect place hidden among this copse of trees*, she thought. *A comforting place, built against a sand hill not far from the river's edge. She felt safe here and that would let her sleep. Physically and mentally drained, the comfort of this place would be her escape from the night's agony.*

Fresh boughs, a comfortable sleep-robe, the warmth of a body you could trust lying nearby, what more could she ask for?

The question hung on the tip of her tongue. There was something, but the answer lay in the haze of sleep that was quickly overtaking her and she could not put it into words. Still, whatever it was flickered at the edge of her mind. Tired, she would soon be asleep and the answer would have to wait till another time. Time. The question... and the answer had something... to... do... with... time....

Muffled sounds, the call of a bird she was not familiar with, a twig snapping, they seeped into Bright Moon's sleep. She stirred, pulled the robe closer against the brisk night air, and rolled toward Wikvaya. He wasn't there.

Startled awake, her eyes flew open. Cautiously, she lay still and listened. The sounds of muffled steps moving away from her were suspicious, but not an immediate danger. Raising her head slightly, she saw two figures—one was Wikvaya—disappear up the trail, swallowed by the fog and the night.

Moving only her eyes, she examined the area in front and to the sides of their lean-to. Empty, no one around, nothing moved. She slid out of the shelter and, keeping low, crept from shadow to shadow, up the path Wikvaya and the other man had used.

Wikvaya, and whoever summoned him, did not have much of a head start. If she were not careful, she might run into them in the fog. Just ahead, the unfamiliar bird call—like the one she had heard earlier—followed by voices, warned her. She slid behind a tree hoping its protection would help her remain undetected. Someone uncovered a small oil lamp. From her vantage point, she saw the pair she had followed standing in the midst of a group of men.

Wikvaya, Bright Moon mused, *you thought I was asleep and slipped away in the middle of the night with a stranger. Quiet as a young fawn, I followed you to the clearing where you met up with several others. I could not hear what you said, but I knew you were the center of everyone's attention. You issued orders and the men followed them. Born in a small fishing village, bah!* Turmoil fueled her anger. It boiled up within her. *What did I do, trade one form of imprisonment for another?* The bitter taste of betrayal grew in Bright Moon's mouth and she had to suppress the urge to show her contempt by spitting, lest she give herself away.

Having seen enough, Bright Moon started for the campsite. *What was Wikvaya doing sneaking off in the middle of the night? What were his intentions? What should I do now? Should I run away, escape into the night while I still can? Could I go far enough, fast enough to avoid capture? Depressed, by the realization that running away was not a solution. It had not worked for me so far, so I'd better think of something else.*

By the time Bright Moon arrived back at their campsite, she had formed a plan. *I will stay, pretend to sleep, and let him think he had slipped away and returned unnoticed.* Using her rope belt and a young sapling next to the shelter, she set up a snare—just in case—then crawled back into her sleep robes to fake sleep.

Wikvaya returned fish in hand, just before dawn and began making a fire. Still feigning sleep, she watched him through eye slits. What was he planning?

###

"Did you sleep well?" Wikvaya eyed Bright Moon as he turned the fish over the fire.

Huddled in her sleep-robes, she sat at the mouth of the lean-to where they had slept. Noncommittal, she shrugged. "I've had better, but, considering the night just past, I did as well as can be expected." Shifting her position, she adjusted her robe against the early morning's cold and put on her most innocent face. "You must have been up early. I was so tired, I didn't hear you until you had the fire going," she lied. Her ruse seemed to work.

Wikvaya, busy with the fish, accepted her answer. "I made a quick trip back to the starting place to dispose of the cook-pot, cups, and torches along the path."

"You left nothing behind?" Covering their tracks, a good idea, she hadn't thought about that.

"The things I left will mislead anyone curious enough to look. They will find nothing important." Wikvaya turned the fish over the fire.

"What do we do now?"

"The villagers will be expecting the others to return… to be magic and powerful… and you'll come back alone. We haven't talked about how you're going to handle them." Wikvaya gave her a long, piercing look.

"You need to trust me."

"I trust you. We worked together to accomplish…."

"Since your return to Askook's meeting place, we've spent time together." His impatience showed. "These were busy times, collecting mushrooms and herbs, setting up the starting place and the path you took. You told me what you wanted when you needed to, but you never laid out your whole plan…. You never trusted me."

He took the fish off the fire and divided it between two slabs of bark. "Hungry?" He offered one to her and looked around for a place to sit. The edge of the sun just breached the horizon and had not burnt off the fog blanketing the ground. Night, except in the shadier parts of the forest, was slowly giving up its hold to the early morning's dimness.

She took the makeshift plate and patted the sand next to where she sat. Accepting her invitation, he shifted to that side and was about to take a seat when he stepped on the snare's trigger.

Released, the sapling straightened up, pulling the loop of rope out of its hidden spot. It snapped around his ankle and pulled him off his feet. Wikvaya landed on his back. Bright Moon threw aside the sleeping-robe and her plate and pounced on his chest, knife drawn.

"I never trusted you?" She spat the words out. "You never trusted me."

"What… what do you mean?" Pretending innocence, he looked up at her and blinked. Her face, contorted with anger, the burning rage she felt clearly showing in her eyes, she glared down at him. Wikvaya knew she was not about to be fooled by any fable he had hoped to feed her.

"Something that bothered me was how little time you needed to put everything together and how little time you needed to cover our tracks last night. It wouldn't work unless you had help."

"Help? Where would I get help?"

"Last night, I watched the little boy from the poor fishing village, slink off into the night, make strange bird calls, and gather his men together. That's where you'd get help, but why? What's next?"

"Strange bird calls? I don't understand." He seemed perplexed.

"Strange bird calls," she repeated. Pursing her lips, she tried to imitate the call she had heard. It wasn't even close.

A smile played on his lips. "Strange bird calls... you mean like this." He repeated the call from last night perfectly.

From behind her, there was a scrunch of dried leaves. Bright Moon's smug look faded. Focused on Wikvaya, blinded by her anger, she had forgotten about the group he had met with. She had not heard anyone approach until it was too late. At that sound, she froze like a fawn in danger. It was too late to do anything else. Out of the corner of her eye, she saw a quick motion as someone reached over her shoulder to seize her by the wrist. An arm wrapped around her waist and lifted her, leaving her feet dangling in midair. She did not resist. Another person leaned in and cut Wikvaya free. He sat up and brushed himself off. Whoever these men were, they had been as quiet as the fog that still covered the area and she was powerless against them....

Chapter 18: A Turn of Events

From behind her captor, an unknown speaker announced, "Lord[68] Wikvaya, all is in readiness, as you directed." His voice, low, deep, authoritative, had the sound of one who expects obedience from those he commands but who also willingly defers to his superiors.

To see the speaker and determine how many men were with him, Bright Moon turned her head and strained to catch a glimpse over her captor's shoulder. The speaker, a tall, muscular man in unfamiliar garb, stood amidst a group of several others, all armed. Spread out, they stood noiselessly, some looking forward, others to the sides or back. No one would approach without their knowledge.

"Good. Bring the others and we can get started," Wikvaya said. "We don't have much time."

A nod from the speaker and one of the men whistled. It was another birdcall, but different from the earlier ones. The call was repeated, first by someone possibly lingering near the fringe of the nearby forest. Then again, the birdcall was repeated by others, further out judging from the fading sounds.

Wikvaya turned his attention to Bright Moon. "We are not here to harm you. I had hoped to talk about the next steps before this, but it did not work out that way."

"We could have," was her terse reply, "but you chose

---

[68] Similar to "Chief" or "Excellency", use of the title, "Lord" or "Lady" here is to recognize that some persons possess a rank above the ordinary individual.

to tell me stories and plot with these men, rather than talk with me."

Stern-faced, but silent, he held out his hand. One of the men gave him a coil of rope. Deftly, he looped a noose over her ankle and drew it tight, but not uncomfortably so. The one holding her put her down.

Bright Moon was glad to feel solid ground under her feet again, but was not happy about her circumstance. Wikvaya had tricked her and now he held her prisoner. She took a step toward her betrayer, but was restrained by the guard's foot planted firmly on the rope.

"Am I your prisoner now?" Rage boiled within her and she gave him a cold stare. Frustrated by being held back, she clenched both fists.

"No. The tether is to keep you from wandering off... like you did in the gorge." Wikvaya smirked at the thought.

She shot him a glance that would have stopped a bear in its tracks, but her reply was cut off by the arrival of a group of women. They carried baskets and bundles and were dressed in ankle length white gowns, not animal hides. Wikvaya had sometimes worn a shorter, but similar, garb. These ladies stopped five paces away and waited. Bright Moon could not tell if they were nervous or if they were excited. Wikvaya recognized their presence with a nod, and held out the rope. The leader of the party, a tall, slender woman, a little older than the rest, stepped forward to accept it. Like Wikvaya, her head was shaved except for one long braid. Even more unique, her hair was golden in color, while everyone Bright Moon knew had hair the color of a moonless night sky. Unusual.

"She's devious, Lady Adsila[69], so watch her closely," he told her.

"She is a woman, Lord Wikvaya. Have you not yet

---

69 Cherokee name meaning blossom

learned that all women are crafty?" She smiled shyly at him.

Wikvaya laughed and added, "Yes, but she is shrewder than most, so keep a close watch." He turned his attention to Bright Moon. Hoping to quell her doubts, he told her, "Cooperate with these ladies and they will not harm you." He paused, allowing that thought to set in. Still angry, Bright Moon folded her arms over her chest and continued to glare at him. Wikvaya, unwilling to give up, added, "The outcome will be to your liking and better than anything you can imagine."

Holding the leash loosely in one hand, the woman looped her arm through Bright Moon's as if they were about to stroll through the meadow. "I am Adsila," she said. "We have heard many good things about you and are excited that we finally get to meet. Come with us. It is time to get you ready." The other women surrounded the pair and the group started forward.

Get me ready? Bright Moon thought. *Ready for what?*

Chapter 19: Preparation

The women rounded a bend in the trail and passed through a grove. Reaching the river, they stopped, put down their bundles, and began shedding their garments. Adsila turned to Bright Moon. "Join us," she invited. "It's time for everyone to get clean."

Squealing, some of the women, having already removed their clothes, entered the cold water and began playfully splashing each other and those still on shore. Bright Moon didn't know what to think, but it seemed harmless to go along with her request. It had been a long time since she had the opportunity to enjoy a luxury such as this.

In waist-deep water, they scrubbed their skin and hair with sand[70] before rinsing thoroughly. The women brought out jars of oil and combs—some made of wood, others made from animal bone. Gathering around Bright Moon, they worked the oil through her hair and combed it out.

Adsila watched, inspecting their work carefully. With a wave of her hand, the women ceased their labors. Two women, one on either side of Bright Moon, took her gently by the arms. Adsila said, "We make perfume out of flower petals. We're going to pour some over your head so close your eyes now, and keep them closed until I tell you. The girls will lead you out of the water, okay?"

Bright Moon nodded and closed her eyes. She felt the water wash over her head and down her body, leaving its delicate scent to linger in the air. The women led her to

---

70 Before soap was invented and before hot waters became available, sand was used to remove dirt and exfoliate the skin.

the shore. "Open your eyes now," commanded Adsila.

Bright Moon found herself at the waters' edge, walking on a white mat. At the end of the mat, two women held an ankle-length tunic decorated with shells and colored pebbles. It was made of the same material as Adsila's but with more decorations. On seeing it, Bright Moon's face lit up.

Adsila let her enjoy the feeling for a moment and then, clapping her hands, she said, "Hurry along, now, we have a lot of work to do."

The women helped Bright Moon into her tunic, combed out her hair again, and finished by weaving in a crown of flowers. Adsila gave her a final inspection and smiled her approval. Turning to one of the women, she said, "Run and tell Lord Wikvaya that all is ready. It's time for him to join us."

At a signal from Adsila, one of the handmaidens stepped forward and cut the rope around Bright Moon's ankle. If she wished, Bight Moon could have turned and fled and probably outran any of the women here. Her curiosity and the excitement of the moment kept her from acting on this impulse.

Adsila interrupted the girl's thoughts of escape. "Come here, to the water's edge," she beckoned. "Take a look and tell me if what you see meets your approval."

Unsure of what she would see, Bright Moon eased forward to join her hostess. The pair looked into the water. Lady Adsila's reflection peered back at them. Next to that likeness, Bright Moon saw a girl she did not recognize. Looking closer, she realized it was herself and gasped in surprise. Still mystified by the morning's events, Bright Moon could not imagine what would be next. She did not have to wait long.

Chapter 20: Entrance

"I see you've worked magic of your own, Lady Adsila," Wikvaya said. Walking around her, he eyed Bright Moon up-and-down as if she was some kind of prize. Something he was thinking as offering in trade.

Bright Moon felt cheated. *All the tricks I've had to play to survive; my efforts to escape from Long Tusk; to have the caravan leader banished and then to rid the world of Askook only to arrive here and be dressed up for... for... for what?* Humiliated, her cheeks red with anger, she choked back tears.

"Does Lord Wikvaya plan to throw me into the sacrificial fire or am I to be traded for some favor?" Bright Moon spat the words out like bad food and looked him in the eye knowing he could easily read her rage. *Why did I let myself be lulled into his trap by this woman and her handmaidens?*

Wikvaya flinched and drew back under this sudden verbal assault. He had thought their treatment of her would encourage her trust. Up until now, she had been calm. What had gone wrong? It was Lady Adsila who stepped in and salvaged their efforts.

"We have no plans to sacrifice you or to trade you," Adsila said. "In fact, you are free to go if that is your wish... but I beg you to stay and help us."

Bright Moon stared at the woman. Questions welled up in her. *How could I be of help to them?*

"Because of you, Askook banished Long Tusk and his people from his lands," Adsila reminded her. "At your bidding, Askook had his people swear allegiance to you. They did, but some were unhappy and we expect turmoil. From the time you arrived, you claimed to be a Great Shaman. Everyone had heard stories about you and they

179

have expectations. We want the Great Shaman to also look like a great queen. It will encourage their beliefs and help our cause."

"You... you... all this was to... make me look good?" Bright Moon was dumbfounded. *I was wrong. They did this for me.*

"I hoped Lady Adsila's work would build your confidence in us and you would feel you can trust us... trust me." Wikvaya let that sink in but did not give her time to reply. "We did not get a chance to talk about what we should do after dealing with Askook. I had to come up with a plan and hope you'd go along." He looked her in the eye. "Are you happy with the changes?"

"Yes," she said. She could no longer hold his gaze. The bitter taste left in her mouth was from her own fallen pride. She dropped her eyes and swallowed hard. "Lady Adsila and the others have been most kind." Her resentment gone, her anger faded, she now felt a need to please these people.

"Good," he said and he waved a hand in the air. Men, from the group that had surrounded her earlier, arrived carrying a platform slung from poles. The platform contained two seats—slings made of cords woven like fish netting—that faced each other. Curtains, open now, could be arranged to hide the passengers.

Taking Lady Adsila by the hand, Wikvaya helped her aboard. After she was seated, he turned and took Bright Moon's hand. She carefully mimicked Adsila's movements, cautiously lifting the hem of her skirt, tucking the excess aside so she could step up without tripping.

While helping her board, Wikvaya said, "There's no time for us to talk now. While you travel, Lady Adsila will explain our plans, your role, and tell you about us."

Wikvaya left them. Strolling forward, he joined his guard detail, two banner carriers, and several handmaidens at the front of the group.

The two women sat facing each other. After the

men—four in front and four in back—shouldered the poles supporting the platform, the procession started forward. Behind them, Bright Moon saw another group of handmaidens and another set of guards.

Their seats swung and swayed with the rhythmic movement of the bearers. Bright Moon, used to sitting or standing on solid ground, hung wide-eyed, onto the frame with a white-knuckled grip. This did not escape Adsila's attention.

"Once you get used to the ride, you'll relax," she said. "The men that carry us have done this before and are very good."

"That's nice to know," Bright Moon said and laughed nervously.

Adsila smiled at the unsophisticated girl and decided the best way to ease her mind would be to tell her their plan. "No doubt, you've noticed we—Wikvaya; myself; our people; are different from any you're used to seeing." She paused, giving the girl time to focus on the idea. "Lord Wikvaya's father's father was the leader of a great tribe in a far-away land. It was a place where people from all over came to share ideas and learn." She grew silent for a moment, as if remembering the tales she heard.

"In a far-away land? How did Wikvaya come to be here?" Caught up in the story, Bright Moon unconsciously relaxed her grip on the swaying ride that carried her and leaned in toward Adsila.

"Alas, nothing lasts forever." Adsila feigned scanning the passing scenery in an attempt to hide the tears she felt forming. "There came a time when a great comet appeared in the heavens. Our wise men watched it for a long time. Fire began falling out of the sky. The ground shook and split open. Our great cities fell down and mountains came to life, spewing burning rocks. Many lost their lives." She bit her lip, as if in pain, when she recalled stories of a place she hadn't seen—probably would never see. "The air filled with smoke and ash. Our leaders, Lord Wikvaya's father's father among them, gathered the people, at least the ones who would leave, along with those goods they could carry, and took to their ships."

"I don't understand... what has this got to do with me?" Bright Moon gripped the side-rails in wide-eyed disbelief. *Do these people believe I am truly magic? Do they believe I can conjure up a remedy to the tragedy that struck them?*

"To know your role, the role we need you to play, you need to understand where we came from, and the dark rule we have lived under all this time," Adsila told her.

Still awe-struck, Bright Moon nodded quietly.

"The people were at sea for three moons. They ran out of fresh water and suffered many hardships. There were storms—great storms—and our ships were separated from each other; some may have broken up and sank. Finally, the ship of his father's father came to a new land, but not before many of our elders and much of our knowledge was lost. We've wandered ever since, always searching for our people."

Adsila looked away as if she examined the terrain, but Bright Moon knew differently. A glimpse of her companion's quivering lip confirmed her suspicions. She remained silent, giving her hostess time to recover her composure.

Adsila cleared her throat, took a deep breath, and continued. "As we wandered, we talked with every caravan we met, with people in every village we encountered."

"What did you learn?"

"We learned nothing from our search. Our methods failed us. We began looking for a new place, one where we could invite people to learn and share ideas as our ancestors did. We still continue to question everyone who crosses our path. Our hope now is that if we cannot find our people, perhaps they will hear about our work and find us... at least, by honoring our ancestors, we will keep their memory alive."

Bright Moon patted Adsila's hand. "Has there been

any word of them?"

"No one had heard of our people," she said. "We had lost hope... until just recently."

"Until recently? What happened to give you hope?"

"You arrived." Adsila giggled like a young girl as she answered. "The vessel, the one you rode when you surprised Askook and Long Tusk, was similar in design to the ships Lord Wikvaya's father sailed. We have no idea where it came from or how it got inside the Great Ice, but it gave us hope that others had survived. Hope that they were out there."

"How did you end up with Askook?"

"We settled in this area and lived in peace with our neighbors. Askook, the tyrant, raids where he wants. Two summers ago, Askook and Long Tusk invaded our lands. We've lived in bondage ever since. Every year, Long Tusk returns with some gift for Askook, who gives him permission to bleed us dry with his demands. Long Tusk's people, the pigs, come through our villages and took what they wanted. We were powerless to stop them, but you solved that problem for us."

"Me? What did I do?" Bright Moon, still reeling from the morning's events, was at a loss.

Adsila smiled. "By having Askook require his people to swear their faithfulness to you as an equal to him, it gave you authority over them. As deceitful as Askook was, we believe he meant to enslave you as soon as he had the key to your magic."

"Yes, but by arranging to get rid of him, it was Askook who was surprised." Comfortable with her swaying seat, Bright Moon leaned back and thought about Askook. *I recognized his greed and didn't trust him. The task was repulsive, but it was Askook or me. If Long Tusk returns I will deal with him also.*

"Yes you did, but before that, you had Askook banish Long Tusk," Adsila said. "Now, they're both gone."

A ram's horn trumpeted, announcing their arrival.

Adsila pointed over Bright Moon's shoulder. "The village is just ahead. We'll be there shortly."

Bright Moon twisted in her seat to get a better look. She could see a walled city strung out along the palisades[71] that rose up along a curve in the river. Boats, similar to the one Bright Moon found earlier, were drawn up on the beach, anchored off shore, or engaged in hauling in nets.

"I expect that you will stand before the council, the elders, and the rest of the clan leaders this evening, it will take that long to get everyone together. In the meantime, we'll tell everyone you are too weary to have visitors and take you to our quarters."

"Won't council members come looking for me?"

"They may, but the guards will turn them away," Adsila looked with pride at their escort.

Bright Moon shook her head. "I'd just like to get through this."

"You will, but first there are things we need to cover. The sleeves of your garment are purposely loose. We can hide a small weapon in the left sleeve. It's a bola—I understand you are familiar with such a device. This is made with special details. In case things get out of hand you may need to work some magic. I think it will suffice."

"Do you think there'll be trouble tonight?"

"I don't know." Adsila shrugged. "Everybody will be expecting Askook and the others to return, to be magically powerful. I don't know if you planned on returning, but if you did, we knew you'd be alone."

"Askook made them swear their allegiance to me. Wouldn't that be enough?"

---

71 A line of steep cliffs usually along a river. An example of such exists in NE New Jersey and SE New York extending along the W bank of the lower Hudson River. It is about 15 miles (24 km) long and, in places, reaches some 300–500 feet (91–152 meters) high. Alternately, a fence of pales or stakes set firmly in the ground, as for enclosure or defense. Any of a number of pales or stakes pointed at the top and set firmly in the ground in a close row with others to form a defense. Finally, to furnish or fortify with a palisade.

"Askook's guards helped keep everyone in line. If you returned alone, the clan leaders could easily forget their pledge and a power struggle might begin. That would be a problem. We decided that it would be in both our interests to act as your honor guard when you returned. We would give you protection, and you would give us leadership and freedom."

Bright Moon nodded. *Wikvaya and his people had thought this out ahead of time and then acted quickly.*

"I think you should tell them that Askook and his men were so excited by their new abilities, they changed into great birds and flew away." Adsila flapped both arms in the air to emphasize her words.

Adsila's imitation of a bird in flight made Bright Moon laugh at the thought of Askook flying through the air. "Yes, I can see their faces when I tell them that Askook flew off and may never return."

"And remember—Wikvaya, his guards, myself and my handmaidens—we're here for you." Leaning forward, she gave Bright Moon a reassuring pat on the knee.

Comforted, the young girl craned her neck to see villagers gathering to greet them..

Chapter 21: Acceptance

A walled village[72] stood atop the palisades overlooking the river. The council house stood in the center surrounded by a large, open common area. Separate stockades, one for each family group, hugged the walls and stretched out toward the center.

Adsila's stockade was similar to those of other families. A privacy fence, made of light poles taller than the average man, surrounded each compound. A common-house and individual huts—sleeping quarters for her and each of her handmaidens—lined the inside walls. In addition, there was an open area where vegetables and flowers were grown. Immediately after they arrived in the village, Adsila brought Bright Moon to her compound to isolate her from others, especially council members.

Arm-in-arm, Adsila led Bright Moon to her new quarters as she explained, "Meeting the council this evening is very important. Askook ruled with an iron fist. With him gone, Wikvaya feels that some of the clan leaders will rebel. If they do, they will try and push you aside and a power struggle will follow."

Bright Moon's heart rose in her throat. "Are we safe? Is there anything we can do to stop them?"

"You are secure here and can rest if you'd like. My

---

72 A walled village is a type of large traditional multi-family communal living structure that is designed to be easily defensible. It is completely surrounded by tall walls, wooden or stone, protecting the residents from the attack of wild animals and enemies

guards will keep everyone out," Adsila explained. "I've had food prepared if you want something to eat. When you're ready, we can talk about the meeting with the council and I'll show you the bola."

"Show it to me now," Bright Moon said. "When I'm comfortable with it, then I'll be able to eat and rest."

She hardly spoke the words when a handmaiden, a covered basket in one hand, a bola clutched in the other, was at her elbow.

Holding the rigging out for Bright Moon to examine, the girl said, "Like similar tackle you might be familiar with, this one uses rocks for weights."

Bright Moon looked it over. "The threads that hold it together are as thin as a spider's web," she said.

"They are made of strips of gut twisted together," the girl said. "If you have to use them at council tonight, they'll be harder to see."

Bright Moon shrugged. "I don't understand. How will this help me?"

The handmaiden held up the basket and smiled. There was fluttering from inside. "Your help is in here. We'll replace some of the rocks and you'll be ready."

Curious now, Bright Moon lifted the corner of the cloth covering the basket. It was her turn to smile.

Dressed in a long flowing robe, Bright Moon stood on a raised dais on the sunrise side of the council house. She faced the seated council and village elders. Villagers knelt a respectful distance behind them.

Wikvaya had the dials strategically placed to make the gathered community face the setting sun in order to see her. Adding to the effect, he had his people discreetly place torches, not to push back the darkness, but to created irregular puddles of light and shadows and set them dancing around. These changed in size and luminance in the wispy evening breeze effectively painting her shadow as a large, looming, ephemeral figure against the face of the council house. In the low light, and because the audience had been looking into the setting sun, their placement diminished the crowd's ability to detect any signs of nervousness on Bright Moon's part.

The ceremonial drums stopped. A low undercurrent of chatter filled the air. Bright Moon recognized her signal to begin. She took a deep breath, stepped forward, and raised both hands in the air. Everyone fell quiet.

Bright Moon looked directly at the council. "Askook made me his equal. Each of you accepted that. In front of him, you freely swore your allegiance to me," Bright Moon said. "I am your leader and, until Askook's return, I am your sole leader."

Pandemonium buried grumbling until a clan leader rose and held up his hands. When quiet resumed, he issued a challenge. "How do we know you speak the truth? Maybe Askook is not a great bird. Perhaps he is sleeping the-sleep-from-which-no-one-wakes."

Bright Moon glared at him. "You do not know, but it makes no difference. You freely and willingly pledged your allegiance to me and I am here."

The clan leader was not appeased. Shouting loudly, his supporters got to their feet. Their actions stirred the crowd to greater frenzy. Holding up his hands to signal quiet, he stood his ground and continued to voice his objection, "You are a mere girl, not a shaman. Prove yourself. Perform some magic," he commanded.

The torches flickered in a light breeze bathing the scene in eerie light. Bright Moon gave him a long, cold stare. "I am Shaman and your leader," she hissed. "I am the one who commands!"

The clan leader flinched, but, unsatisfied, he would not be silent. More clan leaders and villagers—some appeared to support her while others did not—were now on their feet, their voices raised in disagreement. Protests soon turned to shouts.

Unnoticed, Bright Moon slipped her free hand up her sleeve, retrieved the weapon, and took a step back with her right foot, before turning her profile toward the group. With her right hand behind her, shielded from view by the darkness there, she began twirling the bola.

"Silence!" She shouted over the din and raised her left hand high in the air, slowly moving it in a circle.

Clan leaders and villagers, startled by her action, stopped, and looked her way. Everyone focused on her raised hand.

Swaying, eyes half-closed, she tilted her head back and brought it around in a series of sluggish circles as she began an incantation. Low, throaty, it gradually rose in both volume and pitch until it reached a pinnacle. Every eye was on her as she halted her ritual, turned to face them, and quickly brought her right hand forward, as if pointing at her accuser. Released from her grip, the bola flew through the air, barely a blur in the scant light, and wrapped itself around the protesting clan leader's throat.

Exchanged for some of the rocks, the small bats extended their wings and began flapping frantically. Clutching at his throat, the clan leader croaked a scream and fainted. Those closest to him, scrambled away. Those remaining hurriedly lay prostrate, never glancing Bright Moon's direction lest they suffer the same fate as the outspoken clan leader. Much to everyone's relief, Wikvaya's men arrived with a litter and carried the clan leader's unconscious form away.

Once out of view, the litter-bearers were joined by Adsila's handmaidens who cut the bola's cords and released the bats. When the clan leader recovered, the bat attack would be but a memory. For Bright Moon, tonight's ordeal was over.

###

Bright Moon's sleeping quarters, the largest of the several huts within Adsila's compound joined the group's common-house. Each morning, Bright Moon rose with the sun to begin the same monotonous routine.

Their bath ritual was not held at the river's edge with the rest of the females and their small children, but in a secluded spot set apart for use by Bright Moon, Adsila and her handmaidens.

Nodding a greeting to the men, she boarded the sedan chair and was surprised by a young woman—one of Adsila's handmaidens—sitting opposite her.

"Will Lady Adsila be joining us today?" Bright Moon asked.

Dropping her eyes, the girl answered quietly, "No Miss, she is spending time with her mate."

Her mate...? Bright Moon hadn't thought about it and was surprised by the remark. Since the night she faced the council, there were times when Adsila and her handmaidens seemed to be on edge, nervous about an event unknown to Bright Moon. These same days, she noticed, were peppered with short, whispered conferences that ceased when she approached. Baffled by these actions she hadn't thought about Adsila, or anyone else in this group, having a mate. Yes, she had noticed the number of handmaidens present sometimes changed. Yes, there had been days when Adsila joined them late, but none where she did not join them at all.

The only constant was the men with the sedan chair who waited at their gate each morning, to carry them to the water. From time-to-time, Bright Moon would part the curtain to peek at the villagers as they passed. Unfamiliar with life in a village, everything seemed calm.

"Why is our bathing area set apart?"" Bright Moon asked her companion.

"The people believe you're magic and look up to you," she said. "It is best they continue to think that way."

Bright Moon made a face. It was not the message she wanted to hear. "I would like to move around the village and help where I can. Is there anything I can do?" Bright Moon asked.

"I will speak with Lady Adsila and make your wishes known," the girl replied.

Adsila was there to greet them when they returned to the compound. Bright Moon, not waiting for the handmaiden to ask, took advantage of this time to voice her complaint directly.

"Everyone here is so busy, and I am doing nothing." Turning, she looked around at the others now sitting in the sun outside their sleeping huts. They busied themselves at various tasks.

"Certainly," Adsila said. "Whatever you'd like to try, however you would like to help. There are plenty of children to look after as well as grain to grind, meals to prepare, a garden to tend... many tasks that could use additional help." Adsila waved a hand toward the handmaidens busy with activities "Look around and tell me what you would like to learn, or what you would like to do."

Where should I start? She wondered as she watched a group of youngsters throw pebbles at a wicker basket pulled along a suspended rope.

"They're too young to go hunting, but this practice will help them get ready," Adsila explained.

Nearby, two handmaidens sat on opposite sides of a waist-high scaffold. "What is this?" Bright Moon asked. "I've never seen anything like it."

191

"We call it a *loom*," Adsila said. "We use fur from animals or fibers from plants, like the reeds that grow along the river. These are twisted into cords in the same way we make rope. Some of the cords are strung up and down in rows on the scaffold. With the vertical rows in place, the girls pass another set of cords in-and-out, like a deer running through the forest."

Bright Moon watched the two skillful girls working at dizzying speed, chatting as they did.

"The clothes you wear, your shawl and headdress were made on this loom or one like it. If you wish, I will ask them to show you how it works and you can try your hand," Adsila said. "Our people are eager to share ideas."

Beyond the loom, in a quiet corner, a man sat in front of a hide stretched over a frame. On either side of him, sat a boy and a girl, each had a similar setup in front of them. They watched his every move intently. When the man stopped, the youngsters would mimic the symbols he had made while he observed, sometimes commenting on their work.

Not wanting to interrupt them, Adsila stopped a short distance away and spoke quietly. "Antinanco[73] is a scribe and he records our stories. That way, they can be read at special ceremonies and the people will remember their heritage. The youngsters are learning this skill. He guides them so that they can carry on his work. Because of his efforts, our stories will be told to those who come after us."

From this distance, Bright Moon saw a jumble of marks and colors in neat, orderly columns, pretty, colorful, but meaningless to her. "This one hide tells your whole story?" She asked.

"Oh no, it is just one of the many stories that Antinanco has recorded," Adsila explained. "So, it is your

---

73 Native American Mapuche name meaning "eagle of the sun."

choice. What would you like to do?"

Chapter 22: New Ideas

"You are treated well?" Wikvaya asked. Lady Adsila stood at his shoulder. Bright Moon had not seen him for some time and was relieved to know he had not forgotten her.

"There are so many people waiting on me, I cannot lift a finger to help myself," Bright Moon complained. "I've tried to do the work that the others do, but someone is always at my elbow to help. If I step outside the door, your men expect to carry me in that chair. I'm growing fat... and useless." Her voice clearly carried her contempt for this new lifestyle.

Listening to her comments, he turned to Adsila. "It is as you said, she is unhappy. What do you suggest?" Wikvaya asked.

"It's been longer than a moon since we entered the village." Bright Moon interrupted. "The people, the council all seem to have accepted me, but I feel like I'm held prisoner here. I just don't know how much longer I can go on living like this."

Adsila touched Wikvaya's arm, drawing his attention away from the girl. "My lord, perhaps we can go out among the people, if the danger is over...."

The warning glance Wikvaya shot Adsila cut her off, but he was too late to prevent her words from reaching Bright Moon's ears.

Bright Moon was shocked. "Danger?" There were times, after standing in front of the council, when Adsila and her handmaidens seemed on edge. Whispered conferences were halted at her approach. This was why. "What danger?" She repeated.

"It was nothing, really, we were just being cautious."

Hoping to put the question aside, Wikvaya tried to diminish the events with a display of indifference.

Bright Moon would not let him escape, easily. "Askook's people swore allegiance to me in front of the council and himself. Did they suspect something other than magic at work in spite of the little show we put on?"

Still attempting to appear unconcerned, Wikvaya shrugged. "With Askook gone, some of the clan leaders tried to take his place. Their rebellion was put down and the rebels were given the chance to join Long Tusk in exile."

Bright Moon was ashen-faced at this news. "Things seem calm now."

He nodded. "The worst is over. Since then, mutinous clans that were not a part of the initial uprising have chosen to quietly slip away."

Still looking for reassurance, Bright Moon tentatively asked, "So… everything is good now?"

Wikvaya gave her a warm smile. "Those who remain are loyal to us and our people. We do not have the concerns now that we had when you first arrived."

Isolated, she was not aware there was a problem. Now, she didn't know what to think.

"When we first returned our biggest fear was that when you were out someone would ask you to heal an ailment or perform some magic and you couldn't," Wikvaya said. "That would have damaged our position when it was weakest."

"My handmaidens and I can show her around," Adsila told Wikvaya. Turning to Bright Moon, she added, "I welcome the opportunity to tell you about our people, our beliefs, and show what our craftsmen can do."

Wikvaya nodded. "The men who carry your chair are loyal. They can escort you and provide protection, if necessary."

"If a question of magic arises, we'll quickly change the subject. If we don't wander too far, we should be safe enough," Adsila said. She looked at Wikvaya for approval.

Receiving it, she smiled at Bright Moon and said, "Tomorrow's market day. Everyone will be displaying their handiwork. It will be a perfect day for an enjoyable outing. Does that sound like a good beginning?"

Adsila, Bright Moon at her side, made casual conversation while they strolled through the village. "Ever since we left our homeland, my people have wandered the countryside, looking for a place to settle,"

Villagers spread hides or set up simple booths to display fruits, vegetables, handicrafts, hides, cured skins, stone tools, arrowheads, and spearheads. Some had jewelry made from shells or colorful stones. A few had taken hides and created tunics and leggings. Adsila encouraged Bright Moon to stop and examine the displays much to the craftsman's pleasure.

"There are many items here," Bright Moon said. "In my travels, I've seen objects like these, but never such fine work."

Adsila beamed. "Like our forefathers, we wish to create a place where others can develop their art and share ideas. It would be what our people wanted."

They stopped at a display of bone and wooden instruments. Adsila picked up each item and handed it to Bright Moon to examine while she explained its use. "Here are awls for punching holes through hides," Adsila told her. "That way, pieces can be laced together to make tunics or moccasins."

Bright Moon examined the workmanship and the sharpness of its point. "Very nice," she said. Pleased by her remarks, the owner smiled warmly.

"Here is a display of sharp-edged knife blades, needles—from very fine to very heavy—barbed spearheads, arrowheads, and buttons," Adsila waved her hand at the display.

The next booth contained stone implements: Hoes,

spades, flint-edged grain sickles. Adsila handed her a tool. "Look at this sickle," she said.

Bright Moon hefted the implement. The handle was wrapped in soft leather cords and attached to a flat curved blade of polished wood with "teeth" of flint set in the edge. Well balanced, it felt good in her hand.

"We harvest grain," Adsila explained. "It was hard to harvest until someone came up with this tool. The flint pressed into the edge of the lip provides a sharp cutting edge. It easily slices through the grain stalks."

Rounding a corner, they came upon a group of ladies sitting around a row of waist-high scaffolds. Rolls of colorful fabric, some solid colors, others patterned, lay nearby. "These are looms used to make cloth," Bright Moon said. "They're like the one your handmaidens are showing me how to use."

Their walk took them out of the village and into a meadow. Sheep grazed and several youngsters played nearby, all under the watchful eye of a young woman. Two shields, one larger than the other, dangled from ropes tied to a tree limb. The shields swayed gently in the breeze, rarely touched by the rocks or sticks flung their way by the youngsters.

"The young woman looks after the game-playing youngsters while they look after the animals," Adsila explained. "The game passes the time while it helps them develop their skills. When they're old enough, they'll be ready to go on hunts."

The breeze shifted as they walked along. Bright Moon caught an aromatic whiff, unmistakable in its origins. "You keep other animals here?" She asked.

Adsila smiled and pointed out a new direction. "We keep and use many types of animals, some for their milk, eggs, or fibers, others we put to work at tasks that people used to do."

Following the trail, they arrived at the livestock pens. Nearby, a pair of oxen harnessed to a horizontal shaft, followed a circular path around an upright pillar.

"What are those animals doing?" Bright Moon was mystified.

"See the boulder on the other end of the shaft?" Adsila asked. "It follows a stone-path covered with a thin layer of grain. As the animal walks around the circle, the boulder follows the path, grinding the grain as it goes. The crushed grain is swept up and new grain added," Adsila beamed as she finished her explanation.

"But... but... what about the slaves?" Bright Moon asked.

"What about the slaves?" Adsila questioned her.

"What will they do? There will be no need for slaves," Bright Moon said.

"Yes, that's our point," Adsila said. "There'll be no need for slaves." She touched Bright Moon lightly on the arm and said, "That's a good thing."

###

On their tour, Bright Moon spotted a curious device. It stood taller than two men and sat perched atop a stone platform. In spite of its colorful covering, she could make out the long branches that were lashed together to form its insides. "What's it for?" She asked.

"Our people have stories that tell how our forefathers, in the days before the great comet, had vessels that flew and were called *Travels-the-air-with-the-birds*," Adsila said. "Lord Wikvaya hopes to be able to do the same thing."

"They used equipment like this?"

Adsila smiled at the girl's wide-eyed question. "The knowledge they had was lost. No one knows how they did it... or even if they did it," Adsila said.

"No one knows... if they did it?" Bright Moon was incredulous. "I don't understand."

"It's possible that it was one of the stories told around campfires or to children as they were put to bed," Adsila explained as they walked on. She shrugged. "Lord

Wikvaya built a small version. When it worked, he decided to build a bigger one."

"I don't understand," Bright Moon said. "Why would he take the trouble to do that?" Bewildered, she shook her head

"A man like him needs to keep busy," Adsila said. Smiling, she added, "He made a promise to his father that he would recover our lost glory."

Stone-bladed adze[74] in hand, Wikvaya paused in his work on a log to gaze at the river. On the water, a ship—a platform supported by two dugouts—lowered its sail as it made its way toward shore. Lost in thought, he didn't see the vessel or hear the ladies approach.

Adsila called to him, "Lord Wikvaya, does the river fascinate you?"

His head snapped around at the sound of her voice. "Lady Adsila, how is the tour going?"

"We are enjoying our excursion and I am learning many things about your people," Bright Moon interjected happily. "I felt so confined before. It feels good to be out."

He smiled at her enthusiasm as she bubbled over with excitement like a stew pot on a blazing fire. "It's good that you're enjoying yourself, but we want you to feel that they are your people too" Wikvaya said.

Bright Moon nodded her acceptance of his words and shielded her eyes from the glare of the sun off the water. "What is it you look for on the waters?" She asked. "Is it the boat with that strange shelter?"

"Shelter?" Wikvaya looked at the vessel as if seeing it for the first time. "That's not a shelter, it's a sail."

---

74 A tool used for smoothing rough-cut wood in woodworking. Generally, the user stands astride a board or log and swings the adze downwards towards his feet, chipping off pieces of wood, moving backwards as he goes and leaving a relatively smooth surface behind.

Inexperienced with any water craft larger than a dugout, this was new to her, and Bright Moon didn't mind showing her curiosity. "A sail? What's it for?"

"It's made from woven reeds, like a mat, and is fastened to the limb that stretches over the water. They use ropes to pull the limb up the pole that stands upright like a tree. The sail spread out and catches the wind to make the ship move forward." He and Adsila watched Bright Moon to see if she understood. She did not disappoint them.

"What happens if there is no wind or if you want to go the other way?" she asked.

"It does not always work, sometimes we have to row," Wikvaya admitted. The vessel ground ashore and the crew splashed off and began unloading the day's catch.

Bright Moon felt Wikvaya's concerns had been elsewhere, continued her questions. "So, is this what you were watching?"

"No, I was looking at something else. See those posts?" He pointed toward a few timbers upended in the river, a rope stretched between them. Water lapped against those close by while the ones farther out barely broke the surface. "I put them there a few days ago. The closest one was on dry land while the water barely reached the middle of the farthest. Now, the closest is in ankle-deep water and the farthest is completely covered."

"I sense your concern, Lord Wikvaya, but I don't see the problem," Lady Adsila said.

Bright Moon answered before Wikvaya could. "We should be in the dry season. The river level should be going down, but he discovered the water is getting deeper every day."

Wikvaya nodded. "I became suspicious when I saw your vessel come out of the Great Ice. The amount of water that followed you didn't offer any comfort."

"We are on top of a hill, aren't we safe here?" It was Adsila's turn to show wide-eyed concern.

Wikvaya looked around. "It's true the village sits on top of a bluff, a short walk uphill from here. Is it far enough? That would depend on how deep the waters might get. I need to go up river to learn more."

"We could take a trip up river to see if we could learn something." Bright Moon's thoughts raced ahead. "We could take some men and dugouts and…."

Wikvaya shifted his stance, held up a free hand, and cut her off. "It is the time when the great fish appear." He gestured toward the river and then to the log at his feet. "All our men and vessels are tied up with the harvest so I'm carving a new dugout to use for my trip."

Bright Moon eyed the adze he held. Wikvaya's vessel lay on its side. He had been working on smoothing and rounding the hull. Woodchips littered the ground alongside the log while a small fire nibbled away at the inside. The air was filled with an aroma of freshly cut wood and smoke. She could see Wikvaya's craftsmanship was slowly turning the log into a seaworthy vessel. "It looks like it will become a fine looking craft, but hardly big enough for the two of us and our supplies."

Wikvaya held up his hands. "Wait," he said. "I said I need to go up river to learn more. That doesn't include you."

Adsila noticed Bright Moon's chin jut out as she planted her hands firmly on her hips. "You're not going without me." The girl's posture clearly demonstrated her defiance.

"Your position requires you to remain here," Wikvaya replied, hoping that would quell her objections, but knowing that it wouldn't.

"If I can't go along, I will go by myself," she said just as firmly.

Adsila knew Bright Moon was irritated at being confined and chafed at the prospect of not being included in the adventure. Close quarters with her was beginning to wear on her household, as well. Adsila knew the girl would get her way… and, to return tranquility to her group, Adsila would see that it happened.

Wrapped in animal hides, protected against the chill of night, Bright Moon huddled with Wikvaya, Adsila and her handmaidens, around a tiny campfire outside Adsila's common-house. Overhead, the stars pierced the crisp blackness but did little more than separate earth from sky.

Turning to Wikvaya, Bright Moon broke the silence. "Lady Adsila showed me the vessel you're building, the one called *Travels-the-air-with-the-birds*. If it works, what do you plan on doing with it?" Her question interrupted his thoughts.

"*When* it works, it will lift and carry. For example, it could be used to lift timbers, carry them over hills, out of the forest and into our village. Or, it could be used for travel. We are only limited by our thoughts."

"That would be exciting," she said. It was Bright Moon's turn for deep thought. "How does it work?"

"Put a hand over the fire, like so," he said, holding a hand out to demonstrate.

Duplicating his movements, she held a hand over the fire.

"Feel the warmth rise up." He moved her hand away and nudged the fire with a stick. Embers floated into the night air. "The sparks rise up, carried by the warmth you felt. My vehicle will do the same."

Bright Moon watched sparks float through the air and reach a peak before descending. "Your vessel will need to be warmed before it rises, how are you going to do that?"

"It sits on top of ovens," he said. "Like a ship, it will be anchored in place until it's ready to take to the air." He beamed. She could tell he was proud of what he'd designed.

"Why are you carving a dugout when you could be using this?" Bright Moon was at a loss to know why

Wikvaya was wielding an adze when he could use *Travels-the-air-with-the-birds.*

"It doesn't work." The words left a bitter taste—frustration and failure—in his mouth.

Surprised, Bright Moon's jaw dropped. "I thought Lady Adsila said, because the first one—the little one—worked, you went on to build this?"

Wikvaya shook off the feeling of disappointment. He sat up straighter, squared his shoulders, and explained, "It's not working the way I want, but it will...." His voice trailed off as he thought about this difficulty.

"The little one worked, but the larger craft doesn't work at all?" Mystified, Bright Moon struggled to understand the situation.

"Yes, the small one worked but this one doesn't," he made a face. "The big one raises a little and begins to quiver, as if it wants to go further, but fails," he confessed.

"What keeps it down?"

Exasperated, Wikvaya shot her a dark look. "If I knew that...."

Realizing that it was not the best way she could have asked her question, Bright Moon waved a dismissive hand, cutting off his reply. "No, I mean what did you find when it stops doing what you wanted?"

"The warm air carries it up like the embers from the fire just like the model. But, on the larger vehicle, the air leaks out of the skin."

"How do you know this?"

"I held my hand near the surface. I felt hot air rush by like a breeze on a summer day," he explained. "As soon as I fix that problem, *Travels-the-air-with-the-birds* will be ready to take to the sky." Wikvaya took on a dreamy look as he pictured his success.

Bright Moon made a face. "I hate to disappoint you, but it will only get you as far as the next problem."

Her remarks jerked him out of his daydream. "Next problem?" He smiled, cunningly. "I believe it will fly, but suppose you tell us what you think."

Bright Moon stirred the embers again and used her finger to follow a cinder as she spoke. "The fire warms the sparks and they rise, like your vessel will." Everyone watched as the spark rose from the flame and then descended. "Away from the fire, the embers cool and settle back to the ground. What will keep your vessel from doing the same?"

Wikvaya's smile quickly faded. "My concern with the rising waters has taken all my time. I hadn't thought that far ahead."

Bright Moon could tell her question pained him. Without a solution, it could bring his idea to a bad end. All of his work would be wasted. This gave her the perfect opportunity.

"If I come up with an answer that lets your ship take to the air and stay there, will you let me come with you on your trip up river?" she asked.

"You? What could you do?" His words hurt, but she put them aside knowing that he was tired.

"If I come up with an answer, will you let me come with you on your trip?" Forcefully, Bright Moon repeated her question. *If he accepts, I'll have to come up with a solution quickly... but I'm going whether I'm successful or not.*

Wikvaya thought about it. *If she is successful, my vessel will take to the air; if she's not, then I won't have to take her along. How could I lose?* "If you're successful you can come along, but if you're not successful, you will be bound to a post and I'll place guards around you to keep you here. Agreed?"

His words caught her by surprise. The potential of being bound to a post was not something she looked forward to, but, cornered, she would have to accept his offer. This setback only meant she would have to work harder, think harder, to be successful... and she was going on the trip.

Chapter 23: Troubles

Lost in thought, Bright Moon stood atop the platform. Hand on her chin, she contemplated *Travels-the-air-with-the-birds*. The thought of being bound to a post if she was not successful spurred her actions. She had walked from one end to the other, stopping here and there to examine Wikvaya's creation in hopes she could come up with a solution. The swish of skirts interrupted her thoughts and she turned to see Lady Adsila picking her way across the decking along the length of the craft.

Adsila smiled as she greeted her friend. "I come to see what wonderful magic you are planning."

Bright Moon shook her head. "If it were only that simple, I would be packing for a trip instead of standing here." Her face showed her dismay and she slumped against the side of the craft. It gave under her weight. Surprised, she stumbled and nearly fell inside. Adsila, equally surprised, grabbed the girl, and pulled her back from a humiliating disaster. Slightly shaken, it took a moment for the pair to recover.

Adsila stepped closer and ran practiced fingers along the torn seam, not sure of what to expect. "The pieces are sewn together," she said, "but this one gave out."

Bright Moon nodded. "My guess is that it was put together like all the other pieces." She looked at Adsila for understanding, but found her friend still puzzled so she added, "Wikvaya said the air around his craft was warm. I think the seams are too loose the warm air leaks out through them."

Adsila's face lit up. "It was as if he tried to fill a water bag full of holes."

Bright Moon nodded and tugged on another seam.

It came apart in her hands. "Here's another one; I think we'll find most of them are like this." Not satisfied, she pulled the loose flap further back. Inside the vessels' cavernous body she discovered large supporting timbers. "Lord Wikvaya built *Travels-the-air-with-the-birds* like a great council house."

Lady Adsila frowned. "This is bad?" She questioned.

Bright Moon shrugged. "In the spring, the little yellow flowers that grow in the meadow ripen and shed their thistledown. These float on the slightest breeze and travel far. A council house can sit through a stiff wind and not move." She paused and looked at Adsila, hoping her words would not offend their friend, Wikvaya. "To float through the air, I think *Travels-the-air-with-the-birds* needs to be less like a council house and more like thistledown."

Adsila silently looked inside the vessel while she considered Bright Moon's words. In spite of the gloom, she could see the heavy timbers that supported the ship's coverings. She could also see light shining through many of the seams. After long moments, she broke the silence by saying, "What are you going to do to fix this?"

Relieved, Bright Moon said, "We will have to take the vessel apart. If we had the time to weave enough mats, I would replace all the hides. Not having much time, the hides will have to be overlapped and sealed with pitch[75] or pine sap before they are sown. The heavy frame will have to be replaced with a lighter one. "Adsila looked the vessel up and down, pursed her lips, and finally said, "Tell me what you need done. I can get the villagers to help."

"Night and day, Lady Adsila and I worked on making changes to *Travels-the-air-with-the-birds,* "Bright Moon said. " We are ready for you to test it." Flywhisks[76]

---

75 A resin derived from the sap of various coniferous trees such as the pines
76 A flexible bunch of twigs, feathers, or straw, attached to a handle for use as a tool to swat or disturb flies or other insects.

in hand, their defense against the droves of gnats and flies that filled the summer air, she and Lady Adsila stood with Wikvaya atop the ovens' platform while he inspected their work.

Wikvaya eyed the vessel suspiciously. It looked about the same length and height, but there were many changes. Most of the animal hides were gone, replaced by a new skin. The muted browns the vessel once had were now a patchwork of colors. The heavier scaffolding was gone, replaced by a much lighter frame. A long, curved limb ending in a bird's head decorated the front of the vessel. What else had she done? And why?

Bright Moon didn't give him time to ask questions. "To keep it in the air, the vessel will carry its own fires. Lady Adsila had the people melt animal fat and make oil," Bright Moon explained. "It's stored in the jars suspended over the fire baskets. The oil is allowed to drip down and keep the fire alive; in addition to keeping the vessel in the air, the heat of the fire will keep the fat melted."

Wikvaya bent low to inspect the arrangement. "Why are there sticks with colored bands in the top of each jar?"

"They'll tell how much oil you have in a jar without opening it," Adsila said. "The oil-jars in our household each hold a wood block that floats on top of the oil. The stick is attached to the block inside the jar. As the oil is used, the level goes down and the block and stick lower. The length of the stick and the color showing tells how much oil is left."

"I see," he said. "A long stick showing means the jar is full while a short stick means you're almost out."

Adsila turned to Bright Moon and smiled. "See, I told you he'd understand if we could put it simply enough." The girls burst into hysterical laughter and it took a short time for them to settle down again.

Wikvaya did not join in their laughter. "What other changes did you make?" He asked cooly.

"I ask the people to bring their extra mats and lay them out here," Bright Moon explained. "Lady Adsila was unsure about my plan but she was very helpful in getting everything done." Always gracious, Adsila nodded in her acceptance of the recognition.

Bright Moon turned back to the vessel. "To help lighten it, I had the heavy scaffolding replaced. Now, one ridgepole runs along the top, one along the middle, and one along the bottom. Short ribs are attached to the top and bottom, wider ones to the middle pole Ropes run between the levels."

Wikvaya gave her a quizzical look.

"*Travels-the-air-with-the-birds* needs a pocket to hold the warm air," Bright Moon proudly defended her decision. "This was the lightest way I could think of to hold the sides out. The frame holding each fire basket straddles the lower support just inside the vessel's skin. Oil-jars are suspended from the pole that runs along the middle, over the fire baskets."

He looked at her and nodded for her to continue, but said nothing.

Happy that he did not object, Bright Moon resumed. "The mats were stitched together and sealed with pine sap to plug leaks while the areas closest to the fire-baskets were given a light coating of mud."

"Why use both sap and mud?" Wikvaya asked. Hand on his chin; he looked the vessel over closely while she continued.

"The mud protects the skin from the fire. The pine sap seals the seams stopping the leaks and protects the fire from the rain," Bright Moon answered smugly.

Wikvaya shook his head in disbelief. The women had given this much thought. "What else have you done?"

"Because the ship I found had a totem[77], I had Antinanco, your scribe, carve something from the stories

---

77 A being, object, or symbol representing an animal or plant that serves as an emblem of a group of people, such as a family, clan, group, lineage, or tribe, reminding them of their ancestry (or mythic past).

of your people. Its long curved neck and bird-head will make it at home in the sky. The sails, like those on your ship, will help move the vessel," Bright Moon explained.

Quietly, Wikvaya stood back and looked at her creation. Sitting on top of these mud ovens, it lay like a tree downed in a storm. Impaled on chimneys that he hoped would provide it the ability to take to the air. Midway, a mast, complete with the trappings of a folded sail, rose skyward.

"What else have you done?"

"I had a chair-seat and a net added to the framework."

"What's the net for?" Wikvaya asked.

"I didn't know what you might want to carry for the test. I thought this would be light and flexible."

"Interesting changes," Wikvaya said. "I would like to see if they make a difference."

"The men have been stoking the fires so it should be ready for you to try."

Wikvaya strolled alongside the vessel, stopping periodically to hold his hand near its surface. Satisfied there were no leaks, he moved on to another spot and performed the same exercise. The two ladies trailed behind casually swinging their flywhisks as they chatted.

A bug landed on the side of the vessel. Aggravated by these insects, Bright Moon uttered a sharp word and used a quick snap of her wrist to eliminate at least one of her tormentors. The whisk connected to the side of the vessel with a dull thump. The vessel slowly lifted off, an arm's length at first, and then it rose smoothly and faster.

Bright Moon shrieked and clapped her hands in the air as she realized their success was greater than expected. Adsila hopped up and down excitedly. Wikvaya, fearing that it might fly off, seized a line dangling from the rising craft. There he clung while the vessel kept going up, jarring to a stop when it reached the lengths of its tethers.

On the ground, the men stopped stoking the fires and stared, awestruck. Later, they would tell others *the*

Great Shaman cast a spell and touched the vessel with her wand. It caused the ship to rise up so fast that not even Lord Wikvaya could stop it.

"Rest," Wikvaya commanded. "The current is too strong; no matter how hard we paddle, we'll never get the dugout through the canyon."

Bright Moon glanced over her shoulder. Wikvaya sat in the stern, his paddle resting across his lap. The results of his efforts could be read on his face. "If we can't go any further up river, we'll never find where the water is coming from," she panted, no stranger to the same effort.

"We just passed a spot where we could land," Wikvaya volunteered. "If we drift back, we could go ashore there, pull the dugout out, and hide it in the brush. We'll have to go on foot from there."

Breathless, covered in sweat from the exertion, she was happy to hear about the change in plans and didn't object. He dipped his paddle in the water. A few strokes, the bow came around, and they now pointed downstream. Carried by the current, the boat picked up speed only requiring a few guiding strokes to keep it on course.

Wikvaya looked around. Treetops barely peeked above the surface. "I was surprised when I saw the place where Askook met Long Tusk was almost completely under water," he commented as if measuring the rise in water for the first time. "This looks even deeper."

"Yes," Bright Moon said. "We are two days upstream from there and the river has become broader and deeper. Our village sits on a hilltop, but, if the water continues to rise, Lady Adsila won't be safe there."

Wikvaya nodded. "If there is only a little more, Lady Adsila and the village will be safe. If there's a lot, we'll have to pack up and move. Without finding the source of the water, I can't tell how big a threat we face." For a moment, his concern showed and then, like a rabbit, it darted into hiding again. "There's a landing spot," he said and began paddling toward it.

Bright Moon joined him in the effort. It would be good to get off the river and out of the cramped dugout where she could stretch her legs. They would continue their trek on foot, hoping to find the problem, and, more importantly, a solution. Wikvaya kept the canoe pointed toward shore and they continued to paddle until she heard the satisfying crunch of bow meeting gravel.

"Let's unload, and then we'll pull the dugout into those bushes, "Wikvaya directed. Stepping out of the boat, the pair splashed through the cold water to the riverbank.

Stiff from her confined quarter, she began working the cramps out of her legs. Impatient, Wikvaya tugged at the vessel's bow. Bright Moon let him struggle for a moment before joining in the effort. With it in place, Wikvaya made sure the brush hid it entirely, while Bright Moon used a cluster of branches to sweep away their tracks.

They met back at their equipment and examined the results of their efforts. "I'll carry the packs," Wikvaya said, picking up their gear. "You follow and wipe away any sign we were here."

"Are you expecting trouble?"

He shrugged. "I'm not inviting trouble." He turned and led the way up a trail and into the brush. Walking backwards toward the trail, she bent to the task of eliminating their tracks.

"The sun will be setting soon," Wikvaya said. "We should find a place to camp for the night."

"I can see a thicket on the other side of this beaver pond and it looks promising," Bright Moon said. "It should provide cover and shelter for the night. "

"Good. We are close to the Great Ice, and I don't want to stray too far away."

It proved more than promising. Three trees lay victims of the beavers. Selecting a nearby knoll, he used the tree trunks and branches to construct their shelter.

"Will the beavers bother us here?" Wikvaya asked.

"They believe we could be dangerous. Hear them slap their tails on the water? I doubt they'll come near," she replied nonchalantly. Having gathered firewood, she set about making a small campfire while Wikvaya finished the shelter.

The sun had set, and a chill wind blew lightly from the Great Ice. Their pitiful fire did little to chase away the cold. She wrapped up in her sleep-robe for protection. He held a piece of pemmican out to her, and she slipped a hand from under the robe's warmth to accept it.

"How long have you and Lady Adsila been mated?" Bright Moon asked.

Wikvaya snorted, almost choking on a bite of pemmican. "What makes you think we're mated?"

"I see the way you look at each other. I see how she looks when she talks about you. How long have you been mated?"

"All our lives, our families made the arrangements shortly after our birth. We grew up knowing this. It's our tradition."

"You're mated and have fathered children?"

"Yes, she and I have two girls and a boy.

"She is your only one... your only wife?"

"Oh no, she would never do that. All of her handmaidens are my wives."

"All of her handmaidens!" Bright Moon was amazed. She tried to remember how many there were. "All are your wives? Why do you have so many?"

"Well," he said. "With the children, more help is needed."

"She needs that many handmaidens to help raise three children?"

"Oh no, not just three," Wikvaya explained. "Her handmaidens and I have children together."

"So as more children came along, you found another wife? How does that help?"

"No, you've got it wrong. Lady Adsila makes the arrangements. Finding another woman that would fit into the household is not a task for a man."

"Where do these women come from?"

"Some were widows or orphans. Some are daughters of chiefs and the marriage binds our peoples together. Others were interesting or would add to the family's skills. The household discusses the new person, and, if everyone agrees that she is found acceptable, an offer is made. The woman can choose to accept or reject the offer."

"Who decides if the household is in agreement?"

"I understand that each household member is given two pebbles, one black and one white. These are used to cast a vote, in private, by dropping a stone in a jar. If any black stones are found, it means that someone in the household is not happy and the offer is not made."

"Why would they want to add more women to the household?"

"It lets them share the work, and the children will provide for us when we are old and cannot fend for ourselves."

"You had nothing to do with it?"

"Me? No, I know nothing of how a woman thinks. Lady Adsila runs the household... makes all the arrangements," he said. He leaned across the fire so she could look into his eyes and read the truth he spoke. "I have other things to do. With so many mouths to feed and bodies to clothe, I must fish and hunt... and keep everyone happy."

"She makes *all* the arrangements because she runs the household."

"Yes, that's right." Wikvaya beamed. Bright Moon understood his explanation. They were making progress. "That's why Lady Adsila asked me to bring you on this trip.

Her jaw dropped and she became speechless. What? She asked you to bring me on this trip?"

Wikvaya shook his head. "It wasn't my idea, but she can be very persuasive. She and her handmaidens have accepted you. They are the ones who wove the tunic you now wear... it's up to you now."

Bright Moon stroked her clothes, the layers of soft fabric under her fingers, her fur-lined buckskin vest, the other garments in her bag, all provided by the diligent hands of Lady Adsila and her handmaidens. An ember popped, bringing her out of her reverie. "You're expecting to take me as a mate on this trip?"

He held his hands up defensively. "I don't expect anything. Lady Adsila and her handmaidens, on the other hand, do. The rest is up to you... it's your choice, not mine."

Bright Moon's head spun. She should have kept her mouth shut and avoided this discussion. If only she had the sense to have asked fewer questions... but she didn't. Her head buzzed with everything she had learned. Wikvaya confirmed that he and Adsila are mated, have been mated all their lives and have children together. That Wikvaya is also mated to each of Adsila's handmaidens and they also have had children with Wikvaya. Even more, the household voted and had accepted Bright Moon as a new member. She could choose to accept or not. She had answers to her questions and more, but it just added to her confusion. Finally, she decided it would be best to change the subject.

"Now that your great machine flies, why didn't we use it to get here?" Bright Moon asked.

Wikvaya smiled at the girl's innocent enthusiasm. "Thanks to your changes, the machine took to the air," he said, "but there's a difference between getting into the air and being able to control where you're going. That's going to take more work." He stoked the fire, playing with the coals while he thought. "Before that happens, I need to find out about the river."

"What do you think we'll find when we get to the Great Ice?" Bright Moon asked.

"The source of the river," Wikvaya said. "When we find the source, we'll find out how big a threat we face."

"I don't understand what you're looking for. The river level has always risen and fallen. How will you know when you've found the cause?"

"You were right when you told Lady Adsila that it shouldn't be like this at the start of the dry season. It rises after the rains, yes; but, it hasn't rained, and it still rises. The question is why?" Wikvaya said. "When I find the source, I'll find the answer I seek."

She had no answer for that, and certainly not for Lady Adsila. She didn't even want to think about Wikvaya's vessel, *Travels-the-air-with-the-birds*.

Wikvaya, on his belly at the canyon's rim, peered over the edge. He lay there for some time before turning and motioning to Bright Moon. "Crawl forward and join me."

Leaving their gear behind, Bright Moon lay down and snaked her way to the edge next to him. Hand over the canyon lip, he pointed down. "Look at the river and tell me what you see," he said.

A dizzying distance below, the turbulent river bounced white foam-covered waves around. "I see nothing unusual," she said.

"Look carefully," Wikvaya commanded, "tell me everything you see."

"There's water, it is moving fast," she said.

"Yes and how can you tell?"

"White foam on the waves show the water is moving fast." Bright Moon was puzzled. Something in the water held his attention, but she was at a loss to see what he saw.

215

"Look closer. What do you see?"

She stared at the rushing water. Foam tickled the top of most waves, but in the troughs between the white-tipped crests, something else was carried along. "Ice," she said. "The river carries pieces of ice, and it's not early spring."

"That's right," Wikvaya said. "Now the question is why?" He pulled back from the edge. "That's what we're here to find out." He withdrew and motioned for her to follow.

Chapter 24: Ice

"The canyon walls are close together here," Wikvaya pointed out. "On flat land, a man could easily walk the distance between the two sides in less than a day."

Bright Moon shivered in the cool air while she leaned on her walking stick and listened to Wikvaya drone on about the obvious. From where she stood, she could look down into the canyon or up at the towering face of the Great Ice. "I see the mounds of ice covering the distance between the two walls," she said. "Streams of water, large and small, flow from its face." She shrugged. "Askook's meeting place looked like this."

"That's true, it did, but his meeting place was smaller than this. Because we are higher, this place is normally cooler, even at this time of year. Look down there along the base," Wikvaya said. "The large knolls there show that the Great Ice is melting, shedding its face the whole length. "

"Is that what's making the river high?"

"That and the water you see flowing outward will certainly add to the level, but it might be better to ask how high will the river get?" He paused, thinking about what he was seeing. "The answer depends on how much water the Great Ice holds. We'll have to go there and find out. I'd like to camp at the top, near the ice field, before dark."

Bright Moon nodded, picked up her pack, and slung it over her shoulder. Wikvaya turned and led the way.

###

Long Tusk called his caravan to a halt just short of Chochmo's stockade. Without fail, Kaliska had led them to this spot. Hidden off the beaten track, this was not an easy task but his scout had not let him down. Now, in one long sweeping gaze, the caravan master was able to take in the entire village beyond. He found it appeared as dirty and unkempt as the tribe that occupied it.

Tucked in a cleft near the bottom of the canyon, its location offered security, but little more. Snowmelt dripped from above, or seeped from fractures in the surrounding rock, leaving the ground constantly wet and muddy.

Outside the stockade, gravel and rocks mixed with the mud spread out like a fan. It formed a small plain that tilted gently down to the marshes along the river. Insects were everywhere, biting, crawling, or just plain aggravating. It was no wonder Chochmo's people covered themselves in mud.

Huts huddled around the outside of the stockade. Apparently, Long Tusk mused, Chochmo's people were divided into at least two groups: Those who lived inside the protection of the stockade and those who lived outside and had to depend on a few poles with bramble bushes laced between for their security.

Being inside the stockade offered protection, but little else. Inside or out, small, low, huts crowded together. Men, women, children, their bodies decorated with colorful mud designs, came out of their huts to peer at the strangers. Old animal hides, broken tools, bones not quite scraped clean, and other remains remained where they were discarded. Camp dogs lay around or dug in the refuse. Naked children wrestled, chased each other, and played in the mud.

Not many outsiders had been granted entrance to the village and few were ever allowed to leave. Long Tusk's caravan was met by a group, at least two-hands worth, of

Chochmo's armed warriors.

"Long Tusk my friend," bellowed Chochmo from their midst. "You have arrived. Are you ready to trade?"

"Yes, I have brought many women to trade for horses." Long Tusk smiled broadly in anticipation.

"Good. Have your people camp there on the plain. Come, I will show you the horses. They will not disappoint you."

"And my selection of women will not disappoint you," Long Tusk replied with a hearty laugh.

Mouth open, Chochmo showed his rotten teeth—those left—as he laughed. "We will trade and then we'll have good food and celebrate into the night." He wrapped a dirty hand around Long Tusk's shoulders in a sign of camaraderie.

Stopping suddenly, Wikvaya held an arm out. Bright Moon halted and looked around. She was prepared to run or fight as needed. Birds sang as they flitted from tree-to-tree. Branches waved in the crisp breeze. All appeared normal to her. In the lead, did he see something she did not?

With the crook of a finger, Wikvaya motioned her forward. When she reached his side, he parted branches of the bush in front of him and pointed toward the glacier wall across the rocky clearing. "See the place where the ice cuts across the ridge?" he asked.

"Yes, there are many ridges like this nearby," Bright Moon replied.

"True and at each the Great Ice shed its skin," Wikvaya said. "But, this one is different. Near where that large tree fell, the ridge zigzagged[78] away and the ice

---

78 To change course abruptly; to move in one of two directions, for

buckled up, leaving a cave amid the rubble."

"What does that mean?" Bright Moon asked.

"If it's not occupied by man or beast, this place could shelter us for a few nights," Wikvaya said. "You stay here and act as lookout," he instructed. "I will circle around and approach it from a different direction in case there is someone or something there. Watch to see what happens and decide whether you should hide or come to my aid."

Bright Moon nodded and he slipped away through the brush. Wikvaya wanted to play protector. That was okay with her. She could lean on her walking stick and rest. She knew he wouldn't find anything. From where she stood among the scrub pine and Aspen, she could see the thin layer of snow that lay in front of the cave's mouth was fresh and unbroken. Nothing had gone in or out but it was an opportunity for him to play the role and she was none the worse.

After what seemed like a long time, she saw Wikvaya came out of the trees at the other end of the clearing and crept through the brush toward the opening. Reaching it, he bent low and peered inside before crawling in on all fours. When he came back out, Wikvaya waved to her, and she joined him.

"It is empty and shows no sign of being occupied. The inside is not big and it won't take much to hollow a space large enough to hold the two of us and our belongings," he told her. "Come, take a look."

On all fours, she followed him inside. Beyond the low entry, the cave made a sharp left turn before emptying into a low-ceilinged, icicle-clad room. At some previous time, a tall pine was pushed over by the approaching glacier. It fell across the ridge creating a

---

example to move left then abruptly change to moving right; to follow in a zigzag course: First we zigged, and then we zagged, trying to avoid the bull.

pocket that remained locked in the glacier's icy grip.

Even after clearing out the icicles that hung like stalactites from the ceiling, it did not provide enough room to stand. Tree branches, frozen in the snow, poked down from above. The back of the cave angled up to a dark place where light from the opening did not flow. Bright Moon stuck two fingers in her mouth, pulled them out, and held them up.

"What are you doing?" Wikvaya scowled as he watched her. Had the girl lost her senses? Was this some kind of superstition? With her, he was never sure.

"Do this," Bright Moon commanded, and licking a finger, she held it up.

Wikvaya looked at her with curiosity but followed her example.

"What do you think?" She asked.

"About what?"

"Which side of your finger dried first?"

"I don't understand. Why does it matter?" Wikvaya looked pensive.

"It will tell us if there is a draft for a fire so we won't choke on the smoke," she explained. "It will also tell us if there is another way out."

He shrugged. "I understand the smoke, but why would we need another way out?"

"My father told me that when the fox is at the door, the rabbit needs another way to escape," she said.

He nodded and wet his finger again. "That way!" he shouted, pointing toward the darkness. "A draft comes from that way. What's there may give us a chance to escape if we are surprised."

She smiled at his sudden recognition of the threat as well as the solution. "Let's gather some firewood and then we can start a small campfire. I can use a brand from it to explore what lies back there in the dark while you cut some boughs for our bed."

Wikvaya nodded. "It's still early so if we're quick with these tasks, we can venture out on the ice today and look around." They had a place to stay and a plan. He was happy.

"There, this should hold us for the night." Wikvaya handed the last bundle of boughs into Bright Moon. She spread them over the layers already on the floor and tested the results, finding it satisfactory.

"It's fortunate you located this cave in the Great Ice," she said, "and it didn't take long to get it ready."

"The sun is still high enough to light our way," Wikvaya said. "Leave your pack and grab some rope. I want to go out onto the ice and take a look around."

Outside, Wikvaya fastened a loop at both ends of the rope. He wore one and put the other around Bright Moon. "We shouldn't walk next to each other in case of weak spots," he said. "Take the lead and use your stick to check the path in front of you to make sure it's solid."

"I should take the lead?" Bright Moon asked, raising her eyebrows. "I've already been in a hole at the bottom of the ice and have no interest in revisiting that place."

"It's good we agreed," Wikvaya said. "And, I think we'll also agree that I'll have a better chance of pulling you out than you would of getting me out."

Begrudgingly, she turned and started across the ice. He was right. She hated to admit it, but he was right.

In the distance, there was a low rumble, like distant thunder and the wind began to pick up. "It sounds like a storm's coming," Bright Moon said. "Perhaps we should go back before it hits."

"I hear it too, but the clouds don't look too threatening, and I would like to see what is making that noise," Wikvaya said. "It may be the answer we seek."

Their path was anything but smooth. Fissures split the surface and radiated outward from icy mounds pushed up by the shifting glacier. Cautiously, they zigzagged around these dangers, often backtracking when they reached places where their probes found weak spots. The booming thunder grew louder, the reverberation carried to them on gale-force winds. A gray, icy-snow swirled through the air engulfing them, at times making it impossible to see each other. Wikvaya did not want to turn back because he knew they were close and going the right way. Not only was the sound louder, but, beneath their feet, the ice shuddered rhythmically in tune with each peal of thunder. Though the visibility continued to drop, he was not willing to give up. Not just yet.

They were not alone, but were unaware of that fact. From a distance, Hevataneo[79] peered out from under long, matted hair. He had spotted them lying on the ground peering over the canyon's rim. He continued to watch the pair's movements with animal-cunning. Furtively, he dodged from bush to tree, making use of any piece of cover as he followed them up the canyon to the glacier. From a hidden place, he watched the couple prepare their snow cave for, at least, an overnight stay. Then, he followed as the pair wrapped themselves in ropes and ventured, single file, out onto the ice. They would be gone for a while. It should be safe to check out what was left behind in their den before he reported to Chochmo. He knew he would get a reward. Perhaps it would be the girl. She would be his first... his first outside his own family-group, that is.

---

79 Native American Cheyenne name meaning "hairy rope."

###

The thunderous rumble, punctuated by a staccato pounding, echoed in her head and shook the ice under her feet. The air was filled with ice crystals frozen by the wind. There was no escaping it. A biting, bitter force, it was in her face and seemed to blow colder with each step. In the lead, Bright Moon held up an arm, a temporary shield from the wind-driven snow, and took a bead on a peak beyond the ridge in front of her. She pulled her cloak tight to her body hoping for protection against the cold. It did not help, but she said nothing. This was the trip she wanted. Over Wikvaya's objections, she had asked, even begged, to join this trek, and, over his objections she got her way. Now, being a member, she recognized that she could not complain, no matter how harsh the environment, how abrasive the task.

Since the snow didn't allow her to see further, she focused on what was immediately in front of her, concentrating on each handhold while she climbed up and over yet another crest. Wikvaya kept the rope connecting them slack to allow her free movement. At the top, she rolled over on her belly and rappelled down the opposite side, landing on a flat shelf.

Turning around, she stared out through the swirling snow, hypnotized by the sight of the largest sea she had ever come upon. Mouth agape, cold and snow momentarily forgotten, she was amazed to see open water stretching left, right, and in front of her as far as she could see.

The ledge where she landed was less than a man's height above the water. Surf-like white tipped waves jostled ice cakes against each other or sent them crashing into its base. The landing was continually doused with spray. Towering over her, stood the peak she had used as a landmark. It was the highest point of a giant island of ice, large enough to have easily held Wikvaya's whole village. Driven by the wind, it wallowed in the water in front of her, bumping, grinding, and shaking the shelf under her feet each time it struck. More islands, similar to the one she faced, were emerging from the shadowy snows.

"I think we've found the source of our thunder," Wikvaya said. "There seems to be no end to these floating ice islands... or to the water that carries them."

Startled, she turned and saw him straddling the crest, hand shading his eyes as he peered into the distance.

"How deep do you think it is?" Bright Moon asked.

"There's only one way to find out," There was an ominous tone in his voice. She waited while he clambered down the slope.

Wikvaya bent his head close to hers so he could be heard above the wind. "Follow me over here and we can get started."

She had left her pack in the cave as he had asked and only carried rope. Always in the lead, she hadn't noticed that he carried a parfleche at his side. What did he bring along?

Bent against the wind, she joined him. He crouched down and spilled the contents of his bag on the snow. A rock the size of a ripe melon caught her eye. He had probably picked it up outside their cave, but why would he carry such a thing all this way?

"Untie the rope at your waist," he said, his open hand, extended, waiting to be filled.

She untied her cloak and then unwound the rope around her waist. A difficult chore in the wind. "Here," she shouted as she held out the rope.

He took it from her without looking up. "Now, stretch the line out in rows along here and make sure it's not tangled," he said, making motions with his hands.

He watched as she bent to the task, then, with a

couple of quick movements, he tied the rope around the rock, cradling it tightly in the rope's confines. Standing, he put a foot on the rock and tugged at the tether. The two items remained attached. Wikvaya smiled confidently, pleased with his success.

"Now, to see if we can answer our questions," he said. After securing the rope's free end around his waist, he stepped closer to the edge and dropped the rock.

Untouched by floating islands, left intact by the wind, a flat sheet of ice covered the water. The rock hit the ice sheet and bounced before sliding over the edge into the water. Its entry was greeted with a splash, and it sank out of sight. The safety-line, laid out in orderly paths, followed the rock over the edge with efficient precision, halting its downward motion when it became taut. The water was deep here. The rock had not hit bottom, it just ran out of rope.

Wikvaya made an unintelligible grunt that Bright Moon could only interpret as dismal. Next to them, the iceberg joined in the grumbling as wave action ground it against the shelf, shaking the ice under their feet.

Squatting near the shelf's lip, Wikvaya watched the rope sink still further. "It's still not reached the bottom," he muttered as he stood up and back away. "Give me a hand pulling the line back in," he requested, "and we'll test the depth at another location."

Snow, thick, wet, wind-driven, cut their visibility even more. Together, they brought the sounding weight[80] up, laying out the line as they did. When it cleared, Wikvaya scooped up the rock and an armful of wet rope, nodding toward another spot. Bright Moon grabbed the rest of the rope, an uncomfortable armful, and followed him.

The new spot, closer to the iceberg, let them lie

---

80 A heavy weight tied to a rope and thrown overboard to determine water depth

down and peer over the edge. The waves rolled in to slam against the base covering them with spray. They watched the rock disappear below the surface. The wet snow and mist made the shelf treacherously slick. The rope played out its full length and, as before, would have gone further if it were longer. Getting to their knees, Wikvaya and Bright Moon began retrieving the rock.

Nearby, the iceberg ground into the shelf, shaking their platform before it wallowed away. Wikvaya, hands on his haunches, scanned the mountain of ice while Bright Moon laid the line out along the edge of the shelf to avoid tangling.

The iceberg lurched forward, jarring itself into the shelf. Bright Moon, staggering under the impact. Her feet went out from under her and she landed on her back. Arms flailing, she turned over and searched for some solid hold on the slick surface.

Recoiling, the iceberg drifted back. Weakened, the shelf began to tip downward. With the arrival of the next series of waves, the mountain of ice reversed direction and rammed into the shelf again. With this attack, the shelf cracked and began crumbling under Bright Moon. The iceberg drifted back away letting the shelf tip downward. Bright Moon, unable to secure a grip, slid over the edge.

Wikvaya saw her hit the water along with the broken remains of the shelf. "No!" He shouted, but it was no use. Driven by wind and waves, the iceberg pushed forward again, toward the ledge. It bore down on the place where Bright Moon had gone in, crushing everything in its path.

Chapter 25: Chochmo's Discipline

Chochmo led Long Tusk and his clan leaders to the place of honor: An ornately carved set of benches, centered on an elevated stone platform overlooking the rim of a gorge. The platform bridged a shallow creek, hardly more than a trickle, its waters crept lazily along until they slipped over the edge and disappeared into the black depths below. Members of the two tribes followed this assembly of dignitaries.

Kaliska pushed through the crowd to stand next to Long Tusk. The scout could not see the bottom of the pit, but he could hear something moving around in the dark. A sinister sound—perhaps water hitting water, echoed off rock walls—rose from the darkness, sending a chill up his spine.

Since their arrival at the village, Chochmo made every effort to see that his guests' drinking gourds were filled with chicha. No doubt, this was part of a plan to take advantage of them.

Their trip—single file, over rocky ground, up a narrow, twisting path, to the top of the mesa[81]—only seemed like a long trek. It was not long enough. Kaliska had hoped the effort and the cool evening air would work to sober up the caravan leader, but it didn't appear to do much good. On the other hand, trickery could go both ways. Long Tusk being familiar with Chochmo, and a skilled bargainer himself, would have a few tricks of his own up his sleeve.

---

81 Term used to describe an elevated area of land with a flat top and sides that are usually steep cliffs. It takes its name from its characteristic table-top shape

The servants began lighting torches near the rim but the flickering lights did little to push back the growing darkness. The fissure was a murky gash zigzagging across the mesa before disappearing into the darkness. For reasons not yet clear, a wall—hewn stones plastered together with cob[82] or adobe[83]--blocked the near end. Similarly, carved stones lined the rim's edge and stuck out into the darkness. A double row of sharpened stakes had been forced into the wall below the rim and were set to point downward. Whatever was down there, Chochmo definitely did not want it to get out.

The torchbearers made their way over a footbridge, built on top of the rock wall, to light torches on the other side. They'd done this without instruction. To Kaliska, it meant that it was a well-practiced ritual. This thought did not bring him comfort.

"This must be a special place for Chochmo and his people," Kaliska whispered to his leader.

"Eh? What makes you say that?" Though it took some effort, Long Tusk looked around. Impaired by the chicha, he was experiencing difficulties with his ability to focus his mind or his eyes.

"Look around. What do you see here? Both sides of the rift are covered with long, wavy grasses and a smattering of scrub trees, misshapen by the wind." Disgusted, Kaliska bent close to ensure his grating whisper carried the tone of the message he spat out. "This is not exactly the place you or I would come unless it held some special meaning."

Brow furrowed, Long Tusk squinted, as if by concentration he could extract some sense from his scout's words. He could not. "Why not?" he asked.

---

82 A building material consisting of clay, sand, straw, water, and earth, similar to adobe.

83 A natural building material made from sand, clay, water, and some kind of fibrous or organic material (sticks, straw, and/or manure), which the builders shape into bricks (using frames) and dry in the sun. Adobe buildings are similar to cob and mud brick buildings.

Kaliska straightened up and surveyed the area. There was no use in pursuing the matter. Until the effects of the chichi wore off and Long Tusk has something to eat, he would be useless. That couldn't happen soon enough. Until then, there was no use trying.

Another platform—functional, not ornate—decorated the rim directly across from them. Two tree trunks, riding on the corner-posts of the platform, extended their arms over the pit's darken maw, boom[84] fashion.

Kaliska had seen this type of mechanism before. An ingenious arrangement usually made using two trees, one for the base, and one for the derrick[85] tower. A limb, fastened horizontally near the top, acts as a boom. This arrangement is used to raise, lower, or move heavy objects. What use would they have for one here?

Kaliska's musings were interrupted by Chochmo's smelly, mud-caked, vermin-riddled people as they began to noisily push and shove their way into the best position on either side of the gorge.

"More drink!" Chochmo shouted over the din waving his drinking horn wildly in Long Tusk's direction. "Eat more. Drink more. Enjoy," he commanded.

Eat? Kaliska's stomach churned at the thought of what these people considered delicacies. Earlier, he saw stick-bearing youngsters stir refuse piles and club anything that ran or slithered out.

---

84 A long pole, extending outward from the mast of a derrick and used to support, or guide, objects being lifted or suspended.

85 A derrick is a lifting device with three major parts: a stationary vertical base topped with a moveable tower equipped with a boom arm which runs perpendicular to the derrick tower. The base is used to keep the tower from falling over. The tower sits on the base and can be rotated freely. The tower's movement may be controlled by arms or by lines powered by some means such as man-hauling, so that the tower can move in all directions. A line, with a hook or a loop on the end, runs up the tower out the boom arm.. Like a crane, it is commonly used to lift, suspend, or lower heavy objects.

Rat bodies roasting over an open fire appeared to be the best of the offerings, but were not his choice of fine fare. He knew it could be worse. When the opportunity presented itself, Chochmo's people were known to be cannibals, making a meal of any stranger not enslaved. None of this was to Kaliska's liking. Long Tusk, on the other hand, smiled diplomatically, and dug into whatever was offered—roasted rat or snake—washing it down with ample gulps of chicha. Chochmo, after all, was an ally—his only ally—willing to join with him, and Long Tusk could not afford to upset the man, no matter the cost.

The moon edged over the horizon. Kaliska entertained thoughts of slipping away to the river to try his hand at hunting waterfowl or night fishing. With luck, he could catch one or two and have them roasting over a campfire of his own, away from this mangy crowd. A commotion, near the platform on the other side of the pit, disturbed his reverie.

Three guards led a procession. The first half-led, half-dragged a woman, one of Chochmo's people, behind him. The other two led a string of women bound to a line. More guards followed them, prodding those that were too slow. Until earlier in the day, these women had been Long Tusk's captives. Now they were Chochmo's possessions. With the group's arrival, the crowd became even noisier.

"Ah, our entertainment has arrived," Chochmo roared with enthusiasm.

The procession stopped at the platform across from him. The guards selected two of the captives and forced the rest to kneel near the rim.

Amid chanting and jeering from the crowd, the booms, which had been swung out over the pit, were now rotated to bring the tips over the stage. On each shaft, a rope ran from the base up along the derrick, and then the length of the boom to pass through a hole near the tip where it dangled freely. Released from the tether, the two captives were tied to these lines, hoisted into the air, and swung out over the pit.

Chochmo rose, holding his hands up for silence. The din died out. Chochmo signaled four torchbearers stationed around the rim. One-by-one, they dropped their lights into the pit, illuminating its floor. It appeared to be empty. That impression did not last long. Out of the shadows, along the edges, slunk a sabertooth tiger. One… two… three… others followed. A cheer went up from the crowd.

The third woman, the one from Chochmo's tribe, acknowledging her fate, collapsed in a heap, sobbing softly. A rope was passed from one side of the pit to the other and through the ropes that bound the cringing woman's hands. Several men took up each end of the rope and the woman was pushed, screaming, off the stand to dangle in the air over the pit. Kaliska's stomach tightened into a knot. Now, it was clear to him what Chochmo's people kept in the pit and why the pointed stakes had been pounded into the walls.

From their positions, at the rim or dangling at the end of the derrick, the captives watched, wide-eyed, as the men on the rope baited the animals by lowering and quickly raising the woman. Seeing prey dancing just out of their reach, the tigers roared, bared their claws, and leaped into the air. Sometimes, the woman felt the power of their slap as the animals struck, breaking skin and opening wounds. The big cats charged at their prey, snarling in frustration each time they failed to reach her. The crowds, drunk with anticipation, escalated their noisy merriment, singing and dancing around the rim.

Someone fell. If he was a victim of being pushed or if he—*a victim of his own clumsiness*—tripped Kaliska did not know. The capstone lining the edge gave way when the man went over. It took out nearby stakes in its noisy descent, drawing the animals' attention to this new opportunity.

Arms thrashing, the man slid down the rough sides before he managed to get a firm hold. The tigers, quick to respond, crossed the pit and leaped at this new prospect. Long claws struck the rock wall between his legs. With efforts driven by desperation, the man dug toes and fingers into the hard, rough surface as he scampered higher. A low moan of disappointment arose from the crowd while he continued to climb out of danger. Nearing the top, he was met by a wall of feet. Lined up around the rim, the crowd hindered his way. Both he and the crowd looked to Chochmo for direction.

Standing, their leader approached the edge of the platform, stopping a safe distance back to peer over the rim at the pacing animals. He raised one hand in front of him, palm-edge down, and scanned the waiting crowd, silent until he suddenly turned his hand palm down, making a pushing motion. A cheer went up and the crowd began pelting the victim with rocks and sticks. The man clung to the side as long as he could before giving up. The tigers were on him as he hit the ground. He offered no fight.

The mob, expecting more of a show, quieted. A black mood of disappointment fell over them. Those holding the rope, no longer interested in their game, let it go. The woman fell. The mob, having already lost interest, began to disperse before the sound of her screams reached those left at the top.

Still suspended from the derricks, the captive women could have looked down and witnessed the carnage but were unable to force themselves to do so—hearing was more than enough. They suppressed sobs least they draw attention to themselves.

"Look at me," Chochmo shouted to the captives. "She was punished for breaking our laws," he said. "Obey and live long. Break the law and your fate will be similar." He nodded to the guards by the derricks. The man on the left swung his ax, cutting the rope. Startled by the action, the captive watched in frozen silence as the rope shot the length of the shaft and through the hole at the tip of the boom. The woman fell, screaming to the waiting animals.

The guard on the right drew his ax back, but the remaining girl screamed, "No." It was a long, drawn out wail. "Please... anything. I'll do anything," she begged.

Chochmo considered her plea for a moment. "Of course you'll do anything... you are mine to do anything with." He gave an almost imperceptible nod to the guard who completed his swing and the second girl joined the first.

Her scream cut off midway, drowned out by the big cats roar, brought a gasp from the remaining captives. Some of the women doubled over, their stomachs heaving. The rest looked wide-eyed into the gloom of the pit, witnessing the end of their fellow captives. The crowd, those that remained, cheered, danced and jumped up and down.

Useless slaughter, Kaliska thought; he was repulsed by Chochmo's methods. *The man could have found other ways to enforce his will.*

As a hunter, Kaliska slew his share of animals. In doing this, he acquired his share of wounds and lost his share of friends. But, all of this was expected and a necessary part of hunting. What he had witnessed was unexpected and, in his mind, unnecessary.

A scout—one of Chochmo's—pushed his way through the crowd and prostrated himself in front of his leader.

Chochmo pretended not to notice the man; he was a new, young scout, trying to make a name for himself. Chochmo let him lay there and stew over the interruption. "What have you to say for yourself?" he finally demanded.

"Sir," the scout, called Hevataneo, began, "I bring evidence that intruders have invaded our land."

"An invasion! How many?" Chochmo looked at Long Tusk. Was this invasion somehow related to the caravan master being here?

"A pair of intruders... they made camp and are out searching the Great Ice."

A pair? He thought, *Not too much of a threat, unless they were the advanced guard for a larger group.* "What evidence do you have?"

Pulling a wadded bundle from his parfleche, Hevataneo held it out and waited for Chochmo's next move. He didn't have to wait long.

Still showing disdain, his chief snatched the garment and held it up for examination. Long Tusk recognized it immediately and forgot protocol. "Tell me about the pair," he demanded.

Chochmo, upset about being upstaged, glared at his guest. *What right did he have to intrude? The reason for the interruption had better be good.*

"A man, tall and slim, accompanied by a young woman with long dark hair."

"The witch... she is here," Long Tusk hissed. A shudder ran through his body and his blood ran cold.

"How do you know that?" Chochmo asked, forgetting his anger.

"By the garment; the man Askook sent to get the girl wore clothes like this," he said. "The witch cast a spell on him and then she enchanted Askook as well. It caused him to banish me. Now, she comes here to torment me."

"If she's come to us, then it will save us from going to her." Chochmo smiled ominously. "You! On your feet! Lead us to the place where they made camp. We'll capture her there, tonight."

Chapter 26: Hunted

Nearby, the iceberg ground into the shelf, shaking their platform before it wallowed away.

Wikvaya saw her hit the water along with the remains of the shelf. "No!" He shouted, but it was no use. Driven by wind and waves, the iceberg pushed forward again, toward the remnants of the ledge. It bore down on the place where Bright Moon had gone in, crushing everything in its path.

The mountain of ice ground into the shelf and then retreated. Wikvaya watched Bright Moon splash into the water and disappear under the churning surface. Slipping and sliding, he crawled across the slick surface to the edge and peered into the water hoping to catch a glimpse of her in its depths. Chunks of ice, large and small, swirled around in the frothy wake of the retreating iceberg. The snowstorm grew worse, cutting visibility even more.

The howling wind sent another series of waves and the mountain of ice lurched forward to attack the shelf again. His heart sank faster than the rock weight they had used. He was sure she was gone; either crushed, or pinned between the ledge and iceberg, drowning.

On the ice sheet, an eruption, several man-lengths away, flung water and ice into the air. Gasping, Bright Moon pushed the debris aside and clawed her way to the surface. She clutched at the sheet of ice but couldn't pull herself up. She wouldn't be able to hang on much longer.

Too far away for him to grab her, she was too cold to battle her way through the ice sheet. He looked around frantically for a solution and then found it at his feet.

"Grab the rope!" Wikvaya yelled as he twirled the weight overhead. His cast sent the rock just beyond her.

It slid across the ice and dropped over the opposite edge. Bright Moon wrapped her hands around it and he pulled her out of the water and across the icy surface toward him. The rock dragged along behind her.

"Can you use your hands?" Wikvaya asked.

The cold had done its damage. Her muscles had tightened. Her hands had become numb and useless. "No, there's no feeling left in them."

"Getting you out of the water and on the ledge is not going to be easy," he said.

Exasperated at his stating the obvious, her anger flared. "T... t... tell me something I don't know," she said through chattering teeth.

"I'll drop more rope. Loop it under your feet and grab the part that comes back to me. I'll try and pull you up in a standing position. When you get to the shelf, I won't be able to pull and help you too."

After a struggle, she had her arms wrapped in both sections. With slow, smooth movements, he pulled her out of the water and up onto the shelf. Frozen to the bone, she shivered as she lay huddled like an infant. Slipping and sliding, he made his way over and cradled her in his arms, turning her face up to his. Blue from the cold, her hair coated in ice, she was barely breathing. He pulled his ivory-bladed knife and cut off her wet clothes, leaving them in a heap on the shelf. He stripped off his own vest and tunic. Wet as they were, they were still drier than what she had worn, and dressed her in them.

Wikvaya grabbed his walking stick and left everything else. Scooping up the girl, he held her close to his body as he began the trip back. The storm continued. He couldn't see, couldn't watch for landmarks. He followed the trail they made on the way here. He hurried, trying to reach his goal before the storm hid their tracks, before darkness fell, and before either of them died from the cold.

###

The moon's glow pierced the horizon by the time Wikvaya found the cave. The wind shifted, blowing snow into its open mouth. A drift was starting.

He staggered to the threshold and lowered his burden to the ground. Bright Moon, unconscious and unable to help, moaned as she touched down. Almost frozen himself, he crawled slowly into the cave, dragging her behind him.

A ring of rocks surrounded glowing coals, the remains of the campfire left behind. After placing Bright Moon on the bed of boughs, he threw a sleep-robe over her. Without opening her eyes, she pulled the robe close.

Wikvaya bent over the coals and coaxed a fire to life. Satisfied that it would burn on its own for a while, he blew on his numb fingers before digging through a pack. Finding a clay bowl, he filled it with snow and a few pieces of pemmican before placing it on the rocks over the fire.

The flames soon danced around the edges of the bowl, but produced little heat beyond the container. The wind blowing through the open mouth, drew the heat with the smoke up and out through the makeshift chimney.

Taking another sleeping-robe, he stretched it across the cave's mouth and secured it with chunks of ice. This makeshift door would soon be coated with snow and hidden behind a drift. It would not be a problem as long as Bright Moon's chimney remained open

Pemmican floated in the clay bowl over the fire. Wikvaya poured the warmed liquid into a drinking gourd and moved to Bright Moon's side. With an arm around her shoulder, he lifted her and held the gourd to her mouth. Eyes still closed, she sputtered and then sipped eagerly. When she had finished, he laid her limp body back, covering her once again.

Wikvaya added more wood and the fire blazed up, spreading its warmth around the cave. He held his hands out and allowed the heat to warm his still numb fingers.

Bright Moon, still wrapped in the robe, stirred.

"So… co… cold," she said, "s… s… so cold."

Wikvaya put more snow in the clay bowl before turning to her.

"You need to get out of your wet clothes," he said.

"Co… cold," she said feebly. "Help me." She rose on one elbow and pulled the robe back.

Wikvaya peeled off the vest and tunic she wore then he pulled two rocks from the ring that held the fire slipping them under the sleeping-robe. "Here," he said, "hold these near. The warmth they give will help."

She pulled her arms and legs in and assumed a fetal position, once again creating a furry mound on the boughs. No part of her showed. As a final measure, he tucked the robe tightly around her.

Satisfied that he had done all he could for her, he turned to the wet clothes. By bracing his walking stick between the cave walls near the fire, he was able to hang the garments over it to dry. Under the robe, Bright Moon stirred. "Co… cold," came her muffled voice. Wikvaya left the fire and crawled to where she lay. Bundling the robe tightly around her, he pulled her close in hopes that their combined body heat would help.

She felt warmer, her breathing sounded better. She would survive. He found the source of the rising waters. He could relax.

Tomorrow, they would return. The village… his village… the place that he and Lady Adsila had worked so hard to establish, would have to move to higher ground— much higher ground; but life would go on. Lost in the flickering firelight, comforted by its warmth, Wikvaya lay back… and drifted off to sleep.

"Great Chief Chochmo," Hevataneo said, "they made their camp in a cave along one of these ridges." On foot, he looked up at his mounted leader. Next to him,

Long Tusk and Kaliska, also on horseback, waited and watched. Long Tusk had been included so he could confirm the girl was the witch he feared. He had insisted that Kaliska be brought along. The scout knew the caravan leader wanted him there for protection.

High in the sky, the moon shone through broken clouds casting a silver light across the landscape. A shift in the wind had brought warm air and the recent snowfall was turning to slush. Groups of riders, some carrying torches, milled about. Not knowing what to do, they pretended to search; but in the dark, their efforts only trampled any tracks their prey had left.

Kaliska had been aware of the distinctive, sharp, smell of smoke drifting through the air. He didn't mention it, hoping the others wouldn't notice. The stranger could be Wikvaya and the girl. Whether it was or not, there was no reason they should face the pit for their transgressions.

"I see many ridges," Chochmo replied curtly. "Which ridge holds their campsite?" His mount sensed his irritation. It began pawing the ground, snorting, and prancing. The other horses did likewise. Inexperienced, Long Tusk had trouble controlling his mount. Kaliska's horse, more docile than his leader's, was easier to handle.

"They are close," Hevataneo said. "I can smell smoke from their fire."

"You brought me… you brought my guests out here so we can smell smoke from the fire you can't find?" Aggravated by the delay, Chochmo's anger was ready to boil-over. "Don't stand there and tell me you smell smoke. Find them… or find yourself in the pit."

When Hevataneo first saw the strangers, he had hoped for a reward, not this… not the pit. Quaking at the thought, he looked around nervously and then at Chochmo's guests in the off chance that they might somehow intervene and save him.

His mount now under control, Long Tusk leaned forward, supporting Chochmo's intimidation of the young scout. Not knowing which way to turn, Hevataneo looked from one stony face to another hoping for support. In return, he received only grim stares and feared the worst.

While they were distracted, Kaliska did his best to seem uninterested while he discreetly looked around. Whoever the strangers were, they did a good job of hiding their location. The smell of smoke did not appear any stronger in any direction. The recent snowfall blanketed the terrain and now melting further obscured the tracks.

If Chochmo's scout were more experienced, he would know they were close to the source of the smoke. If Chochmo's scout were more experienced, he would have kept the riders from running over the intruders' tracks. If Chochmo's scout were more experienced, he would have been able to read the tracks before the melting snow wiped them out.

But, Chochmo's scout wasn't experienced. Between the melting snow and the riders milling aimlessly around, the tracks were lost. Kaliska only needed to move the search away from here... but where? If they went upwind, they would leave the smoke-filled air and might discover they had been duped, returning to this area to begin anew.

If Kaliska could lead them downwind, they would remain in the smoky air. He could encourage them to search other ridges, each one further out and away from this location in hopes that eventually the search would be called off.

What had looked like a snow-covered wall suddenly moved. Whether from the breeze or a person's hand, Kaliska didn't know. But, to keep the strangers safe, he knew he had to hustle the others away from here. The melting snow coating the makeshift door began to slough off.

"Is doesn't look like there's anything here," Kaliska said, hoping to move them away from this spot. "Let's go this way, and check some of the other ridges." He urged his mount downwind. Not having a better plan, the pair of leaders wheeled their mounts and started in the new direction, leaving Hevataneo to stand there or follow on foot.

The snow that had held Wikvaya's robe in place, melted, freeing it and it slumped to the ground. Chochmo's young scout jerked his head around at the sound the robe made hitting the ground. "Wait!" he shouted. "It's here! It's here!"

In her dreams, Bright Moon relived the terror of the ice collapsing under her. It had caught her by surprise. She hit the ice-cold water before she had time to cry out. Deep in the dark waters, she struggled to get out of her heavy cloak, to swim away before the mountain of ice crushed her.

She fought to get to a place where surface-shimmer was no longer cut off by the approaching iceberg. It felt as if she was running in mud. Had she swum far enough to be safe? Her aching lungs told her she would have to take a chance. Against the weight of her wet clothes, Bright Moon clawed her way to the surface only to find it blocked by a sheet of ice. A weak point, a crack where sheets joined, gave her hope. She pounded on it until she got a fist through. Two more blows opened the hole wider. Hands on either side of the opening, she lowered herself her full arm's length and then pulled upward, smashing her head against the ice. It gave. Ice flew and she was out of the water. Still, she could not get a breath. Struggling, she tried to cry for help, at least to scream. Arms thrashing, she clawed the air until finally finding a handclasp firmly over her mouth.

"Be quiet," Wikvaya whispered hoarsely. One arm clamped around her, holding her down, his other hand clasped tightly over her mouth. He listened intently.

Bright Moon, fully awake now, quit struggling and looked around. They were at their campsite in the cave.

She had only vague memories of how she got back here. Clothes hung over the fire, now almost out. When he felt her relax, he released his grip.

"What is it?" she asked.

"Someone's outside. I hear them moving around."

"Animals?"

"Not unless they've learned to talk." Wikvaya threw back the sleeping-robe and scrambled to where his clothes hung. "Find something to wear. I think we might be leaving in a hurry and we'll have to travel light."

She grabbed her pack and dumped the contents on top of the sleeping-robe. Her hand came away muddy. "Look," she commanded. "Someone was here while we were gone."

Nodding, he struggled into his tunic, still damp. "Get dressed," he said. "We don't have much time."

Dressed, he dumped his own rucksack on the robe, sorting bundles of pemmican and other essentials into three groups, one larger and two smaller.

Wikvaya looked up to see Bright Moon watching him as she laced her vest over her tunic. "Put everything you don't need back," he explained. "I want it to look like we are out, but expect to return."

"But... but... they'll search for us?"

"If they think we'll return, they'll lay a trap here. It will give us a head start. The larger bundle stays here. The smaller ones are for each of us... in case we get separated."

"Yes...." Bright Moon stopped abruptly leaving her fears unspoken. On all fours, she crawled to the cave's opening and eased back the edge of the robe. The view did not give her a warm feeling.

A trio of mounted men confronted a youth on foot. In the midst of this group, Long Tusk attempted to control an unruly mount. She did not know those with him. One, probably a chief, loudly questioned the youth, who claimed he knew the intruders were close. The young man's explanation did not go over well. His chief exploded, roaring back a reply. The animals they rode pranced nervously. Long Tusk had trouble getting his under control. Another group of men, some with torches, rode past. Having seen enough, Bright Moon let the flap fall back in place and backed away from the mouth.

"It's Long Tusk," she whispered. "They're searching for us."

Wikvaya tossed her a bundle of pemmican. "Tuck this away. It's time for us to try your escape route."

Chapter 27: On the Run

Hevataneo's shouts carried through the night air, echoing off rocks and ice-covered walls. Garbled by reverberations, his excited words still managed to catch Chochmo's attention. Had he heard his scout correctly? He halted abruptly. Close behind, Long Tusk's ride, startled by this sudden stop, reared up and dumped its rider. Kaliska prodded his horse toward Long Tusk's mount, feinting helpfulness while secretly chasing the animal away in order to delay their return.

Tired of the holdup, Chochmo wheeled around and spurred his ride into a gallop, racing toward his scout. Giving up the delaying tactic, Kaliska caught the caravan leader's horse and they joined the race. Kaliska seated, Long Tusk prone across his animals' back and hanging on for dear life.

Hevataneo squatted in the trail. His spear at the ready, he peered at the dark spot in the wall of snow beyond the heap that was the robe and snow. Though the exposed cave entrance was not more than two man-lengths away, there was nothing he could see past the bend, save the dull flickering light cast by a campfire. Feeling he barely escaped the pit, he now wanted to appear intent on not letting anyone get away.

"Here," waving his arms, violently, Chochmo called to his riders, "I need you here!"

From upwind and downwind, groups of riders descended on them. Some remained mounted and alert for unseen dangers while others quickly dismounted, gathering around Chochmo and Hevataneo, their torches lighting the scene. The place erupted in a cacophony of voices as everyone tried to find out what had transpired.

"Silence!" Chochmo roared over the din. Except for the echo of his words, the place fell quiet. "Someone needs to go in and confront the invaders." Turning to Hevataneo, Chochmo said, "You found them. You led us here. The honor should be yours." With a nod, he gestured toward the cave.

Saved from the pit but now sentenced to the possibility of being the first to die at the hands of the intruders, Hevataneo swallowed hard. In the dark, he hoped nobody noticed his reluctance as he started forward.

"Wait!" Kaliska commanded. Everyone looked at him. Long Tusk, jumpy because he wanted his scout close if the witch were there, glared at him for interfering. Chochmo glowered at him for interrupting.

"If the witch followed us here, then I should be the one who faces the risk of confronting her," Kaliska told them. He used his bravest words to convince them. "I have dealt with the man, Wikvaya, and the girl before. She did not enchant me, perhaps, she cannot. I should be the first one to enter their lair."

"Agreed," Chochmo said, accepting Kaliska's judgment. It would, after all, be better to risk one of Long Tusk's men than one of his own. "Go then and tell us what you find."

Kaliska slid off his horse, crept forward, and crawled into the cave. Saved from the pit by the melting snow, Hevataneo realized he was also saved from the witch by Long Tusk's scout. His luck continued. He breathed a sigh of relief.

Not as relieved, Long Tusk watched Kaliska bent low to enter the cave and disappear around the bend. Now he waited uneasily for his scout to emerge.

After rounding the bend, Kaliska halted, pausing to

let his eyes adjust. The chamber before him took shape.
No more than a narrow pocket cradled between rock and
snow, it was too low for him to stand upright. This
pocket was here because a fir tree, toppled by a storm or
the Great Ice, lay propped against a low wall. Successive
snowfalls covered branches and formed the roof while
leaving this niche underneath.

Within a ring of rocks, flames consumed the last
pieces of wood leaving behind glowing red coals.
Crawling in, he stirred the fire into life, added a few pieces
of wood, and looked around.

Across the snow-covered floor, in a corner against
the wall, lay a bed made of boughs and sleeping-robes. A
walking stick and two rucksacks—their decorative
stitching looked familiar--were stashed against the
opposite wall. Beyond the bed, the rear of the cave tilted
sharply up and disappeared in darkness.

Kaliska took a brand and crawled back to examine
the area. Telltale tracks in the snow confirmed that
someone had gone this way. The flicker of his torch
confirmed a natural chimney lay ahead. He followed the
path, knowing it would lead to an opening. The signs he
read confirmed it had become an exit. It was as he
thought, *this is your answer. We come in the front, and you go out
the back. Very good… very smart!*

He propped his brand upright and returned to the
main room where he broke off a section of bough and
grabbed the walking stick. Scampering back to his torch,
he inserted the stick into the chimney and poked at the
walls, scouring snow from them. They collapsed under his
efforts. Putting the pole aside and taking up the bough, he
carefully swept the loose debris around, destroying any
signs of tracks.

Finished, he raised the torch to get a better look. The
flame gently flickered confirming the chimney was not
entirely closed, but closed enough to hide its dual

purpose. Only his tracks remained.

Good, Kaliska said to himself, *I don't know if you're my friends or not, but whoever you are, to help keep you safe from the pit, I've bought you some time.*

With Wikvaya's help, Bright Moon scooted up the chimney to the top. It was almost drifted over from the recent snow and unseen by anyone who would have ventured along. With pursuers at the cave's mouth, it made little difference.

Cautiously, she eased her head out and looked around. Over time, the snow had drifted around the tree branches that had not yet been buried. Moonlight, filtered through clouds throwing long shadows over the landscape, but there was no one about. Voices and shouting arose from below.

"Is it clear?" Wikvaya asked from below.

A bright Moon wriggled out and turned back to help Wikvaya. Behind them, light flared. Someone had stirred the campfire. They drew their knives and held their breath as they waited to strike at anyone who followed. A pole jabbed up the chimney, not at them but at the sidewalls. Below, someone was busy scouring the walls, scraping snow loose in an attempt at plugging the chimney and hiding their trail.

"We have a friend," Wikvaya said quietly. Putting his knife away, he motioned for her to join him. Together, they pushed loose snow and chunks of ice down the place they exited.

"That should help him mislead them," Wikvaya said, and motioned for her to follow. To get away before the sun came up, they would have to act quickly. He crouched low behind the snowdrift and crept along the slope to the crest of the ridge. Bright Moon trailed close behind. It would be light soon, the first signs were showing along the horizon. Behind them, the voices died out.

"Our unknown friend must have left the cave by now," Bright Moon whispered. "If our plan works, they'll busy themselves laying a trap expecting our return."

"And if they're not fooled," Wikvaya replied, "they'll be after us in no time."

"I checked the cave. There's no one there now, but it looks like they expect to return," Kaliska told the two chiefs "I believe it's the only way in or out."

No one else had entered when Kaliska came out. Knowing the way was safe, others rushed to the cave's mouth hoping to be the next one to enter.

"Wait! Don't let them go in!" Kaliska exclaimed. "It would alert the strangers when they return." Chochmo, not recognizing the scout's deception, agreed and called his men back.

"It would be good if you'd hide your men in places where they can watch the cave but are not seen," Kaliska told him.

At Kaliska's suggestion, Chochmo would post his other men where they could pounce on anyone who returned. The men would not leave their place until their chief called them; delaying pursuit until their leader decided the intruders were not coming back.

Kaliska wanted to keep Chochmo's scout from making any discoveries. If Hevataneo found the fugitives' tracks, the wait would be over and the hunt would begin. On the other hand, if Kaliska could distract Chochmo's scout keeping him busy in the process, the discovery would be delayed. He turned to Chochmo. "I need your scout to show me where the strangers went out on the

Great Ice."

"Why do you want to know that?" The two chiefs chorused.

"They went out there looking for something," Kaliska said. "I don't know what they looked for, but I think it's important to find out."

Chochmo pursed his lips. The horizon showed the first signs of false-dawn. It would be light soon. He nodded to Hevataneo and said, "Go with him."

Wikvaya called a break near the beaver pond where they had camped the first night after leaving the river. The pair plopped down in the shade and searched their packs for pemmican. The sun was high overhead and they had not seen anyone since leaving the ice field. Wikvaya had moved cautiously in the dark, but, as dawn broke, he stepped up the pace. Bright Moon followed closely behind him. Travel downhill had been easier. They moved quickly, especially once they had passed the snow line, but they were near exhaustion and needed a break, however short.

"Do you think we're safe now?" Bright Moon asked.

Wikvaya shrugged, tiredly. "We have a lead, I hope a long one," he said, "but, it really depends on when they discover we're not coming back."

Weary, Bright Moon lay back and put one arm over her eyes. "Other than following in your footsteps, we haven't been doing much to cover our trail so it shouldn't be too hard for them to track us," she said.

"And, they'll be mounted. They can travel faster," Wikvaya added. Anxious to make good their escape, he hadn't given much thought about hiding their tracks. Apparently she had and did her best to confuse the issue by stepping where he stepped. Was their scout good enough to know she had done this?

Bright Moon sat up. "There is only one answer for us," she said. Although they were both bone tired, Wikvaya could see the determination in her eyes. "We have to split up," she said.

"Split up... but why?" Wikvaya could not believe what he was hearing.

"If we remain together, they'll have a better chance of catching up with us, and if they do, they'll catch both of us," she answered. "Someone must warn the village. If we split up, take separate trails, it will be harder for them to track us. It will give one of us a better chance to get back and warn the others."

It made sense to Wikvaya. He didn't like it, but he couldn't think of another solution. "Yes," he said, "you're right. I don't like the plan, but you're right."

"One more thing," Bright Moon said quietly. "Whoever gets to the dugout first... cannot wait for the other person."

Shocked, he looked at her as he realized what she was not saying. She would sacrifice herself so he could escape and warn the villagers. "No, I cannot...."

"Yes, you must." Her sharp response cut him off. Bright Moon continued quickly, "Every day, the risk is greater. The water will rise beyond belief, but they cannot just move to higher ground."

Wikvaya looked at her questioningly.

"We've ventured into Chochmo's lands and, in spite of his efforts, we have escaped. He cannot let that go unpunished without losing stature with other tribes and his own people. Lady Adsila and the others must hear of this danger ... they will have to leave everything... everything... and flee and they will be reluctant to do so. Someone has to convince them. She will listen to you... they will listen to you."

Bright Moon's mind was set. Wikvaya knew she was

right. He also knew there was no argument he could make
that would change anything.

Chapter 28: Pursuit

It was midday by the time Hevataneo and Long Tusk's scout returned from the Great Ice.

"Did you find them?" Chochmo demanded.

"We followed their tracks to…." Hevataneo began, but was cut off by a sharp look from his leader.

"They aren't out there," Chochmo said quietly. "They're not returning." Pulling himself together, he motioned to the waiting men. "Check for signs. Find out where they went."

The men, scattered and began searching the area. Hevataneo, eager to regain some prestige, entered the cave only to exit after a short time. Eager to join the search, he began looking where others had not, scrambling across mounds of snow-covered ice, he looked around for a way to climb up the ridge. By reaching the top, he hoped to see farther, perhaps see the fugitives as they escaped and be the first to raise the alarm. He did not find them, but what he found was almost as good. Hevataneo raised both hands high, and jumping around excitedly, he shouted, "Tracks! I found tracks." He was successful where the others were not. This should raise his prestige.

"Which way?" Chochmo answered, cutting off his scout's celebration all too soon.

"This way," Hevataneo replied as he started off on foot along the trail they had left on the ridge. Below him, Chochmo and his men followed, their horses in a slow gait, while Long Tusk and Kaliska tagged along behind them, each with their own set of concerns.

###

Bright Moon watched Wikvaya disappear into the forest. He moved quickly, but with great care, leaving little to hint that he had passed that way. Sighing, she turned to the task of making their pursuers follow her and not him.

Her tunic, tied off at the bottom, made an excellent pouch. Bright Moon filled it with rocks gathered from several places so their absence would not be obvious. Their weight would give her footprints depth similar to his. Shouldering her bundle, she started up the trail, away from Wikvaya's route, toward the ridge that skirted the Great Ice. As she traveled, she would discard a stone until all were gone, not only lightening her load, but also changing her footprints ever so slightly. Her pursuers would not notice the change.

"They stopped here," Hevataneo offered.

Mounted, Chochmo watched his scout hover over scattered imprints and listened to his report before speaking. "Where did they go from here?"

"Up the trail, that way," Hevataneo answered.

Chochmo, stone-faced, sat quietly for a moment before turning to Long Tusk and Kaliska. "What do you see," he asked them. They both knew the question, while directed at Long Tusk, was meant for Kaliska.

Kaliska dismounted and strode over to join the dejected young man. Squatting to better read the prints left behind; he studied the markings for a long moment and then said, "They stopped here. I see steps leading up the trail."

Kaliska confirmed Hevataneo's findings, putting a smile on the man's face and a prideful swell to his chest. Kaliska smiled back. *Yes, they rested here. Yes, the tracks go up the trail*, Kaliska said to himself, *but, if you had more experience, you'd see that those tracks are different. As if one person wanted to appear as two. It had to be the girl... and she had fooled*

Chochmo's scout.

"How far ahead are they?" Chochmo questioned.

Kaliska looked up and pointed to a curl of white smoke beyond him, "Judging from the smoke, not too far," Kaliska said, stone-faced. *Why would someone running away do such a thing... unless it was bait for another trap?*

###

A small cookfire, laid in a hollow scooped out of the dirt, devoured the green sticks she had gathered, turning them into gray-clad coals. Nearby, two young lambs bleated quietly. Tied, one on each end of a carry pole[86], they started thrashing about again.

"Lay quiet now," she scolded them. "I rescued you from that hole where you would have starved so you're mine. I could cook you now, but I will need you later." *Good for you but too bad for me,* she mused as she added dry grass and green wood to the embers. *If I didn't need you, my supply of pemmican would last longer.*

White smoke curled upward. Bright Moon, wanting smoke and not flame, slowly added more greens to the fire. After the last of it had shriveled and turned to ash, she covered the coals with sand, leaving a few burnt lumps exposed. Sitting back on her haunches, Bright Moon checked her work and thought, *If you're watching, Long Tusk, you and your friends should see the smoke and come this way.*

She bit off a piece of pemmican then shouldered the pole with her captives and trotted along the ridge, alert for a suitable spot to ambush her pursuers.

###

"The intruders stopped and cooked a meal,"

---

86 A pole used to carry items of approximately equal weight. For balance, the items are fastened to each end of the pole which is carried across the individual's shoulders.

Hevataneo said. "The remains of the fire are still warm."
He held up a burnt stick as proof while continuing,
"Tracks lead that way, along the ridge."

"Lead on," Chochmo commanded. This time, he
accepted the evidence without looking to Kaliska for
confirmation.

Hevataneo beamed with delight as he stepped out
along the path Bright Moon had left for him. Glancing
toward Kaliska, the young scout was rewarded with a
reassuring smile.

The trail followed the ridge and lead uphill. As they
neared the Great Ice, the landscape changed from trees to
scrubby, ill-shaped brush sprouting among boulders.
Ponds and bogs were abundant.

The tracks meandered amidst rocks and
outcroppings, as if its makers were lost. Even on the
rocky ground, Hevataneo was able to follow the trail.
Perhaps, Kaliska thought, *Chochmo's young scout does so well
because there are always clues for him to find. Probably left by
someone wanting to lead him into a trap.*

The pathway, caught between the brush-covered
ridge and a turbulent stream, narrowed allowing only two
riders to travel side-by-side. A man-length below, the
torrent pounded over rocks, and cut away at the bank in
its rush downhill.

On its way, the river had cut away much of the strata,
but it found an unyielding rock to be a challenge that
forced the river to go around. The bend it left behind
became a flat, green peninsular, defiantly thrusting its
presence into the raging torrent. Rounding this bend,
Hevataneo raised a hand signaling a halt before retreating
to the group that followed.

Chochmo leaned forward. "What's wrong?" He
questioned.

"Ahead, voices," Hevataneo said, and pointed toward
a rock cliff.

"Show me." Chochmo dismounted and led his horse
by its reins; the others did likewise. The young scout led

the way to the bend and pointed. In front of him, at least two spear-throws away, stood a wall, a stepped waterfall decorating its rim. A narrow shelf, divided the upper and lower falls.

From the path, it would be a steep climb up the slope over sharp-edged rubble to the foot of the wall. The base of the upper falls appeared to be another man-length above that.

Chochmo listened intently. Mixed in with the reverberation of the waterfalls and water pounding over rocks came another sound. Words? A sound, as if people were talking, drifted in and out on the breeze. "Where are they?"

"There's a shallow cave near the underbrush by the foot of the upper falls," Hevataneo answered. "Watch closely and you'll see bushes move. Someone's there, but I can't tell what they are doing."

The path leading forward was barely wide enough for the men to travel single-file and certainly too narrow for the horses.

"Leave the horses here," Chochmo commanded. "We will go forward on foot. Be ready, the intruders are close."

His command was greeted with glum looks from everyone. The men had heard stories about the witch. Kaliska had made sure of that and they were not eager to act.

Chochmo recognized their reluctance. "There will be a special reward for the one that captures the intruders," he promised. Looking at Hevataneo, he said, "You have done well. Stay with the horses," and he threw the reins to his scout.

Spurred on by their leader's action, as well as the promise of a reward, the men left their horses and followed him. Kaliska and a reluctant Long Tusk trailed everyone, leaving the lone man with their animals.

Hevataneo watched the party start out, not sure whether he was disappointed by being left behind or relieved to be on safer ground. He glanced over his shoulder at the horses. They were content to graze quietly and shuffled around in their search for new foliage. He turned his attention back to the others.

Chochmo's men halted near the base of the lower falls. In a sudden fit of bravado, some had scampered over the rubble and up the slope. Now, closer to their goal, their exuberance cooled and they turned to help their slower comrades.

Their chief stood at the edge of the rubble, watching the men above him. Long Tusk, less than eager, stood sandwiched between his ally and Kaliska, and craned his neck to see.

Working together, Chochmo's men boosted the first member to the upper shelf. He turned to help the second and together they brought up a third member. Weapons ready, the trio edged toward the cave. Behind them, additional men gained this ledge while all eyes on the ground focused entirely on the three closest to the cave.

Feet clutching a narrow ledge, fingers wrapped around a branch, Bright Moon crouched under the overhang a scant hands-width above the river's torrent, and listened to Chochmo's arrival.

Before hiding, she had watched their approach, taking a tally of the number—two hands' worth—of men trailing her. Now they were finally here and she waited, tucked into this hidden spot, to put the next part of her plan into action.

The scout halted the expedition, reporting voices. His chief sauntered forward to listen for himself before ordering them to go ahead on foot. She listened to the group's movements, their footfalls as they crept forward. The sounds of their departure soon mixed with the rumble of the falls, leaving only the shuffling of the horses where they grazed.

It was time to act. Bright Moon raised her head and peeked over the edge of the embankment. In front of her was a cluster of horses. Familiar with animals from birth—her father occasionally used horses and other pack animals—she was an experienced rider.

Intent on grazing, they paid little attention to her. She peered through a forest of moving horse legs and saw a lone man, his back to her, loosely holding a set of reins. He was focused on the action near the falls where Long Tusk and two others stood. The trio watched as Chochmo's men scurried up the precipice and edged toward the cave. They would be there soon. When they did, they would find she had tied the lambs there and know they had been tricked. She had to act now.

Soundless as a cat, she pulled herself up onto the pathway. Hiding behind the horses, she let her cramped legs recover. Unable to delay further, she skulked through the herd to a place behind the man. He stood less than a forearm's length from the edge. Bright Moon covered the remaining distance in a couple of quick, powerful steps crashing into him. The body blow sent him tumbling forward into the water. Startled, Chochmo's horse reared up, whinnying in surprise. The other horses picked up their ears. Alert for danger, they were ready to move fast. Bright Moon caught the reins of the startled horse and calmed the animal. Glancing over her shoulder, she saw the young scout surface, gasping and spluttering. The current carried him downstream and he fought it until finally reaching a protruding log.

She peeled off her vest and swung up on Chochmo's horse. Wheeling her mount around, she waved the garment in the air and shouted, driving the pack ahead of her. Surprised, the men on the cliff could only watch, dumbfounded, as their horses disappeared up the trail.

For them, it would be a long walk back to the village.

Chapter 29: Surrender

Reins in one hand, legs firmly clamped around the animal's midriff, Bright Moon yipped, shouted, and waved her vest as she drove the herd ahead of her. Panicked, the horses ran until they were covered in lather and ready to drop. Now, some distance from the waterfall, she slowed their pace, turned the horses toward rolling, grassy hills and let them go. They would scatter across the meadows and fend for themselves in this area of lush grass and stream-fed groves.

Satisfied she had accomplished this goal, Bright Moon sat astride her mount and watched the exhausted animals as they grazed. It was time to find answers to the questions she had pushed away during the long ride.

Did Wikvaya make it back to the village? Was he able to rally his people? Would they have enough time to gather their most precious belongings and flee? Even if Wikvaya and his people fled, would they be able to get far enough away to be out of Chochmo's reach?

Her efforts would delay Long Tusk and Chochmo, but do little more. Neither of these leaders could afford to have such an affront go unpunished. If anything, these setbacks would only increase their determination. As soon as they were able, these tyrants would march on Wikvaya's village.

The answer to all the questions came down to one thing. What Chochmo and Long Tusk really wanted was her. If she allowed herself to be captured, Wikvaya and his people would no longer be important and soon fade from memory.

Wikvaya, Adsila, and the others in their tribe had befriended her and then, during the rebellion, they risked their lives to protect her. Bright Moon swallowed hard. She had avoided thinking about a solution and now this, even though distasteful, was the only idea that presented itself. She shrugged. There was no way out. She owed this to her friends. Accepting her role, Bright Moon turned her mount toward Chochmo's village. It would be sunset soon and there was work to do.

"Truly, the girl is a witch," Long Tusk said, "a worker of many spells and much evil." Pausing, he held out a drinking mug, and waited while one of the women refilled it. Hungry and exhausted, it had been a long walk back to the village and it was well past sunset by the time they arrived. Women scurried quietly about the long hut, lighting lamps, making sure drinking gourds were filled and bringing trays—made from slabs of wood—loaded with food for the hungry men.

"My scout, Hevataneo, said he had no warning," Chochmo said. "She came out of nowhere and attacked him. In spite of her size, she was able to throw him into the river."

Long Tusk nodded. "I had Kaliska, my scout, look around. He found no tracks other than right behind your man. You see what a problem she has been for me."

Chochmo nodded but remained silent, thoughtful.

A tall, cloaked woman, her face in the shadows, bent low, dropped a wad of animal fat into the fire in front of them and offered a tray. "Perhaps, Chief Long Tusk, it is you who are the problem," the bearer said softly.

The fire, prodded into action by the fat, flared up and pushed back the gloom of the hut long enough to illuminate a face he dreaded seeing. Long Tusk jumped—could not have jumped any higher if someone dropped a flaming torch in his lap. The image, framed by the cloak's hood, jarred him from his doldrums. He had recognized that voice. Staring across the fire, he recognized the face that went with it.

Chochmo, cup to his lips, choked when he heard her words. "Foolish, brazen girl, who are you?" he bellowed. "I'll have you beaten and thrown into the pit."

The young woman, still bent over, disdainfully dropped the tray into Chochmo's lap. Straightening up and stepping back, she let her cloak slump to the floor. "I am Bright Moon, Shaman of the People," she said, her reply loud enough for all to hear.

Long Tusk's heart raced. It was true. He had heard her. She was here. Kaliska thought he heard his leader whimpering. The young scout was enjoying this moment.

Shocked by the intrusion, Chochmo sat mouth ajar. "How did you get in here?" He finally managed.

"I was invisible, just as I was when I shoved your scout into the river and drove your horses away," Bright Moon said. "There or here, no one saw me until I showed myself."

"Invisible?" Chochmo choked out. "I don't believe you."

"Don't believe me," Bright Moon answered defiantly. "But did your scout see me?" Waving a hand around, she challenged, "Ask those here if they saw me before now?"

Chochmo looked at the others in the hut. They clung to the walls, not brave enough to get close. No one volunteered a response.

"Why are you here?" Chochmo demanded.

"I've come to warn you. Take heed while you can." Rebellious, she stood there glaring at him.

"Warn me? Warn me about what?"

"Because of Long Tusk's evilness, I've called up great waters to carry him away," she said. "Now you have given him shelter and plan to join him in his evil deeds. You will suffer the same fate unless you give up your ways and leave this place."

"You lie!" Chochmo shouted.

"I believe she speaks the truth," Kaliska interjected.

Bright Moon stole a glance his way. Was this her

secret ally?

All eyes were on Long Tusk's bold scout. Chochmo scowled at him. "What is it you're saying? Explain yourself." Rage smoldered in his eyes.

"We, your scout Hevataneo and I, went out on the Great Ice," Kaliska said. "It holds back great waters, more than either of us has ever seen. The ice is breaking and will not hold much longer. Already the river is higher than before we arrived. Go to the river's edge and see for yourself."

Before Chochmo could reply, one of his men—a squat, barrel-chested loudmouthed man named Growling Bear—jumped up. Two others joined him and the trio started toward Bright Moon. "Reward us, my chief," he boasted. "We'll take her as our prize. Once she learns respect, she won't be a problem."

Bright Moon turned to face them and said, "Come to me and your man-sticks will wither like summer grass and then fall off." She spoke softly, confidently, and with a voice as cold as ice. "After that happens you will die a slow and painful death."

Hearing her words, knowing her reputation as a witch, the pair that followed Growling Bear had second thoughts and stopped in their tracks, wondering how they could separate themselves without losing face. The trio's leader knew he could not back down without appearing weak and had to continue toward her. It was now her turn to show bravery, but she knew that if he reached her unharmed, she would not have a chance. It was time to come up with a new trick.

She sized up her barrel-chested opponent. Shorter than her, his head, face, and body was a mass of matted hair partially concealed by mud. Closer now, she could see the eager glint in his eyes, like the burning embers of a fire. Hanging nearby, a lamp—a clay bowl filled with animal fat turned to oil and set with a wick—reminded her of something her grandfather had done. She lifted it from its mount, looked him in the eye, and asked, "Do you want a witch's kiss?"

Her question and her action caught him off guard. Barely two steps away, he could have reached out and touched her, but was now unsure. Fascinated, he watched as she lifted the bowl to her lips and sipped a portion of the warm liquid. Lowering it just a little, she looked down at him and smiled encouragingly.

Growling Bear stood rooted in place not knowing what either one of them would do next. Bright Moon took a step toward him, the lamp still positioned between them and the wick at mouth level. She breathed deeply through her nose and exhaled forcefully through closed lips[87]. The contents spewed out of her mouth—an action, much like a baby's—spraying the oil in fine droplets through the flame of the lamp. It ignited, and her assailant was met with a tongue of fire and a cloud of oil. His hairy body, now oil covered, burst into flame. Screaming, stumbling blindly around, he finally fell in a corner, a smoldering heap. No one came to his aid.

Trembling, afraid to look the witch in the eye, everyone crowded into a recess behind the two chiefs. Witnesses to the event would say that she had breathed fire and her assailant burst into flame.

Chochmo recovered just enough of his wits to call for someone else to take the risk. "Seize her, slay her," he shouted. Warily, a few men rose, weapons in hand, but were unsure of how to advance or even if they wanted to proceed.

---

87 In more modern times, fire eating was a common part of Hindu, Sadhu, and Fakir performances to show spiritual attainment. It became a part of the standard sideshow acts in the late 1880s and is often seen as one of the entry-level skills for sideshow performers. Skilled fire performers, such as those who can utilize the difficult and dangerous vapor transfers and produce large breaths of fire are regarded as equals in the circus community for their skill and devotion to their art. It is because fluids, even solids, when reduced to small particles and accompanied by the right mix of air/oxygen can become flammable, even explosive. Do not try this at home.

"Wait," Kaliska said, jumping in front of the girl. "Slaying the girl still leaves you with the rising waters to deal with. If she called them up, she can make them go away."

"What are you saying?" demanded Chochmo

"Hang her over the pit for a night or two and see if that changes her mind," Kaliska answered.

Chochmo paused to consider Kaliska's plan while Bright Moon's thoughts of a secret ally quickly faded.

"Here's an even better idea," Kaliska offered. "If she is as powerful as she claims, think what you could do with someone like that."

Chochmo sized up the scout, a man of unknown potential, "You have no fear of her?"

Kaliska's chest swelled and he said, "Her magic has no effect on me."

Chochmo nodded agreement. Clearly, Long Tusk's scout seemed unaffected by the girl's magic. Even better, the young man's plan had merit. "Seize her," he told Kaliska. "Tie her securely and we'll hang her over the pit."

Hardly had Chochmo's commitment left his lips when Kaliska, rope in hand, turned to Bright Moon. "Hold out your hands, woman," he demanded loud enough for all to hear. As he looped a thin rawhide strip over her wrists, he lowered his voice to a whisper and added, "Don't make a fuss. I will be out to free you as soon as I can. I don't know why you didn't keep running, but I've just bought you some time... again."

Bright Moon stood quietly while he tied her hands. It gave her time to study him, to study his face. She had heard his whispered voice before; and had looked into those eyes.

Bound, Kaliska at her side holding her tether, Bright Moon was led out to the pit. They were anything but alone. A string of torchbearers and drummers led the way, and the pair was followed, although at a safe distance, by guards their spears at the ready. The curious—men, women and children of the tribe—completed the procession. A thick overcast blocked the moon and stars, making the night darker than usual. The day's heat hung in the stagnant, clammy air.

At the platform, workers hung their torches in brackets before they crowded around the derrick to rotate the boom inward. After winding its rope around those that bound her hands, they tied it off and hoisted her aloft. The boom was pivoted out and she found herself treading air over the dark abyss next to the illuminated platform.

The ropes cut into her wrists and she knew she could soon be losing the feelings in her fingers. Those were the least of Bright Moon's problems. Someone tossed a couple of torches into the pit. Disturbed, the big cats under her made their presence known. The onlookers stood silently waiting for the witch to do something. They did not have to wait long.

The wind, previously still, flared up, shifted direction, and blanketed the area with a sudden chill. Dust devils threw sand around. Fire-from-the-sky struck a tree on the nearby ridge. The crowd froze in place as if petrified. Before they could recover, the overcast broke open drenching them with a cold rain. Only two of the torches on the platform remained lit.

"Take heed," Bright Moon shouted through the downpour. "Your days are numbered. You have been warned."

With Bright Moon's words ringing in their ears, panic set in. The crowd turned into a mob. In their rush to get to a safer place, people were pushed, shoved, trampled, some even knocked over the edge into the pit.

###

In the dark void below her, the big cats moved around, fought, and snarled at each other while they waited for her to slip, to fall, to become their next meal. Meanwhile her Mother's dying words kept running through her mind. *You are wise beyond your years, but... you must be wary... lest your wisdom... gives you false confidence... it will be your downfall.*

She had not had time to question Kaliska about his role and his motives for helping her were a mystery. He had promised to come out and free her as soon as he could. His choice of words only provoked her interest. Did he say that to keep her from rebelling or was he her secret ally. Alone now, with only the rain beating down on her, Bright Moon decided she could not wait for his arrival and began struggling with the bindings. He had tied the rawhide tight enough to pass inspection but not so tight as to cut off circulation. That part gave her hope. While she knew they would have been easy to slip off if dry, the rain soaked rawhides complicated her efforts, making it a nearly impossible task.

Frustrated, Bright Moon gripped the rope, pulled her legs up over her head, wrapping them around the strand that held her. Upside down, she inched her way up until she could gnaw at the binding. It would be a slow process, but she would free herself. Glancing down, she saw the platform, but only counted one torch. The other had gone out. Not a good omen.

###

"I knew I could count on you," Hevataneo told Growling Bear. "You would want revenge for the burns she gave you and the humiliation you suffered."

His companion, lumbered on silently through the mud. The cold rain, practically a constant lately, wasn't a problem for him. In fact, it felt good on his burns. *He would make the witch pay for what she did. He would....*

"I saw them first," Hevataneo interrupted his

thoughts. "The girl is rightfully mine, my reward for warning Chochmo when she and the man first arrived."

Heads down as protection from the rain, each lost in their own thoughts about how they were going to celebrate once they got their hands on the girl. Neither one saw the tall, lanky guard until they were on top of him.

"Stop," the guard commanded. "Go no further." Wrapped in a hide, he had curled up in a niche, out of the weather.

"What? Why?" Hevataneo said. Pictures of the fun he would have, the torment, he would dish out, quickly dissolved. "What are you doing here? What right do you have stopping us?"

"Long Tusk's scout asked Chochmo to post guards," he said. "Least someone harm her before she has given up her secrets."

"But...." Hevataneo's reply was cut off by a quick jab from his companion.

"Good," Growling Bear said. "We are your relief. You can go back, dry out, and get warm now."

The guard looked them over carefully. In the dark, it was hard to tell if they were truthful, but if they lied they would answer to Chochmo. It wouldn't be his problem.

He bent over to gather the few items—a goatskin of chicha, an amulet as protection against evil—he had brought with him. At the same time, Growling Bear picked up a fist-sized rock and hit the unwary guard before he could straighten up. The man went down in a heap and lay still.

"What... why'd you do that?" Shocked by his partner's action Hevataneo stood there wide-eyed.

Growling Bear shot him a poisonous glance, unnoticed in the dark. "We can't have him returning to the village right now," he said. "People would ask questions and it would ruin our fun. You wouldn't want that to happen now would you?"

Understanding, Hevataneo nodded. In the darkness,

it was an invisible, useless gesture.

"Good," his companion said. He picked the guard's hands up and added, "Give me a hand. Grab his feet."

Together, the pair lugged the heavy body toward the edge of the pit.

Through the drumming rain, Bright Moon heard voices. Not clearly, but bits and pieces carried by the wind. Someone was coming this way. It spurred her to work harder. Chewing her way through the bindings was going painfully slow, but she had to be careful not to trade being tied and hung up to being free and falling into the pit. *When I get free, what should I do next? Could I climb up the rope to the boom then along the boom to the derrick and the safety of the platform? I would be safe there, at least from the pit, but what about my next step? What would I do then?* Her thoughts were interrupted by noises terminating in a heavy thud. Then, all was quiet.

Bright Moon continued working at freeing herself until she felt the boom jerk as the derrick began to turn. She lost her grip and tumbled into an upright position, jerking to a halt at the end of the tether. Dangling in the rain, she swung back-and-forth in the dark. Below her, the lone torch still burned valiantly as it tried to force back the darkness.

Men grunted and their grunts became louder as the derrick neared the platform. Suddenly, hands reach out, seized her, pulled her in, and stilled her sickening swing. Fire-from-the-sky lit up the night. She recognized the scout—the one she pushed into the river—and the blistered face of the loudmouth warrior that threatened her earlier that evening.

Hevataneo wrapped his hands around her waist while his companion, cut the rope above her bindings. Letting herself go limp, she became dead weight in the scout's arms. He staggered under the load and finally allowed her to slump into a pile on the deck, but not before she managed to steal his knife. She pulled her body into a ball hiding the knife as she did.

"Grab her legs. We'll have to carry her," Growling Bear snarled. He seized her under the arms. Following the other man's commands, Hevataneo scrambled to Bright Moon's feet.

As the scout bent to grab her, she kicked out catching him at the knee and was rewarded with a sharp crack. He let out a howl, clutched his leg, and rolled away in the darkness. Surprised, Growling Bear stopped but didn't straighten up fast enough. Knife clutched in her bound hands, Bright Moon jabbed upward catching him high in the chest, striking bone. He yelped and knocked her hands away. She lost the knife. It bounced off the platform and clattered onto the rocks. Furious, he struck her. His huge fists rained blows through her raised arms. Bright Moon rolled away, slipping off the edge of the platform, landing face down in the mud. Hands under her, she felt the snap as the rawhide bindings broke, freeing her. A rock, fist-sized and sharp, dug into her ribs. She pretended unconsciousness.

Growling Bear followed. "No tricks left Witch-Woman?" Panting, his sweat dripped down on her. He grabbed her by the hair on the back of her head; lifting it, he bent low, his fetid breath overpowering everything as he spit his words out between gasps. "Well, too bad because you're mine and I'm going to make you pay for what you did to me."

Chapter 30: Captured

The burly man's rasping breathing joined the drumming of the rain and the sporadic roll of thunder, the only other sounds, as he rolled the compliant girl over. She lay still. Had he gone too far in the beating he gave this witch? In the dark, he could not tell her condition. Should he bring the lone torch over for a closer look?

Deciding it didn't matter, he grabbed her by the tunic and dragged her back to the platform where he stretched her out unaware that her hands were free and she was armed with a fist-sized rock.

He drew his knife and knelt by her side. Still pretending unconsciousness, Bright Moon moaned, rolled away and pulled her legs up to hide the hand embracing the rock. Her assailant, upset because her movement ruined his handiwork, cursed as he rolled her onto her back and moved to straighten her legs. *Had that idiot scout remembered to bring some cord,* he grumbled, *he could have used it to tie her down and have avoided this problem. No matter. He would have his way with the girl and then make sure that idiot scout didn't live to talk. There was no point in leaving loose ends.*

Bright Moon eased her eyes open and peered through the rain to watch her attacker's movements. She could make out his silhouette in the flickering torchlight. Near her feet, he had his back turned to her. Quietly, she sat up, rock poised, and waited for him. The rumble of thunder and the drumming rain covered her movements.

Growling Bear turned around to see the girl. She swung her weapon. The blow caught him on the side of the head. Stunned, he pitched back on his heels.

Rocking back, she pulled her legs up, knees almost touching her chin, and shot them straight out. Her feet caught him square in the chest. The blow, not enough to finish him, pushed him further back and off-balance. *Where is Kaliska? He promised to come rescue me. He is not here.* Her antagonist might win and she could picture the scenes that would follow if she didn't get away.

She rolled over, rose on all fours, and scrambled to get to her feet. Hands clamped around her ankles and jerked her feet out from under her. The landing knocked the wind out of her.

Having recovered from her last blow, Growling Bear leaped forward to grab her leg near the knee. Her heart sank as she tried to kick out, but was unable to connect with anything that would do damage, anything that would slow him down. He rewarded her efforts with grim, menacing laughter and pulled her toward him, using his body to hold her down. Together, they rolled off the platform and she landed face down in the mud. An arm across her shoulders, a big hand on the back of her head, he pushed her face into the mire and held it there. She squirmed but could not get free nor could she breathe.

Exhausted, he rested while he waited for her struggles to wane, to signal him that he could begin her torment.

A sharp poke between his shoulder blades upset his thoughts. "Stop!" Kaliska's hoarse whisper broke the silence.

In no mood to have his work halted, Growling Bear shouted, "Who are you? Why are you interfering?" Bitterness rose in his mouth. He was so close to extracting his revenge.

The jab came again. This time the spear point was more forceful. "Let her up and back away," Kaliska commanded.

Reluctantly, the burly man rolled away and took up a squatting position nearby. The whites of his eyes glowed with rage even in the dim light. The scout watched his adversary's eyes because he knew this animal would attack the first opening he saw.

Kaliska knelt at Bright Moon's side and rolled her over. She did not react and, if she breathed, it was too shallow to be noticed. He slapped her sharply several times to revive her. Spitting mud and water, Bright Moon raised her head, nosily sucked in air, and began flailing her arms around, ready to fight.

"Be still!" Kaliska commanded. His words, though a hoarse whisper, were forceful and quickly got her attention.

Bright Moon recognized Kaliska's voice. *He did come to rescue me.* She stopped thrashing about and brought her arms close to wrap around herself in a tight hug. Her gasps became sobs that shook her body and she began to rock back and forth.

"Who are you?" The burly man demanded. "Why are you here?"

"I am Kaliska, a scout for Long Tusk," was his quick reply. "The witch forced your leader, Chochmo, to demand I come here and check on her." It was a lie but the man had no way of knowing unless he asked his chief and Kaliska was sure that wasn't going to happen.

"Ha! Not possible,' the burly man said. "She was a little busy. How could she do that?"

Kaliska shrugged a movement barely noticeable in the low light. "I don't know, but Chochmo woke greatly disturbed. He said she haunted his dreams and he demanded I come here."

Kaliska knew he couldn't trust the man to keep quiet, nor could he let him go free. Unable to tend to the girl until her assailant was gone; Kaliska had to goad the man into taking action. It would not be difficult because the burly guard was determined not to be caught. "When I report back to your leader, he will not be happy," Kaliska said.

The rage burning in Growling Bear's eyes flared as the guard realized the punishment that would come his way. He leaped toward the scout, hoping to surprise him. Kaliska expected it and was ready having quietly raised his spear.

The bone blade sank to the hilt. Surprised, the man shrieked. Bright Moon snapped around to face the sound, ready to defend herself.

Fire-from-the-sky lit the night. The torch flared up in a sudden gust of wind. She saw Kaliska and her assailant get to their feet. Her tormentor moaned as he clutched at the intruding point. He tried to push it away but Kaliska held the spear tightly in place. The burly man stepped backward in a futile attempt to back away from the offending blade. He stumbled over the rough ground until he finally tumbled over the edge of the pit and disappeared into the darkness. Bright Moon shut her eyes, squeezing them tight in hopes she could push the night's events from her memory.

Kaliska scooped Bright Moon up and carried her to a cleft in the rocks. She did not resist, but pressed close to him. He sat her down there thinking she would be all right and knelt beside her to unveil a shrouded lamp and a cloak he had stored there. Wide-eyed, shaking, the mud-covered girl looked around frantically—her breath came in short, shallow puffs

The lamp's feeble glow showed the emotions in the girl's face. Exhausted and now traumatized by the night's events, she was on the verge of panic. He grabbed her by her wrists and pulled her close. So close, the only thing she could see was his face. Forcefully, he told the panicked girl, "He's gone. It's over. You don't have to worry about him anymore."

A few heartbeats went by and he could feel her relax. Taking his knife, he cut the remnants of cords that had held her, freeing her from the last material evidence of her bondage. Bright Moon rubbed her wrists, made sore by the bindings while she digested what he said. Then she broke down sobbing, collapsing against Kaliska's side. He wrapped her in the cloak, put a comforting arm around her shoulders, and held her close. Eventually, she slept.

Kaliska gently shook Bright Moon awake. "It's time we get started."

Recovered from her ordeal, Bright Moon now seemed torn between being upset and being happy to see him. She growled, "What are you doing here?"

"Just what I said. I came to rescue you. I was nearly too late."

Bright Moon shuddered at the thought. "Yes that is true," she agreed.

"I was on my way here," he explained, "and I almost ran into your foe and Chochmo's scout, Hevataneo. I held back to see what they were planning. Their intentions were clear when I saw what happened to the guard."

"Where's the other one... the scout?" Bright Moon asked. Having forgotten about him, she now looked around nervously.

"He hobbled off after you gave him something to think about. I knocked him over the head and tied him up. He's over there on top of a boulder."

"What now?" she asked.

"I don't know where you learned to ride a horse but I was happy to see you seemed to know how," Kaliska said. "It's a long trip on foot to Wikvaya's village. If you're up to it, I think a few of Chochmo's best horses will be just what we need."

"My father had tried using horses. They were great on flat ground, but not as good as human porters in the rough, high country," Bright Moon explained. "While they eat grass, they don't live on grass alone, so, in place of trade goods, we had to carry extra food for them. To survive, a caravan depends on what they can trade and has to live off the land. He felt that horses were okay, but they just didn't fit his needs."

Kaliska nodded. What she told him fit into his plans. "The sun will be up soon. In order to make good our escape, we've some work to do."

"Work? What are your plans?"

"Wait here while I fetch something." He disappeared into the darkness.

When he returned, she saw he brought a long pole. He motioned for her to bring the lamp and follow.

Lamp held low to light the path, she fell in step behind him. The trail was rough. All the way back to the platform, she had to watch her step as well as dodge the pole Kaliska shouldered. He stopped, letting the tip of the pole rest on the ground while he looked around.

Bright Moon had no idea what he was thinking so she asked, "What's the pole for?"

"We'll need, a distraction while we escape," he said and looked at her for some sign of agreement. A smirk crossed his face. "I thought we'd get rid of Chochmo's toy" he said. "Give me a hand."

Stepping to the back of the platform, he planted the end of the pole under its lip. "Roll a rock in behind the tip, and then come back here with me," he instructed.

Together, they heaved on the pole. The heavy platform lifted, slid off the edge of the gorge and down the slope into the darkness of the pit. Noises came from the depths as the big cats, surprised by this new intrusion, made their objections known.

"Quick, come back here, we're about to have company," he said and he took her by the hand. Holding the lamp close to the ground, the pair retreated to a butte. Using a rope Kaliska had tied there earlier, they climbed the two man-lengths to the top. No sooner had they arrived than the first large cat clawed its way out of the pit. Others followed.

"Chochmo's toy took out some of the stakes that kept the cats at bay, and the platform gave them something to climb on," Kaliska whispered.

Silence was pointless. Noses to the ground, the cats followed the pair's scent and soon gathered near the base of their hiding place. The largest animal rose on hind feet and stretched its full length up the wall. From the top, the pair peered over the edge. Below them, not a forearm's length away, the animal's eyes glowed in the lamp's feeble light. Its knife-like teeth, longer than Bright Moon's hand, were dangerously close. Its black nose sniffed the air checking their scents. Kaliska wished he had chosen a higher hiding spot.

Before he could stop her, Bright Moon held a hand out, palm up, close to the animal's nose. Kaliska's heart stopped. If the animal wanted, it could clamp its jaws around the girl's forearm and pull her down in a flash. He held his breath and watched. Sniffing, the animal ran its nose along the girl's hand and then looked her in the eyes.

Each—the cat and the human—held the other's gaze for several heartbeats before Bright Moon whispered, "We are the ones who set you free, not the ones who imprisoned you. If it is revenge you want, follow the path to the village. You will find those you seek there."

The cat blinked, as if it digested her words, then it lowered itself to the ground and started down the path toward the village. The rest of its pride followed.

"I've seen it, but I don't believe it," Kaliska said. "But that leaves the way open for us. It's time to climb down and follow them."

###

Streaks of pre-dawn light edged along the horizon as Kaliska led Bright Moon along the path behind the cats. Not wanting to attract attention, he had extinguished the lamp once they had left the gorge.

The trail split: One branch, the one the big cats followed, went to the village. The other, the one Kaliska and Bright Moon took, went to the main corral. They left the path before they reached the guard dozing near the enclosure.

Kaliska motioned for Bright Moon to stop and keep low. Crouching, he moved on alone, quiet as fog, leaving the girl in the shadows. A dull thump sounded and, moments later, he returned carrying two small knapsacks and a bundle of apples. Putting his mouth next to the girl's ear, he whispered, "One guard. I left him under a tree. I'm afraid his head will hurt when he wakes, but with him out of the way, we can choose some mounts."

Bright Moon nodded. It felt good to have someone else carry the burden of planning.

###

The big cats followed the scent of Chochmo's people to the village. Fires burned low near the huts outside the bramble stockade. All was dark. The animals moved quietly along the paths until they reached the gates of the inner village. Finding them closed, they sniffed around and then found hiding places. The dark shadows gave them cover to wait until the gates opened.

###

Noiselessly, moving as one, Kaliska led Bright Moon

past the guard propped against a tree, to the far side of a bramble-laced enclosure. Wielding his knife, the young scout cut the strands that held the barbed brush in place. The animals, alert for danger, stirred at these new sounds. Bright Moon crawled through as soon as the opening was big enough. Inside, she slowly got to her feet. She did not want to panic the horses, not yet. The sun, just breaking the horizon, painted the scene in long shadows. Bright Moon held an apple out and waited quietly. The nearest animal, curious at this new arrival, pressed forward. She felt his soft muzzle touch her hand as he sniffed and then snatched the offering.

More of the enclosure's wall parted under Kaliska's knife as he finished cutting the bindings. Carrying both knapsacks, he joined her. "I see you've found a friend," he whispered. "Chochmo has other enclosures, but this is where they keep their best mounts. If we can lead them away, it will delay his coming after us. "

Setting the packs down, he took out a rope, looped it over the animal's muzzle, and threw the loose end back over the animal's neck.

He handed her a pack. "I managed to sneak some food for our trip. Wait here. I'll go to the back and get ready. When you see me mount up, you do the same. We don't want to be trapped in here. Move slowly so you don't spook the animals while you lead them. I'll herd the rest behind you and signal when I'm out. You can go faster, then. Our efforts won't stop Chochmo, but it will slow him down."

Bright Moon watched Kaliska make his way through the herd. The animals, sensing something was different, snorted and pawed the ground as they moved around. Finally, Kaliska mounted and waved to her. She swung herself up on a horse's back and walked it toward the opening. Behind her, the herd milled about and then, as if reaching a group decision, followed. Kaliska was quiet until, on the last horse, he exited the corral. He waved a cloak in the air and began shouting. "The witch is loose. Help me catch her. She is taking the horses."

Taking this as her signal, Bright Moon applied her heels to her animal's flanks, urging her mount into an easy lope. The guard stirred and staggered to his feet. He was in time to see the herd thunder down the trail. Kaliska rode by shouting for help as he pretended to give chase. The guard turned to sound an alarm, but a saber tooth's roar split the silence. Hearing this, Kaliska knew their escape was secure. No one would be free to give immediate pursuit.

Chapter 31: Cornered

Hevataneo fidgeted nervously. He could feel the cold stares, not only from both Chochmo and Long Tusk, but also from council members and knew he was in trouble unless he could persuade them to accept his story. "Growling Bear, the one the witch breathed fire at, wanted revenge for what she did to him," he proclaimed. "I went to talk to her... to warn her. I hoped she would be grateful and tell me how she worked her magic, but he lay in wait and attacked me." The young scout paused to add some drama to his storytelling. "We fought, but he overpowered me. When I came around, I was on top a boulder all tied up and gagged. I have no idea what happened or how I got there."

Chochmo eyed the young man. The sentry he had posted at Kaliska's request could not be found. The other man—the one who suffered from the witch's fire—had disappeared. He probably had a hand in the disappearance of the sentry, but neither of them was here to question. The scout was nervous, but held his ground, telling the same story each time he was asked. There was no tripping him on the details. True, he showed signs of having been in a scuffle, but was he telling the truth? Chochmo could not tell.

Leaning close to Long Tusk, he lowered his voice and said, "You told me she was powerful and devious." Only Long Tusk could hear his remarks. "I don't know what happened, probably never will." He shook his head.

"I tried to warn you," Long Tusk said, "and now you know why."

"Unbelievable!" Chochmo continued. "Not only did she escape, she wrecked the platform from which she hung and set my big cats loose. Then she ravaged my village before she fled. If that wasn't enough, the witch rode out of here with a herd of my best horses."

"What will you do now?" Long Tusk questioned.

"Others will have no respect for me if I let her get away," Chochmo said. "I've sent my scouts out. They will find her. She must pay!"

###

A day and a night's ride later, they brought their remuda[88] to a halt on the hilltop overlooking Wikvaya's village. Bright Moon and Kaliska could see the river and a few people moving around the settlement. The water was high enough to block all but one path in or out of the village.

From the village, the trail took a serpentine route downhill to a meadow that ended on a beach. From that sandy spot, rafts carried goods to a ship at anchor. The trail in front of Bright Moon mirrored the one from the village.

"Last part of our trip," Kaliska said. "I'll race you to the...."

Bright Moon slipped over to a fresh mount and whipped her reins, leaving her companion in the dust before he had completed his challenge. Kaliska dropped the reins to the other horses as he urged his mount into action. Being herd animals, the other horses would automatically follow.

By the time they had covered half the distance, someone in the village sounded a trumpet. Focused on their contest, they paid it little attention and raced through the gate. They were surprised to find themselves immediately confronted by guards, spears at the ready.

---

[88] A word of Spanish derivation, roughly meaning "change of horses" and refers to a herd of horses from which hands select their mounts.

Behind the guards, a few villagers ran up, weapons in hand. Two more followed.

"Is this how Lord Wikvaya treats his companions?" Bright Moon demanded.

The spear tips did not waver. The gathered crowd parted, allowing a haggard Wikvaya through.

"You're here!" He exclaimed. "When we parted, I was afraid I had seen the last of you."

The sun sat low on the horizon. Lady Adsila and a handmaiden scrambled to find clothes and make a meal for the pair of weary travelers. Bright Moon watched the villagers prepare the night fires. It was good to be back.

"If circumstances were different, we would have a great celebration," Adsila apologized. "But, at Lord Wikvaya's urging, everything is packed and ready for loading aboard the last ship."

"Packed? Last ship?" Bright Moon was shocked. Had they arrived any later, they would have found an empty village.

"Lord Wikvaya was torn between leaving and waiting for you," Adsila said. "The waters rose so fast he had to send the others on ahead."

"So everyone—the children, the craftsmen, your other handmaidens—are gone?"

"Yes, the few of us that are left here expect to sail tomorrow," Adsila said. "Ours is the last ship. We could wait no longer." She paused, a tear rolled down her cheek, her voice cracked with emotion when she continued. "There were not enough ships, not enough space on the ones we do have, to take everybody and all our wonders. We can only take the most essential items. To take all the people, we've had to leave much behind."

Bright Moon looked around. Outside of the huts, now vacated, families had placed their best items—woven cloth, beaded furs, carvings—to be sacrificed to the waters. Beyond the village, on the platform, sat the flying ship they had built. Like many other belongings, it would not be going with them. Unwilling to destroy it, but not wanting it to fall into the wrong hands, the ovens beneath the craft were started. When the air in the vessel grew warm enough, it would rise up, never to be seen again.

In the village, a trumpet sounded again.

Kaliska stood next to Bright Moon and Wikvaya in the watchtower. On the next hill, an army of riders and foot soldiers had gathered.

"I had hoped the chaos we caused during our escape would delay them, maybe even discourage them," Kaliska said.

"It gave us a head start," Bright Moon said, touching his arm tenderly. "The important thing is that you risked everything to save me," she said, "more than once."

From the tower, the trio watched a group of riders come toward the village.

The riders stopped within shouting distance of Wikvaya's stockade.

"Turn over the witch, and we will leave you alone," the speaker shouted. "Resist and we will destroy your village and everyone in it."

"There is no witch here," Wikvaya shouted back. "You're wasting your time."

The speaker ignored his reply. "We will give you until the morning to change your mind." The riders wheeled their mounts around and returned to Chochmo's camp. As the sun sank below the horizon, a mob of foot soldiers, accompanied by women and children, came down the hill and set up camp in the meadow near the beach.

"Apparently, our friends want to keep us company through the night," Wikvaya said.

"You don't think it's because they want to make sure

we don't sneak off? " Kaliska asked. A sparkle in his eye and a wry grin on his lips told his companions he was joking.

"Well, whatever their reasons, they're in a position that will keep us from getting to the ship," Wikvaya said.

Bright Moon peered into the fading light, examining the terrain. Campfires marked the place where the group of soldiers and camp followers settled in for the night.

It was the lowest point along the path. From there it would be uphill either direction. More importantly, it was the closest place to the river's new shoreline. Dugouts and rafts, used by Wikvaya's people, lined the beach. These would be needed for their final departure. Before her arrival, the villagers biggest concern was setting sail before the flood came. Her arrival brought Chochmo and his tribe of cutthroats and that changed things.

"They are here because of me," Bright Moon said. The lump in her throat became heaviness in her chest. Tearfully, she lowered her head and told her friends, "I will turn myself over to them. They will go away and leave you alone."

"No!" The men chorused loudly.

Startled by their response, she jumped back.

"It would not change things," Wikvaya said in a softer voice. "Certainly, they want you, but they won't be satisfied with that."

"What... why?" She asked.

"Having you will only feed their appetite, not satisfy it," Kaliska said. "Chochmo and Long Tusk always want more; always want what they cannot have."

"So... we have until morning to come up with an escape," Bright Moon said. "Do either of you have any ideas?"

Long Tusk sat with Chochmo and his council and watched flames from the fire try to hold back the night.

He knew that recent events had weakened his influence, his stature, not only with Chochmo and his people, but also within his own tribe. To regain his position, to be a leader again, he needed a plan.

He could see the night fires burning in the village on the opposite hilltop as well as those of the guards in the valley between them.

After the pair escaped, Chochmo's search parties spread out across the countryside to look for them. Now, his guards built a fire that lit the sky, signaling searchers to gather here. Throughout the night, small parties would arrive. In the morning, there would be enough to force the gates and take everything and everyone in the village. The people in the village knew this, and so did Long Tusk. The villagers would have to act before morning, and so would he.

Long Tusk turned to Chochmo. "I will lead a small group to the village tonight," he said.

"Why?" Chochmo asked. "My people will be here by morning and we can take them then."

"I know the witch better than anyone," Long Tusk said. "She is sly. If you give her that much time, she will set a trap for you. I don't plan on letting that happen."

Chochmo nodded. "Your scout is gone, captured by the witch. Take my scout, Hevataneo, along to guide you in the dark."

Long Tusk didn't know if Chochmo believed him or just saw it as a way to get rid of him. *It didn't matter*, he thought. *One way or another, I will have the witch, she will pay, and I will regain my prestige.*

###

Previously, Bright Moon had traveled the path from the hill to the village many times. She knew that the trail from the hilltop skirted a rock wall on one side and the river on the other. Narrow most of its length, at its lowest point the trail widened to form a small meadow bordering the beach.

She leaned against the stockade gate and peered at the few small campfires clustered at this crucial spot. They went almost unnoticed in the darkness, unlike the blaze that capped the hilltop beyond. *A signal fire, it's calling others of Chochmo's tribe to join them at this place. By morning, enough of his people would have gathered to easily overrun the handful of those who remained in the village.*

The group in the valley was all that stood between them and the beach, but too many had gathered there for the villagers to attempt escape. If they did try, Chochmo's people on the hill would soon be there to crush their plans. Wikvaya's people needed to get to the ship before morning. The alternative would be death or enslavement. She had to find another way. Go through, go around, or go over. What they needed was another ship....

That's it! Another ship! Bright Moon turned and ran through the village hollering, "Wikvaya! Lord Wikvaya, I have a solution."

"So, let's go over the plan once again, "Bright Moon said. She pointed to Lady Adsila.

Adsila nodded, needing little prompting to start her narration. "The ovens are being fired as we speak," she said. "My handmaiden collected the clay jars left behind. Half of these are being filled with oil, the other half with hot coals. They'll be lashed together."

"I hope you're right about this being enough of a diversion," Kaliska said.

"I am right... about not wanting to be a slave," Bright Moon said. "I will risk death to avoid it."

"So will many others," Wikvaya added. "And, we haven't been able to come up with another plan." He nodded and looked at Bright Moon to continue.

She turned to Kaliska.

"The men and I will follow you and wait for your signal," he said.

Adsila's handmaiden arrived. "The fires in the ovens are burning," she told them. "When it is ready, Lord Wikvaya's vessel, *Travels-the-air-with-the-birds*, will leap into the air and float away. They will never seize it."

"Good," Adsila said. "Guards have the sedan chair ready. The villagers have their shields ready as instructed. I will lead them out behind Kaliska. When the commotion begins, we will run to the beach and the dugouts."

"We won't have much time, "Wikvaya said. " The dugouts won't wait for anyone—not even me—so don't delay."

Hevataneo led Long Tusk's small group down the path toward the foot soldiers' camp. Most of the campers slept. Even the guard dozed.

"What goes here?" Long Tusk demanded. "Is this how you keep watch? The witch could have slipped by you."

"They slept," Bright Moon said from the darkness, "because I cast a spell on them." Wrapped in a cloak, she stood on the sedan chair and appeared to tower above everyone. The feeble glow of a small oil lamp under her chin showed only her pale face. It was a ghostly apparition. "Since you're here," Bright Moon continued, "I have another reward for you."

"I have something for you," Long Tusk shouted. "Slay her!"

The air filled with spears, clubs, and rocks. Misguided in the dark, few of the weapons hit anywhere near their target. Bright Moon, protected by a shield, unseen in this low light, remained untouched.

"Once again, you've brought this on yourself," Bright Moon shouted. "Soon, a *Fire-dragon-in-the-sky* will visit his wrath on you. Before then, I will I bring you fire from the sky. If you want to save yourself, run!"

Behind her, hidden by their own shields, Kaliska and his men flung the oil-filled jars into the campsite. Crashing to the ground, the containers broke open. The camp was engulfed in flames.

Panicked, screaming people dropped everything and followed the foot-soldiers uphill toward Chochmo's camp, Long Tusk's escort with them.

Long Tusk collared Hevataneo before he could get away. "Stay with me," he commanded. "This is another one of her tricks."

Adsila, seeing Chochmo's campers flee, signaled the villagers, hidden behind Kaliska's group. They rose up and headed for the beach. From the hilltop, Chochmo heard the ruckus and started downhill toward them. The panicked mob, rushing away from the wrath of the witch, streamed up the narrow path and Chochmo's guards couldn't pass.

Adsila, focused on getting her people to the beach, didn't see Long Tusk until he was next to her. She felt his arm around her waist. He jerked her off her feet and threw the surprised woman over his shoulder.

His prize, an unknown value, struggled while he turned and headed for the village. It would be unwise to fight his way through the chaos and added humiliation if the woman turned out to be no one. Thanks to the witch, he believed the village would be empty. He could figure out his next step there.

"Help, Lord Wikvaya," the handmaiden cried out. "He has taken my Lady!" She jumped in front of the rotund Caravan Master in an effort to slow him down, but a swing of his hand knocked her aside.

Lord Wikvaya? Long Tusk could not believe his ears. *Wikvaya was the one who was supposed to escort the witch. The prize slung over my shoulder was becoming more valuable with each step I take.*

Turning from his pursuit, Wikvaya saw a pair of men

head for the village; Adsila was flung over one of their shoulders. "Adsila!" He cried out and started after her.

Seeing this, Kaliska grabbed one of his men. "Get everyone to the beach," he commanded. "Leave one dugout for us, but load the others and head for the ship. Get it ready to sail."

Adsila's handmaiden staggered to her feet and into Bright Moon's arms. "He took my Lady and I was not able to stop him," she sobbed.

"Come with me," Bright Moon said. "We will get her back." They followed Kaliska and Wikvaya up the hill toward the village. Chochmo's men were fighting their way through the mob and would soon be at the campsite, but not before the villagers were aboard the dugouts. There would only be a handful of people left behind. Thanks to Long Tusk, Bright Moon would be one of them.

Seemingly empty, the village was quiet. Night fires burned low. Soon, it would be dawn. Kaliska and Bright Moon, weapons at the ready, followed Wikvaya through the open gates. They were trailed by Adsila's loyal handmaiden.

Suddenly, Adsila was shoved into view. She stood in a hut's open doorway in front of Hevataneo and Long Tusk. The Caravan Master's dirty fingers wound through her hair, holding her in place.

"I am a reasonable man, willing to make a trade," he roared and, pulling her head back, he flashed the knife held at her throat. "Give me the witch, and I will let her go."

It seemed like a fair trade to him. In the turmoil of the camp, he recognized his captive, from her dress and manner, as an obviously important woman. Now that Wikvaya, himself, came after her, Long Tusk knew he had found a good bargaining prospect, especially when both the witch and his scout turned up. Before Chochmo could arrive, Long Tusk would have the witch in custody, maybe even the others as well, and his stature would be without question.

Wikvaya started forward, directly toward the hut where Long Tusk held Adsila. Kaliska circled to the right; Bright Moon to the left.

"Stop where you are!" Long Tusk commanded, and jerked the knife closer under Adsila's chin, this time drawing blood. "

Adsila gasped. Everybody stopped, frozen in place. Heartbeats measured the passage of time while Long Tusk sized-up his situation. "I offered you a good trade. However, if this one means nothing to you, then I have nothing to bargain with. I might as well be rid of her." He pulled her close and made a gesture with his knife.

"No!" The trio chorused.

"Good," Long Tusk crooned and relaxed his hold.

Adsila slumped a little and looked Wikvaya's way through sad, tear-filled eyes. "Leave me. Go, and lead our people to a new place."

"I cannot," he told her softly.

"Now that we understand her value," Long Tusk said. "We can begin bargaining. I had offered an even trade, this woman for the witch. But, I've found that her value has gone up. I am still willing to trade this woman for the witch… and my disloyal scout."

"Agreed," Bright Moon said, and threw down her weapon. "I will surrender."

Hearing those words, Adsila's tears became a flood. "No," she wailed. "You have done enough. Don't sacrifice yourself for me."

"Be still you," Long Tusk said. "It's time she learned her place."

He nodded to Hevataneo. "Take some cord and tie her. When you're done, tie up my scout," Long Tusk said. "Hurry up, we don't have much time."

Meekly, Chochmo's young scout walked toward

Bright Moon.

Adsila twisted in Long Tusk's hold, but a jab from the knife's tip, stilled her movement. *When Hevataneo gets those two trussed up,* Long Tusk fantasized, *it will be Wikvaya's turn to feel the bite of rawhide bindings. He won't put up a fuss with his friends tied up and the woman held at knifepoint. By the time Chochmo arrives, everybody will be my prisoner.* He smiled broadly, pleased with how well his plan was working.

"Hold your hands out," Hevataneo commanded, wagging cords in front of her and smiling gleefully. Along the way, he had traded his timidity for arrogance.

Bright Moon despised him and his smile, but she was stuck. She had hoped for more time, but things were coming to a close. Long Tusk held Adsila captive. Chochmo and his mob would be here soon. They were cornered. She was out of tricks when she needed one the most. Her heart sank as she held her hands out in surrender.

Long Tusk felt a sharp poke in his back. A woman's voice commanded, "Drop the knife and let her go." Chochmo's worthless scout, Hevataneo failed to account for everyone who came through the gate. He failed to warn Long Tusk that another person trailed behind the others and now held a spear on him.

Adsila's handmaiden, entering after the others, saw her lady's imprisonment and everyone else held at bay. Creeping through the shadows, no one noticed her slip behind a line of huts to reach the one where Long Tusk made his demands. Entering the back, she eased her way forward, spear at the ready.

"I will slit her throat," Long Tusk told his unseen assailant, through clenched teeth. He hoped his bluff would work, but his words were greeted with another jab, deeper, more insistent, this time.

"Do as I say or I will push my spear through you."

The knife clattered across the stone threshold and Long Tusk released his hold. Everything he had hoped for was fading before his eyes.

Adsila and Wikvaya rushed toward each other. Hevataneo's brash smile quickly faded and he forgot his task. Bright Moon hit him. The scout stumbled backward, more humiliated than hurt.

Long Tusk felt the spear-holder behind him relax. It was the opening he needed. He whirled around and tore the spear out of the surprised girl's hands, knocking her aside. Driven by frustration, he hurled the spear after the fleeing Adsila and then turned and ran off, swallowed by the darkness.

Reaching Adsila before the spear, Wikvaya threw her aside. The spear hit him in the shoulder, and he went down.

Hevataneo, taking advantage of the confusion, got to his feet and ran away. Bright Moon and Kaliska gathered around Adsila, Wikvaya's head in her lap. They pulled the spear free before Bright Moon could stop them. A quick look told her that her friend bled freely and the wound was not deep.

"I have no medicines here," Bright Moon said, "and we have no time."

Adsila nodded, understanding their plight. "Go," she said. "You've done all you could, now save yourselves."

"We will not leave our friends," Kaliska said.

Adsila's handmaiden, a large red welt across her cheek, now knelt next to her ladyship.

Wikvaya's eyes fluttered and he moaned slightly as he tried to sit up. "Can you get me ready to move?" He asked. "We must get to the beach."

Bright Moon looked at the handmaiden. "Find some cloth, and bring it to me." Turning to Kaliska, she said, "Go to the gate, and see if it is clear. We will get Wikvaya ready to travel."

The handmaiden returned, a bundle of cloth in her arms, and the three women bound Wikvaya's wound.

Kaliska returned wearing a look of grave concern. "It looks as though Chochmo has fought his way through the swarm and is at the beach," he told them. "The people from the campsite told of the attack and no one wants to come closer. Chochmo is yelling at them, trying to get them to move, but they are refusing. For the time being, they're stalled there, but it won't last long. I saw Hevataneo run out the gate. When he gets there and tells his story, Chochmo's people will regroup and head this way. We won't be able to get by them. It will be light soon, so there is little chance of hiding." He hung his head "I'm afraid all is lost."

Exhausted, everyone was silent, lost in their own thoughts. Adsila's handmaiden started to cry quietly, and Adsila wrapped a comforting arm around the young girl. The clamor of Chochmo's people at the beach grew louder. Hevataneo must have reached them and told his tale. Now, Chochmo would rally his people. They would be here soon.

Chapter 32: Airborne

Bright Moon looked at her small group. Wikvaya, wounded, leaned against Adsila while their handmaiden sat close by, tearfully waiting for what she feared was capture and a life of slavery. Kaliska—who would fight to the end—stood near, spear at the ready, to prevent a sneak attack by Long Tusk. Not far away, the blazing fires in the ovens devoured timbers, turning the wood to ash. Smoke drifted her way. Exhausted, it took a moment for an idea to form. When it did, it struck her like Fire-from-the-sky.

"We still have a chance!" Bright Moon exclaimed and jumped to her feet. "But, we must act quickly, before the sun comes up."

All eyes were upon her.

"To get to the beach and escape, we need another diversion," Bright Moon explained. "Chochmo's people are already afraid. Hevataneo is not too believable so it won't take much to panic them again," she said.

Wikvaya winced as he tried to sit up. "The last trick worked because we caught them off guard. To fool them again will take something really big."

"Your plan has been to let *Travels-the-air-with-the-birds* float away so they would not capture it, but now we can use it to aid our escape." Excited, Bright Moon beamed with pride.

Wide-eyed, the others looked at her with open mouths. Had she gone mad?

"It will take to the air," Wikvaya said, "but it will never carry all of us."

Bright Moon nodded. "It doesn't have to carry all of us; it just has to create enough panic that you can get away."

Before they could recover, she pulled Lady Adsila aside. "Kaliska and I will ready the vessel to fly," she said. "Get Wikvaya to his feet and start for the beach. If Chochmo's people catch you, act terrified. Tell them the beast, *Fire-dragon-in-the-sky,* is loose and comes for them."

Adsila, a new spark of hope showing in her eyes, understood her task and nodded agreement.

"Oh, and one more thing," Bright Moon said. Laying a gentle hand on Adsila's arm, she lowered her voice to a whisper, "Take good care of your man. Our people need him to lead them and, right now, he needs you to lead him to the beach."

Before Adsila could protest, Bright Moon gave her a gentle shove toward Wikvaya, her handmaiden, and her new role as leader. Adsila, willing to try anything to avoid captivity, was shocked by the idea, but she had no better plan.

Kaliska watched Wikvaya, aided by the two women, hobble through the gate and disappear into the darkness. With them out of sight, he turned to Bright Moon. "What now?"

"Come, we have work to do," she said, and she turned toward the ovens.

Chochmo's men had their hands full halting the stampeding mob that had once been guarding the beach. Using their torches like spears, they pushed the terrified group back along the narrow path to the place they left in such a hurry.

"You were sent here to guard this place," Chochmo yelled. His guards held their torches high so he could read the expressions of these frightened people. Moments before, the flames had been poked in their faces in order to stop their stampede and force them back to the meadow. This new change was a relief to the crowd because they feared Chochmo less than they feared the witch.

"Why do you run?" Chochmo challenged them.

"The witch appeared and threatened us," they said. "She floated high in the air, only her face showed."

"You act like old women," Chochmo said. His voice clearly showed his disgust. "You should have slain the witch." His words were greeted with a cacophony of garbled replies, their words lost in the babble of voices.

"Enough!" He shouted. Pointing to one man, he barked, "You! Speak! Tell me what happened and be quick about it."

"We did attack," the man said, wishing someone else had the honor of explaining, "but our weapons were useless against her powers." He made a futile attempt at reading his leader's face in the flickering light before finally adding, "She said a *Fire-dragon-in-the-sky* would soon come after us." He wrung his hands nervously. "She said if we wanted to save ourselves, we should run. Then, she made fire fall out of the darkness. Seeing it drop on us as she commanded, we ran."

Chochmo made a face, his lips curled in rage, but his reply was cut off and his anger defused by Hevataneo's arrival.

"They surprised us and captured Long Tusk," he yelled, "but I got away."

Chochmo was pleased to hear of Long Tusk's capture. The caravan master was too old, too soft, and too... too... too much in the way. "How many are there?" Chochmo asked.

"Before they attacked, I saw four—the man, Wikvaya, Long Tusk's scout, a woman, and the witch— but I was barely able to escape with my life."

Chochmo leaned forward. "While you were there, did you see anything of a *Fire-dragon-from-the-sky?*"

"I saw no such thing," Hevataneo said. "If they had a *Fire-dragon-from-the-sky*, why did they need so many people to fight Long Tusk and me?"

###

Long Tusk ran headlong through the darkened village, until, winded, he crept into the shadows around a raised platform and plopped down. Shaken, his rotund body covered with sweat, out of breath, he needed time to collect himself.

In all his exploits, he had wielded many a spear, but had never felt a spear in his back. There must have been more than the four he had held in front of him. How many, he did not know, but he was sure that he escaped only by his quick wit.

Nearby, voices signaled someone approaching. He needed a different place to hide. The platform walls were hot to the touch. The voices were too close for him to risk running. He lay on the ground in the dark and hoped to go unnoticed.

Long Tusk watched the witch, carrying a torch, and his scout, climb a ladder at the far end. What were they up to? None of the others were in sight. *Maybe*, Long Tusk thought, *I still have a chance to capture them.* Getting up, he crept along the wall toward the ladder.

###

"The pockets in the netting not only holds cargo— furs, bags of grain, anything you might carry on a ship—it also gives us a place to sit," Bright Moon explained as she lead Kaliska around the vessel. Along the way, they pulled the ropes allowing the sails to unfurl and lit the fire-bowls under the double row of oil-jars lining the underside. The last tether, secured at both ends, ran alongside the fire-bowls the length of the vessel and met mid-ship.

"What's it for?" Kaliska asked. He walked quickly, both because she was in a hurry but also because the scaffolding over the oven-tops was hot. He had never seen anything like this. Why someone would build it and put it on top of the ovens was beyond him.

"Are you ready for a new adventure?" Bright Moon asked. Her lips curved into a small smile she added, "This is our way to escape."

"If it gets us away from Chochmo, I'm ready," he said. "But, how will this help?"

"You've heard me talk about something called *Travels-the-air-with-the-birds?*" She asked.

He nodded. He heard them use that term many times but had no idea of what they were talking about.

"Well, this is it," she said, waving her hands around. "We're going to fly out of here."

Kaliska stopped in his tracks and looked at her. She was serious.

"Wikvaya created it and it works! We've been up in it!" She said reassuringly.

Threatening sounds from the beach cut off any argument he would have made.

"What do we have to do?" He asked.

"We're ready," she told him. "Climb in and I'll cut us free."

Kaliska crawled into the shaky netting. Pushing two ram's horns out of his way, he turned to see Bright Moon using a hand ax on the ropes with little to show for her efforts.

"Here," he yelled, "join me and we can use our knives."

She threw the ax onto the seat next to him, climbed in, and drew her knife. When the mooring lines parted, *Travels-the-air-with-the-birds* rose smoothly.

As Kaliska's view of the village spread out in front of his eyes, his heart rose in his throat and he tightened his grip on the webbing that held them.

Remembering the sail ropes beside her, Bright Moon gave them a tug releasing the booms that held the sails. "There, that should make the vessel look pretty threatening," she said.

###

Long Tusk slowed his climb as he neared the top of the ladder and peered over the edge, ready to duck out of sight if they were near. He was at the end of a huge structure. Resembling a bloated fish caught in a net. It sat atop several chimneys. The girl and his scout were ahead, picking their way over scaffolding as they moved toward the other end. Both were too engrossed in explanation and lighting fire bowls to notice him.

Long Tusk climbed up and crept after the pair, hiding in the security of the shadows while he watched for the opportunity to capture them. Reaching the far end, his scout climbed into a pouch in the mesh while the girl took an ax and began flailing at a tether in front of this device.

Long Tusk edged forward, his knife drawn, stopping in the shadows just short of the pouch. The scout called the girl back. She joined him in the netting and they began cutting through the rope. Long Tusk wrapped his free hand in the netting and leaned forward to strike just as *Travels-the-air-with-the-birds* lifted off. Feet suddenly clawing the air, Long Tusk looked down to see the platform, bathed in the early dawn light, a few man-lengths below him and getting smaller. Panicked, he looked at the witch and her companion. Seemingly unconcerned, she pulled a cord and a boom on either side of the ship slammed into place, unfurling sails.

Hevataneo, hands on hips, leaned back and laughed. "They have no *Fire-dragon-from-the-sky*."

Chochmo's people stood In front of the scout rooted to the ground and stared over his shoulder at the village. In front of their eyes, *Travels-the-air-with-the-birds* rose up, stretched its wings, and headed their way. Wide-eyed, their own leader was heard to utter one word, "Unbelievable."

"Run! It's the *Fire-dragon-in-the-sky*." Someone yelled.

The crowd, frozen in place until now, broke and began running in every direction.

Aboard *Travels-the-air-with-the-birds*, Bright Moon and Kaliska put the ram's horns to their lips and blew a long, low note. The sound drifted out over the valley, its echo bouncing off rock walls, stirring the commotion. Below them, on the meadow near the beach, terror erupted even among the people who had stood immobile.

They could see the sun cracking the horizon, throwing long streaks of golden light across a still dark landscape. Movement behind Bright Moon caught her attention. She turned and saw Long Tusk, just two arms' lengths away, tangled in the webbing. Panic on his face, he hacked away at the ropes.

"No!" She yelled. "Stop!" Turning fully around, she tried to climb through the netting toward him, but Kaliska held her back.

Long Tusk's knife became caught and he worked to free it while the cords slowly unraveled, dangling him lower. Wheezing, the fat old man pulled himself up the rope until he reached the row of fire-bowls along the underside. He reached out and grabbed the framework surrounding the closest set.

Built to hold the oil-jar and fire-bowl, it could not take his weight and broke loose. By the time he realized his mistake, he had fallen too far away to save himself. In his panic, he became tangled in the cords and framework. The oil-jar flipped over, spilling its contents on him. Within a heartbeat, he turned into a blazing torch. It marked his path through the sky until he hit the ground in front of Chochmo.

Burnt, broken, Long Tusk lay there, the remains of his life fading away and recalled Silver Water's warning, *I looked into your future and see you die, falling from the sky covered in flames.* Those close by heard his final words, "The... witch... was... right...."

Travels-the-air-with-the-birds, freed of the weight of both Long Tusk and an oil-jar, lurched upward. This sudden movement knocked a second jar loose. Like the first, it tumbled through the air and hit the ground in the middle of the fear-struck crowd. A ball of fire erupted. One-by-one, several more jars joined those already fallen.

Bursting into flames on impact, these bonfires made short work of any lingering discipline in Chochmo's camp. Believing her warning to be true, the guards joined the crowd—blind with panic—and stampeded, running in every direction, unaware that two women and a wounded man hobbled through their midst to a dugout on the beach.

Travels-the-air-with-the-birds floated gently over the countryside. Kaliska relaxed his grip just a little. The sails flapped and crackled in the breeze. Beside him, Bright Moon quietly hummed a tune unknown to him as she watched the birds glide around them.

From their height, Kaliska felt as if he was looking out from a high mountain. The river's twists and turns, the forests, and even the water beyond the Great Ice were all clearly visible. Behind them, the sails of Wikvaya's ship glistened in the early morning light as it made its way downstream.

"See the waters over there?" Bright Moon asked. "As Wikvaya thought, the Great Ice grows thin. It will not hold back much longer."

He nodded. "When the ice is gone, the water will rush down the river," he said. "Who knows where it will go?" He leaned forward and craned his neck, "Perhaps over there to that river or to the plains, beyond." He shaded his eyes to make out other landmarks.

Bright Moon watched him take in the sights. He had relaxed his grip and was more at ease now, but she felt she should prepare him for yet another surprise. "Do you like the view," she asked.

Kaliska nodded. "I didn't know what I was in for,

but it was worth the risk. I didn't want to end up in Chochmo's hands, and I didn't see another way out."

"Enjoy it while it lasts," she said, "I think we're dropping down."

Kaliska sat up, and tightened his grip on the ropes. "What? How can you tell?"

"I'm not seeing as far as I did just a short time ago and landmarks—animals, trees, bushes—on the ground are getting clearer. The oil in the remaining jars may be gone or the fires under them went out."

"What do we do now?"

She shrugged. "I don't know."

"You told me you were up in this before," he said, his voice tinged with fear-driven anger. "How did you get down then?"

"It was always tied to ropes, and we were pulled back down," Bright Moon replied in the same angry tone. "This is something new. I don't know if Wikvaya even thought that far ahead." Tearfully, she shook her head. *How could she be expected to think of everything?*

Trees were closer now. They both leaned forward to see what lay in front. The river glistened through the leaves. Beyond it, low, rocky hills stood tall... too tall for them to cross. A scraping sound as treetops ripped along the base of their vessel, tearing out the remaining fire-bowls and oil-jars. These crashed to the ground, starting fires.

Free of their weight, *Travels-the-air-with-the-birds* rose clear of the trees, only to dip back, tail low, as it aimed at a brush-covered ridge in the river.

"Make yourself into a tight ball and hang on," Kaliska shouted excitedly.

Behind them, pillars of black smoke marked their passage.

Chapter 33: Crashed

Chochmo watched the beast the witch called the *Fire-dragon-in-the-sky* float by overhead. He heard its snarl, an ear splitting high pitch combined with a low rumble, echo off the canyon walls. Suddenly, the beast cast off Long Tusk's burning body. Everyone watched it plummet out of the sky and land at Chochmo's feet. To add to their duress, the beast's flaming eggs began dropping on them.

The horses reared up, throwing their riders. The men scrambled to keep the animals from running off. With the guards occupied, there was no one left to keep the crowd in check and they ran off. Feeling the witch had laid a curse on Chochmo and his tribe propelled them into a blind panic. There would be no stopping them. It would take days before any of them might be found. Some, Chochmo knew, might never be found.

However, Chochmo was not left alone. A few of his mounted guards—having regained control of their rides—remained nearby, along with Hevataneo, his worthless scout. He didn't know if they remained due to loyalty or fear, but here they were and he didn't question it further. A sound, rolling like distant thunder, broke into his trance.

"There," pointing, Hevataneo shouted, hoping to regain lost prestige. "The *Fire-dragon-in-the-sky* went that way and now there is smoke." The young scout danced around merrily. "All is not lost! All is not lost!" He sang.

Chochmo shaded his eyes and peered at the column of smoke. "Perhaps the beast is in trouble," he said. "We will go and see."

###

Travels-the-air-with-the-birds slid over the treetops and crossed the water that separated the ridge from the mainland. Scattered along the ground behind them, lay the remains of the framework that once held oil-jars. Free of the weight, the tail-heavy vessel rose and then sagged low to skim the tops of bushes. The tangle of branches and vines along the ridge grabbed at the vehicle's netting.

Travels-the-air-with-the-birds made a valiant attempt to bore its way through the brush. Bright Moon lost her grip on the netting and slid toward the mass of vegetation rushing by. Kaliska's strong arm wrapped around her, pulling her back to the safety of the corner he occupied.

The sounds of cracking brush and calls of startled birds rose to a fevered pitch. The vessel finally dragged to a halt leaving them in silence, broken only by the fluttering sails dangling from broken yardarms.

The craft lay on its side, forcing Bright Moon and Kaliska to crowd into a corner of the pouch. His arms wrapped around her, he still clutched the netting tightly.

"That wasn't so bad," Bright Moon finally said. She smiled reassuringly at Kaliska, but quickly freed herself from his embrace.

Kaliska gave a nervous laugh. "Well, I guess I can breathe, again." He let go of the ropes and flexed his stiff fingers.

"Come on," Bright Moon said. "Let's see where we are." She seized the edge of the net and lowered herself to the ground. Kaliska picked up the ax and followed.

From the front of the vessel, the pair hacked their way through the brush to reach a ledge overlooking the river. Chunks of ice, some larger than huts, jostled each other as they floated downstream.

"Won't be getting off on this side. Let's check the other side," Kaliska suggested. "Maybe over there, we'll find a way off the ridge."

Travels-the-air-with-the-birds left a cleared trail behind it so getting to the other side didn't prove a great challenge.

On one knee, Bright Moon looked across the brink at the chaos their passage had left. Kaliska stood beside her, a hand at his brow to shield his eyes and scanned the horizon.

Bright Moon looked at the water-soaked swamp in front of them. Creeks flowed down the hillside and fed the wetlands. Added to this, upstream the rising river now spilled over into the bog further separating mainland and ridge. Before they came down, she remembered seeing the ridge set apart by this band of shallow water. Tufts of marsh grass decorated its surface, but their grassy tips— normally high above the water—barely cleared the waves now.

"There's more ice and the river's getting deeper, just as Wikvaya said it would," Bright Moon said. "It's not normal for this time of year. Think we can get across that?" she pointed at the flooded marsh.

"It looks like a bog," Kaliska said. "You can never be sure of the base. Some places are muck and will pull you under. These spots can be so deep you'd never find the bottom. We'll need to build a raft, but there aren't enough trees here to make one."

From their vantage point, they could see that the opposite shore sloped down from the forest to the water's edge. The oil-jars that had fueled their flight now fueled a fire, clearing the land of brush and grass. The smoke marked their location and provided a beacon for Chochmo. He would be here soon.

Kaliska eyed the column rising into the sky. "We need to get away from here, or get ready for guests."

Bright Moon sighed. "We could gather some stones in case we have to fight, but let's go back to Wikvaya's ship for right now," she said. "Maybe we can put something together from its remains."

Chochmo's meager group halted at the edge of the forest. The burnt over ground in front of them sloped away to willows and reed beds at the water's edge. Smoke from nearly exhausted fires curled up from blackened trees.

Across a water-filled channel, sat a low, brush-covered ridge. Obviously, the crash site, its surface was also marred by recent cuttings. There was no question in his mind: he found the place where the witch came down. "Come," he said. He urged his horse forward.

On foot, Hevataneo ran ahead and tested the depth of the water with his spear. "It is shallow here," he said, holding the spear's end up as evidence.

Chochmo leaned forward and grunted an acknowledgement. "See if this is a good crossing place," he ordered.

"Sir?"

Chochmo was interrupted before he could reply.

"Who is it you seek?" From across the bog Bright Moon called to them. She stood on a rock, hidden behind bushes, about halfway up the slope. It was a position of superiority and power because it gave her the appearance of being taller than they remembered.

Chochmo jerked upright. His horse pranced nervously. Getting the animal under control, he looked across and sized up his opponent. "I have come for you, witch!"

"You have come here after I warned you of the great water?" There was a twinge of sadness in her voice.

"Your warning is a hoax like your other tricks," he said. "Where is your *Fire-dragon-in-the-sky* now?"

"Alas, the *Fire-dragon-in-the-sky* has devoured my

powers, but they will soon return. In the meantime I am vulnerable."

"Then I will send my men to seize you. You will be mine."

"Yours?" She asked. "Why yours?" She acted as if this was a puzzle she did not comprehend.

"Did you not hear me?" Chochmo shouted. "My men will seize you. They will bring you to me, and you will be mine."

"If your men come, then the first one who reaches me will be the one who will benefit from my powers when they return. Do you men want to be powerful?"

She searched their faces hoping her words would appeal to their greed. While Chochmo's men stood frozen, a few glanced slyly at their comrades. Confident that her plan was working, she continued. "Would you men want to fly, to become invisible, to breath fire on your enemies? Who would be the first to come and claim me? Which one of you deserves that honor more?"

"I'm the one," Hevataneo shouted. "I found her. I deserve her. She is mine."

"Shut up, you fool!" Chochmo roared. He had had enough and swung his club to silence his young scout.

Holding his spear up, Hevataneo parried the blow, danced back out of range and then lunged forward, his spear catching Chochmo in the side.

A guard, war-club raised high, urged his mount forward, but Hevataneo pulled his spear free in time to dance away from the guard's attack. Before the guard could turn his mount, Hevataneo knocked him from his horse and impaled him as he hit the ground.

Everyone began swinging their weapons. In order to protect himself, Chochmo joined in the melee. Before the bedlam stopped, his left arm hung limp, and a leg wound bleed freely. In addition, he sported several additional wounds, but he was the last man left.

Chochmo looked at the carnage around him and then across the water at Bright Moon with the knowledge that the witch had not only watched everything, she was the cause of it.

"You still have time to save yourself," she said quietly, even though she knew what his answer would be.

"I will make you mine and you will pay for this." He ignored his wounds and urged his horse forward into the water.

Two man-lengths from the bank, the animal was up to its belly. At a signal from Bright Moon, Kaliska rose from his hiding spot. Together, they began throwing rocks at the animal. The horse reared up under the assault, dumping Chochmo, who disappeared under the surface. When he found his feet, he came up sputtering.

The animal continued its violent movements under the barrage of stones the pair flung its way. Chochmo grabbed at it, but couldn't remount. His attempts managed to drag him further away from the shore he had left before he lost his grip. Free of its rider, the animal turned and headed back to where it had entered the water, leaving him alone in midstream. Filled with blind rage, he seethed as he stumbled forward toward Bright Moon. So sure that he would eliminate the man and have his way with the girl, he ignored the fact that the water was nearly chest-deep. His rage grew even louder when he realized he had become caught in the muck beneath the water and it was dragging him down. No matter how he tried, he could not get free. His rage turned to panic as he sank lower into the ooze. "Help me," he shouted. "Save me!"

Her emotions cut through her exhaustion and rose quickly to the surface. "You had a chance to save yourself," fist in the air, Bright Moon shouted back. "Instead, you came after us."

Bright Moon felt relief as the constant fear of pursuit lifted from her shoulders. Tearfully, she turned her back to the struggling man.

Kaliska wrapped a protective arm around her as he led her away. "He is the last one. No one else is left to pursue us. It's over." His voice soft, he comforted the sobbing girl as they returned to the vessel they had started making from pieces of *Travels-the-air-with-the-birds*.

Chochmo's horse clamored out near the spot where he had entered the water. The animal trotted past the carnage the guards had made of each other and disappeared into the forest just as two tigers, their long tusks glinting in the sun, slunked out of the brush. Ignoring the horse, they seemed to make themselves comfortable near the water's edge and watched until Chochmo disappeared below the surface. The waters became calm, the ripples died away, and the big cats turned and left.

Chapter 34: A New Life

The ridge where they crashed, although covered with dense brush and vines, lacked trees even scrawny ones. It was just as well. If one had existed, Kaliska and Bright Moon knew they lacked the time needed to carve an adequate dugout. Not having a choice, they did the next best thing.

What remained of *Travels-the-air-with-the-birds* was salvaged: Sails, riggings, reed bundles, and hide removed and then its skeleton taken apart. All these items were laid out on the rocky beach near the river's edge. They would build their craft from this assortment.

When Bright Moon and Lady Adsila redesigned the vessel, they substituted light poles and bundled reeds for the heavy timbers Wikvaya had used. Wood of any size was scarce so they improvised. They started by binding poles together to provide a hardcore to build on. Bundled reeds were bound to these poles. They continued the process until they were able to form a makeshift log. This would be the craft's hull. To keep it from rolling over, outriggers were added. Finally, a mast completed the vessel. The remnants of the sails their airship had once worn would now live on to propel this new vessel.

Kaliska stood back and looked at their creation. Originally, he had talked about making a raft from the mast poles. It would have been small and simple, but large enough to carry them across the marsh to dry land. "We could travel on foot from there," he had explained.

Bright Moon had other ideas. "Travel where?" She challenged. "If we go back to Wikvaya's village, we face the risk of running into the rest of Chochmo's guards. If not them perhaps we would end up face-to-face with some of his people. I would like to find Wikvaya, but I am not looking forward to running into anyone else."

In the end, the pair compromised on this solution.

Bright Moon looked over their creation with a jaundiced eye, but, since it was her demand they travel by river, she could not object to the vessel's crudeness. The hull, nothing more than a collection of sticks and reeds lashed together, would have to suffice. She would sit atop this cylinder with her feet propped up on the outrigger frame. Kaliska would stand behind her and work the sweep to steer them past obstacles. Because the sail was directly in front of her, it blocked much of her forward view. To see anything, Bright Moon would have to lean forward and crouch low to peer under the sail's bottom lip. In such an awkward stance, she had little hope of seeing an obstacle in time to avoid it.

As if he had read her mind, Kaliska broke the silence. "It doesn't look like much, but we did our best with what we could salvage. If we had better materials and more time, we could have come up...."

Drained to near exhaustion by the night's episode, Bright Moon cut him off sharply. "You're sure this will float?"

Equally tired and irritated, Kaliska responded. "Do we have a choice?"

Bright Moon shrugged and glanced at the rising water, the abundance of ice in the river, and then back at their contraption. "There is only one way we'll know if it will hold together long enough to at least get us to the other shore," tired resignation showed in her voice. Getting to shore was not her goal. She hoped it would last long enough to carry them down the river where travel would be faster than on foot and should provide fewer dangers.

"The water has gotten deeper since *Travels-the- air-with-the-birds* came down," Bright Moon said. "We both know it's too cold and the current is too fast to let us swim across. This is our only hope so we should get started."

Kaliska motioned her to the front of the boat and he stood at the back.

Irritated, her thoughts boiled up but she kept them to herself. *No, it's not a raft. It's better! There were times when we just need to act,* she thought. *His constant explanations could be so irritating.* Together, they lifted the vessel and carried it into the shallow waters.

Now that this is built, travel by river will be faster, Kaliska thought, *but if we had built a raft when we first started, we'd be across the swamp and on our way by now. Chochmo's people are gone, so should her concern for them.*

"It floats," she said. "Let's get going." She swung herself up and took a position near the bow, feet braced against the outrigger frame, and sail ropes firmly in hand.

Kaliska pushed it a little further out before climbing on behind her. He guided the craft into the current. Smugly, he thought, *the vessel not only floats, it handles nicely,* and his chest swelled a little. The breeze, as if it wanted to confirm his feelings, filled the sail and they began their trip downstream.

From the beginning of the trip, their vessel leaked. By the afternoon of the second day, the reeds were so soaked that their sturdy little craft rode low in the water. Kaliska knew he would have to repair it soon or they would be swimming. Playfully, he bent down, scooped a handful of icy river water, and flung it at Bright Moon. His aim was true. It hit her bare skin and he was rewarded with Bright Moon's surprised squeal. Furious, she turned quickly and gave him a look that would have stopped a stampede of buffalo.

"Our vessel is getting waterlogged," he said and emphasized his point by bouncing in place. This caused the perch where she sat to rise and fall in time with the rhythm of his movements, dunking Bright Moon's seat.

Her scowl darkened and she tightened her grip on the ropes controlling the sail. Kaliska knew that they were substitutes for his neck and, having made his point, stopped his demonstration.

"Unless you plan on swimming, steer over there." He pointed at a beach near a steep cliff. "We need a place to dry it out and tighten the cords or we'll be in the water."

Bright Moon pulled on the ropes adjusting the sail while Kaliska worked the sweep. They watched as the bow came around and were soon rewarded with the grating sound of their vessel hitting the beach. Ashore, they pulled their craft high on the sand and tipped it over to allow the wood and reeds to dry.

"Clear a spot," Kaliska said. "We can use the sail to make a tent." He laid the mast out on the ground and began stripping the sail from the yardarm.

"A tent?" Bright Moon questioned. "Are we going to be here that long?"

"It will take a few days for the canoe to dry out and for us to gather enough pitch to coat the ropes and make repairs," Kaliska said. "While we wait, we can stretch our legs and do some hunting. It will give us something besides fish to eat."

Bright Moon nodded, but said, "I don't want to put the tent here."

Kaliska made a face. *What now?* He thought. "If we're going to be here a few days, I think we'll need a tent, don't you?"

"Yes," Bright Moon agreed. "But not here," she said and pointed to the top of the bluff. "We need to put it up there, where there's a forest and animals. We can look for Wikvaya's ship."

Kaliska craned his neck, and then he looked at the goat track leading from the river. It would be a long, steep climb. "Do we really need to be up there?" He asked.

Bright Moon, having gathered the sail, had already started up the trail. She paused and turned his way "Yes," she replied. "We don't have to take everything, just the things we'll need." Pausing, she looked at him and then smiled. "From up there we will be as high as when we were in *Travels-the-air-with-the-birds,*" she coaxed. "We can see and our signal fire can be seen."

Signal fire? What next? It is a good thing she has a pretty smile because she is starting to really get under my skin. Kaliska kept his thoughts to himself. *There is no point in stirring up a bee's nest. I will go hunting after we make camp. Time away from each other would improve both of our outlooks.*

She shifted the bundled sail over her shoulder and started up the path again, calling, "After you finish with the canoe, bring anything else you think we might need."

Hunting! Once our camp is set up, I will go hunting! He thought. Yes, the solitude of the forest and time away, that's what

###

By the time he got to the top, Bright Moon had a tent set up and a fire started. She sat near the edge looking out over the valley. He dropped the few items he brought near the tent and then flopped down next to her to rest. The forest behind them seemed to call his name, but right now, he was tired. It had been a long two days on the river capped off by the uphill climb. He needed a rest.

Together they took in the view. She was right. They were as high as when they flew in *Travels-the-air-with-the-birds.*

"From here, the river we followed is but a silver band winding through rolling hills," he said.

"Yes, "Bright Moon agreed, "and back the way we came, there is a storm."

"How can you tell," Kaliska asked.

"See the sky there, near the edge of the world, clouds have gathered and their dark forms are alight with Fire-from-the sky."

The sound of thunder rolled through the air

confirming her observations, and a cold breeze came up. The thunder seemed to continue. They got to their feet. She turned and started toward their makeshift tent when she felt the ground begin to shake. Kaliska made a surprised gasp. Had he spotted Wikvaya's ship? She turned back quickly to see the cause of his excitement.

"Look!" He yelled and pointed upstream, toward the storm.

She looked where he directed and saw a wall of water, nearly as tall as the bluff, bury the hills and careen along the river valley toward them.[89] The source of the thunder, it carried blocks of ice the size of boulders and smashed them explosively against the canyon's rocky walls. Pieces flew in every direction. The noise grew louder as the wave approached.

When Bright Moon explored the Great Ice with Wikvaya, he tried to measure the water's depth, but could not. From that, they knew the water was deep. He told

---

89 (see Missoula Floods) In geomorphology, an outburst flood, which is a type of mega flood, is a high-magnitude, low-frequency catastrophic flood involving the sudden release of water. During the last de-glaciation, numerous glacial lake outburst floods (GLOF) were caused by the collapse of either ice sheets or glaciers that formed the dams of pro-glacial lakes. Examples of older outburst floods are known from the geological past of the Earth. This is similar to The Missoula Floods (also known as the Spokane Floods or the Bretz Floods) which all refer to the cataclysmic floods that swept periodically across eastern Washington and down the Columbia River Gorge—creating the 'Channeled Scablands of Washington state'--at the end of the last ice age. These glacial lake outburst floods were the result of periodic sudden ruptures of the ice dam on the Clark Fork River that created Glacial Lake Missoula. After each ice dam rupture, the waters of the lake would rush down the Clark Fork and the Columbia River, inundating much of eastern Washington and the Willamette Valley in western Oregon. After the rupture, the ice would reform, recreating Glacial Lake Missoula once again. Geologists estimate that the cycle of flooding and reformation of the lake lasted an average of 55 years and that the floods occurred several times over the 2,000-year period between 15,000 and 13,000 years ago. By calculations, it is estimated that the maximum speed of the flood waters approached 36 meters/second (130 km/h or 80 mph).

her when it came; nothing would stand it its way. He was right. She had believed him, but in her wildest dreams, she had no idea it would be like this.

"Get down!" Kaliska yelled. Captivated by the scene unfolding in front of her, Bright Moon remained frozen in place. In a heartbeat, Kaliska hurdled himself her way. His quick action had her off her feet and on the ground. He was on top of her, sheltering her body with his. They lay that way while ice chunks whizzed overhead or rained down around them. The ground where they lay shook under the impact.

The rushing waters swallowed everything in its path. Nothing—bushes, trees, or boulders—could stand in its way. The deluge crashed onto the beach where their canoe rested. In the blink of an eye, their little vessel was gone, crushed under the onslaught, the pieces swept away. Eventually, it seemed like forever, the crest of the flood rushed on leaving a white-capped sea where a valley had been but moments before. Five days passed before the water subsided. When it was gone, the land in its path was barren and unrecognizable. It was another five days before they worked up the courage to move on.

Having finished weaving herself a crown of flowers, Bright Moon reached up to search for the right spot between her braids to place this unusual ornament. Kaliska sat across the fire from her working on yet another spear. *How many did he need? What was it about this one that he spent so much time and energy on it? Why was putting so much effort into making this smaller one? So engrossed in his work, had her traveling companion noticed when she returned from the river, even her tunic had been scrubbed clean? Had he noticed the special care she'd taken preparing the evening meal? If he had, he failed to mention it. There he sat, applying another coat of wet sand to the wooded shaft and rubbing it smooth. What to do? I guess I will have to come up with a way to tell him my thoughts and see where he stands.*

"How long has it been since we left the river?" Bright Moon asked.

Kaliska put aside the spear and picked up the hand-ax to count the marks he had made on the handle. "We were on the river two days and then on the bluff overlooking the flood for another two-hand's worth of days," he said. "Since then, we've been traveling on foot for three-hand's worth of sunrises." He looked up from the ax to see if his answer satisfied her before going back to work on the spear.

"We were lucky," she said.

He shrugged. "It wasn't luck," he answered. He sighted along the length of the spear, turning it to check for imperfections. "Our canoe was getting waterlogged and needed a chance to dry out. I was tired of eating fish and wanted to come ashore so we could hunt." More attentive to his work than to her words, he hefted the spear, checking its balance before continuing, "You're the one that wanted to climb to the top, build a signal fire, and look for Wikvaya's ship. You insisted we make our camp on the bluff."

"We were lucky," Bright Moon repeated. Green wood in the fire sang and popped as it burned. She played at stirring the coals and adding more wood.

Kaliska went back to work on his spear, but added, "I suppose we could have been on the river, or camped on the beach, when the waters came, but we weren't. The only thing we lost was the canoe. We had brought the sail with us to make a tent."

Luck? Who could say? Bright Moon was determined that it was luck, but it was not something that she felt Kaliska gave much thought. Now that the waters were gone and they'd left the river, it didn't matter to him. It mattered to her.

Lost in these thoughts, Bright Moon sat staring into the campfire's hypnotic flame. A green stick in one hand, she poked at the coals without thinking about her actions while she mulled over his words, balancing them against her memories....

Bright Moon might have been killed had it not been for Kaliska's quick action. Before she could blink, he shoved her to the ground and threw himself over her. Faster than an arrow in flight, chunks of ice whizzed by their heads, finger-lengths away, and knocked down their tent.

Pinned to the ground, Kaliska's arms around her holding her down. She was unable to run, but managed to push unsuccessfully at his rock hard body. In doing so, she became aware of his wildly beating heart and realized that he was as frightened as she. Instead of running away, he chose to stay and protect her... once again.

Like the floodwaters that had covered the hills and valleys, memories of past experiences engulfed her. When she upset Long Tusk's planned attack, he was the one who saved her. When she and Wikvaya had to escape from their camp near the Great Ice, it was Kaliska who covered their trail. It was Kaliska who came to her aid at Chochmo's council, as well as at the lion's pit. He was the one who helped her getaway on horseback. He was the one who protected her.

As quickly as it started, the initial tumult faded. She was not sure how long they remained locked together before she finally whispered, "Kaliska."

"What?"

"I think the worst is over."

He raised his head, slightly, and looked around. "Yes, I believe you're right."

"Good," she said. "Then... can you let me up?"

"Oh," he said. Shyly, he rolled away and sat up, seemingly embarrassed.

###

Kaliska fastened a decorative collar of feathers and clamshells around the neck of the spear. Satisfied with his accomplishment, Kaliska looked up from his work. He made this spear for her and now, free of this preoccupation, he needed to find a way to present it to her.

He looked across the campfire at Bright Moon, still lost in thought, and realized she looked different somehow. It reminded him of the way the women of his tribe prepared themselves before a big celebration. But, that was nonsense. What would they celebrate out here? Who would they celebrate with? How should he start a conversation? "Still thinking about the flood?" He finally asked.

Jarred out of her musings, Bright Moon looked up from the fire and directly at him. It was now or never. She took a deep breath before she spoke. "Did you know that in Wikvaya's tribe, the women choose their mates?"

The abrupt change in subjects lost him. *The words he had planned went differently.* He rushed to catch up. "What brought that up?"

"We've searched for his tribe and haven't found them," she said. "We haven't found anyone else, either."

Kaliska thought about it. "No," he said. "I don't know if they survived the great waters, but I never saw signs of Wikvaya's village so I can't be sure we're on the same river."

She dropped her eyes, looking at the fire before beginning again. "What happens if we don't find them? What do we do then?"

He shrugged. "I think we'll find someone," he said. *This was not the subject he wanted to discuss, not the conversation he had planned.*

"But if we don't, what do we do?"

Tired of her questions, he thought he'd turn the problem back to her. "What do you think we should do?" *Maybe once she got these questions out he'd have a chance.*

She raised her eyes and smiled shyly. In a soft voice,

she said, "I think we should start our own tribe."

Her soft reply was not what Kaliska expected her to say. "What?"

"I choose you as a mate!" Her heart in her throat, eyes fixed on him, she waited for his answer.

Kaliska looked at her, dumbstruck. He finally realized what celebration she had had in mind… and that they were thinking alike. Holding the spear out, he smiled and said, "I made a present for you."

She smiled. "It is beautiful. Thank you."

Kaliska tossed a handful of light snow in the air and watched the tiny crystals drift on the breeze. "We are downwind from the doe. Move that way and ease in behind her before you spring," he whispered. "She should bolt this way and we'll have food and another nice pelt to keep us warm."

Bright Moon nodded and did not voice any objections. She was familiar with the role he wanted her to play. Each time they were ready to close in, he gave the same instructions.

Heavy with child, Bright Moon waddled through the light snow. To keep from spooking the animal, she held her cloak—the remainder of their canoe's sail—close to her as she inched her way behind their prey. Even though she felt they had enough meat and pelts to last them, he continued to hunt. *Laying stores aside for later, for after the baby, when she wouldn't be able to join him*, he told her. She knew that he was trying to bury his clumsy concerns for her well-being.

In position, she jumped up and yelled. Her cloak flapped in the wind. The doe, startled, bolted downhill toward Kaliska and he downed it immediately.

"I got it," he yelled. "We'll have food and hides for a while." There was no reply. Had something happened? Leaving his kill, he hurried to the last place he had seen her.

He found her in blood-soaked snow, bent over a form half-hidden in the rocks, and exposed grass. It was a young lad, his lanky figure covered with claw marks. His eyes closed, a bloody knife frozen in his grip. The lad lay atop a dead sabertooth. The cat, a victim of recent knife wounds. A bloody spear shard lay nearby. A short distance away, Kaliska found another big cat's body pinned to the ground by the remains of the broken spear. The boy had downed the animals, but not before they inflicted injuries on him.

Bright Moon used snow to clean the wounds and treat them with the few medicines in her parfleche.

With a practiced eye, Kaliska surveyed the area while he tore strips from her cloak and handed them to her. "From the tracks, it looks like there were three of them," he told her. "All are young, but the boy here is the largest, probably the oldest of this group."

Bright Moon grunted an acknowledgement of her mate's ability. He is very good at this task.

She carefully wrapped each of the boy's injuries, but her duty did not keep her from being concerned. "I wonder what they were doing out here all alone?"

"The smallest one left many tracks. Probably got separated from her clan and got lost. The other two were out searching for her."

"I can't do anything more for him here. We'll have to move him to our camp. We should use our spears and the rest of my cloak to fashion a litter."

Bright Moon leaned over the youth laid out on her sleeping robe. She clutched her side as the baby within stretched and flexed. These movements were coming more often now, and Bright Moon suspected that it would not be long before the child demanded to see the light of day.

Kaliska, returned to their campsite from the last of his trips to retrieve the kill. He was in time to witness her wince. "Are you all right?"

Bright Moon looked up at him and smiled. "I am fine. The baby is fine. He heard his father return from a great hunt and wanted to greet him."

The youth moaned and Bright Moon turned her attention to him.

Kaliska smiled. "Maybe, the baby wishes to help her mother, the Great Shaman."

The youth's eyes fluttered open cutting off the reply on Bright Moon's lips. He stared up at her, trying to focus, trying to place her face. He moaned again. It was not a face he recognized.

"What's your name?" Bright Moon gently pulled the warm furs she had wrapped him in, closer to his body.

"How... Howling Wolf," he said. His voice was but a hoarse whisper.

"Howling Wolf, Slayer-of-Lions." Bright Moon motioned to the place where Kaliska had their doe and the boy's cats hung. She hoped the knowledge that he had been successful would buoy his spirits and bolster his will to live.

It brought a weak smile to the boy's lips.

"We're about to have company," Kaliska said.

From high up on an adjoining hill, another youth led a group of hunters as they scrambled across the rocks. It was clear they were not finding what they were looking for.

"Good," Bright Moon said. "Get their attention." Another labor pain forced her to clutch her side. "He needs more help than I will be able to give him."

Kaliska recognized the quandary that faced her. She could not tend to the boy and deliver the baby at the same time and the baby was not going to wait. A shout from him and the group stopped, formed into two clusters, and began making their way downhill. Outnumbered, Kaliska was not sure that shouting had been a good idea. If he had not attracted their attention, the hunters would follow the tracks. It would have delayed their arrival, but the trackers would have found them, and they would have been irritated by the delay.

Bright Moon looked up from her work to see Kaliska quickly looking around their camp. She knew that he was considering the chance he would have if he had to defend the two of them. Overall, their compound provided shelter from the weather and wild animals, but it would provide little protection from a determined group of warriors.

Arriving at the compound, the two groups of men stopped short. The nearest, formed a half-circle about ten paces outside the woven brush gateway, the second group, formed another half-circle about ten paces behind them. One man, apparently, the group's leader, strode forward and stopped about halfway between the gate and the first group. The youth that accompanied them, trailed after this lone man and stopped quietly near his side.

Bright Moon could see that the boy wore the same trappings as the lad she tended. It helped to know that it was his people who were searching for him. She breathed a sigh of relief and went back to her work. It was apparent these strangers were not looking for a fight. All the men carried their spears relaxed, but ready. They were winded from their scramble across the rough hillside. Kaliska adopted a stance similar to theirs, standing quietly in the entrance and returning their stares.

Bright Moon looked up from her work and saw this standoff. It was something she knew she needed to break up right away. "You men," she commanded, "use your spears and tunics to make a stretcher. You need to get him back to your village."

The group's leader nodded and a few men stripped off their tunics threaded the spears through the open bottoms and out the sleeves. Kaliska stood aside to let them enter. The men placed the youth on this makeshift stretcher and started down the hillside toward the river.

Bright Moon rose to follow, but the remaining hunters stood in her way and would not let her pass.

The group's leader turned to Kaliska. "What are you doing here?"

"This is our village," Kaliska said with a sweep of his arm. "We were uphill, hunting, and slew a doe when we discovered the boy. We brought him here to treat his wounds. Up the hillside near where we made our kill, there is evidence that he killed two great cats; one with a spear and the other with a knife. He is a brave lad. His kills are hanging there next to our own. There had been two others with him. I suspect that the smallest one had been lost—perhaps threatened by the lions. This lad sent his companion to grab the child and escape while he remained behind to keep the big cats at bay."

Bright Moon saw the leader glance at the youth who gave a confirming nod. It was apparent to her that this was the one who spirited the child away. After safely delivering his charge, he led the others back.

Though expressionless, the stranger asked, "How do you know all of this?"

It was Kaliska's turn to remain stone-faced. "I studied the tracks in the snow. I read the signs. With his back near the wall of a bluff, the lad chose a good place to make his stand. The lions were dangerous, but young and inexperienced. Instead of striking together, they came at him one-at-a-time. The more aggressive one attacked from the front, the other approached from the side, but held back. The first lion leaped and found himself on the tip of the spear. The butt of the spear jammed against the wall while the point drilled its way through the lion. The shaft broke under the animal's weight, but it was over for that one before he hit the ground. With the second cat close at hand and his spear tip buried in the first lion, the lad grabbed the broken shaft and used it like a club. Their fight covered some ground as he parried the cat's claws and stabbed at it with the point of the broken spear shaft. In the end, it became a wrestling match and he finished it with his knife."

The leader nodded to another hunter. The man and two companions charged up the hill in the direction Kaliska had indicated. He had not attempted to hide his tracks and the men would follow these to the place where Bright Moon had found the boy.

Still outnumbered—though by fewer men—Kaliska remained silent. Bright Moon stood quietly behind him, wincing now and then from early labor pains. If there was a fight, she was in no condition to help.

Her plight did not go unnoticed by these strangers. From her actions, they knew the baby would be coming soon. They made no attempt at entering the camp, nor did they threaten Kaliska or Bright Moon. Instead, their leader quietly inspected Kaliska's campsite from where he stood. He could see that this man and woman had taken great pains to care for the boy. They had also done well in choosing this site.

This location gave a good view of a stretch of the river and of the plains beyond. It lay nestled among boulders in a clearing near the base of a cliff and had its own spring-fed pool assuring them of a constant water supply. Overflow from the spring, fed a creek that flowed downhill to the forest attracting animals. Two animal pens, one holding goats and one holding geese, stood inside the camp. A sleep-hut stood close to the back wall. Their efforts to secure it against animals' intrusions were evident. To fill the voids between the boulders, they stacked rocks, creating solid walls and placed fences made of brush to restrict the entrance.

A hide stretched on a frame that stood near their sleep-shelter caught his attention. The fur had been removed, and the surface was covered with drawings of animals. It showed the plains across the river filled with great herds grazing peacefully. Hunters hid in the nearby bush waiting for the right time to attack. He had seen this type of art before. It was used when a shaman wanted to summon animals to the hunt. He looked from the drawing to the plain, itself. Herds grazed there. While not quite as plentiful as those in the drawing, there were more than he had seen in several summers.

His men returned, and they held a whispered conference while eyeing the animal's bodies. The lad's two lions and the pairs' doe hung from poles, confirming what they had been told.

The stranger turned to Kaliska and waved a hand toward the animal pens, "You brought these animals with you?"

Kaliska looked at the animal pens. "No, we captured them here. My mate is with child and we'll need them when the baby comes. We were wandering when we found this place and decided to settle here."

"Who are you?" The leader asked.

Kaliska slapped a hand across his chest. "I am Kaliska, hunter and scout," he said. "My mate, Bright Moon, is a Great Shaman. We are weary travelers and have made this our home."

The chief made a gesture similar to that made by Kaliska. "I am Gray Wolf, Chief of the Narwikin. The boy, Howling Wolf, is my son. He and this lad were searching for one of our lost children. My scouts looked at the place where the lions were taken. It is as you said."

It was Kaliska's turn to ask questions. "Where is your village?"

Gray Wolf, unaffected by the bluntness of the question, did not blink as he replied, "My people had lived in the hills near the river that flows along the edge of the great plain. One hand's worth of summers past, a drought came. The river went dry and the animals left. There's been no game here since. My people had to leave to search for lands where game is plentiful."

"Have you found such lands?"

"No, we did not. Wherever we went, we found barely enough to keep us alive. At one time, game was abundant here. We kept coming back only to find that nothing had changed..." Gray Wolf paused, weighing a decision.

Another cramp. Bright Moon put a hand on her side, trying to comfort the baby inside her. This man, Gray Wolf, was thinking, but about what? *Was he recalling the hardships his people had endured, possibly considering the benefits of having a man with Kaliska's scouting ability join them?*

Whatever it was, Gray Wolf reached his decision. Interrupting Bright Moon's thoughts, he gestured toward the pair and said, "We found no animals here until the Great Shaman arrived. My people will camp here, protect you, and give you aid. You are both welcome in our tribe for as long as you want to stay."

(The End)

Glossary and References

Name	Definition
Abyss	In geology, a relatively narrow, often deep, fissure.
Adobe	A natural building material made from sand, clay, water, and some kind of fibrous or organic material (sticks, straw, and/or manure), which the builders shape into bricks (using frames) and dry in the sun. Adobe buildings are similar to cob and mud brick buildings.
Adsila	Cherokee name meaning blossom. Lady Adsila is the wife of Wikvaya.
Adze or Adz	A tool used for smoothing rough-cut wood in hand woodworking. Generally, the user stands astride a board or log and swings the adze downwards towards his feet, chipping off pieces of wood, moving backwards as he goes and leaving a relatively smooth surface behind.
Aggregate	A collection of items that are gathered together to form a total quantity. In construction, an aggregate may include sand, gravel, crushed stone, or slag
Algard	The younger of the two guards wounded by Little Fawn (associated with safety)
Antinanco	Native American Mapuche name meaning "eagle of the sun."
Arroyo	A Spanish word translated as "brook", it can also be called a "wash" or "dry wash" as it is usually a dry river, creek or stream bed—a gulch that temporarily or seasonally fills and flows after

	sufficient rain. "Wadi" is a similar term in Africa. In Spain, a "Ramblahas" has a similar meaning.
Askook	Native American Algonquin name meaning "snake." Long Tusk's friend and Chief of Mattocks. Older now, but in his younger day, led his tribe to conquer surrounding areas. After years of soft living, he is very interested in Bright Moon's magical powers as a means of retaining his power.
Attikamekey	The Attikamekey (Whitefish People) are Little Fawn's original tribe
Bandy Legged	This is also called bow-leggedness or bandiness, is a deformity marked by medial angulations of the leg in relation to the thigh, an outward bowing of the legs, giving the appearance of a bow.
Bending Willow	A Sabala woman that Little Fawn meet while being held captive
Bog	Wet spongy ground; especially a poorly drained usually acid area rich in accumulated plant material. Also known as a mire or "muskeg", bogs consist of a thick ground cover layer of sphagnum moss or similar growth. Acidic in nature and very low in nutrients they may support thin amounts of black spruce, Pin Oak, or Tamarack Larch forest. Open water is rare, but the water table is very close to the surface and the ground soft with many hidden sinkholes that act similar to quicksand.
Bola	Weighted cord for entangling an animal's legs: a strong cord with weights attached to the ends, used for catching animals, large or small, by throwing it to entangle the animal's legs.
Bolt	To run off quickly; to depart in haste.
Boom	A long pole extending outward from the mast of a derrick and used to support, or guide, objects being lifted or suspended.
Bore/Drill	To make a hole in or through something in the form of a hollow cylindrical chamber (a tunnel, for example) or, to form by drilling, digging, or burrowing as if with a chisel.
Brand	A piece of burning wood.
Breechcloth	A form of loincloth consisting of a strip of material (usually a narrow rectangle) passed between the thighs and secured, in front and behind, under a belt or string. (See loincloth).
Bright Moon	Daughter of Silver Waters, as a young girl she

	traveled with a trade caravan and later became a tribe's medicine shaman, responsible for treating the sick and wounded. The main purpose of shamanism is to understand nature and heal the sick.
Bright Star	The name Bright Moon used when she was undercover in Kam Udo's city with Crooked Foot ("Crow")
Running Buffalo	The chief of the Attikamekey and Waving Grass'father.
Buttes	From a French word meaning "small hill", this .is a conspicuous isolated hill with steep, often vertical sides and a small, relatively flat top; it is smaller than mesas, plateaus, and tables.
Cairn	A pile of stones used to mark a path for walkers and climbers.
Calico	Any small repeated print design. This snake was probably a Water Moccasin, also called a Cottonmouth, and is poisonous.
Canyon	A canyon or gorge is a deep ravine between cliffs often carved from the landscape by a river. A canyon may also refer to a rift between two mountain peaks.
Capstan	In its earliest form, the capstan consisted of a timber mounted vertically through a vessel's structure which was free to rotate. Levers, known as bars, were inserted through holes at the top of the timber and used to turn the capstan.
Carrion	(From the Latin caro, meaning meat) refers to the carcass of a dead animal. Carrion is an important food source for large carnivores and omnivores in most ecosystems.
Carry Pole	A pole used to carry items of equal weight. For balance, the items are fastened to each end of the pole and balanced across the individual's shoulders.
Chicha	A term used for several varieties of fermented beverages, most commonly made from maize, grapes or apples, but which also describes similar non-alcoholic beverages. Chicha may also be made from manioc root (also called yucca or cassava), or fruits, and other ingredients. The drink is often consumed during festivals or provided to visiting guests.
Chochmo	Native American Hopi name meaning "mud mound." This is the chief Long Tusk meets with after he is sent into exile.

Clam Shell People	This is White Badger's tribe in dire straits. After meeting them, Red Deer, he invites them to join the Narwikin.
Cleft	Geologically, a crack or a long narrow opening in a rock face; an opening, fissure, or V-shaped indentation. A hollow between ridges or protuberances.
Cob	Cob, cobb or clom (in Wales) is a building material consisting of clay, sand, straw, water, and earth, similar to adobe.
Canyon	This is a narrow chasm with steep cliff walls formed by running water
Copse	A thicket of small trees or shrubs; a coppice
Coulee	A term applied rather loosely to different landforms, all of which refer to a kind of valley or drainage zone.
Counting	In this culture, counting is done in sets of five. One hand is a count of five; two hands are a count of ten. Individual numbers are: Da (1); Jar (2); Cha (3); Tug (4); and Mux (5). For numbers six through ten, Pra plus the count, as Pra-Da (6), Pra-Jar (7), etc.
Creeper	A clinging plant especially one that grows by means of tendrils, suckers, or roots that anchor it to a surface
Crooked Foot	A boy from a prehistoric, ice age tribe called The Narwikin ("The People")
Crow	The name Crooked Foot used when he was undercover in Kam Udo's city with Bright Moon ("Bright Star")
Cudgel	A short heavy club: a heavy stick used as a weapon.
Da	See Counting.
Derrick	A derrick is a lifting device with three major parts: a stationary vertical base topped with a moveable tower equipped with a boom arm which runs perpendicular to the derrick tower. The base is used to keep the tower from falling over. The tower sits on the base and can be rotated freely. The tower's movement may be controlled by arms or by lines powered by some means such as man hauling, so that the tower can move in all directions. A line, with a hook or a loop on the end, runs up the tower out the boom arm. Like a crane, it is commonly used to lift, suspend, or lower heavy objects.
Drill/Bore	To make a hole in or through something in the form of a hollow cylindrical chamber (a tunnel, for

	example) or, to form by drilling, digging, or burrowing as if with a chisel.
Drinking gourd	A container made from the dried shell of a bottle gourd or any of numerous inedible fruits with hard rinds.
Dugout	A dugout or dugout canoe is a boat which is basically a hollowed tree trunk
Dust Devil	A miniature whirlwind strong enough to whip dust, leaves and litter into the air.
Emissary	Someone sent on a mission to represent the interests of another person.
False Dawn	Also referred to as the Zodiacal Light, is a faint, roughly triangular diffused white glow seen in the night sky that appears to extend up from the vicinity of the Sun along an imaginary line called the ecliptic or zodiac. It is best seen just after sunset and before sunrise in spring and autumn when the zodiac is at a steep angle to the horizon. It is caused by sunlight scattered by space dust in the zodiacal cloud.
Fen	An area of low, flat marshy land where decomposing plants accumulate, forming peat
Fire eater	In more modern times, fire eating was a common part of Hindu, Sadhu, and Fakir performances to show spiritual attainment. It became a part of the standard sideshow acts in the late 1880s and is often seen as one of the entry-level skills for sideshow performers. Although skilled fire performers, such as those who can utilize the difficult and dangerous vapor transfers and produce large breaths of fire are regarded as equals in the circus community for their skill and devotion to their art. It is based on the fact that fluids, even solids, when reduced to small particles and accompanied by the right mix of air/oxygen can become flammable, even explosive. Do not try this at home.
Fire-dragon-from-the-sky	A fictional beast Bright Moon used to panic Chochmo's people. In truth she used Wikvaya's hot air balloon, Travels-the-air-with-the-birds
Fire-from-the-sky	This is how they described lightning because they recognized that it sometimes started fires.
Fissure	In geology, a crack or crevasse in a surface, ice or land.
Fly-Whisk	A flexible bunch of twigs, feathers, or straw, attached to a handle for use as a tool to swat or disturb flies or other insects.

Gachi	The chief of the guards in Kam Na Udo; one of Romnog's Lieutenants.
Gray Wolf	In Book One, this is Howling Wolf's father. In Book Three, this is a different person. He is a member of the rescue party.
Great Elk	Two different individuals. In Book One, he is the mate of Silver Moon and the father of Bright Moon. In the Book Three, it is the name of the master brick maker of the Sabala. He befriends Little Fawn during her captivity.
Great Ice	The glacial ice-sheet, in their view, an area that the people saw as seemingly going on forever.
Great Otter	Tribal chief of the Sabala, the White Clay People
Gorge	This is a deep narrow passage with steep rocky sides formed by running water
Gulch	This is a deep V-shaped valley formed by erosion. It may contain a small stream or dry creek bed and is usually larger than a gully. Occasionally, sudden intense rainfall may produce flash floods in the area of the gulch.
Gully	A landform created by running water, sharply eroding the soil, typically on a hillside. Gullies resemble large ditches or small valleys, but are meters to tens of meters in depth and width.
Gut String	A tough thin cord made from the treated and stretched intestines of certain animals, especially sheep, and used for stringing musical instruments and tennis rackets and for surgical ligatures
Hands old	See Counting.
Hantaywee	A Sioux name meaning "faithful." He is a clan-leader for Chief Honovi
Hardpack	Soil that has been packed down either by feet or nature, into a firm layer of dirt that is structurally developed enough to prevent much penetration or deformation. It is the most common soil condition if the weather has been dry, and the trail is in good condition without much loose dirt on top.
Hevataneo	Native American Cheyenne name meaning "hairy rope."
Hobble	This is a device, such as a rope or strap (around the legs of a horse, for example) used to impede action and restrict, but not prevent, movement.
Hogback	A ridge formed by tilted strata; hence, any ridge with a sharp summit, and steeply sloping sides.
Honored	A term of respect and endearment often used by

Mother	Bright Moon when she addresses her Mother.
Honovi	Hopi Indian name meaning "strong deer."
Horse	History of Modern horses (Wikipedia): Equus: The oldest species of "true" horse, Equus stenonis, was discovered in Italy, and is believed to have evolved from Plesippus-like animals at the end of the Tertiary or the beginning of the Quaternary periods. Equus stenonis proliferated into two branches, one lighter in body mass and one heavier. Equus stenonis crossed into North America, where similar forms known as Equus Scotti are common; some types (Equus Scotti var. Giganteus) exceeded the modern horse in size. However, all the horses in North America ultimately became extinct approximately 11,000 years ago. The causes of this extinction (simultaneous with a variety of other American megafauna) are still a matter of debate, particularly given the suddenness of the event and the fact that these mammals had clearly been surviving for millions of years before their disappearance. Often-mentioned possibilities include climate change, pandemic, or hunting by the possibly simultaneous arrival of humans. Recent studies by a team of geneticists headed by C. Vila indicate that the horse line split from the zebra/donkey line between 4 and 2 million years ago. Equus Ferus, ancestor species to Equus caballus, appeared 630,000 to 320,000 years ago. Equus caballus was formed from several subspecies of Equus Ferus by selective breeding widely over Eurasia for an extended time. The details of this process are currently a target of research by archaeologists and geneticists.
Howahkan	A Sioux name meaning "of the mysterious voice".
Howling Wolf	Crooked-foot's grandfather; an elder of the tribe and leader of the tribal council
Jaleti	Salmon, the giant fish
Attikamekey	The tribe that was attacked and finds refuge with the Narwikin. These are Little Fawn's people.
Jerky	A meat that has been cut into strips, trimmed of fat, marinated in a spicy, salty, or sweet rub or a liquid, and dried or smoked with low heat (usually under 70°C/160°F) or is occasionally just salted and sun-dried. The result is a salty, savory, or semisweet snack that can be stored for a long time without

Term	Definition
	refrigeration. The word "jerky" comes from the Quechua term charqui, which means to burn (meat). Jerked meat was one of the first human-made products and is derived from this crucially important food preservation technique. It was essential for survival.
Kaliska	A Miwok name meaning "coyote chasing deer." He is a scout for Long Tusk, and is befriended by Wikvaya and Bright Moon.
Kam Na Udo	The tribal name of the raiders – the 'People of Kam Udo'
Kam Udo	The tyrant leader who wants the city built for him to rule.
Kamaja	The great wandering herds; Mastodons, buffalo, antelope, deer, reindeer, horses
Kolata	The moon in the sky
Kolenya	A Miwok name meaning "coughing fish".
Lackey	A servile follower; toady.
Liminaka	The one that travels on its belly; a snake
Little Fawn	A young woman, daughter of White Owl
Little Wolf	Son of Running Wolf, Chief of the Sea People
Loincloth	A one-piece male garment similar to a breechcloth, sometimes kept in place by a belt, which covers the genitals and, at least partially, the buttocks. (See breechcloth).
Long Tusk	The caravan master and bandit leader who leads his people on raids of settlements and other caravans.
Lord, Lady	Similar to "Chief" or "Excellency", use of the title, "Lord" or "Lady" is to recognize that some persons possess a rank above the ordinary individual.
Magram	The local overseer in the village, he accompanied Romnog at the air shaft and the wood gathering
Makata	The Mastodon that Ti-gal uses in his caravan
Mamuta	The sun in the sky
Mangy	A class of persistent contagious skin diseases caused by parasitic mites. These mites embed themselves either in hair follicles or skin.
Mattocks	A tribe that is led by Long Tusk's friend, Askook. The Mattocks trade with Long Tusk's caravan and he hopes to use Bright Moon in exchange for trade goods. The tribe gets its name because they use a digging and grubbing tool with features of an adze and an ax or pick.
Meltwater	The water released by the melting of snow or ice,

	including glacial ice. When meltwater pools on the surface rather than flowing, it forms melt ponds. As the weather gets colder meltwater will often re-freeze. Meltwater can collect or melt under the ice's surface. These pools of water, known as sub glacial lakes can form due to geothermal heat and friction.
Mesa	Spanish and Portuguese for "table", the term is used to describe an elevated area of land with a flat top and sides that are usually steep cliffs. It takes its name from its characteristic tabletop shape.
Missoula Floods	The Missoula Floods (also known as the Spokane Floods or the Bretz Floods) refer to the cataclysmic floods that swept periodically across eastern Washington and down the Columbia River Gorge at the end of the last ice age. Ice dam on the Clark Fork River would form and create Glacial Lake Missoula before failing. These periodic, sudden ruptures generated glacial lake outburst floods . After each ice dam rupture, the waters of the lake would rush down the Clark Fork and the Columbia River, inundating much of eastern Washington and the Willamette Valley in western Oregon. After the rupture, the ice would reform, recreating Glacial Lake Missoula once again. Geologists estimate that the cycle of flooding and reformation of the lake lasted an average of 55 years. It is estimated that during a period between 13,000 to 15,000 years ago, this massive flood cycle occurred several. By calculations, it is estimated that the maximum speed of the floodwaters approached 36 meters/second (130 km/h or 80 mph).
Missoula Floods: Slideshow (Internet)	http://www.angelfire.com/hugefloods/Video.html
Missoula Floods: Channeled Scablands (Internet)	http://hugefloods.com/Scablands.html
Missoula Floods: Scablands (Internet)	http://www.pbs.org/wgbh/nova/earth/explore-the-scablands.html
Mochni	This pudgy out-walker is a lackey/minion of Long

	Tusk. She is a constant nemesis of Bright Moon. The name is a Hopi name meaning "talking bird."
Mud brick	A brick made of a mixture of loam, mud, sand, and water mixed with a binding material such as rice husks or straw. Brick makers use a stiff mixture and let them dry in the sun for 25 days. In warm regions, with very little timber available to fuel a kiln, bricks were generally sun dried. In some cases brick makers extended the life of mud bricks by putting fired bricks on top or covering them with stucco
Narwikin	'The People'. The manner in which many primitive tribes simply referred to themselves
Night Fires	Campfires set at night to ward off wild animals or keep raiders from attacking.
Nukimba	Rats
Nunashki	When the flowers come, spring
Nunavik	Musk Ox, long haired, heavy tusk, 8 feet long, 4-5 foot tall, can weight anywhere from 450–800 pounds. Wool is soft and a good insulator.
Ogdun	The architect and construction project manager for Kam Udo
Out-walker	A person who walks next to, in front of, or behind a procession and acts as a guide or escort. They may also be employed to keep porters from acting up, getting out of control, or running away. On occasion, they may be sent to catch runaways.
Palisades	A line of cliffs, examples of such exists in NE New Jersey and SE New York and extend along the W bank of the lower Hudson River. It is about 15 miles (24 km) long and, in places, reaches some 300–500 feet (91–152 meters) high. Alternately, a fence of poles or stakes set firmly in the ground, as for enclosure or defense. Any of a number of poles or stakes pointed at the top and set firmly in the ground in a close row with others to form a defense. Finally, to furnish or fortify with a palisade.
Parfleche	A Native American rawhide bag. It is similar in construction to an envelope but can be as large as a suitcase. They were often painted, decorated and used to carry personal and ceremonial objects. In everyday use, they were typically used for holding objects such as dried meats, jerky, and pemmican.
Paxotori	A sub-chief in Kam Na Udo army; one of Romnog's Lieutenants.

Pemmican	A concentrated mixture of fat and protein (usually meat) used as a nutritious food as a mainstay while on the trail or as a supplement when other food was available. Traditionally pemmican was prepared from the lean meat of large game such as buffalo, elk, or deer. The meat was cut in thin slices and dried over a slow fire or in the hot sun until it was hard and brittle. Then, using stones, it was pounded into very small pieces, almost powder-like in consistency. This was mixed with an equal amount of fat. When available, nuts and dried fruits were pounded into powder and then added to the meat/fat mixture. The resulting mixture could be packed into rawhide pouches for storage until needed.
Pinnacle	Any pointed, towering part, or formation.
Pitch	A resin derived from the sap of various coniferous trees such as the pines.
Plateaus	Also called a high plain or tableland, is an area of highland, usually consisting of relatively flat terrain. Plateaus can be formed in many ways. One is due to the erosional processes of glaciers on mountain ranges; in this case, the plateaus are left sitting between the mountain ranges. Water can also erode mountains and other landforms down into plateaus.
Porridge	Depending on availability, they boiled cereal meal (oats, rice, semolina, etc.) in water, milk, or both.
Porter	A person, or people, whose job is to carry burdens or baggage
Poultice	Medicine that might be converted to a paste and applied as a salve or, used dry, worn in a small bag. Its purpose is to heal bruises, break up congestion, reduce inflammation, withdraw pus, toxins and embedded particles in the skin, and to soothe irritation.
Quirt	A weighted, short-handled, whip usually made of braided rawhide or leather
Ravine	A deep narrow steep-sided valley or gorge in the earth's surface worn by running water
Red Bird	After the Narwikins are attacked, she speaks out at the tribal meeting. Her family elects not to move to the island retreat and end up captured (slaves)

Red Deer	A young man, whose parents had died and he is the adopted son of Howling-Wolf
Remuda	A word of Spanish derivation, roughly meaning a "change of horses". It refers to a herd of horses from which hands select their mounts.
Rift	An opening made by splitting, cleaving, etc.; fissure; cleft; chink.
Romnog	The chief of the army in Kam Na Udo
Running Buffalo	Chief of the Attikamekey (Whitefish People), father of Waving Grass and leader of Little Fawn's people.
Running Elk	Hunting companion of Little Wolf of the Sea People
Running Wolf	Chief of the Sea People
Sabala	The village and tribe that Kam Na Udo invaded and now occupies.
Saboniti	A large wild feline with curved tusks; a Saber-Tooth tiger
Sand	Before soap was invented and before hot waters became available, sand was used to remove dirt and exfoliate the skin.
Sanity	The older of the two guard wounded by Little Fawn (associated with Algard)
Satchel	This is a bag with a cover, similar to a saddlebag but often with a strap. The strap is usually worn so that it crosses the body diagonally, with the bag hanging on the opposite hip, rather than hanging directly down from the shoulder. Satchels are most commonly made of leather or cloth.
Scablands	Also called "The Channeled Scablands", these are a unique geological erosion feature in the state of Washington. They were created by the cataclysmic Missoula Floods that periodically swept across eastern Washington and down the Columbia River Plateau during the Pleistocene epoch—approx-imately 2.588 million to 12,000 years before present (BP). River valleys, when formed by erosion normally have a 'V' cross section, while glaciers leave a 'U' cross section. The Channeled Scablands have a rectangular cross section and are spread over immense areas of eastern Washington. (See Missoula Floods).
Score	A set of twenty members.
Scorpion	These are predatory arthropod animals of the order

	Scorpiones within the class Arachnida. They have eight legs and are easily recognized by the pair of grasping claws and the narrow, segmented tail (called a telson) carried in a characteristic forward curve over the back with the tip ending in a venomous stinger.
Scrub	A stunted tree, shrub, or bush.
Shining Waters	From the legends of 'the people', in an earlier time, she was the medicine shaman who brought fire.
Shaman	A "medicine elder" (not always a male) who uses naturally occurring products, such as herbs, to treat ailments/illness. In order to attend to the tribes' physical, spiritual, and mental needs, they had to be adept at reading body language and using primitive psychology. They were often required by situations to think and act quickly. To become a Shaman, a person would apprentice themselves to a teacher for 20-30 years
Silver Fox	Crooked-Foot's peer and (sometimes) tormentor.
Silver Leaf	The second child of White Bird and Little Rabbit, she tells Howling Wolf that she heard a baby's cry on the Attikamekey's rafts. This was when Small Turtle was captured.
Silver Waters	The mate of Great Elk and mother of Bright Moon. She was a great shaman whom many thought of as magical. She trained Bright Moon to follow in her footsteps
Skewer	A wooden shaft used to secure or suspend meat and/or vegetables during cooking.
Skid	A plank, log, etc., often one of a pair or set, used as a support or as a track upon which to slide or roll a heavy object. A low pallet on which goods are loaded for handling or transport.
Small Turtle	Captured by Waving Grass and her people, he acts as diplomat in order to bring the two tribes together.
Sounding weight	A heavy weight used to determine water depth
Spire	The slender, tapering part of a structure or formation, such as a steeple or a newly sprouting blade of grass that tapers to a point at the top.
Spit of land	A peninsula, possibly an island, that appears to protrude from the main land mass.
Stalactites	This is a type of formation that hangs from the ceiling of caves, hot springs, or man-made

	structures such as bridges and mines.
Stocky	Compact, having a short and solid form or stature
Strokes	Typically imposed on an unwilling subject, this is a form of corporal punishment which involves methodically beating a person or animal. It has also been called flogging, whipping, birching, and caning. Some specialized implements for it include rods, switches, and the cat o' nine tails˙
Switchback	A path, as in a mountainous area, having a series of tight zigzag curves arranged for climbing a steep grade.
Table	When used with landforms, this is a hill, flank of a mountain, or a mountain, that has a flat top. This landform has numerous names in addition to "table." The term "flat" is relative when speaking of tables and often the name or identification of a table (or table mountain) is based on the appearance of the terrain feature from a distance or from below it. An example is Mesa Verde, Colorado, where the "flat top" of the mountain is both rolling terrain and cut by numerous deep canyons and arroyos, but whose rims appear quite flat from almost all directions, terminating in cliffs.
Tawasiki	The one who roams along the Great Ice; a large bear
Telson	The rearmost segment of the body of certain arthropods, or an extension of this segment, such as the middle lobe of the tail fan of a lobster or the stinger of a scorpion
The Great Ice	The glacial ice-sheet. An area that the people saw as seemingly going on forever.
The Long Cold	Winter. Seasons occurred even in the Ice Age
The-long-sleep	Death was associated with sleep, and is referred to as "the-sleep-from-which-no-one-wakes" as well as "the-long-sleep".
The-sleep-from-which-no-one-wakes	Death was associated with sleep, and is referred to as "the-sleep-from-which-no-one-wakes" as well as "the-long-sleep".
They-That-Make-Honey	Bees. From ancient times, Bees were known for their ability to produce honey and through the ages, many cultures used honey not only as a sweetener but also in many other home remedies.
Tigal	A merchant with the caravan and friend of the Narwikin

Till	Sediments composed of a mixture of grain sizes which were deposited directly onto the sub glacial landscape during basal melting.
Till Plain	A gently irregular plain of till--mixed grain-sized sediments—deposited by an actively retreating glacier
Tinder	Fine, dry grasses and other materials for starting a fire.
Todie	A person who flatters and ingratiates himself in a servile way; sycophant: to fawn on and flatter (someone). A servile self-seeker who attempts to win favor by flattering influential people.
Tolinka	Miwok name meaning "flapping ear of a coyote." He is the advisor to Chief Honovi.
Totem	A being, object, or symbol representing an animal or plant that serves as an emblem of a group of people, such as a family, clan, group, lineage, or tribe, reminding them of their ancestry (or mythic past).
Travels-the-air-with-the-birds	The name given to Wikvaya's hot air balloon because it flew through the air with the birds. Later, Bright Moon called it the *Fire-dragon-from-the-sky* in order to panic Chochmo's people.
Travois	A frame structure that was used by indigenous peoples to drag loads over land, ice, or snow. The basic construction consists of a platform or netting mounted on two long poles, lashed in the shape of an elongated triangle. Sometimes additional poles, bound across the two main poles, were used to stabilize the frame and support the load being carried. When dragged by hand, the travois was sometimes fitted with a shoulder harness to ease the work. A travois could be loaded by piling goods atop the bare frame and tying them in place or by first stretching leather over the frame to hold the load being dragged. It is considered more primitive than wheel-based forms of transport. Wheeled vehicles excel on roadways, however, a travoise is superior when used on forest floors, soft soil, snow, etc., where wheels would have encountered difficulties. It is possible for a person to transport more weight on a travois than can be carried on the back.
Tree hollow or	A semi-enclosed cavity which has naturally formed

tree hole	in the trunk or branch of a tree. These are predominantly found in old trees, whether living or not. Hollows form in many species of trees, and are a prominent feature of natural forests and woodlands, and act as a resource or habitat for a number of vertebrate and invertebrate animals
Tunic	A short, usually to hip line or slightly longer, sleeveless, straight, tubular garment, gathered at the waist, sometimes belted.
Valley	A valley is a depression with a predominant extent in one direction. In its broadest geographic sense, it is also known as a dale. A valley through which a river runs may also be referred to as a vale. A small, secluded, and often wooded valley is known as a dell, or in Scotland as a glen. A wide, flat valley through which a river runs is known in Scotland as a strath. A small valley surrounded by mountains is known as a hollow. A deep, narrow valley is known as a coon. Similar geological structures, such as canyons, ravines, gorges, gullies, and kloofs, are not usually referred to as valleys.
Vest	A sleeveless garment, worn usually over a shirt or blouse and, in modern day, sometimes as part of a three-piece suit. A waist-length, sleeveless garment worn for protection
Walking Stick	A device used by many people to facilitate balancing while walking. It may be used as a defensive or offensive weapon, and may conceal a knife or sword as in a swordstick. Walking sticks come in many shapes and sizes.
Walled Village	A walled village is a type of large traditional multi-family communal living structure that is designed to be easily defensible. It is completely surrounded by protecting the residents from the attack of wild animals and enemies

Water under Glaciers	Glaciers form because snow collects faster than it melts. Time, cold, pressure from the weight of the snow, and additional water, turn some of the snow into ice. The surface may appear as one continuous expanse, but seasonal changes cause the ice to push forward or draw back, creating fissures. These may be partially or fully buried under a shroud of snow. The glacier's immense weight, combined with the friction of its movement, produces heat which creates small amounts of water. Fast flowing rivers may have been swallowed but not frozen. Beneath the surface, protected from the intense cold, the water collects, drips down, trickles, and forms rivulets. The rivulets combine to form creeks, streams, and rivers. They burrow ravine-like tunnels and eat away at the snow and ice overhead.
Waving Grass	Daughter of Running Buffalo; she is the one that Little Fawn rescues from the intruders and then she later comes searching for Little Fawn
Wawakin	Their name for cold wind which blows off of the Great Ice.
Welt	A raised mark on the skin (as produced by the blow of a whip), may also be called a wale
White Badger	Red Deer encounters the remnants of this tribe on his way back to the Narwikins. At his invitation, they later join the Narwikins.
White Eagle	One of the youngsters that went berry picking with Little Fawn, Silver Fox, and Crooked Foot.
White Hawk	Running Wolf's, of the Sea People, advisor.
White Owl	Father of Little Fawn, also shaman of the Attikamekey, an elder of the tribe and a council member
White Rain	Snow was called 'white rain' to distinguish it from regular rain.
Why is Glacier Ice Blue?	In simplest of terms, think of the ice or snow layer as a filter. From the surface, snow and ice present a uniformly white face because almost of the visible light striking its surface is reflected back. Light that is not reflected is scattered by the icy grains filtering out most of the light spectrum. If the ice is thick enough, mostly blue light makes it through.
Wikvaya	Native American Hopi name meaning "one who brings."
Yellow Flower	Howling Wolf's first wife (deceased)

Wye	The name of the letter Y; A Wye-shaped object: a Wye-level, Wye-connected.
Zagged/zigzagged	To move in one of the two directions followed in a zigzag course: First we zigged, and then we zagged, trying to avoid the bull; also referred to as a zig-zag or zigging.

Book II: The Sojourner

(Draft excerpt – forecasted release: Fall 2014)

Agitated with the delays, Red Deer, unwilling to continue with Tigal's caravan and they agreed to part company early that morning. The lone young lad watched them depart. In line, they marched across the rolling, grassy hills. Pack animals, mastodons and camels alike, stopped here and there to enjoy the grasses until prodded to move on by a drover.

Not having a drover to prod him, Red Deer was, once again, on his own. He made good time in the lowlands by following an animal trail through the forest. The travois was heavy, but the path was wide and free of obstacles so he did not have to fight with it.

Reaching the foothills changed everything. The path became narrower and rock strewn as it circled upward out of the forest and skirted around a cliff face. Traveling uphill, the travois had become harder to pull and his progress slowed. The day wore on. As night approached, he heard wolves howl in the distance. How far away were they? He listened intently as he tried to gauge the distance, but the sound echoed off the rock walls and over the icy terrain making it impossible to locate them. A chill ran up his spine. At this altitude, trees had become scarce making it necessary for him to pick up scraps of dry wood for his nightly campfires.

Red Deer made camp for the night in a crevasse in the rocks. For protection, he sat with his back against the rock wall and a blazing fire at his feet. Taking his travois apart, he used his knife to scrape off the remaining bark and any nubs giving the shafts a flatter side. With nothing left to snag obstacles along his path and flat runners, it should allow the sled to ride easier across ground or snow. He could quickly cover more ground and go farther before tiring. That would shorten his trip.

When morning came, Red Deer stirred the dying coals into life long enough to give him some warmth while he reassembled his travois. The shafts thumped and bumped over rocks but didn't snag, confirming its smoother surface meant improved progress. By nightfall he reached the big ice. The snowfield, peppered with outcroppings, pinnacles, crags, and places where the ice had buckled, flowed out through the pass between mountain peaks. The field was tilted from side to side. He stood at the highest point and looked down across the expanse. It ended in a crumpled mound of snow and ice just beyond here, but the other end was over the horizon and beyond his view. He knew that it would look like it could go on forever.

A cold wind swept off this sea of ice chilling him to the bone, or was it the fact the ice field was bigger than he remembered. Backtracking a little, he found a spot to make camp. The lee side of a rocky ice-covered mound, it provided a pocket out of the wind.

A wolf's howl split the night air waking him. It was near dawn. His fire was but glowing coals. He debated about throwing more wood on it, a nice blaze would certainly warn him, but his thoughts were interrupted by another wolf howl... than another... then a chorus joined in. He had heard them last night, but these were closer. They were on his trail.

He suspected the smell of smoke had attracted them. A fire now would hold them off until he ran out of wood, and then it would be another story. Ending the debate, he packed his travois and broke camp.

Before striking out toward the ice field, he stirred the embers and arranged the remaining firewood to kindle a new flame. As a last item, he placed fragments of dried meat on the fire near the back wall. If they wanted the meat, they would have to cross the fire. The smell would attract them, the fire would hold them at bay, and the delay would give him time to get away. That was the plan. The howls grew louder, closer.

With each step he took, the wolves took two. A quick glance over his shoulder confirmed that there were enough to count on the fingers of one hand. Alone, there would be too many to fight... and win.

He reached the ice field before the wolves and started across. The snow had a crusty glaze caused by constant thawing and freezing. It was strong enough to hold his weight. The travois slid smoothly along, allowing him to gingerly break into a gentle lope.

Slipping and sliding along behind, the wolves pace had slowed, but they continued to close the gap. He would not be able to keep his pace up for long, but he would be able to do so long enough they'd tire and look for other prey? If it didn't work, he'd need to find another solution.

The field in front of him curved away downward in a series of gentle ice-covered slopes. There was his answer. He slipped the travois in front of him and pushed it along. It gained speed as he jumped aboard. The prow of his craft dipped down, and his sled picked up speed as it as it crossed the slope. Behind him, the wolves, surprised by his maneuver, skidded to a stopped and stared at him as he disappeared down the hill.

The pace of his descent didn't provide time for him to watch them. The only way to control his direction was by leaning left or right. That worked fine until a wall of snow appeared before him. He had reached the other side of the glacier and needed to kill off his speed. Clinging to the webbing, he leaned away from his direction of travel. A runner on his sled hit a rock hidden by snow and ice jerking it around and his makeshift sled began spinning across the ice toward a pinnacle of rock. Not having time to think about another solution, he let go of the webbing, grabbed his pack, and rolled off this makeshift toboggan. The sled smashed into the rocks sending its contents flying. Red Deer slid to a halt near the wall. He lay there for a minute and then starting laughing. Thanks to the wolves, he made it across the ice field in record time with little more than a few scrapes and bruises.

Book II forecasted release Fall 2014

Book III: Crooked Foot

(Draft excerpt – forecasted release: Fall 2015)

"Is it fresh?" Crooked Foot watched as his grandfather, Howling Wolf, crouched down for a closer look. The paw prints in the soft mud were the largest that the boy had ever seen, but then he had not seen much.

By the time boys were two-hands old, they knew how to read many animal signs, follow game and find their way in the woods. From an early age, they had been taken hunting. As an orphan, he had not gone. However, he had listened carefully when the hunters and would-be hunters gathered around campfires. He listened when they told of their adventures. From their stories, he learned to make a pouch sling by attaching leather cords to a piece of animal hide. He practiced all day, every day.

Howling Wolf replied to the boy's question in a quiet tone, "It rained before we started out." He pointed to the edges of the imprint, as he went on, "See here, the mud is still soft. Mamuta, the sun, came to chase away the darkness and the rain. But look, there is no sign of rain in the print. It was made after the rain stopped."

He paused to let the boy take it all in and then patiently continued. "At the edges, the mud is still soft. The sun brought warmth but hasn't had time to make the edges dry." He poked a finger into the soft border and held it out for Crooked Foot to examine. Satisfied the boy understood, he continued, "The cold tongue of Wawakin, the wind which blows off the big ice, hasn't made it solid."

He looked at the lad for confirmation. Did he

351

understand?

"The rain came and made the ground soft and wet," Crooked Foot acknowledged. "The animal that made this print came here after the rain. There wasn't enough time for the warmth of the sun or the cold breath of the wind to change things."

Satisfied the boy aptly demonstrated that he understood Howling Wolf nodded in agreement. That was good. What lay ahead would be a shock. He spread his fingers wide, palms down, leaned in close, and used both hands to measure across the paw print.

"It's wider than your hands," Crooked Foot gasped. "What kind of animal made this?"

"Look here." Howling Wolf pointed to the ground in front of them. "Front feet." He stood up and pointed at another set of tracks. "Over there. Hind feet... tell me, what kind of animal do you think made this?"

Crooked Foot looked down at this print and then at the other tracks, more than twice his grandfather's height away.

Memories flooded in. Gathered around campfires, men loudly proclaimed stories of their hunting exploits except when it came to this creature. Then, they only spoke in hushed voices least they disturb the beast and give it a reason to come looking for them. It seemed like his heart stopped and then began beating again... fast... and in his throat. His mouth went dry. He was hardly able to speak. Finally, he managed to squeak out one word, hardly more than a whisper, "Tawasiki." The creature of bad dreams had been here.

Howling Wolf nodded. "When you were a baby strapped to the carry-board, Tawasiki, the great bear who roams the hills along the big ice, came upon your mother and father. Your father fought bravely while your mother put you up in a tree. He took them both."

Howling Wolf fell silent for a moment. His gaze wandered out over the horizon as if he watched something. Finally he continued, "Tawasiki has been gone such a long time... we thought he had gone away... we thought we were safe." He dropped his gaze back toward the paw prints. "It looks like he has returned."

"What should we do?"

Howling Wolf directed his attention back to the boy. "We must go back and warn the people. The council will have to decide whether the Narwikin should stay or leave."

He stood up and scanned their surroundings for any signs of trouble. If they had to run, he knew the boy's lame foot would slow them down. All seemed quiet. Clumps of low brush, scrub trees, and Pinon Pine dotted the grassy meadows that border the river. The trail followed along the river's edge, skirted around a tall, old tree, and turned to climb uphill. The hill, a major outcropping forced a bend in the river. A mound of debris--brush, stumps, and whole trees left here year-after-year by spring floods--lay jammed in the bend.

Farther inland, away from the river's edge, the meadow and the scrub gave way to tree-covered hills. Behind the trees, snowcapped mountains rose up. From the high valleys between the mountains, glacial ice crept outward and threatened to swallow everything. Nothing seemed out of place. "Come, we must go now."

"Grandfather, the Narwikin are hungry," the boy protested. "The long cold has left them with pains in their bellies. So far, we've only managed to slay two rabbits." He held up the animal carcasses. "This won't be enough to feed everyone."

Howling Wolf smiled modestly, He wondered if the boy's concern were about lack of food or lack of time to enjoy hunting.

Earlier, they had come across a rabbit. Through hand-signs, Howling Wolf encouraged the boy to try his hand with a sling. He had watched quietly, patiently, as the boy selected a smooth rock from his pack and loaded it into the pouch. Twirling the sling over his head, Crooked Foot aimed and let the missile fly. Struck, it lay stunned. They rushed up and dispatched the animal. In their wanderings, they found more rabbits and repeated the process each time, but not always with the same success. Still, Crooked Foot was elated with his efforts and his chest swelled with pride. Howling Wolf did his best to suppress his own delight.

The old man watched ice floated by on the river. "The sun has returned to warm us. Soon, we will see the spring floods and then Jaleti, the giant fish, will return to the river. Flowers will appear on the plains and the grasses will grow green and tender. When that happens, we will see Kamaja, the great wandering herds, return. Then there will be plenty to eat. But not yet."

Howling Wolf put a tender hand on the boy's shoulder. Like his father before him, Crooked Foot already showed signs of being a great leader. The sun was near the midpoint but clouds gathered and would once again cover it. The smell of rain was in the air. Crooked Foot waited for an answer.

Howling Wolf looked into his grandson's eager face and knew the answer he had to give wouldn't be as a grandfather but as a tribal leader. "We're not the only hunters. The Narwikin sent out many hunting parties since the sun returned to chase away the darkness."

The boy was dejected. It wasn't the answer he hoped to hear.

Howling Wolf tried to soften the blow. "Before they left, each group agreed to return by the time the sun reached the midpoint. Now, it looks like the rain will soon be on us. Perhaps the others did better."

He watched as the lad scanned the skies as if to see if he could wring out just a little more time for them to be together. As young as he was, the lad realized the elements weren't on their side and they should return.

Howling Wolf offered another reason, "Tawasiki has also been hunting. He has driven the game from the area. We need to get back and tell the others he has returned and he is hungry." Howling Wolf turned and started up the animal trail toward their encampment. His action cut off further discussion.

Crooked Foot fell in step behind him and tried to match Howling Wolf's long strides with his own bouncy quick ones. Since birth, his foot had turned inward. Being born with a clubfoot made his movement awkward, but he hadn't allowed this to keep him from trying to do what the others did. What he lacked in speed he made up for in other ways.

The trail they followed paralleled the river before turning to coil uphill through stands of scrub brush, pine, and cedar. It started to rain, lightly at first and then heavier as the wind picked up. Howling Wolf peered through the rain and scanned the barren bush with wary eyes. Game, normally attracted to the water, would be plentiful in the area along the river. The only movement came from Wawakin, the cold wind, as it stirred the bushes and trees.

Rain, interspersed with snow and ice, picked up as they reached the crest of the hill. Rounding a bend found them walking directly into the storm.

They hadn't gotten far from the river when Howling Wolf froze in mid-step. Crooked Foot almost ran into him. He looked up at his grandfather and then peered through the driving rain to see what caused him to stop.

He too froze in his steps. Ahead, a few stones' throw away, Tawasiki, his winter white coat just beginning to turn to the browns of spring, stood on his hind feet, and sniffed the air. He looked as tall as three men. Upwind and slightly turned away, the bear hadn't seen them. It would only be a matter of time before he did.

Howling Wolf whispered through clenched teeth, "Don't make a sound... just back up."

Following his grandfather's instructions, Crooked Foot moved slowly... quietly.... backward. If they could back around the bend without being discovered, they would turn and move faster, possible making good their escape

Fate wouldn't allow that. From somewhere behind them a long dead tree surrendered to Wawakin's cold breath. It collapsed with a crash. The sudden noise launched a covey of startled birds into the air.

The sound caught Tawasiki's attention and his head snapped around. Their eyes locked. Howling Wolf and Crooked Foot stood frozen hoping they wouldn't be noticed.

This would not happen. The bear dropped to all fours, turned, and started lumbering toward them, head lolling side to side with each step.

"RUN!" Grandfather yelled, "Quickly... to the tree by the river."

Book III forecasted release Fall 2015

ABOUT THE AUTHOR

The author's career spans 40 years in Information Technologies. During this time, whether working on large-scale computers, PC's, networks, or communications systems, the author found the success of any application was highest when the materials were tailored to the audience.

Understandable, this is a major factor in writing fiction. The author tailors his writing to the type of material he believes his audience will enjoy: Interesting, action-packed adventures, with a historical bent, and chapters that tend to end as cliffhangers.